Charles,
Thanks for coming to
Mini-U. Hope you
enjoy the story!
			Dan June 2016

**OTHER NOVELS BY GENE COYLE**

The Dream Merchant of Lisbon
The game of Espionage

No Game for Amateurs
The Search for a Mole on the Eve of WW II

Diamonds and Deceit
The Search for the Missing Romanov Dynasty Jewels

A Spy's Lonely Path

# Nazi Gold, Portuguese Wine, and a Lovely Russian Spy

Gene Coyle

authorHOUSE

*AuthorHouse™*
*1663 Liberty Drive*
*Bloomington, IN 47403*
*www.authorhouse.com*
*Phone: 1 (800) 839-8640*

© 2016 Gene Coyle. All rights reserved.

No part of this book may be reproduced, stored in a retrieval system, or transmitted by any means without the written permission of the author.

Published by AuthorHouse 01/12/2016

ISBN: 978-1-5049-7255-0 (sc)
ISBN: 978-1-5049-7256-7 (e)

Library of Congress Control Number: 2016900265

Print information available on the last page.

Any people depicted in stock imagery provided by Thinkstock are models, and such images are being used for illustrative purposes only.
Certain stock imagery © Thinkstock.

This book is printed on acid-free paper.

Because of the dynamic nature of the Internet, any web addresses or links contained in this book may have changed since publication and may no longer be valid. The views expressed in this work are solely those of the author and do not necessarily reflect the views of the publisher, and the publisher hereby disclaims any responsibility for them.

## AUTHOR'S NOTE

Many of the characters of the story, such as Ian Fleming, Kim Philby, Duncan Lee, and British double agents GARBO and TRICYCLE are true historical figures, as is the fact that Lisbon was indeed the spy capital of WW II, given Portugal's neutrality and convenient geographical location. The other main characters are purely fictional and any resemblance to real people and facts in the classified files of the WW II Office of Strategic Services is purely coincidental and unintended. Descriptions of Portuguese wine as being superb and its women beautiful are absolutely true.

Many thanks to Kallen Picha for her fine editing assistance.

# Chapter 1

# Berlin 1943

Admiral Canaris signed the last of several documents that his personal assistant, Ewald, had placed before him on his large and ornate desk. A desk that had once belonged to the famous Prussian Field Marshall Helmuth von Moltke. He rang the buzzer on his desk to call one of his lesser aides and then leaned back in his large leather chair while he lighted a cigarette. Major Fritz von Hesseburg entered the office of the commander of the Abwehr, the German Army's intelligence unit, halting at attention just a few feet before the desk.

"See to it that these documents are forwarded to the proper offices." Without waiting for a response from von Hesseburg, the tall, thin admiral rose and turned to Ewald. He not only looked like a leader of the Teutonic race, he even walked like an admiral, with determined long strides. "Let's take a walk out in the garden before I go to lunch." It was a heavily overcast day in late July, 1943 with thick, low clouds. It was raining lightly, but at least with the bad weather, it was unlikely that there would be a daytime bombing raid that day on the city. No great damage had been caused yet on the capital of Hitler's Third Reich, but the raids were becoming more frequent and effective. The British bombed at night in their Lancasters and the American 8th Air Force with their B17s during the daytime. With their raincoats draped over their shoulders, the two officers and longtime friends began their stroll outside, along the paths of the garden. The two career military men had known each other since serving together in the First World War.

"There's something quite pleasant about strolling in the rain," noted Ewald.

"Yes, plus we don't have to worry about Gestapo microphones while walking outside," replied the Admiral.

"Nor do we have to worry about the ears of Fritz out here!" Both men laughed grimly.

"It's a shame that he's an informant for the Gestapo," commented Canaris. "He really is an excellent aide. I suppose that something should be done to be rid of him, now that we are going to be moving forward with Operation Grandfather. Nothing too obvious. Perhaps some sort of accident could be arranged?"

"Leave that to me," replied Ewald. "I have been giving that some thought and I think I have an idea on how to be rid of our young friend, but without there being any follow-up investigation by the Gestapo."

Not too surprisingly, with the downward trend in the fortunes of the German military, there had been muted but growing opposition to Hitler's leadership, especially within the Army, and even rumors of several assassination plots. Allegedly, these plots had been thwarted by the Gestapo, but then one never knew if there had really been such plots or if such allegations were just a convenient way for Heinrich Muller, the head of the Gestapo, to make himself look good to Hitler and also to do away with perceived rivals. Admiral Canaris himself had fallen under a cloud of suspicion because a number of the alleged plotters had been personal friends of Canaris and fellow members of the Abwehr.

The two had been discussing the basic concept of Operation Grandfather for several months, as the Americans continued to march northward through Italy and bad news continued to flow in from the Russian front. The propaganda machine of Dr. Goebbels naturally announced news of victory after victory against the inferior race of Russians, or at worst, the "consolidation" of the German lines. However, the reality as known to the senior leadership of the German Army and Hitler's inner circle was that the fighting was not going well anywhere. Canaris and Colonel Ewald Gehlen had concluded that if things continued as they were currently going, Germany would eventually lose the war. They had both also been appalled by the atrocities carried out in Poland and in the occupied parts of the Soviet union by the SS troops and by the establishment of the concentration camps for the "final solution" of the Jewish problem. They had no great love for Jews themselves, but felt it was a great waste of scarce men and resources to be rounding up and imprisoning Jews, gypsies and other so-called

"Untermensch." They knew that there would be retribu[tion from the] Allies for such crimes, on top of the general chaos and su[ffering that] would follow the military defeat, as there had been after the F[irst World] War. Canaris felt that as the Abwehr had had no role in the [crimes] ordered by Hitler, nor in the insane decisions by him which were leading to the nation's defeat, his officers should not suffer the consequences that were coming. He couldn't help everyone, but he intended to make arrangements to save as many of his younger officers as possible before those dark days arrived. Perhaps it would be fair for the senior officers, such as himself, who had not had the courage to speak the truth to Hitler about the conduct of the war, but it was a different situation for young lieutenants, captains and majors, and their families, who up to then had only been following the orders of their commanders. If Germany somehow managed to win this world war or at least come to some stalemate, then the preparations for Operation Grandfather could later be scrapped. But if the Admiral's predictions for the outcome of the war and post-war sufferings, were correct, certain steps needed to be put in play now for the future welfare of his young colleagues. He had heard rumors that similar measures were being contemplated by second tier Nazi leaders, who claimed that they were only making provisions so that the struggle for the "Thousand Year Reich" could be carried on from other places, such as South America. He suspected that many of those particular Nazis were much more concerned about their own futures than they were for the future of Hitler's Reich. In any case, they had their secret plans and he had his.

"Approximately how much gold have we managed to set aside to date?" asked Canaris.

"Calculated as American dollars, which is how it will be deposited when the money arrives at the bank in Rio de Janeiro, we have some $4 million of gold and close to $1 million worth of diamonds, which were obtained out of various banks in Amsterdam at the start of the war. It's a bit harder to calculate the exact worth of the diamonds, as their value fluctuates more than the gold does, but even after the various bribes and transportation fees are deducted, we should still have close to $5 million available for our men and their families in Brazil."

"Excellent! Excellent! I will have Wolfgang work on the issue of false documentation and travel permits for our officers. Hopefully, those will not be needed for many months or perhaps even a couple of years, ut we need to start making preparations for the travel of our people now. Your responsibility is for making the final arrangements with the Portuguese bankers and others who will be needed to physically transport the gold and diamonds to the ships in the harbor of Lisbon for their onward shipment to Rio de Janeiro. Have you identified yet a Portuguese banker that we can trust?"

"As you know, I was in Lisbon last week and discreetly discussed this matter with our Abwehr chief there, von Karsthoff. He told me that he has narrowed the selection down to two or three candidates. One of them, who is a senior official in the Espirito de Santo Bank, which has a major branch office in Brazil, seems particularly promising. He has a German mother and appears to have certain emotional ties to the Fatherland, but is not a fanatical Nazi idiot."

"Very good. Tell him to continue with his evaluation of the candidates, but that I will find a reason to visit Lisbon to personally make the final assessment of the chosen banker before the formal proposal of our plan to him. I will explain exactly what his role would be. We will be trusting everything to this banker and we must be absolutely certain that he will neither betray us nor simply disappear himself with our money."

"I'm sure that von Kasrsthoff will make it perfectly clear to the banker and others involved in the transportation what would be the consequences to them and their families should they betray us. By the way, do you wish to know the details of how I plan on dealing with Fritz?"

"No, I shall leave that matter in your competent hands. Just make sure that his disappearance cannot be traced back to me. I am distrusted enough by the Gestapo as it is, without making them suspect that I have had anything to do with the 'accidental' death of our dear Fritz. And now I must be departing for my official luncheon with Air Marshal Goering. That fat ass has just received another trainload of artwork that he has had plundered from France and wishes to show it off to his friends and colleagues."

"Perhaps this weekend, I can arrange for the tragic death of Fritz. Enoy your lunch." Ewald proceeded on down the path to return to the Headquarters building. His boots making an authoritative crunching sound in the gravel. Admiral Canaris stayed a few minutes more in the garden, inspecting some of the small flowers. Without the sounds of bombing one could almost imagine that a horrible war with the deaths of hundreds of thousands was not underway. He was tired. The stress of running the Abwehr and the disastrous results of the war to date were taking their toll. If only something could be done about that madman Hitler running the country into the grave. Aside from the planning for Operation Grandfather, there were other ideas circulating in the clever mind of the Admiral. Perhaps he might pursue several goals while in Portugal, if he managed a discreet trip to Lisbon.

On Sunday afternoon, the Berlin city police received an anonymous phone call informing them that they should check out apartment 3B at 27 Windmuhlenweg. Upon their arrival, they found two men dead, both nearly naked and with stab wounds. One was known to the local police as a fairly notorious queer from the music hall world, who had managed to stay out of the military because of his bad foot. The other dead man was initially unknown, but from the bra and panties he was wearing, it was presumed he was a fellow pervert. The knife was found in the chest of this man. The conclusion by all three middle-aged policemen present was this had been some sort of lover's quarrel or robbery attempt gone bad. No need to waste much time on the mutual murders of two perverts. Unfortunately, one officer then looked in a closet and found the military uniform of the second dead man and his identity card – Major Fritz von Hesseburg, assigned to the Abwehr. The senior police officer on the scene knew that this was going to be embarrassing to somebody and that a great deal of discretion was going to be needed. He put the identity card in his pocket and told the other two officers to list the man on the official police report as "unknown." He would deliver the identity card to police headquarters and would leave it to some poor bastard much higher in rank than himself to deliver the news to Abwehr Headquarters.

## New York City

U.S. Army Captain Charles Worthington came down the stairs from the main entrance of Grand Central Station. Charles looked good in uniform. His six foot tall, average build filled it out nicely and he had a face that most women would refer to as handsome. It was pouring down rain and Charles figured it would be quite difficult to find an available taxi in such weather, especially with wartime gas rationing. Standing at the bottom of the stairs, holding a large umbrella, was a familiar face. It was Salvatore, the Italian-American gangster that Vincent Astor had arranged as Charles' bodyguard back in the fall of 1941. Charles had been assisting Mister Astor in a search for an American intelligence officer working for the Japanese as the threat of America being drug into the world war grew in the final months of that year. Salvatore was nattily dressed as ever, in a dark pinstriped suit, complete with a carnation in his buttonhole. He gave Charles a sharp salute and then pointed over to the large black Packard driven by fellow Italian, Lou. It was the same automobile and the same two "gentlemen" who had taken Charles to the train station for his departure from the city back in mid-December 1941. Charles began to ask Salvatore how it was he knew that Charles would be arriving that day and at that time from Washington DC, while traveling under secret orders, but decided it was best not to ask.

"Sally, you son of a gun! How are you?"

Salvatore extended his hand and gave the young captain a hearty shake. "I'm fine, just fine. And how's youse doing?" inquired the native of Brooklyn, with his unmistakable accent. "Let me help youse with your bag, Sir." Charles didn't even try to argue with his former gangster friend and simply handed over his leather suitcase. The two of them headed over to the Packard and a similar warm greeting occurred with Lou.

"Since you knew when I was arriving, I assume you know where I'm headed?"

"Sure, youse is headed for the Harvard Club, to have lunch with Mister Astor and Mister Kermit Roosevelt."

"I don't mean to embarrass either of you, but when I was leaving New York City back in late 1941, you two told me that you were planning on joining the Army. What happened with that plan?"

Both men looked a little sheepish. Sally finally answered for both of them. "Well, that was da plan and after we wrapped up a little business in December and celebrated the New Year, we wents down together to da Recruiting Office to sign up. Seeings as what soldiers do, youse knows, shooting and killing people, we figured that they would be ecstatic about havings experienced guys like us. But afters they did a little checking, they told us that because we had criminal records that we couldn't join their Army and go kill Germans and Japs! What kinda logic does that make?"

"That does seem a little narrow minded on the part of the Army. So what do you do when you're not picking me up?" Charles offered a big smile, so that neither man would take offense at his question.

"Well, youse might say that we're in the improving the morale of our soldiers business. Not only was the Army narrow minded as youse called it, about letting us join, but they don't wants their soldier boys that they do let in to have no fun. Guys always like to play a little cards, drink a little liquor and meets some girls, on a short term basis, ifs youse get my meaning? So, me and Lou makes dem recreational activities available to our boys in uniform. We's just as patriotic as dem Hollywood movie stars that do USO shows for the troops!"

Charles flashed a large grin. "Indeed you are! I suspect that Eleanor Roosevelt will be giving you a phone call one of these days to personally thank you for your service to the morale of our soldiers."

"Youse wants us to call you Captain, or can we still call you Charlie?"

"Unless we're in front of some colonel or general, it's fine to still call me Charlie."

"Youse still spying around over there in Portugal?" asked Salvatore. "I knows that's where you been caused Mister Astor told me, but I don'ts go spreading that around to just anybody."

"Yes, that's where I've been and I'm heading back there on Tuesday via the Pan Am Clipper."

The car pulled up to the curb in front of the Harvard Club and an elderly doorman in a bright red uniform with red braid opened the door for Charles. War or no war, the club maintained its standards. "Will I see you boys again while I'm in town?" asked Charles as he climbed out of the car and started to reach for his bag.

"Sure, Mister Astor has booked us to look after youse while youse is in town. You can just leave your bag here for now. We's taking you over to one of Mr. Astor's houses after your lunch. That's where youse will be staying."

Vincent Astor and Kermit Roosevelt were already seated at a luncheon table, awaiting the arrival of Charles. After the usual greetings, both men started questioning Charles about the situation in supposedly neutral Portugal. Kermit was technically in the US Army, but had continued to struggle with depression and alcoholism. Vincent still officially had his position as Coordinator of Intelligence in the New York area, but as the war effort had gotten into full swing and the intelligence units of the Army and Navy had grown immensely, there was less and less for Vincent to actually do on a weekly basis. President Roosevelt had appointed him to several advisory boards to make sure that the American economy was working efficiently and cranking out all of the necessary war matériel needed for the American troops and for America's allies.

"Can you tell us why General Donovan brought you back to Washington for meetings?" asked Vincent. "Is he perhaps sending you somewhere where there is a little more action?"

"No, nowhere new. I'm flying back to Lisbon on Tuesday. He just wanted to go over a few things with me about activities in Portugal."

Both men clearly looked a little disappointed. They had been talking before Charles' arrival and had concluded that as Charles had been in Lisbon for over a year, perhaps he was going to be moved on to some country where there was real fighting underway. Kermit spoke first, "Well, Donovan knows best where you're needed."

Charles tried suppressing his smile. "The general did mention to me that he was sending me back to Lisbon as the Chief of the OSS Station in Portugal and had arranged for me to be promoted to major, so that I would have the appropriate rank to go with the position."

The two older men were both trying to pat Charles on the back at the same time and big smiles had come to their faces. "Congratulations, congratulations," they were both saying with loud voices, drawing stern looks from fellow diners. Vincent might be one of the richest men of the country and Kermit the son of a former president and a cousin of the current one, but there were proper rules of decorum to be observed in the dining room of the Harvard Club! Vincent lowered his voice and inquired if there was any particular event that had led to Charles' promotion.

"Well, as you probably know, Major Robert Solborg had been the Chief in Lisbon since his arrival in early 1942, but General Donovan fired him late last year for being just a little too forward-leaning and taking actions without checking first with Washington. The strange thing is that Solborg has stayed on as an assistant military attaché for the Army at the Embassy, which has made it just a little bit awkward in our relations with him. David Delaney was made the Chief, but he was suddenly transferred out a couple of weeks ago because of his ability to speak Arabic. It's supposedly a secret where Delaney was sent, but you don't have to be a genius to figure it had to be North Africa."

"So, dominoes have been falling and you were the logical choice to be named the new Chief in Lisbon?"

"That's about it; although it may make things a little easier around the embassy with Delaney's departure. Solborg has always suspected that Delaney was behind his dismissal by General Donovan. I don't think that was the case, but there were very strained relations between the two of them. Fortunately, I don't think Solborg holds any particular animosity towards me."

Kermit turned to Vincent. "You remember Solborg don't you? His ancestry is Polish and he'd even been in the Polish cavalry at some point early in his career, if I'm not mistaken. We met him at some receptions down in Washington a few years back."

"Yes, yes I do, but the reason that I remember him is because I found him a rather arrogant individual who believed that he'd been denied several things in life to which he was entitled," replied Vincent. The two older men then looked to Charles to hear his assessment of Solborg.

"He seems a competent individual, but not the hardest working person in the military attaché's office. Perhaps that's the result of his feeling that he was treated unfairly by General Donovan. He arrives promptly on time in the mornings, but also leaves promptly at 5 PM each day and appears to spend a good deal of his time in Lisbon just enjoying life."

"I've heard the latter comment about me, though not always in Portugal," joked Kermit. "As long as he's getting his assignments done, more power to him in enjoying what might be a short and dangerous life for an Army officer these days."

Vincent turned the conversation back to his curiosity as to what interesting projects might be underway in Portugal. "Anything really sexy going on in Lisbon for the OSS these days? I hear secondhand that Lisbon is the spy capital of Europe. I trust that you're earning your pay in that regard."

Charles gave him an enigmatic smile. "The British tell us that there are people from some fifty different intelligence services of the world present in Portugal. You'd think that I must be able to find something to do while there!" He had just found out two days earlier from General

Donovan that in fact a couple of the most secret double agents working for the British were handled out of the British Embassy in Lisbon; one of them code-named TRICYCLE and the other GARBO. Charles was to meet with the MI6 Lisbon Commander about these cases as soon as he returned to Lisbon, in order to be ready to offer any American assistance in an emergency. While these were British operations, MI6 had decided to let a few Americans in on the cases involving Portugal, and upon Donovan's insistence, that included the OSS Chief of Lisbon.

"Speaking of different intelligence services, have you run across any attractive female Russian spies named Olga?" Charles hesitated a moment before answering, so Vincent continued. "Yes, Salvatore told us about the postcard you had received just before you left New York to go off for training in Canada back in December 1941."

"No, by the time I arrived in Lisbon there was no sign of Olga anywhere in the city. But then, the Salazar regime is not particularly fond of the Soviet Union. There's no official Soviet presence in the country. And I've had no further postcards from her."

The arrival of their food brought to a close any further conversation about the mysterious and gorgeous redheaded Russian "journalist" from the days when Charles was searching for a Japanese mole within the US government in New York City.

Charles spent the next several days doing some shopping for items which he wished to take back with him to Portugal. Not surprisingly, Salvatore was of great assistance in knowing where hard-to-find items could still be purchased. Charles dined with a few other acquaintances while waiting for his departure date for Lisbon. Come Tuesday it would be time for him to get back into the war, even if it was one that occurred in the shadows and more often involved martinis than bullets.

Aside from promoting him, General Donovan had also given him a sensitive assignment that he was to discuss with no one else in the American Embassy for the present. In a rather déjà vu task, Donovan had told him of the possibility of an Axis mole within the OSS Station of Lisbon or a possible breach of its classified communication system. One of the activities that had contributed to Solborg's dismissal had been the tasking of a Portuguese clerk working within the Japanese Embassy in Lisbon, who also earned a second salary from the OSS, for stealing items out of trash baskets in the offices of the Japanese officials for whom he worked as a translator and general gopher. Several pieces of paper that he stole one day turned out to be parts of a coded message. It turned out to be a rather low-level code that the Allies had long ago broken and not a message that had been done in the top-secret system involving the Purple machine and at the time, the stolen sheets had simply been filed away at OSS Headquarters.

The proverbial bureaucratic shit had hit the fan about a month later when a coded message from the Italian Foreign Ministry in Rome to its embassy in Lisbon had been intercepted and deciphered. The message instructed the Italian Ambassador to go to the Japanese Ambassador in Lisbon and inform him that his codes had been broken. The American fear was that the Japanese might correctly conclude, but for the wrong reason, that their highest-graded code, PURPLE had been broken and change it. That would bring to an end the American code-breaking program named MAGIC, which had been responsible for the great successes against the Japanese Navy throughout the Pacific Ocean. A special task force was examining the problem at the Washington end. Charles was to handle the investigation in Portugal. Ironically, while he couldn't tell Vincent about his assignment, General Donovan had chosen to trust Charles because of Vincent's assurances on several occasions that Charles was above suspicion and how helpful he'd been back in 1941. Charles was to suspect and investigate everyone in Lisbon who might have even possibly known about the theft of the few sheets of code paper from the Japanese Embassy. Anyone who knew about that operation might have tipped off the Italians, or there was always the possibility of hidden microphones in some part of the American Embassy in Lisbon. Without being able to trust anyone else in Lisbon, Charles was going to have a difficult time investigating everyone else on his own. As Salvatore and Lou were escorting him around town one afternoon, a bizarre thought came to his mind. Once at the mansion on 41st Street owned by Vincent Astor, where Charles was staying, Charles placed a call to General Donovan down in Washington.

# Chapter 2

Salvatore and Lou came to the Astor home Tuesday morning to pick him up at 10:00 a.m. as arranged, but Charles instructed both of them to come into the house, rather than him simply coming out with his bag when Sally knocked on the large ornate door of the elegant townhouse, which had belonged to the Astor family for several decades.

Charles directed them into the living room. "Have a seat fellas. We need to chat just a little before we head to the pier."

"Yeah, we suspected that after we both had visits last night at our apartments from some hush-hush guys in civilian clothes, that youse might have had something to do with that. They was carrying IDs saying they were with Army Intelligence,"

"A visit by Army Intelligence you say?" He smiled slightly.

"They told us that our applications to join the Army had been reconsidered and that we're supposed to shows up for physical examinations tomorrow morning. Youse arriving and our applications being 'reconsidered' might be what you'd call quite a coincidence."

"Indeed, it's no coincidence. I can't go into the details right now, but I've been given a very important assignment to carry out in Portugal and I need the assistance of a couple of mugs that I know I can trust. It might be just a few weeks or a few months. Hard to say right now. I hate to cut into your 'morale building' activities here in New York, but could you get away to Lisbon via the clipper in about ten days to give me a hand?"

The two looked at each other, shrugged their shoulders and gave him a salute. "Youse see Lou. I told youse when we picked him up at the train station the other day that soon he'd realize that he could use ours help."

"I take that as an affirmative response. How long will it take you to arrange for alternative management of your 'local businesses' while you'll be away?"

Sally shrugged again. "Well, I gots a few associates that I know I can trust not to lose our percentage of the profits while we're off fighting Nazis. I figure that in about a week or so, we's could be ready to travel."

"Excellent," replied Charles. "I knew I could count on you two. You have any further questions?"

Lou spoke up. "Yeah, just one. Youse gonna supply us with guns, or should we brings our own?" He patted the inside vest pocket of his suit jacket.

"I think the U.S. Army can find you a couple of guns and all the ammunition you need. Will 45's be OK?"

"A couple of 45s for each of us will be just fine," replied Salvatore without even a hint of a smile.

"OK, I think we're all set. The people you both met last night will be in touch once you've passed your physicals. They're the only two you should say anything to about going to Portugal. If by any chance Mr. Astor wants anything of you before you leave town, just tell him that you're doing something for me, but leave it at that. He won't press you for any details."

"Understood. Youse still wants us to take you to the pier this morning?"

"Absolutely, I think you two bring me luck when I'm starting a trip. Anything else need covering?"

Lou had one more question. "Could we just come over on a ship instead of the airplane? I ain't never been on a plane and the idea don't sound real assuring to me. I hear all the time about those things crashing."

"You'll be perfectly fine. I'll need you there sooner than a ship could get you there. Besides, on a ship you'd have to worry about a German U-boat putting a torpedo in you. The PanAm clipper is much safer." Lou still didn't seem real convinced, but saw that he was stuck with the airplane.

"Let's head down to the pier."

## Lisbon

The four-engine Pan American Clipper made a lazy circle over Lisbon, the capital of Portugal, before lining up for its amphibian landing in the bay. The flight from New York to Bermuda to the Azores and then on to Lisbon had been uneventful. Charles loved looking down on the picturesque city with its many red-tiled roofs, cobble-stoned streets and ancient churches. He enjoyed the Portuguese food and especially its wine. Because of its official neutrality, and with its travel connections to England, America, Germany, Italy and various countries of North Africa, making it a crossroads for people of all sides in the war, it was indeed the spy capital of the world. Because of the dozens of foreign intelligence services present in the country and the thousands of Portuguese citizens who had found employment serving those various services, watching other spies or renting non-descript apartments where an intelligence officer could secretly meet one of his agents, espionage was also one of the major professions of the country! And then there were the thousands of members of the Portuguese Security Service, the PVDE, which watched the foreigners (who were often watching other foreigners) and also any locals suspected of being disloyal to Prime Minister Antonio Salazar. He had come to power in 1932 and planned on staying in office for many years to come.

His government of "Estado Novo" was a mixture of nationalism and conservatism; he was opposed to democracy and communism. His basic political policy was simply that whatever assisted him to stay in power was good policy for the country. While maintaining friendly relations with Germany and Franco's totalitarian Spain, he kept Portugal neutral in the war, seeing no advantage for getting actively involved on either side. The mining and sale of the mineral wolfram, better known as tungsten, to Germany was very profitable for Portugal. Its extraction and export employed 100,000 people and brought in some hundred million US dollars each year to Portugal. Wolfram was very important to the Nazi war effort, because of its hardness and use in various military projectiles.

Neither the American nor British governments liked the sale of wolfram to Germany, but accepted it as the lesser of two evils rather than "insisting" on the halt of the supply to Germany and thus possibly pushing Portugal to join the Axis alliance. There was also the distinct possibility of the Nazis using such a cutoff as an excuse for simply invading and taking over the country so as to assure the continued supply of wolfram. The Germans could then also use Portuguese airfields and ports to attack shipping entering the Mediterranean Sea, choking off supplies to North Africa. One assignment for the OSS officers in Lisbon was to prepare for the sabotage of these mines, should either of those "negative" steps occur.

The British had only opened an office of its intelligence service, MI6, in Lisbon in September 1939. There was, however, a long history of good British-Portuguese relations and many citizens were privately in favor of the Allies winning the war. On the other hand, times were hard and a lot of Portuguese were quite amenable to being bought, if the price was right. There was a joke among the OSS officers that you didn't really recruit a Portuguese, you simply rented him for periods of time. Of course that always left open the possibility of the other side paying him more at an inopportune moment.

After landing and passing quickly through customs, given his diplomatic passport, Charles took a taxi first to his apartment. He wanted to drop off his suitcase, take a shower and grab a few hours of sleep before going to his Embassy late in the afternoon. It was nearly 4:00 p.m. when he showed up at his office on the third floor of the quaint, old building. They had been informed via a secure telegram of his planned arrival that day and of his promotion to becoming the head of the OSS Station in Lisbon. That was rather expected, but of more interest to most everyone was to hear what was the latest gossip out of Washington, about the war or simply about whose careers were headed up or down at OSS Headquarters.

It took Charles a few days for his body to adjust to Portugal-time and get back into the swing of OSS work. Being Chief wasn't all the fun that most people presumed it would be. He now had to sign off on all outgoing messages, sign off on the time sheets, approve leave requests and all the other bureaucratic necessities that readers of spy novels never associated with a spy organization. Fortunately, he had a very good secretary, Mary Beth, who knew the ins and outs of how to run the Station and politely took over doing most of it, while pretending that Charles was actually in charge of the place. She'd been in Lisbon since the OSS office had opened and not only knew all the ins and outs of the Embassy, but everybody had learned that you couldn't sweet talk your way around the middle-aged lady for any needed favor. She was a very plain Jane and knew that if any of the men in the office tried flirting with her, it was simply because they wanted a favor. The few other female employees of the Station, all much younger than Mary Beth, really liked her. If one of them was supposed to work late and a "hot date" suddenly came up, she was always willing to fill in for the younger gal.

One afternoon shortly after his return, Charles had her bring him all the personnel files on the 17 people who made up Lisbon Station, explaining to her that he simply wanted to be familiar with all the skills and backgrounds of the staff. Naturally, he knew most of the people and their backgrounds just from chatting over coffee or lunch, but he wanted to see if there were any clues as to who might have had reason to leak the information about the theft at the Japanese Embassy to the enemy. The personnel records showed the names and background of parents and even grandparents. Nobody seemed to have an Italian grandfather hiding in the closet. No other indications leapt from the pages as to why any of them would willingly provide information to the Italian government. That, of course, left the possibility of doing it unwillingly, as in blackmail over some indiscretion, or good old-fashioned greed. Investigating those possibilities would be where Salvatore and Lou would be useful. He hoped that the Italian and Portuguese languages were close enough so that the two could get around on their own and be more or less understood.

A few days later, Charles went to the British Embassy for a meeting with Nigel Pendergast, listed on the diplomatic roster as an assistant attaché in the Passport Control Office, but actually the MI6 Chief in Lisbon. He had been informed by London Headquarters that Charles would be dropping by for a conversation. He was to advise the American, in general terms, about the existence and work of two of the British double agents based in England who were working against the Abwehr and who, on occasion, would travel to Lisbon to meet their Abwehr handlers. A junior officer met Charles at the front door of the stately 19th century edifice and politely escorted him up to Pendergast's office, while discussing in typical British fashion the "beastly" weather they'd been having recently. After a quick knock on the large oak door by the junior officer, Charles was shown into Nigel's office. Charles had to suppress an inclination to grin. The trappings of the office, from the large ornate mahogany desk to the portraits on the walls of various English kings and queens, were straight out of a Hollywood movie version of how an upper class British study should appear. Nigel himself also perfectly fit the image of an English gentlemen, by his clothes, his pure Norman features and his public school accent.

"Charles, so good of you to drop by. I know we've met briefly a few times about the city at receptions, but we've never had a good chat have we?" He rose from behind his magnificent desk and came around to shake Charles' hand. He pointed to a couple of large leather chairs over by the window. "Would you care to join me for some tea, or is it late enough in the work day for you to enjoy something a bit stronger?"

"Tea will be fine for me."

"Excellent. Sadly, it's actually a bit hard to get good tea back home. I do feel a bit embarrassed that we have easy access to it here in Portugal. Whenever I travel back to London, I actually take a few tins with me as gifts for the chaps stuck there at Headquarters."

"I'm sure they appreciate your thoughtfulness." Charles took his seat.

Nigel poured their tea. "I understand you're a Harvard man?"

"Yes, that's correct. And yourself?

"Cambridge," was the reply, with a tone as if to say, "but of course, where else is there for a proper education in England."

After a few more minutes of the obligatory chit chat, they got down to the appointed business.

"Well, I've been instructed by "C" to brief you on the operations of TRICYCLE and GARBO, two of our double cross agents, as we refer to them. The understanding is that it is to be you alone from your office who is to know about them and that there will be no written records kept at your Embassy."

"That is the understanding that I was given by General Donovan when I met with him just before I left Washington to return to Lisbon." If Nigel was going to drop the name of Stewart Menzies, "C", the chief of MI6, then Charles figured he would mention General Donovan.

"Very good, let's begin with our little Spaniard, agent GARBO. He's quite the clever fellow in his late twenties. My colleagues over in Madrid had turned him down when he'd volunteered back in early 1941, as he had no connections of any interest, so the cheeky fellow went over and volunteered at the German Embassy, claiming he was about to move to England and had lots of friends in government. They gave him a bottle of secret ink and some accommodation addresses in Spain and wished him well. Well, that was all a fabrication. He simply moved here, bought a few used books about England and started making up 'reports' about the war effort and mailed them off to Madrid."

"Didn't the Germans notice the letters were mailed in Lisbon, not London?"

"Ah, well, that was part of his ingenious mind. He'd told his Abwehr handler that he had a friend with the airline that flew between London and Lisbon and the friend would smuggle his letters to Portugal to mail from here and thus the Portuguese post mark. The silly German buggers bought his fanciful stories and forwarded his information via radio to Berlin."

A smile of admiration had come to Charles' face. "Quite the crafty fellow. Glad he's on our side. You are convinced he's really on our side?"

"Yes, we are quite certain. I was told you are aware of our, uh, very special intelligence?"

"Yes I am, in general terms."

"Good, that will make it much easier. When we started intercepting messages out of Madrid in mid-1941 about their great new agent in London, I can tell you that the MI5 boys started pulling their hair out in panic as they thought they had all the German agents in jail or under control. Then they really carefully read the agent reports and realized they were nonsense. I won't bore you with the long story, but in early 1942 the Spaniard contacted your OSS colleagues in Madrid and told them the whole story. They came to us about the fellow, we remembered his volunteering and we realized he was the mysterious German agent with the codename ARABEL we'd been reading about in the intercepts. Everyone at the MI6 Station in Madrid felt rather embarrassed at having turned him away in the first place, but we swallowed our pride and recontacted him. He asked us if now we thought he had any useful contacts! Anyway, we moved him, his wife and son up to London and have continued to run him as a double agent. Occasionally, he can explain a trip back to Lisbon or Madrid, but he has his own shortwave radio link to the Abwehr and cranks out several bogus reports a day to their offices in Madrid."

"Sounds like a great case. And the Abwehr really believe his radio reports?"

"From their own messages between Madrid and Berlin, it certainly appears that they do, though I have a peculiar thought on that, which I'll return to in a moment. Now, we here in Lisbon are much more directly involved with the second fellow. He's a Yugoslav, from an upper class family, with a good education and who is quite the handsome playboy. He had first been approached in Belgrade by the Abwehr to work for them. He agreed to their offer, but came straight to the British Embassy the next day and offered to do whatever we instructed him to do. He's been an excellent double agent for us ever since the first week."

"He's in London as well?"

"Yes, the Germans think he has some sort of low-level job with the Yugoslav government-in-exile, but that he also has some personal business dealings which occasionally bring him to Lisbon. In fact, he's scheduled to arrive here in just a few weeks time. The London Controlling Station, which actually runs all these double agents, is sending out one of their bright young lads from Naval Intelligence to oversee everything. He isn't really needed, so I suspect that young Ian Fleming is just using the travel of TRICYCLE as an excuse to get out of England and come to Portugal for a few weeks!"

"And what is your peculiar thought about whether the Germans truly trust these agents?"

"Ah, yes, that. It's just my own personal view mind you, but we know a good bit about the Abwehr chief here, Karsthoff, and the Madrid chief, Kuhlenthall, and both of them seem pretty sharp fellows. Also, there have been a few minor inconsistencies in both agents' reporting over time. Bit hard to fathom that both men have been completely fooled by our efforts, yet their official reports praise them highly month after month."

Charles was quite attentive. "And, your explanation is?"

"The Abwehr does seem to be a bit of a dog eat dog organization. Second, it is much colder and much more dangerous on the Russian Front than here. Three, handling star agents here looks very good in those men's personnel files and probably guarantees their continued presence under the Iberian sunshine. It might even be a subconscious inclination to simply believe the best about their agents. Reminds me of an old mentor of mine in British Military Intelligence, Major Gill, who had a plaque on his door saying 'no wishful thinking allowed here.' Perhaps those two are just allowing themselves some 'wishful thinking,' or perhaps it's even a bit more cynical, but it appears that they have no intention of upsetting the boat and suggesting in official reports back to Berlin that their star reporters might be controlled and are sending along bogus information."

"I suspect you're more acquainted with the German mind than I am, but if you're correct, it certainly tells us something about the mentality and professional ethics of Colonels Karsthoff and Kuhlenthall!"

"Just a theory of mine for now."

"Very well. I think that's all I need to know as background. If there's ever anything I can do to assist, please don't hesitate to ask."

"Thank you. I guess there's just one more thing – their true names, in case you do ever stumble across any mention of them from your assets. GARBO is Juan Pujol Garcia and TRICYCLE is Dusko Popov. But as I said, please do not write those names down anywhere in your files."

"Understood. I do have one other topic for today. Do you by chance have much information about who the Italian Intelligence Service people here in Lisbon are?"

"I think we might know a few of the names. Can't say as we pay much attention to the Italians here as we've never seen them do much of anything, except enjoy the food, the wine and the women of Portugal! But I'll check our files and send over to you in the next day or two anything that we have. Any particular reason you're inquiring about the Italians? With the way the fighting is going on there now, I can't imagine that there will be an Italian Service in a few months from now."

"That may well be. I simply noticed recently that we didn't have much in our files on the Italians and thought we ought to at least have an accurate listing of who is here in town from their service." Charles hated lying to Nigel, but he had no brief to share with him the intercept information indicating a leak out of the OSS office in Lisbon. Hearing that fact wouldn't have made Nigel feel particularly comfortable, having just handed over to an OSS officer the true names of two of their most valuable double agents!

Charles made his farewells and returned to the American Embassy just as the work day was ending. He signed off on the release of a few telegrams to Washington and then was headed out of the building when he ran into Bob Solborg.

"Charles, I heard you were back. How was your trip?"

"Good, thanks. It's always nice to get back home for a few days and see a few friends. How have you been?"

"Alice and I went down to the Algarve beaches for a week. We just returned yesterday. By the way, I understand that congratulations are in order. I hear they made you the chief here in Lisbon."

Charles wasn't quite sure how to deal with this potentially sore point with Solborg and decided to just minimize the issue. "I think I was just the next in line in terms of having been here the longest and they decided I couldn't screw up things too much. Are you in a big hurry to get home? Or do you have time to join me for a drink over at the Club Copacabana?" Charles had been wanting to get a better feel for Solborg as a possible suspect of the leak about the Japanese Embassy operation and this seemed as good a time as any to get started.

Solborg took a quick look at his watch and replied, "Sure, I have time for one or maybe even two before I need to head home for dinner. I presume that you will be buying, now that you have been promoted to being the chief."

They both smiled. "Sure, drinks are on me."

The club would not be busy until later in the evening, so it was quiet and easy for the two of them to converse in private. Charles shared with him news from America on how everyone down to the local taxi drivers of New York City thought the war was going. After about fifteen minutes of idle chitchat, Charles shifted the conversation to slightly more valuable topics. "Bob, is it true that you were really in the Polish cavalry when you were a young man?"

"Indeed, I was. If you ever need someone to lead a cavalry charge, I'm your man!" They both drained their glasses in a mock toast and Charles signaled to the waiter for another round of drinks.

"So you're ancestors are all Polish? Any place in Poland I would have ever heard of?"

"My father's side of the family all lived near Warsaw, but my mother was actually born in Sicily. That's why I'm so good looking," he quipped. "Unfortunately, my mother died when I was still a young teenager."

"Sorry to hear that. Do you still have any relatives back in Poland or Italy?"

"Everyone left Poland for America at the same time. As for Italy, I suppose I might have some distant cousins somewhere, but after her marriage, which was frowned upon by her family, it doesn't appear that my mother ever maintained any contacts with people back in Sicily."

After finishing their second round of drinks, Bob announced that he really should be getting home for dinner and departed. Charles decided to stay on and have one more glass of wine and think about Solborg as the possible leak. He would have the hypothetical motive of seeking revenge against the OSS for his being fired and now Charles had learned of his Italian ancestry as well. Hard to say if his mother having been Italian actually meant anything to Bob or not. For some people, one's ancestry was very important, for others, it really meant nothing at all. They simply thought of themselves as Americans.

Two days later the Pan American Clipper arrived with two ghostly white Italian-Americans among the passengers. Once they were on the dock and Charles had led them away from the other people, he joked with them, "Good thing that you two joined the regular Army; I don't see a real future for either of you in the Army Air Corps!"

"I'll be staying here in Portugal until the war is over, so I can go home on a ship," replied Lou.

Charles had personally and discreetly booked them into a small family-run pension away from the center of Lisbon, which would also provide them their meals. He didn't want others at the Embassy to know of their association with him. Charles took them directly there, registered them and told them to get some sleep. He would be back at 7 p.m. to take them out to dinner, at which time he would discuss with them their tasks while in Lisbon.

Charles had arranged that same day to have lunch with Captain Antonio Lourenco, the head of the Lisbon branch of the PVDE. Nobody knew for certain how many people were in the Police for Vigilance and Defense of the State, but it was the primary organization for making sure that Salazar and his associates stayed in office and seemed to have officers and informants everywhere numbering no doubt into the thousands. They didn't mind if foreigners spied on, recruited or even assassinated each other, but anything that appeared to be a threat to the stability of the regime was not allowed and was cracked down on immediately with no subtlety at all. Many of the senior PVDE officers, including Lourenco, had the reputation of being pro-Nazi, but Charles suspected that many of them were mostly just looking out for number one, i.e. themselves. As the war had started to turn in favor of the

Allies, he'd noticed that a number of the local police officers seemed to be much more "open minded" and neutral than they had been back in early1942.

Once they were seated at a seaside fish restaurant in the suburb of Estoril and the waiter had poured both gentlemen a glass of vinho verde wine, Lourenco raised his glass to Charles. "Congratulations on your promotion to major and to becoming the chief of your office." They clinked their glasses and drank. Supposedly Lourenco knew a good bit of English, but always insisted on speaking in Portuguese if a foreigner had any command of the language. Perhaps he felt it gave him an advantage in the conversation, or perhaps simply felt it a matter of courtesy – that if a foreign intelligence officer was coming into Portugal, he should speak the language.

"I've only been back about ten days and you already know of my promotion," replied Charles with a smile.

"Well, I am the head of the secret police here in Lisbon; it would be a poor reflection on me if I didn't know such things." They both laughed. "So, what is new in America? Is it true that Betty Grable married Harry James?"

"Yes, back in early July. Quite an affair I heard, all sorts of Hollywood stars were there."

"Ah, my heart is broken. She has married someone besides me. I'd heard it on a BBC shortwave broadcast, but one never knows what to believe on those broadcasts. There is so much propaganda!"

"I don't think there'd be much reason for the British to lie about who Harry James married," teased Charles.

"Perhaps not, but then according to the BBC, the Allies have taken Italy, the Russians are advancing everywhere and the war might be over next year."

"You don't think the tide of the war has turned?"

"Well, Colonel Karsthoff describes the situation a little differently," responded Lourenco, with his own slight smile under his thin Errol Flynn mustache. "He talks of 'tactical withdrawals' and 'straightening of the lines' and seems to think that being rid of Italy as an ally is actually an improvement." Both men laughed at the snide comment about Italian fighting capability. "I believe Mr. Churchill supposedly said something similar in 1939 when Ribbentrop stated that if there was to be a future war, Italy would be Germany's ally. Churchill responded

23

that that would only be fair – England had been burdened with them in the last war. But tell me, what are they saying in Washington about how this war is going?"

"If I tell you, will you then pass that along to Colonel Karsthoff?"

"Only if he asks me when I have lunch with him this coming Friday at his home. Have you ever been to his home? No, of course not. How silly of me. It's a beautiful place with a lovely view of the ocean."

"Perhaps I'll have a chance to see the inside of it when the war is over."

Lourenco smiled. He liked Charles' sense of humor. "Shall we order? The head waiter told me when I came in that they have fresh swordfish today."

"Excellent, why don't you just order for both of us. I hate to torture him with my poorly accented Portuguese."

I will do that, but you're much too modest. You're Portuguese is very good. I think you must spend a lot of time speaking our language, especially at night with your secret agents."

"Perhaps it's from talking so much at night with the beautiful Portuguese women!"

"Perhaps," replied the police chief with a nod of his head. "Perhaps."

The two ordered and continued their light-hearted banter throughout the leisurely meal. Charles turned serious only once, over dessert, when he mentioned in passing that when the Allies had won the war, they would remember who had been their friends and who had not during the war. It might be nearing the time when many people should be getting off the fence, even in neutral Portugal.

Once again, Lourenco smiled and simply responded, "Perhaps."

At the very end, it was the police chief's turn to be serious. "You should be careful when out late at night on the streets of my city, whether to meet agents or beautiful women. Unfortunately, there are a lot of criminals out at night these days who don't care that you have diplomatic immunity. This is no game for amateurs."

Charles almost laughed.

"I am not joking my friend. These are difficult times for many Portuguese and many have turned to crime to survive."

"I do take your warning seriously. I wasn't laughing at your comment; it's just that someone told me almost the exact same thing a few years ago." Charles stared off into the ocean for several long seconds, remembering fondly the lovely Olga's warning to him back in New York City. "By the way, are there any Soviet representatives of any kind here in Portugal? I know you don't have diplomatic relations, but are there any sort of charitable organizations or journalists?"

"I don't think there is anything official. Of course, the various leftists are always seeking donations to help Russian orphans or something like that. If it looks like something legitimately helping children or wounded Russians, my office tends to look the other way. I am really a compassionate person. Besides, if their money is going off to some Russian charity, it's less money they have to be printing up Communist flyers, etc. here in Portugal."

Charles didn't make Lourenco ask as to why he was inquiring. He immediately explained that he had brushed elbows with a few NKVD officers back in New York City before America got in the war and he was simply curious if there were any around Lisbon. Presuming Lourenco's denial of knowing of any such presence was true, Charles seemed out of luck on getting any word on what had happened to Olga after she mailed her postcard to him from Lisbon back in late 1941.

When the check came, Charles started to reach for it, but Lourenco took it and put it in his pocket. "Please, save your money for your agents. It's only a little game the manager plays with me. He gives me a bill, I tear up the bill. The lunch doesn't cost either one of us."

"Thank you. This has been very pleasant. We shall have to do this again soon. Give my regards to Colonel Karsthoff on Friday!"

## Chapter 3

The handsome passenger with short-cropped hair in his early 30s came down the B.O.A.C. flight portable stairway while still flirting with one of the stewardesses, as he had been for most of the flight from London to Lisbon. Unfortunately, she already had plans for that evening in the city and would fly back to England the next day, so the charming Yugoslav had to settle for only getting her phone number back in London. He was relieved to have landed safely in Portugal. Generally, the flights between the two capitals circled far enough out to sea to be safe from German fighter planes, but one had been shot down just a couple of months earlier carrying the famous English actor Leslie Howard on his way back to England.

The check-in clerk at the front desk of the Hotel Estoril looked attentive as the well-dressed man approached, followed by a bellboy carrying a very expensive-looking leather suitcase. He was not enough of a regular that the clerk recognized the man by name, but simply the way he carried himself and his well-tailored clothing told him that this was a client accustomed to being treated well and perhaps tipped well in return.

"Good afternoon, Sir. How may I help you?" inquired the elderly clerk in excellent English.

"I'm fine thank you. I believe that you have a reservation for Dusko Popov. I requested a room on the back side of the hotel."

The clerk placed a registration card and fountain pen on the marble counter for Mr. Popov and then searched in the wooden registrations box. "Yes, here we are. You are in Room 427, with a balcony. The young man will take you to your room now if you are ready."

After being shown the room, the guest gave the young man a full English pound note and a gracious thank you for his assistance. Popov knew that it was always good form to exceedingly over-tip the first employee of any hotel. Word would then spread quickly and he would be assured of excellent service and a good dining table for the rest of his stay. He checked his gold watch. It was only two o'clock. He had plenty of time for an afternoon nap before he was due in the casino at 7:00 p.m. He phoned down to the front desk and requested a wake-up call for 6:00 and also instructed that he was not to be disturbed before that time. He then lay down and fell quickly asleep. Plane travel always wore him out.

Wearing a white dinner jacket and black bow tie, Popov entered the casino portion of the hotel just a little before seven o'clock. Some men looked exceptionally elegant in formal attire; Popov was one of them. He purchased some chips and then went straight to the one roulette table that was operating. It was still early for the usual gambling clientele and there were probably only 50-60 people present at the various tables around the beautifully decorated gambling hall. Popov only made a few small and unsuccessful bets until a beautiful blonde woman came to the table. She paid no attention whatsoever to Popov, or any of the other dozen or so players. She placed a small wager on number 3 and lost. This was followed by wagers on 21 then 20, upon which she also lost. She then seemed to lose interest in the game and headed to the bar area of the casino. Even if anyone had recognized her as Elizabeth Sahrbach, personal secretary to Colonel Karsthoff, they would have simply concluded that she'd decided to have a few flutters before going for a drink. A few minutes later, Popov also left the table and the casino, now knowing that he should be waiting the next night at pre-arranged site number 3, at 2120 hours military time. With luck it would be Fraulein Sahrback driving the car. He never made but the slightest token passes at her, as it was generally assumed around the German Embassy that Elizabeth did more than just typing and filing for Karsthoff. It wouldn't be good to get the head of the Lisbon Abwehr office angry at him. Still, she was very pleasant to look at while she was driving him to Karsthoff's home for his secret debriefings by him.

While Popov was losing at roulette, Charles was having dinner with Sally and Lou at an obscure chicken piri-piri restaurant. There was nothing elegant about the place, but the roasted chicken coated with the fiery African spice was delicious. Charles' nose had discovered the small family-run hole-in-the-wall one Sunday afternoon as he was just wandering on foot about the city. He'd suspected from the wonderful smell emanating from the door that there had to be something delicious inside and he had been correct. He'd eaten there numerous times since that first day.

A week earlier, Charles had provided the two men a list of the home addresses of all of his OSS colleagues in Lisbon and they were to be discretely investigating everyone as the potential leaker to the Italian Service. Most all were bachelors or unaccompanied by spouses, but a couple had managed to bring their wives, as they worked as clerks within the OSS office in the Embassy.

After the initial chitchat they got down to business. Charles asked, "Anything interesting turn up yet?"

Sally gave a big grin. "Yeah, the married guys here without their wives are having more sex than the actual bachelors of your office!"

"Any of them sleeping with nice Italian girls?" inquired Charles.

"Naw, it looks like they's all Portuguese broads."

"Too bad. And to what do you owe the greater success of the unaccompanied married men to their true bachelor colleagues at finding local girlfriends?"

Lou and Salvatore looked at each other. Finally, Lou answered. "Maybes cause they appreciate the opportunity more and try harder."

"Hmm. An interesting observation about the condition of mankind during the stress of wartime," noted Charles.

That was one of those rather erudite comments that sometimes came out of Charles' mouth that the two street-wise, but graduates of only junior high school, simply ignored and waited for him to say something that they understood.

"And how about any unexplained spending?"

"First thing youse ought to know is that the locks most of these guys have at their apartments are worthless. Anybody who wanted to sneak in and steal something, or just looks around, would have no problem at all with dem locks. And if any of youse colleagues have extra money, they sure ain't spending it on good clothes or other stuff in their homes. Youse working with a number of real slobs."

"I shall be sure to send an office memo around tomorrow about personal hygiene." Another comment simply ignored by the two Italian-Americans.

"Now, we's asked around of a number of da neighbors, to get a feel for whats they think of your guys. We only came up with two people who sort of stand out from the others." Salvatore opened a small notebook. "One guy whose name is John Clark apparently never goes out and never has company in. Once he comes home, he turns on his shortwave radio and just stays there till its bedtime."

Clark wasn't a guy Charles knew well and indeed he did seem to keep pretty much to himself, even at work. "And who is the second 'unusual' fellow?"

"His name is Gary Powell. Apparently, he goes out in his car late at night several times a week and sometimes he drives away on a Friday evening and doesn't come home till late Sunday night."

"Not terribly incriminating in either case, but I'll check back in the records and see when Powell normally meets his agents. If it's usually late at night, that might well explain his nighttime behavior. As for Clark, I don't know what to say. God knows what he does at home alone every night, but he doesn't seem like a man who is out having secret meetings with an Italian intelligence officer."

"Youse told us to look for some behavior that was unusual. Everybody else is out and about or having women in for sex, but this guy apparently just sits alone at home."

"True. If he is my man, maybe he wants to be alone because he feels guilty about what he's doing, as in betraying his country? I'm just grabbing at straws here. Frankly, Solborg is my first candidate, but weirdly enough, he looks so guilty I just can't believe it could be that obvious." Charles slid a large envelope across the table to Sally. "Here is a photo of Solborg and his wife Alice, and his home address. Even though he has not been part of the OSS Station for many months, why don't you two take a look at him for the next few days and get a feel for what he does with his nights."

"Whatever youse thinks is best, boss. I wish we could wrap this up. We thinks it would be a lot more fun following around dem German spies rather than our own guys."

"I couldn't agree with you more. Spying on my colleagues isn't much fun, but we need to find who the mole is, if there is one. Then we could all get back to our real job – the Nazis."

The following evening, Dusko Popov, wearing a well-tailored, dark suit, first took a taxi from his luxury hotel to downtown Lisbon. He walked around a bit, then took a second taxi and did more walking in back streets. As he was really working for the British, he didn't actually have any concerns about being followed by the British to his meeting with the Germans that night, but as the Germans had told him to do such surveillance checks, he did them. On the off chance that they were watching him, he needed to be seen doing the checks. If he didn't, they might wonder why he wasn't concerned about being followed to his meeting with the Abwehr. It was all such a complicated world of mirrors within mirrors. After several hours of "checking," he took a taxi to a small café out near the Boca de Inferno – the Mouth of Hell. It was so named because of the natural geography of the coastal spot, which forced the waves to crash violently on a small section of the coastline. Upon arrival to the parking lot of the café, he waited till the taxi had driven away, then he started walking the last few hundred yards to reach the pick-up spot. He had only been at the spot for a few minutes when a large Mercedes sedan driven by Katherine pulled up.

"Good evening, Fraulein Sahrback."

"Good evening, Herr Popov. Did you have any luck at the roulette table last night?"

"No, seeing you was the only good thing that happened for me yesterday."

"Oh, Mr. Popov, you say the sweetest things." She gave him a smile, then headed back in the direction of the city. The two continued their polite chit chat as they drove.

"Should we not have turned back there for Colonel Karsthoff's home?"

"Yes, we should have, if we were headed to his home. You and he are meeting somewhere else tonight." After another fifteen minutes of driving, she turned in to a rarely used gate for the airport. "We've just about arrived."

As she pulled up to a plane, Colonel Karsthoff came over and opened the door of the car. "Good evening, Dusko. I trust you had an uneventful trip."

Popov did not like the situation, but tried to maintain a calm appearance as he stepped from the vehicle. "Have you just arrived back to Lisbon?" he inquired of the Abwehr chief.

"No, you and I are about to take a trip to Paris. There is someone who wants to meet you. I'm sorry for the short notice, but we can get you some personal items and a change of clothes once we land. Please, come with me. We must leave immediately, so that we arrive there early in the morning. We're much less likely to encounter Allied fighter planes if we arrive at first light."

Popov definitely didn't like the idea of a trip to German-occupied France, but Karsthoff had already turned his back and headed for the steps to board the plane. Popov flirted for a moment with the notion of making a run for the gate, but saw that there were two other Germans standing nearby the plane as well. His running would certainly prove beyond a doubt that he had betrayed the Abwehr. He decided to bluff it out. After all, if they wanted to interrogate or even kill him, they could just as easily do that in Karsthoff's home. No need to fly him all the way to Paris.

"I hope you have some food on board. I was expecting dinner at your home and I'm starving." He hoped that made him appear as a man with nothing to worry about. As soon as the two men were seated, the engines started and in a matter of minutes they were on their way northward.

Karsthoff did indeed have a basket with food and a bottle of good German white wine on board, which was opened once they were at their cruising altitude. "So, who in Paris wants to see me?"

"I'm not supposed to tell you; it's to be a surprise, but I can tell you that you will be quite honored!"

"The Fuhrer is coming to Paris to meet me?" asked Popov, with a slight smile.

"Not quite that much of an honor, but you will be impressed. Once you've eaten, I suggest that you try to get some sleep. When we arrive in the morning, we will be going straight to the meeting."

Seeing that he would learn nothing more from Karsthoff, Popov finished his roast beef sandwich and another glass of wine and then leaned back to try to sleep as suggested. With no other facts to go on, there was little point in worrying about what would really be happening upon arrival in Paris. He had always been a self-confident and optimistic person and he would remain so that night. The droning of the propeller engines and steady vibration of the plane did fairly quickly put him to sleep. When he awoke, he could see the sun just rising on the right side of the plane and they seemed to be descending. It was not Orly they were landing at. It seemed to be some sort of rough, military airfield still south of the city.

A large, black Mercedes sedan was waiting for them as soon as their plane came to a stop on the grass field and there was an escort vehicle as well. There was some captain there who greeted them, but he appeared to have no role other than to get his two passengers into the vehicle and take them somewhere. Within about twenty minutes, their vehicle entered the grounds of a lovely country chateau. One which no doubt the owner had "donated" to the German Army, thought Popov as they pulled up to the front entrance of the main house. Two armed soldiers snapped to attention as he and Karsthoff exited the Mercedes. Another Army captain impeccably dressed and a high shine on his boots appeared as the large wooden door of the 17th century home swung open.

"Good morning, gentlemen. I trust you had a good flight," was his opening comment as he gestured for them to enter the mansion. There were more armed guards inside the grand hallway. He may not be meeting Hitler, but whoever it was must be somebody of importance to merit such quarters. The captain said nothing further and simply led them in silence up the stone stairway and opened another door to a large study. There was a man standing with his back to them, looking out the window at the surrounding fields.

The captain came to attention. "Admiral Canaris. May I present Colonel Karsthoff and his guest."

The Admiral turned abruptly and came over to the small group with a broad smile on his face. "Welcome, Ludovico, how have you been?"

"Fine, Admiral, and yourself?" The two had never met in their lives, but if the head of the Abwehr wanted to pretend that they were old friends, he was happy to go along with the charade. He knew that personally escorting Agent Arabel to Paris had been a good idea.

Canaris ignored Karsthoff's question as superiors generally do to questions by subordinates and simply turned his attention to his guest. "Dusko, how are you? I'm glad that we finally have a chance to meet. I've been reading, of course, all of your excellent reporting. Please, come over here and have a seat. Would you like some coffee or something to eat?"

Popov shook the Admiral's extended hand and followed him to a setting of chairs near the window. "Yes, some coffee and a roll would be quite good." He acted as if he met with important men on a daily basis.

The Admiral indicated to the escorting captain to bring some refreshments and took a seat as the captain clicked his heels and departed the room. Karsthoff sat in silence as Canaris and Popov discussed the weather of Lisbon and whether one could still get good coffee back in London, even with the war going on. The captain and a corporal actually carrying coffee, croissants and some fresh cut fruit in bowls returned in a few minutes and placed it on a small table. The corporal poured coffee for all and served up a croissant for Popov. As the Admiral took only coffee, Karsthoff decided he should only take a cup of coffee as well, even though he was quite hungry.

"Tell me about the general situation in London. About the mood of the people and the situation of food supplies."

"Well, if I may speak freely, I'd say the situation has been improving throughout this year in terms of food supplies and in general, the mood of the populace is improving every month. This has been greatly helped by the ending of Luftwaffe bombings of the city, and the news from Italy and the Russian Front is making the English optimistic that they will win the war within the next year or so."

Colonel Karsthoff was fidgeting a bit in his chair, wondering how such a negative assessment by Popov would go down with the Admiral. He had a reputation for being a realist, but there is honesty and then there is honesty. Karsthoff waited to see how such a senior figure of the Reich would react to such frank views.

"Yes, that's generally the impression we hear from a number of sources. I've known a number of Englishmen over the years and they are a resilient race."

Canaris asked further questions about the types of contacts that Popov had within the British government or military, mostly just listening in silence and giving the occasional head nod. Finally, he turned to Karsthoff. "Ludovico, would you please give me and Dusko a few moments alone. There is one subject I would like to discuss with him in private."

Karsthoff stood immediately. "Certainly, Sir. I shall wait out in the hall until I am again needed."

Canaris sat in silence until the door closed behind the departing Colonel. "What I am about to discuss with you is to remain strictly between you and me. You will not discuss it with Colonel Karsthoff. Is that perfectly clear?"

"Yes, Admiral, I understand perfectly." He rose and went over to the table and poured himself some more coffee. He thought to himself that this day was turning out to be an excellent one.

"Do you know anyone within the British MI6 organization?"

Popov did not flinch. "Yes, I am acquainted socially with a few officers who have told me they are attached to MI6, though in what capacity has never been discussed."

"I want you to seek out as high a level contact as possible and arrange an appointment for yourself with Stewart Menzies, the Chief of MI6. Try to keep to a minimum the number of people who know of your request, but you are to explain that you are bringing an oral message from me for Menzies and for him alone."

"That will not be easy, but I will certainly try my best."

"I know that this must seem a strange request, but I know that you are loyal to the Reich and I can assure you that this is in the best interest of Germany."

"Yes, Admiral. And what is the message that I am to deliver?"

"I want you to inquire of Menzies what terms might be available for the surrender of Germany. A surrender to be made only to England and the Americans, not the Bolsheviks and in which we would then expect protection from further attack by the Russian Army. No Russian soldier is to set foot on German territory."

Popov was stunned. He thought of himself as a cool, professional man of the world, but this was shocking even to him. "If I am able to deliver such a message as you request, I'm sure there will be many clarifying questions asked of me. Are there any other details I might pass along? Such as, is this a proposal from the Fuhrer himself or from you?"

"You may tell Menzies that this surrender would not include Adolf Hitler in a postwar Germany. Tell him that if he is willing to discuss such a proposal I am prepared to fly to Portugal in two weeks time and secretly meet with him. Only with him."

"And how am I to get an answer back to you if Ludovico is not to know any of this?"

"As soon as you have secured a meeting with Menzies and presented my proposal, you will then return as soon as possible to Lisbon. The Lisbon Abstelle will report your arrival and I will personally come to Portugal to meet with you to hear his response. If it has been a positive one, tell him to travel to Lisbon as well within a few days after you do and we will use you as our intermediary to set up a personal meeting between Menzies and myself. Once I'm in Lisbon on other business, I will simply tell Karsthoff that as we are both in town at the same time, I would like to discuss the situation in England again with you and he will set up our meeting."

"I understand."

"Good. I knew I could depend on you. Karsthoff will of course be curious as to what we've been discussing in here alone. Refuse at first, but as he persists, simply tell him that we have another sensitive agent in London, about whom he has no reason to be aware of, and that as we've lost contact with him, I've instructed you to do some checking on him."

Popov smiled. "Yes, first saying no and then letting him in on an alleged secret will make Karsthoff very happy."

"I thought it would. Now, go open the door and have the Colonel rejoin us."

It wasn't until they were back on the plane that night for the return flight that night that Popov really had time to think about his extraordinary private conversation with Canaris. He wondered why the Admiral would take the chance of entrusting such a mission to someone who was working as an agent for the Nazi regime. Popov could have simply left the chateau and told Colonel Karstoff what had transpired and Canaris would have been shot within a matter of days. He was either quite the gambler or a fool. The Admiral didn't really seem either of those. It slowly came to him that there was a third possibility. Perhaps the Admiral knew or at least suspected that he was really working for British Intelligence and thus he would have no problem getting an appointment with MI6 Chief Menzies. By the end of his mental gymnastics, he also realized what a dangerous spot Canaris had put him in. As the Admiral's proposal was for a Germany without Hitler, he presumably had also been making plans for his overthrow and probable assassination. The Gestapo wouldn't like that. If Canaris was lucky enough to know they were coming for him, he might be able to shoot himself. If they took him alive, they would torture him until he revealed all – and that "all" would no doubt include the name of Dusko Popov.

The enterprising Yugoslav also had to decide whether he should simply report all that had transpired at the chateau to Nigel and Ian Fleming back in Lisbon, or do as Admiral Canaris had requested and tell no one except Menzies directly. After that, Menzies could tell whomever he wanted. He admitted to himself that as much as he disliked Germany, he had to admire the personal courage of Canaris to have taken such a step to try to save Germany from total destruction. Too many angles to calculate all at once. He finally gave up and just leaned back in his seat and went to sleep. Perhaps an obvious course of action would come to him in the morning when he was safely back in Lisbon. His final thought as he drifted off to sleep was that it was rather telling of how the war was going that they only thought it was safe to fly over Nazi-controlled territory in the dark of night!

# Chapter 4

Upon landing back in Lisbon, Karsthoff took Popov back to his home for further discussions, ostensibly dealing with his tasks to be conducted back in London, but after breakfast, he slipped in a question as to whether Canaris had given Popov a particular task during their private session. Apparently he'd not had the courage while still on the ground in France or even while in the air to ask Popov what had transpired, but now feeling bolder back on his home ground, he decided to tactfully inquire.

"Ludovico, I would love to tell you what we discussed, but the Admiral gave me very specific directions that I was to say nothing to anyone about the conversation."

"Naturally, you shouldn't go in to specifics. I just thought that if there was anything I could do to help you carry out whatever assignment you had been given, it would help us both if I had just a general idea of your task." He gave Popov a smile and a look of "we're good friends aren't we."

Popov stayed with his plan of refusing to initially tell Karsthoff, but when the German managed to bring it back into the conversation an hour later, Dusko pretended to relent.

"Well, it does impact somewhat my work for you in London, so perhaps I should give you a rough idea, as long as this stays strictly between you and me."

"Naturally, strictly between the two of us." Karsthoff gave him his most trustworthy look.

"Well, Canaris has another sensitive agent in London with whom they have lost contact and I'm to discreetly try to find out what has happened to him. Please, let me just leave it at that."

"Of course, of course. I'm only asking to see if there is anything I could do to help you in any way."

"By the way, I told the Admiral that I would prefer to make you aware of my mission, as you are my direct commander, and that I totally trusted you, but he was quite adamant that this was to be strictly between me and him. He replied that while he had total confidence in you, it was a matter of 'need to know' for the present. If I can recontact this agent, perhaps he will be run from Lisbon in the future, when naturally, you would be made aware of all details of the case."

Popov's recounting of the alleged praise of him to the Admiral had the expected effect on Karsthoff. "Well, that was nice of you to try, but the Admiral is quite correct. I won't need to know more details until Lisbon is possibly brought in to handle the case." He then looked at his watch. "I suppose we should be getting you started on your way back to your hotel. They're perhaps wondering why you've not slept there for the past two nights."

Popov grinned. "Oh, I think they might jump to the conclusion that it has had something to do with a beautiful woman."

Karsthoff laughed. "Of course, of course. There is just one more bit of business to transact before you leave." He went over to his desk and took from a drawer an envelope and passed it to Popov. "Here is US$25,000 to cover your expenses in the coming months and your salary. Unfortunately, acquiring English pounds is becoming harder and harder, but you'd told me last time that American dollars would be acceptable. That you could easily exchange them on the black market, now that there are so many American soldiers in England."

"Dollars will do just fine." He signed the receipt for the money and then he was off in the Mercedes sedan, again driven by Elizabeth. She would simply drop him somewhere in the city and he would catch a taxi back to the Hotel Estoril.

Popov debated what to do with the money until his scheduled meeting with his British handlers the following day. The front desk had a safe, but they generally insisted on knowing what they were storing, so there would be no "unpleasant" moments when a guest retrieved a package and claimed something was missing. He'd prefer that all of Lisbon not know he had $25,000 in his possession, which was likely to happen once the hotel staff started gossiping. No, he decided. It would be better if he just kept the money on him for the next 24 hours. Once

*Nazi Gold, Portuguese Wine, and a Lovely Russian Spy*

he was back in his room, he decided that first he needed to rest, not having slept well on the plane. He put the money under his pillow, right next to the Webley pistol he carried for protection.

He had dinner in the hotel restaurant. Still carrying all the money in the inner vest pocket of his white dinner jacket, he figured it safer if he didn't go traveling around the city that night. After eating, he wandered into the casino to pass the evening. He saw Ian Fleming having a drink at the bar. The British knew he was supposed to be getting his money supply refreshed by the Germans on this visit. Perhaps they'd sent Fleming to make sure nothing happened to him or that money before their scheduled meeting on Thursday, or maybe they were wondering where he'd been for the last 48 hours. He presumed that the British had informants working at the hotel, given its popularity with foreign guests from many countries. Popov went over to try his hand at the baccarat table. The "bank", the holder of the wooden dispenser of cards, was unfortunately in the hands of an obnoxious and loud former Dutch banker of Amsterdam, who had fled to Portugal early in the war. He'd probably absconded with the bank's money.

The game was similar to blackjack, except the goal was nine, not twenty-one and the player holding the "bank" served as the dealer. Before each game that night the annoying Dutchman would loudly shout out, "no limit on bets." Disliking pretentious people almost as much as Nazis, Popov had finally had enough and after one such statement of "no limit", he took the entire $25,000 from his coat and disdainfully tossed it on the table, saying "Will you cover that bet?" The balding banker sputtered, then passed the wooden shoe to the next player as he rose and fled from the table. Popov picked up his money and returned it to his white dinner jacket. He looked over at Fleming who'd almost had a stroke when he'd seen Popov lay down the bet of all the money that he'd presumably recently gotten from the Abwehr. He'd heard that Fleming fancied himself a writer. Popov thought to himself, "Perhaps that will give him an idea for a story someday for a debonair spy in a casino!" He headed into the bar area to see if there were any unattached women there that night.

The following afternoon, Popov arrived on foot at the "pick-up point" of a bus stop in a middle-class residential neighborhood of the city, exactly at 2:55 p.m. The ever-prompt Nigel pulled up in his sedan just a minute or so later and drove to a non-descript block of apartments.

A one-bedroom apartment on the second floor had been rented for just such secret meetings by a trusted Portuguese support asset. After parking the vehicle nearby, Nigel had gone first to the apartment and Popov arrived about five minutes later. He immediately saw Ian Fleming sitting in the living room, but didn't recognize the third man present. He went over to Fleming. "Ian, how are you? Did you have any luck at the casino last night?"

"I just made a few small bets, with my own money," was the cool reply. He'd not told Nigel about Dusko's flamboyant move at the baccarat table, so the others didn't understand the hidden meaning of Fleming's reply.

Nigel stepped forward, "Let me introduce you to Charles of the United States."

"A pleasure to meet you," responded Dusko. The two men shook hands and found sitting positions in the small living room. The plain and modest furnishings matched the outside of the building. Unlike most agents, who were always worried about more people knowing their identity, Popov seemed to enjoy being introduced by name to ever more colleagues of Nigel. His unusual behavior in that regard had on occasion made Nigel wonder if Popov might in fact be a triple agent, as he showed so little concern about how many people knew he was working for the British. For the present, Nigel's conclusion was that Popov was so egotistical, he simply liked as many people as possible to know he was the famous double agent TRICYCLE.

Early that morning, Popov had pretty well decided not to share with Nigel and Ian the portion of his trip about the secret proposal from Canaris. The presence of the American, whom he didn't know, clinched his decision. He would take the Admiral's amazing offer directly to Menzies and no one else.

Nigel started the formal part of the meeting. "So, where did you disappear to for several days? You and von Karsthoff off on a drinking binge?"

Popov waited several seconds for dramatic effect before answering. "No, the Colonel and I flew to Paris Monday night where I met with Admiral Canaris at a lovely chateau south of the city."

The British were accustomed to what they believed were certain exaggerations at times by Popov, but fortunately, Nigel had read just that morning a report from an informant at the airport. The control tower employee had passed along word about a special German flight on Monday night that had listed its official destination as Madrid, but had headed directly north after takeoff. "And just what did the Admiral want to discuss with you?"

"He had a number of questions about the food and living conditions in London and what was the attitude of the Londoners about the future of the war."

The other three were a bit underwhelmed by the subject matter of the special conversation with the Chief of the Abwehr. It was Ian's turn. "He had you secretly flown all the way to Paris just to ask you if there was coffee available in the shops of London?"

"Naturally, he discussed some of my military-related reporting and my sub-sources, but he really seemed more interested in what you English call 'atmospherics' – about whether the English people seemed optimistic or pessimistic about the outcome of the war. And afterwards, Karsthoff was quite happy that Admiral Canaris had wanted to personally meet one of the agents that he is in charge of in Lisbon."

Nigel dryly noted, "Yes, that should ensure that he won't be sent to the Russian Front for at least the next six months."

Charles had remained silent up until this moment of the meeting, but as the debriefing seemed to be nearing an end, he did pose a question to Popov. "Tell me about Canaris - what was your impression of him as a person, or even his appearance? I've never seen a photograph of him."

"Well, he looks just like an admiral should – tall and straight. He walks like someone who has spent decades in the military and he treated the subordinates around him like, well, subordinates. His questions were direct and focused. I've seen many photos of him over the years in German newspapers and magazines. This wasn't some impostor, if that is what you are wondering about."

"No, no. I don't doubt it was really Canaris. I was just wondering what he was like in person."

Popov pulled out the envelope with $25,000. "Here is my monthly payment from the Abwehr for the next three months and to cover my expenses for all those subsources I've supposedly recruited and am running throughout the British government." He laughed. He knew that most all of the money that he turned in went directly into the petty cash box of MI6. He thought it quite funny that the Abwehr was helping to fund MI6 operations against Germany.

Another fifteen minutes of discussion and they were done. Popov would be thoroughly debriefed once back in London. The purpose of the Lisbon meeting was simply to receive any "timely" intelligence that Popov might have acquired that should be acted upon immediately, or if he needed instructions on what to do regarding questions or tasks from Karsthoff that needed to be handled while Popov was still in Portugal. Nigel gave Popov a ride back to an area of the city where he could catch a taxi, then returned to the safehouse for further discussion with Ian and Charles.

Once the three were back together, Fleming asked Charles "Why were you so interested in Canaris' demeanor and appearance?"

"Because I know someone, Kermit Roosevelt to be precise, who had met Canaris a couple of times before the war started and who had described him once to me back in New York City. Popov's comments match quite well with Kermit's. I just thought it would be another way to help confirm Popov's story of having met with the Admiral. I believe him. Perhaps the more interesting question is why Canaris so wants to know what the living conditions in London are and what the attitude of the British public about the war is?"

"Maybe he's trying to assess the impact of the German bombing raids on London, though those pretty well ended months ago," responded Fleming.

Charles suggested that maybe Canaris just wanted to have a justification for a trip to Paris and to look like he's really trying to gather all the intelligence he can, by meeting personally with one of their supposed top agents. "Given all the German setbacks and since nothing is ever Hitler's fault, Canaris may sense he is being set up for the blame and wants to appear that he's working very hard to gather intelligence."

"No doubt he's under great pressure. Or perhaps he's thinking of moving to London and is wondering how life will be there. If he is, I have a flat in Mayfair I'm not using these days that I could let him have at a very reasonable rate," added Nigel. All three men had a good laugh.

"Ian, when are you headed back to London?" inquired Charles.

"Won't be back there for about a week or so. I'm flying on to Madrid tomorrow for a meeting with General Clarke of A Force, who's flying in from Cairo. He's the chap in charge of our deception campaigns throughout the Mediterranean area. We're having a bit of a conference on such things and my boss decided that since I was so close, I should pop on over and attend."

"With you away, who will handle the in-depth debriefing of Popov once he's back in London?" asked Nigel.

"Graham Greene is the Portugal desk officer these days for MI6. He might do it or his boss, Kim Philby, who is the Iberian Branch chief. Both are first rate men and would do a fine job with Popov."

That same day, Colonel Karsthoff had to his home for dinner Pedro da Silva, one of the vice directors of the Espirito de Santo Bank. Da Silva came from a long line of Portuguese bankers, though his mother was German, a fact that greatly interested Karsthoff. According to the dossier that the Abwehr had assembled on him, Da Silva was 62 years old, happily married, with one daughter who was married to a man who owned a large cork farm in the center of the country. There was one young grandson.

The banker thought that he was to be but one of several guests that evening, but in fact it was just the two gentlemen. As they were having coffee and brandy in the living room after an excellent dinner, Karsthoff brought the conversation around to Da Silva's ancestry.

"Did I hear correctly that your mother is German?"

"She was born in Germany, near Flensburg, but at the age of ten, her father was transferred from Hamburg to Sao Paulo, where she really grew up. I think she considered herself as much a Brazilian as a German. My father and she met when he was assigned to our office in Brazil and she simply swept him off his feet. My father tells the story that he knew within a week of meeting her that she was the woman for him."

"How romantic. Do they still live here in the Lisbon area?"

My mother unfortunately died of a heart attack in 1939, but father lives out on a small farm, not far from Lisbon, so he and I get together with some regularity."

"So sorry to hear about your mother. Your German is quite good. Did you learn your German from her?"

"In part, but I took German when at university in England and of course, I've visited Germany a number of times – before the war."

"What a man of the world you are. Connections to Brazil, Germany and England. Have you spent much time down in Sao Paulo?"

"I've made a number of trips there. My colleagues always kid me after such visits that my Portuguese has been ruined by the Brazilian accent I pick up while there."

Karsthoff laughed appropriately. "Ah, I must visit Brazil one day. The pictures I've seen of Rio de Janeiro are quite appealing. Perhaps when I retire after this terrible war, I might just move down to Brazil. Despite my Prussian background, I've never really liked the cold and snow of my home state. I've enjoyed my time here, but think I could easily get accustomed to warm weather year round."

"Yes, Rio is quite lovely. I think you and your family would enjoy living there."

"Tell me Pedro, is it difficult to transfer money to Brazil?"

"No, not at all. My bank has a large branch in Rio and we could easily transfer your money from here to our branch there."

He leaned forward in a conspiratorial manner. "Are there any particular reporting requirements to the government about such transfers, or can they be done almost anonymously? Special bank 'handling fees' for discretion I would naturally expect, but I do value my privacy, if you understand. In fact, I have several other military colleagues who might also be interested in moving to Brazil, so if done as one lump transfer, it might be a fairly sizeable amount."

Da Silva understood perfectly. He too read the newspapers and listened to the BBC reports of how the war was going. He suspected that in the future there might be a number of Germans exploring the possibility of moving to Brazil. "Normally, all international transactions are recorded and if above a certain amount, even require prior permission by the Portuguese authority that oversees banks. Salazar doesn't want to see too much money being sent out of the country, you see."

The German looked a little disappointed that there would be a record of where money was sent.

Da Silva quickly added, "Of course, any time there are regulations, there are usually ways to circumvent those regulations, but naturally there might be higher 'fees' involved in using those alternative ways."

"Naturally," replied Karsthoff with a slight smile.

"Banks sometimes send secured pouches with ship captains who are sailing to other countries. He keeps the pouch locked up in his safe and delivers it to a banking representative once he arrives in the foreign port. This is used when perhaps someone has kept jewelry or rare coins in a safe deposit box here, and then wishes to send those items to say a relative in Brazil, but in principle, most anything could be shipped in this way. Naturally, it's important to find an honest and reliable ship captain to entrust with such a pouch."

"And how big a 'pouch' can this be? What if perhaps someone wished to send a painting or something heavy like gold bars?"

"I'm sure that for a slightly larger fee, the right captain would be willing to take on any securely sealed crates. He, of course, in good faith, simply registers on the manifest whatever the owner of the cargo tells him is in those crates. If he's told there is small farming equipment in the crate, he has no reason to doubt the owner's word, nor even the name of the person sending the shipment. Sometimes, a shipment is simply in the name of my bank."

"I understand. That does sound like a possible solution for me and my friends. I will give that some thought. And what might be the fees for sending a few hundred kilograms of 'farm equipment' to Brazil?"

Da Silva took a sip of his coffee and smiled. "Fees vary depending on the weight, the time of the year and certain other variables such as the value of the farming equipment being discreetly shipped. Once you have a rough idea of the value of the items you are thinking of shipping, I could make some discreet inquiries and get back to you with a price."

"Very good. Well, let me discuss this with my friends and I'll be back in touch with you in the next week or two."

"That's fine. And by the way, some of these cargo ships at times can even make accommodations available for a few passengers, if that is desired."

"That's also good to know." Karsthoff finished the last of his coffee, sat down his cup and rose from his chair. "Let me see you to your car."

"Thank you for a wonderful meal and delightful conversation," replied Da Silva.

The following morning, Karsthoff sent off a classified telegram to Abwehr Headquarters, which simply read that it was time for Herr Vogel to come to Lisbon for discussions. Upon its arrival and decoding at Abwehr Headquarters in Berlin, Colonel Gehlen personally brought a copy to Admiral Canaris. "We have some good news from Lisbon," he commented as he handed the telegram to Canaris.

Canaris smiled -- not something that Gehlen had seen his boss do very often in recent months. "Excellent. It appears as though Karsthoff has found us the needed banker." During Gehlen's recent visit to Lisbon, it had been arranged that all that should be said in a telegram was that it was time for the visit by Herr Vogel. There should be no further details mentioned about a banker, so there would be no need to worry about who else within the Abwehr read it. While they were rid of the Gestapo informant von Hesseburg, there could be others. Plus, Canaris had never felt as completely confident in the security of the Enigma machines used by the German military to encode their wireless communications as most of his military colleagues were. Not that he had any real proof of there being a problem, but as a cautious intelligence officer, he found being suspicious of all potential threats a wise attitude to maintain. Too bad, he often thought, that Hitler didn't have such an attitude.

Gehlen could tell from the wrinkled forehead that Canaris was deep in thought and just remained silent. Finally, the Admiral turned to speak to his trusted assistant. "The next time that we hear that ARABEL will be traveling to Lisbon, I will seek Hitler's approval to secretly travel there to personally debrief him and also agent OSTRO. For the time being, simply respond to Colonel Karsthoff that we are working on the Vogel trip and will advise when that agent is ready to travel."

"Very well. Anything else for me to do right now?"

"Reconfirm about the availability of the gold and diamonds and brief me in the morning on that point and also what the transportation plans to get those items to Lisbon are."

"Colonel Gehlen clicked his heels and left the Admiral to himself behind his desk. Canaris lighted a cigarette. He wasn't that much of a smoker, but he'd found that having one in his hands when he was thinking seemed to help. He contemplated the various wheels of deception within wheels, all simultaneously in play for his scheme. His German colleagues must think that he's going there to debrief the two agents. If the British somehow learn of his travel, they must think he's only coming to receive Menzies' answer via Popov about a possible surrender plan – and who knows, that might even be an avenue to pursue in the future. But of course, the real reason for the trip would be to personally meet with the banker Karsthoff had lined up and come to a formal agreement with him about secretly moving the gold and diamonds to Brazil. Canaris had set in motion an intriguing game of international chess.

## Chapter 5

Dusko Popov was searching through pants pockets of various suits, on his small desk in his London flat and in the leather suitcase he had used to travel to Lisbon. Somewhere, there had to be that scrap of paper upon which the airline stewardess had written her London phone number. He noticed the clock and realized it was time to leave. He would search again later upon his return, but he never liked to arrive late for his sessions with MI6. His father had taught him from a young age that punctuality was the first step in making a good impression. Given the sensitive nature of his being a double agent, Popov never set foot in the MI6 Headquarters or any other official installation. The British maintained a small flat where he alone was met. They had a different flat for every Double Cross agent, that way there could never be any mistakes of scheduling two agent meetings at the same time and letting one become aware of the other.

When he arrived at the modest one-bedroom flat just before 10:00 a.m., he found Kim Philby already seated in what served as the living room, smoking, as he always seemed to be. He'd hoped that Ian Fleming would be back from Portugal to handle his debriefing, but at least he'd met Philby a couple of times before, so it wasn't like he was being handled by a complete stranger. He'd heard that the man had grown up as a small boy out in India, where his father had been something in the Colonial Service. He was another Oxford man and had tried his hand for a while as a journalist down in Spain during the Civil War before, like most of the English upper class, he'd ended up in some government position. The two men were really quite different people. Popov was the epitome of the socializing extrovert. Philby seemed to do well with people he already knew and were of his social class, but meeting perfect strangers was not something he enjoyed. He also had a slight stammer. At least he did seem to enjoy drinking alcohol, regardless of the time of day, and had already poured himself a large Scotch and left the bottle and another glass on the coffee table. He presumed that Popov would have one as well, despite the early hour of the day.

"Good morning, Dusko. Did you have a good journey to Portugal?"

"Yes, and not only to Portugal, as I presume you've read in the initial report from Lisbon. I had a special trip up to Paris, not that I got to enjoy that lovely city and its beautiful women. The Germans are even worse than you British when it comes to making everything about work."

"Well, thank you. I'm glad to hear that you think we're superior in at least one category to your German friends." Popov never understood why at every meeting he'd ever had with Philby, the man always seemed to go out of his way to be insulting. It was almost as if he was trying to provoke him into quitting.

Philby was a meticulous individual, as it seemed that all Oxford graduates that he'd ever met were. They spent nearly two hours going over in the finest detail of every hour of his time on the trip and exactly who said what to whom when he was actually in meetings with the Germans. The British were, quite rightly, always looking for the slightest sign that the Germans had tumbled to the fact that Popov was a double agent.

Popov waited till they had covered all the typical topics and Philby seemed to be winding up before he decided to launch into his special agenda item. "I do have one special request for you to pass along."

Philby knew, as well as every other officer who had dealt with Popov, that "special requests" from him usually had some connection to the topic of money or some other perk for him. "Yes, and what would that be?"

"I need a private meeting with MI6 Chief Menzies."

Philby managed to suppress a grin and simply replied, "And what is it that you wish to discuss with him?"

"I need a private meeting, as in, I have something to tell him and him alone."

"Well, he's a very busy man and unless he has some idea of what it is you wish to raise with him, I'm afraid that really isn't going to happen." Philby put away his fountain pen, to indicate that the question was closed.

The two stared at each other in silence for several long seconds. "I have a message from Admiral Canaris that I am to deliver personally to Menzies or not at all." Philby might have already put away his pen, but Popov was calling his bluff. The Brit was tempted to just shrug his shoulders and say that he guessed then that there would be no message delivered, but he knew that Popov would be seeing other officers in the coming weeks and would simply repeat his request.

Philby knew that Popov was considered highly enough by MI6 that eventually they would humor him and let him in to see Menzies – maybe not completely alone, but he would get a meeting. Philby calculated that it would be best if he maneuvered the situation so that he would get to be that other officer in the room with the Chief. Otherwise, he might never get to know what the message was – and he had to know what high-level communication was being sent from the head of German Military Intelligence to the head of the British Secret Service.

"Very well, I'll pass along your request, but surely you know that someone else will sit in on such a meeting, probably me. And to be honest, you'll have a much better chance of getting a meeting if you at least give me a rough idea of what the nature of this message is."

Popov had spent a lot of time in casinos and was a very good card player. He knew how to bluff as well as some Oxford graduate. "If Mr. Menzies wishes someone else in the room, that's his choice, but the first words I will say about this message I am delivering will be said in front of him." He then shrugged his shoulders and stood to leave.

"I'll see what I can do, but the answer may be simply that you first tell me what the topic is and then he'll decide whether it's worth his seeing you or not."

"Fine, you know my phone number." Popov shook hands with Philby and departed.

Philby stayed in the room for another twenty minutes trying to decide what the best way to handle this awkward situation was. He finally concluded that MI6 management would be too intrigued as to what Admiral Canaris wanted delivered to completely turn down the unusual request. Therefore, the best Philby could do was to try to ensure his presence at the high-level meeting.

His decision made, he then went straight to MI6 Headquarters and sought out Menzies' Chief of Staff, Benjamin Braithwaite, to present

*Nazi Gold, Portuguese Wine, and a Lovely Russian Spy*

Popov's demand. As Chief of the Iberian Branch, he was senior enough to get in to see Braithwaite, though after a half hour's wait.

The Chief of Staff wasted no time on pleasantries, even for a fellow Oxford man. "My secretary tells me you have something terribly important. I know you were to meet TRICYCLE this morning. Might I presume that what you're about to say is connected with that meeting?"

"Yes it is. After we'd finished the usual debriefing issues, he announced that he had a message from Admiral Canaris, whom he claims to have met a week or so back, and he is to deliver it directly to Mr. Menzies. He mentioned nothing about such a personal message when Ian and Nigel met him right after his alleged return from Paris, so this is probably all utter nonsense, but I figured I should bring it to your attention. I tried getting him to share with me at least a hint as to what the topic of this alleged message is, but he refused to budge. Said he either delivers it directly to Menzies himself or he won't deliver it all. The best I could finally get from him was an agreement that I could be at the meeting – that it didn't have to be totally private, as in just him and the Chief."

Braithwaite had continued to lean back in his large leather chair with the fingers of each hand interlaced on his stomach, while Philby had presented the situation. "Well, that was very generous of him to include you," he responded. He was known around the building for his sarcastic quips.

The two then sat there in silence staring at each other for a while, rather as Philby and Popov had done earlier in the day.

"Oh well, I suppose we need to humor him. Clearly the Germans like and trust him and we will be needing him when we get to planning a cross-channel deception package." He checked the official calendar of appointments. "Bring him around to the Chief's home tomorrow evening promptly at 6:00 p.m. and he can have exactly ten minutes. He has a dinner at 7:00 to go to, so be on time. Bring him in through the servants' entrance and put a hat and some fake glasses or whatever you field fellows do so as to disguise him. This better be a bloody good message!"

"Right. We'll be there promptly at 6:00 tomorrow." Philby hesitated a moment and then added, "And shall I sit in on the meeting, so as to take notes or be ready to take any needed follow-up action?"

Braithwaite had already started shuffling through some papers, looking for something on his desk. "Yes, yes. You sit in on this meeting and take notes. Tomorrow evening is my wife's birthday party and I intend to be at home, or there'll be hell to pay."

Once he'd left the Headquarters building, he stopped at a public call box and phoned Popov and told him to be back at the meeting flat the next day promptly at 5:30 p.m., to be ready for a 6:00 meeting as he'd requested. "The front office initially wanted to tell you to go fly a kite, but I argued strongly on your behalf. You will have your meeting, but he insisted that I be present."

"If he wants you present, that's his choice. I'll see you tomorrow at 5:30."

While on the phone with Philby, Popov had idly started turning the pages of a book and out fell the scrap of paper with the sought-after phone number of Phillipa. He now remembered that he'd taken the book on the flight to Lisbon. He thought to himself that things were starting to look up, on both the professional and personal parts of his life. Who knew if this crazy proposal from Canaris for a separate surrender to England would go anywhere, but if it did, surely it would merit a serious bonus payment and possibly even a knighthood!

In the meeting flat the next evening, Philby tried once more to get an inkling out of Popov as to the nature of the secret message, but the handsome Yugoslav would not budge. Having already agreed to the Popov-Menzies meeting, Philby had no leverage to use with the calculating double agent. In a begrudging way, he almost admired how Popov had manipulated his way into a personal meeting with the Chief of MI6. Philby explained the mechanics of how the meeting would occur and at about 5:45 told Popov, "We should be on our way. It wouldn't do to be late." Popov was in an excellent mood. He'd had a very exciting time with the airline stewardess the night before, which had included her roommate when they'd gone back to her flat with a couple of bottles of very good champagne. It would have been so rude not to have invited the roommate to share some of the bubbly. (The MI6 selection of his cryptonym as TRICYCLE had been a fine example of the British sense of humor among the insiders who knew well his background and predilection for threesomes!) And today he was about to bring about Germany's surrender. He'd put on his very best Savile Row-tailored suit for the meeting with Menzies.

Having slipped quietly in through the servant's entrance, Philby escorted Popov up to Menzies' study, and the two of them were seated, engaged in idle chatter, when the MI6 Director entered the room about five minutes past the hour.

"Dusko, so good of you to come by this evening. Sorry to have kept you waiting. Kim, good to see you again." Menzies had not become the Chief of MI6 without having learned long ago how to be charming and making perfect strangers feel comfortable.

Popov greatly enjoyed the treatment he was receiving. Not that he'd come from a peasant background himself in Yugoslavia, but to be received in such a manner, in the personal home of one of the ruling "old boys" of England, made him very pleased.

After the obligatory two minutes or so of chit chat, Menzies got down to business. "So, I understand you had the opportunity recently to meet with Admiral Canaris. How is he doing these days? I guess it was 1938 or so the last time I saw him and he looked rather tired even back then. I should think he must look positively haggard now, the way the war is going."

"He did look like a man who could use a good night's sleep, or perhaps a week or so of total vacation."

With perfect English understatement, Menzies replied "that he would be perfectly happy to send him into permanent vacation."

"Perhaps there will be an opportunity to do so." Having gotten the two Englishmen's attention with that comment, Popov proceeded to deliver the personal message from Canaris to Menzies. "The Admiral wants to know if the British and presumably the American governments would be interested in negotiating a surrender of a Germany that does not include Adolf Hitler? And need not necessarily involve the Soviet Union."

All three men sat there for several moments in absolute silence. Having rather expected something more mundane from Popov and along the lines of some way for him to receive more money, the Englishmen were quite taken aback. Menzies had seen and heard many amazing things in his 53 years of life, but that had to be the most unexpected proposal he'd ever heard. Philby was in absolute shock.

"Well, let's suppose hypothetically for a moment that the Allied position of demanding unconditional surrender might be modified, just how is Admiral Canaris going to deal with Mr. Hitler? I rather doubt he's going to willingly step aside from being the Fuhrer of the Reich."

"He didn't go into details, but I took it that Canaris is not alone in his view that Germany would be much better off at this point without Hitler as its leader and that a group of senior Germans would take care of the removal of the little corporal. And he implied -- yes, that's the correct English word I believe -- implied that it would be much easier to convince other leading military officials to go along with such a plan if they thought there could be a negotiated surrender, leaving them a better Germany than just fighting to the bitter end. And part of that negotiated settlement would be protection from the Russian Army coming onto traditional German territory." Popov then shrugged his shoulders as if to say, "That's it." "Admiral Canaris himself will show up in Portugal to hear your answer through me two days after I return to Lisbon for another meeting with Karsthoff. If it is a 'positive' answer, he will expect to meet you there in Portugal to discuss the fine details of an agreement. And, by the way, to justify another trip so soon back to Portugal, the XX Committee will have to come up with some fairly exciting sounding intelligence to pass along to the Germans."

"It's certainly an interesting offer. Too bad he and these other German officers didn't make it a year or so ago. Because politicians don't actually have to go out and do the fighting, I suspect now that the war is going so well for the Allies they'll feel that they don't have to make compromises with anyone in Germany."

Popov again shrugged as if he couldn't care less one way or the other. "Winning in North Africa and even in Italy is one thing. Making a successful cross-channel landing and then invading the German Fatherland will be quite a different matter."

"You're correct, but reality and politics are not always the same thing and the Allies have had the joint policy for some time now that only unconditional surrender will be accepted. However, I will forward Canaris' proposal to Mr. Churchill and when I have an answer, you will have one as well, to take back to the Admiral. It might be some sort of counter-proposal. We shall see."

Menzies turned to Philby. "In the meantime, you'd best inform the XX Committee that Dusko will need some 'hot stuff' to justify another trip very shortly back to Portugal. Regardless of the Prime Minister's answers, Dusko will have to go deliver that answer to Admiral Canaris as expected."

"Yes, Sir. I'll see to that right away. And may I suggest, Sir, that I should go down to Portugal as well. As I am aware of what is really afoot, and our Station there does not, it would be best if we had someone on the ground fully apprised of the situation."

"Yes, yes, good idea. You get the various wheels ready to roll and I shall arrange to go see the Prime Minister tomorrow. And now if you will excuse me gentlemen, I have a dinner that I should be departing for, so as not to arrive late. American Ambassador Winant is one of those people who expects everyone, war or no war, to arrive promptly on time. Only Mr. Churchill's daughter, Sarah, is forgiven for arriving whenever she feels like it, but that's another story." Menzies was alluding to one of the worst kept secrets among the top circles of the British Government, excluding Churchill, that Winant was having an affair with Churchill's daughter. Menzies stood, shook hands with both visitors and then was out the door.

Once back in the car, Popov observed to Philby that "I think that went well. You have any feel for how long it will take your government to come to a position on the proposal?"

"It might take several days, or even weeks. Depends if Mr. Churchill and Mr. Roosevelt just want to stab our Soviet allies in the back, or if they will take this up with Stalin."

Popov thought his response a rather odd one, but said nothing. Popov figured he could find a variety of pleasant ways to spend his time while in London, waiting for his instructions.

Somewhat to Philby's surprise, Stewart Menzies sent for him only two days later to come immediately to his office. Despite the message to come immediately, upon arrival Philby had to wait an hour for Menzies to return to his office. When finally told to go in, he recalled the comment at Menzies' home about Canaris looking tired and haggard. He thought to himself that Menzies also looked quite tired and in need of rest. Whether German or British, running an intelligence service in wartime obviously took its toll on the leader. Philby himself knew about stress, but couldn't imagine the daily decisions and burdens placed upon Menzies.

"Good afternoon, Sir."

"So sorry for the delay, but I had an emergency meeting with the Americans. Come in and have a seat. I have an answer for TRICYCLE to deliver to Canaris."

"That was certainly quick." Philby literally held his breath, waiting to hear what that answer was.

"A decision came so quickly because it's a simple one. Allied policy is for unconditional surrender, with or without Hitler. Mr. Churchill would certainly welcome that surrender sooner rather than latter, but there will be no negotiating."

"He didn't even raise the question with his inner circle or with the Americans or the Soviets?"

"He said that it would be a waste of time. He shared my view that the politicians think we're on the homeward stretch to victory now and there's no need to negotiate with any group of Germans who might take control of the country from Hitler."

"If I may, Sir, I think I have to agree with that view. Germany needs to be crushed good and proper so we're not going through this again in just another twenty years' time."

"Perhaps, though leaving such a power vacuum in Central Europe practically invites that butcher Stalin to move in and take over a dozen or so countries. Mr. Churchill did like the idea of keeping the Russians out of a post-war Germany, but that wasn't enough of an enticement to get him to even want to enter into negotiations with Canaris. You're to tell our agent to tell Canaris that it will be unconditional surrender now, or simply fight on, and be crushed. When the German military is ready to surrender, they need only start hanging out white flags along the fighting lines, not send back channel messages through secret agents. By the way, was the XX Committee able to come up with some sexy-sounding information to justify TRICYCLE's immediate travel?"

"They have, Sir. They're going to play on the German fears that an invasion force will soon be building up in England, and start laying the groundwork for the deception of the creation of a massive new American Army Group called FUSAG. This mythical First United States Army Group is to camp where one logically would, if planning on invading the Pas de Calais area, not Normandy. Such a report should guarantee our man a warm welcome. I'll make arrangements for TRICYCLE and myself to leave for Portugal immediately."

"Excellent. Have a safe journey and come give me your personal assessment of how things went as soon as you're back."

Philby was pleased with Churchill's answer and to see that the British Government was going to live up to its agreement with the Soviet Union for demanding unconditional surrender, though he was still surprised that Churchill didn't even want to discuss the offer with the Americans. Not that the bombings of British cities had not been terrible, but only the Russians had felt the brutal consequences of Nazi invasion and deserved to show the German people what it was like to be invaded.

Philby met with TRICYCLE later that afternoon back at the safehouse and briefed him on his meeting with Menzies. He accepted it, knowing there was no point in debating the wisdom of the response, but thought it was rather shortsighted. To pass up the chance of even discussing with Canaris how to possibly end the war a year or more sooner seemed to condemn to death tens of thousands of soldiers on both sides and also the massive civilian casualties that would come with further war, for no real purpose. Was it that important to remove the traditional rulers of German society and the military class? And there was also the personal impact on him. There went his chance for a medal and a handsome cash award for his part in bringing about an end to the war. He also contemplated how Canaris would react and what that might mean for his relationship with the Abwehr. Germans were not known for reacting well to being told "no." Now that the war would simply continue on and probably with Hitler in command, Canaris might want to ensure that there could be no leaks about his having tried to negotiate with the British. Him being dead would eliminate any risk of him ever telling anyone else about Canaris' attempt. He knew he would have to be very careful about where and how this meeting with Canaris took place in Portugal. There was also an impact at the London end of Menzies' decision on Popov. If he and Philby would be departing in just a day or two for Lisbon, it also cut into his social plans he'd made for while in London!

## Chapter 6

Admiral Canaris passed through the outer checkpoint of the German High Command at Wunsdorf, some twenty miles south of Berlin with ease, as the guards were regular Army personnel. However, at the second and third checkpoints, he actually had to produce his identity card for the SS guards who manned those inner perimeters. "What idiots!" he thought silently to himself. If some Allied commando attack had managed to put together several staff cars and motorcycles with German-speaking men and German military attire, didn't the SS think they could forge a few fake ID cards? Finally, his vehicle entered the underground parking facility connected to the massive underground command bunker of the OKW. So far, it hadn't even been bombed, but given the thickness of the concrete with nearly 50 feet of earth on top of that, nobody was particularly worried even about direct hits of aerial bombs. The complex was a model of German architecture and engineering, completed in early 1939, it was the brain center of the German military. Reports came in from all Naval, Air and Army commands and out went orders from the hundreds of officers assigned to the OKW. They not only worked down in the bunkers, they slept there as well. Only when the "Clear Skies" indicators were posted did they venture out to enjoy the sunshine and fresh air. There was no above-ground housing within miles of the complex, in hopes of drawing as little attention as possible to the OKW Headquarters. Multiple underground cables ran to the radio antennas hidden in the nearby forest, so as to minimize the possibility that air attacks could prevent them from communicating via radio with German commands around Europe. There were only a few token anti-aircraft batteries around the facility, again in hopes of minimizing the chance that any enemy would even think the complex was worth bombing.

Admiral Canaris entered the personal quarters of General Alfred Jodl, Chief of Operations of the German High Command. There were no windows, of course, in the underground bunker, but the walls of the living room were covered with expensive tapestries or wood paneling with tasteful landscape paintings of Germany. Jodl came in about five minutes later and went directly to a sideboard to pour both of them a glass of schnapps. He gave one of the beautiful Czech crystal glasses to Canaris. He raised his and said, "To the Fuhrer!"

"To the Fuhrer," repeated Canaris.

Both men smiled. One never knew quite where the Gestapo might have installed hidden microphones so as to uncover anyone disloyal to Herr Hitler. Canaris observed that in addition to the tasteful landscape oil paintings, there was only one portrait – and not of Hitler, but of the 19th century German Chancellor, Otto von Bismarck.

Admiral Canaris wasted no time asking for updates from the various military fronts, which would only be depressing for both men. He came more or less straight to the point. He didn't come straight out and ask for permission, but rather for Jodl's "opinion."

"I'm thinking of making a discreet trip down to Portugal in order to meet personally with two of our best agents, ARABEL and OSTRO. I don't wish to throw any doubt on the ability of our Abwehr people in Lisbon, but sometimes it's good to meet directly with people, be able to look them directly in the eye, and ask questions."

"Indeed it is. Face-to-face is always better than just reading second-hand reports. I'm sure, however, that Gestapo Director Muller would be very worried about any Allied attempts to kidnap you while on such a trip to a neutral country like Portugal. I believe he might insist that some of his people accompany you on this trip, for your safety."

"I think that would be an excellent idea. I'm sure I'd feel much safer with his people providing security in addition to my own security detail." Canaris said that in a slow, loud voice so that any microphones might record it clearly. After a few more minutes of inquiries about the wellness of mutual friends, Canaris rose and made his exit. It was another lovely day of thick, low cloud cover, so there would be no worry about possible American bombing raids during the trip back to Berlin that afternoon.

As soon as he was back at his office, he called in Ewald. "Please send a message to von Karsthoff that Mr. Vogel is ready to travel whenever it is appropriate, but would like to combine the travel with a meeting with ARABEL with his next trip to Lisbon, and a meeting with OSTRO as well."

"Understood. I'll take care of that immediately."

"After that, phone over to Gestapo headquarters on a secure line and talk to Director Muller's chief of staff. Alert him to my possible journey soon to Portugal and that General Jodl and I agreed that it might be safer if I were to travel with an additional security detail provided by the Gestapo – perhaps just three or four of his men."

Ewald gave a broad grin. He understood that by taking along Gestapo guards that would make Director Muller feel comfortable that Canaris would be returning from such a trip to a neutral country and thus raise no objections to the secret mission. "I shall get on that as soon as I send the message to Lisbon." He also placed on the Admiral's desk a folder. "The latest casualty reports from our forces at Kursk. We have finally managed to stop the Russian counteroffensives, but at terrible losses. Casualties are nearly 100,000. We have lost several hundred tanks and nearly 500 planes of the Luftwaffe have been destroyed."

Canaris sat in motionless silence as he read the report. Finally, he let out a deep sigh and simply mumbled, "The end is coming." He hoped that ARABEL would return from England with a positive response and there might be some way to at least prevent the German homeland from being overrun by Stalin's hordes, murdering everyone and looting everything in their path. Far better to surrender to the civilized British. He then turned to Ewald and added, "It's definitely time to proceed with some haste on Operation Grandfather."

The coded Abwehr message from Berlin to the Lisbon Abstelle about the upcoming travel of Mr. Vogel arrived on a Tuesday. On Wednesday night it received a brief coded shortwave message from ARABEL that he would be arriving Saturday and would await contact in the usual method. Colonel Karsthoff understood that to mean that Popov would again be at the roulette table in the Estoril Casino on Saturday night watching for Elizabeth's betting pattern. He in turn then sent a brief message to Berlin alerting Admiral Canaris of ARABEL's travel plans. He understood that this would set in motion the predictable falling of various dominos, but sometimes in the spy business, unpredictable events occurred as well. One domino that needed his immediate attention was to arrange for a meeting between Canaris and his banker friend, Da Silva.

Canaris set out on his long plane journey first thing Saturday morning, accompanied by two of his own security men and four from the Gestapo. He'd initially turned down Ewald's request to accompany him, arguing that he needed someone he trusted at Headquarters in case something important came up. However, in the end, he gave in to Ewald's desire to see Lisbon, and his point that they would only be gone 3-4 days and surely the Reich would not collapse in four days without either of them present!

It was an uneventful flight, and after the first eight or nine hours, even the Gestapo men finally took both hands out of their coats and relaxed. Up to that point, all four had clearly been sitting with at least one hand on a gun in a pocket. It appeared that they had been briefed to be more worried about the possibility of Canaris defecting to the enemy than of any enemy's possible attempt to kidnap the Admiral. The head man of the Gestapo detail was probably curious as to what was making Canaris suddenly smile at one point of the flight. The truth was, Canaris was thinking to himself that all such Gestapo security men appeared almost identical – early twenties, at least 6 feet in height, athletic build, usually blue eyes and not a very intelligent looking face. He wondered if they all came from the same village, or if perhaps Dr. Mengele had been conducting his genetic experiments much longer than was known and he'd produced all these "ideal" security men from the same test tube.

Eventually, the Lisbon airfield came in to view. Despite the cabled instructions to keep the arrival of "Mr. Vogel" quiet, not only was von Karsthoff waiting at the airfield, but half of his staff had found some excuse to be there as well. Even if British intelligence had not known in advance courtesy of TRICYCLE who was coming to meet him, news that someone of high importance had arrived that night from Germany would have reached British and American ears by the following morning.

Nigel had decided to share with Charles a day earlier the news that TRICYCLE was about to return to town and even that Admiral Canaris was coming to Lisbon to ostensibly meet with a few of his star agents. It was a fine August morning when the two intelligence officers met at a quaint outdoor coffee shop in the old part of the city.

Before Nigel even had a chance to bring up the TRICYCLE visit, Charles had started with his own big news. "I've got General Donovan showing up here tomorrow. He's making a swing through the Mediterranean theater and was supposed to be going to Gibraltar, but for some reason that got cancelled at the last moment and he's stopping here for 48 hours instead. Our Ambassador is still putting some social event together, but keep your calendar open the next few evenings if you can, as there will surely be some dinner or cocktail party being held."

Nigel smiled. "It's going to get rather crowded around Lisbon in the coming days. We have TRICYCLE flying in from London and none other than Admiral Canaris himself coming down to meet with him and another one of their star agents called OSTRO."

They both had the same thought at the same moment. Intelligence officers didn't believe in coincidences and it was impossible not to wonder what might really be afoot. The heads of the Abwehr and the OSS both going to be in the same neutral city over the same time frame – that was one hell of a coincidence!

Charles was the first to speak. "Do you think there is something going on, far above our pay grade?" In typical British understatement, he replied, "I'm sure there are many things going on all the time that our masters do not share with you and me." He paused briefly. "It might possibly explain why Kim Philby is down here in Lisbon, without any particularly good reason. I guess if something is really going on, our superiors will let us know what that is when they think we need to know it."

"True. In the meantime, I guess he should get back to the topic of what we do know Canaris is doing in Lisbon. So, who is this second agent that Canaris is coming to see?"

"The German code name for him is OSTRO. His true name is Paul Fidrmuc, a Czech by birth, but generally an international citizen of the world. He's a professional con man who holds a variety of passports in different names from various countries. He first came to our attention almost two years ago when the ULTRA intercepts started showing that the Germans had a source that we had not been previously aware of who was allegedly running a number of sub-agents within England. That of course made our MI5 security people go crazy as they tried to figure out who this source was and who his sub-agents were. As we continued to analyze the reporting, it finally became obvious that this was all a scam by someone who was simply making up reports from his imagination and from reading the newspapers. No one would have really cared if he was deceiving the Abwehr, except that on a number of occasions his speculations on the next planned steps by Allied military units turned out to be very accurate."

"Have you British ever thought about directly approaching the man yourself and formally turning him into a double agent, since the Germans apparently already completely trust and value him?"

"You make me wonder who's reading whose classified cable traffic," replied Nigel with a faint grin. "That is precisely the first option that we considered, but he keeps a very low profile and it's difficult to know exactly where he is on any given day. The second option considered was for Mr. Fidrmuc to simply fall down a staircase late one night. Again, there was the question of where to find him and I suppose a small ethical question of why to do that to a man simply trying to make a modest living by lying to the Nazis. For the present, we are still just watching and waiting to see if any particular action is needed. I have to say, there is a begrudging admiration for a man who totally out of whole cloth can make up such wonderful reports and has convinced the Germans that his insights should be sought out on future possible moves by the Allies."

Now it was Charles' turn to smile. "He does sound like quite an amazing fellow. I suspect that he's not the only agent working for the Germans, the British or us Americans, who is at least a partial fabricator of the information we are buying. And here in Portugal, providing information, truthful or false, to various intelligence services does seem to be about the third or fourth largest profession among the residents of this country!"

"Yes, indeed, my Ambassador commented a few months ago that if one ran a restaurant which sold wine, provided ladies of the night and sold a few secrets on the side, you would have all four major avenues of income generation in this country covered."

"So when are Canaris and Popov supposed to meet?"

"According to Popov, he is to meet the Admiral two days after his own arrival in Lisbon. Presumably, Karsthoff will be involved in arranging such a meeting. We will learn from Popov the following day what Canaris has wanted to discuss with him."

Nigel was not being deceptive with Charles about what was to be the topic of discussion between Canaris and Popov, because his colleague, Kim Philby, had not shared that information even with him. Nigel had found Philby a bit evasive as to why he had traveled to Portugal to be present in country during this next round of meetings between Popov and the Germans, but had basically chalked it off as simply another Headquarters officer wanting a trip to Portugal. Coming to neutral Lisbon was as close as they were likely to come to the fighting and it did seem to make them feel as if they were a more active participant in the war effort. As long as such people stayed out of his way, he didn't mind such bogus trips. He had, however, found it a bit odd that Philby had booked a room at a rather out-of-the way hotel instead of staying at the Hotel Britannia in the center of the city, near the Embassy and which even gave a discount to British diplomats. But on the other hand, he found Philby a bit of an odd duck in a number of ways and that was even in comparison with a number of others within a wartime intelligence service that seemed to specialize in attracting most every upper class eccentric in the British Isles.

One of the first things Philby had done after arrival at his modest Henry the Navigator Inn was to go into the bar area and ask to use the phone at the bar. He spoke no Portuguese, but apparently spoke reasonably good Spanish – at least so it sounded to the barman who partially overheard the call the Englishman made. It sounded as if the guest had called a bakery and had asked if they baked French croissants with cinnamon. He then gave the number of the hotel and hung up. One more person who thought Philby was a bit odd, but then the Portuguese bartender had found most Englishmen over the years a peculiar bunch. About 30 minutes later the phone rang and when the barman answered, a man speaking Portuguese asked if there was someone there interested in fresh croissants.

The barman turned to Philby, the only person in the bar and asked him in halting English, "You want to buy croissants?"

"Yes I do, thank you very much."

All the barman heard over the next 60 seconds was the thin, well-dressed Englishman saying "Allo", "Si" and "Bueno" several times. He then hung up, looked at his watch and went back to reading a several days old London Times, as if the call had never occurred.

Precisely one hour later, Philby walked out of his hotel and started strolling leisurely through the city. Had anyone been following him -- which he concluded after about forty-five minutes of walking that no one was -- they would have probably concluded that he was simply killing time and exploring the city. Near the top of the next hour, he sat down on the bench of a bus stop, clearly to take a short rest, fanning himself with the same London Times newspaper that he had been reading earlier. Precisely at 4 p.m. a slightly battered old Vauxhall sedan pulled up to the bus stop, Philby got into the car and it slowly drove away. There were, in fact, so many spies having so many clandestine meetings in Lisbon on any given day, the maneuver of a man getting up from a bus stop and quickly getting into a car without having made any hand or vocal acknowledgment to the driver of the vehicle, did not seem odd at all.

Some twenty minutes later, the car made a quick turn around a corner and stopped briefly. Its passenger exited the car and headed directly for the entrance way of a working-class apartment building. As had been directed by the driver of the vehicle, Philby went to apartment six on the third floor and knocked softly. Just a few moments later, the door was opened by a beautiful woman in her late twenties. Her short-cropped, black hair did not seem to go with her facial color of a more northern European woman. She was dressed in the manner of a lower-class, Portuguese working woman. However, she spoke broken English.

"Good afternoon, Mister Smith. How are you?"

Philby replied, "I'm well. And you?"

"I am fine. And how is your older sister?"

"Not well. She is still suffering from a bad cold."

The correct recognition phrases having been completed, the young woman gestured for Mister Smith to come in and she closed and locked the door behind him.

"And what's your name?"

"Forgive my bad English, please. My friends in Portugal call me Maria. I bring you greetings from your friends in Moscow, though they worried when you signaled for emergency meeting Lisbon. Everything good near you?"

"Yes, I'm in no danger. It's just that I came across what might have been very crucial information. Fortunately, it doesn't appear now as if there's as much of a threat to mother Russia as I first feared, but things are still in play. In any case, I wished to pass along the full details of what has been happening involving the Germans trying to make a separate peace agreement with England, which I could only do in a face-to-face meeting."

Maria did not know the true name of the person with whom she was meeting. Obviously, it was not Smith, but it didn't really matter. Her real name wasn't Maria either. She only knew that the Englishman had been for many years a very trusted agent of the NKVD and that he was now someone important within the British Intelligence Service. She indicated to Mister Smith to take a seat at the small table in the room. She brought over a bottle of Portuguese white wine and two glasses. She began pouring wine into a glass for herself and inquired if he would like a drink as well. He accepted her gracious offer.

She had a small notebook laying on the table. "You mind I take some notes of what you about me to tell? If it only few short items I do not need to write down anything, but if there many details, would help me making sure my report back to Center completely accurate. It type of paper that easily dissolve if I swallow, so do not be concerned it falling into wrong hands."

Philby was convinced that she was a Russian. She spoke English as Russians often do, leaving out indefinite and definite articles of grammar. "It might be best if you took some notes. I have no objection." He then began explaining to her the background of Dusko Popov, his role of ostensibly working for the Abwehr while in fact serving as a double agent for the British.

Maria had yet to write anything down. "Okay, I understand background. Now, what occurred that caused you trigger special meeting? And I must you tell, making all these arrangements on such short notice not easy, so I hope what you about tell me truly important comrade."

Philby did not enjoy being spoken to in such a tone, regardless of her grammar. He'd become a secret agent for the Communist cause when the woman before him had still been a young school girl and he expected a certain degree of respect, even from a member of the workers' paradise, where everyone was equal. "I'm certain that Moscow will think it's important to know that Admiral Canaris, the head of the Abwehr, sent a personal message via Popov to Stewart Menzies, the head of MI6. The proposal is that Germany will negotiate a surrender directly with England and America and one of the conditions would be that Red Army troops would be forbidden by the Allies from entering onto traditional German territory. Also, quite importantly, Canaris and other leading German officers would remove Hitler as the leader of Germany. The proposal was taken by Menzies directly to Prime Minister Churchill. He supposedly immediately rejected the proposal without even referring it to Washington or Moscow, stating that the Allied policy is for unconditional surrender and there is nothing to negotiate, regardless of whether Hitler or someone else is the leader of Germany."

Maria looked up from her writing and commented, "It good see that Mister Churchill living up to his agreements with Soviet Union."

"I have reported to you what Popov is allegedly to say to Canaris in the next day or so, when they meet here in the Lisbon area. I must add, however, that several comments by Menzies made to me make me believe that he was unhappy with this decision and I wouldn't put it past him to try to secretly reach some sort of agreement with Canaris. Apparently, the two men knew each other before the war, and Menzies is no friend of the Soviet Union." Philby had become quite animated.

"Please not so fast speak. Let me make sure I have correct. The first part what you told me are facts as you understood them. Your last comment pure speculation your part?"

Philby was coming to dislike this woman more and more. "I would prefer that you accurately pass along what I have said as my informed analysis, not merely speculation." Given her poor English, he hoped her report back to Moscow would be somewhere near what he'd actually said.

Having wrapped up the formal debriefing portion of the meeting, Maria poured them both another glass of wine and he inquired of her of how long she had been working for the NKVD. Despite his disliking her attitude while debriefing him, he did greatly enjoy the opportunity to speak honestly with someone about who he was. It was very stressful to work undercover, pretending every hour of the waking day that he was truly part of MI6 and of the English upper-class. He suspected that he actually had better information about the wartime situation in Russia than she did, if she had been working long down in Portugal and Spain, but he did inquire, "How are things back in Russia, particularly around Moscow?"

She appreciated the stress that he must be under working in London, in the heart of British Intelligence, and that he simply wanted to talk with her, but she had very little information about what was going on back in Russia and honestly told him so. "Unfortunately comrade, I working nonstop in the Mediterranean area almost 18 months and know only what read in local newspapers. I, of course, in radio contact with Center, but messages kept short as possible and deal strictly operational matters."

For the first time since entering the room, Philby actually smiled at Maria. It had finally dawned on him that she too was leading a very difficult life, no doubt posing as some lowly worker and in as much danger, if discovered, as himself. "Of course, it might be that being connected with the British government and sitting in London, I am more up-to-date on the situation in Russia then you are." He then spent the next five minutes bringing her up to date on anything that he could remember about what had been happening along the Russian front and about conditions in general back in Russia. He then looked at his watch and realized, reluctantly, that he should be on his way. He shouldn't be "unaccounted for in his movements" for too long a period.

"I shall probably need to meet with you again, once I know the results of the Canaris - Popov meeting. Can your colleague with the car check each day at that same bus stop at 8 a.m., 3 p.m. and 10 p.m. for the next several days? If I have anything worthwhile, I shall again be at that pickup point."

"We agreed." She extended her hand and they clasped their hands together firmly and silently stared into each other's eyes for several seconds. There was a special bond between fellow secret agents living undercover in a foreign country, with death possible at any sudden moment. She then unlocked and opened the door and he was gone. She stayed another fifteen minutes, concisely writing out a report that she would shortly hand to her radio operator and he would take care of encoding it and sending it via shortwave radio later that night to Moscow.

As she stood to leave the small and sparsely furnished apartment, she happened to look at herself in a mirror. Her lovely red hair was masked with the black dye and was roughly cut. There were bags under her eyes and her face looked like that of someone pushing 40, not that of a 27 year old woman. The constant pressure from fear of arrest, sleeping in the woods and not eating properly for many months had taken a toll on her appearance and probably her health. For some reason, she suddenly thought of one of her last days in New York City and having gone to a beautician to have her hair styled, having a facial and a manicure as a farewell present to herself. She'd also indulged in such capitalist comforts because that night was also going to be her last time to see Charles and she had wanted to look her best for him. Those days and spectacular nights in Manhattan now seemed a lifetime ago. She briefly wondered what had become of Charles. Was he still playing amateur spy for Mr. Astor or had he gone off to war like so many millions of young men around the world? Was he even still… she stopped herself from even thinking about that. She'd already lost one person she'd loved to this horrible war. She didn't even want to contemplate the possibility that Charles was also dead.

She locked the apartment door and headed off on foot for a brief encounter with her radio operator to pass him her notes. He was a young Russian boy who had lost a leg early in the war, but because of his Spanish mother from whom he had learned fluent Spanish, he had been transferred to intelligence work. While he couldn't exactly run quickly if he had to escape, on the other hand, he never needed to do so. Security officials would simply take one look at his missing leg and would stereotypically dismiss him as no threat. In a similar vein, border guards and various city police officials would often feel her up while checking her credentials or supposedly checking her for hidden weapons, but the chauvinistic Mediterranean male mind couldn't really conceive of a female as a threat.

Philby wandered into the British Embassy around 5:00 p.m. and sought out Nigel to see what was happening.

"Ah, feeling better?"

"Yes, yes indeed. When those migraine headaches come on, nothing works better than taking a headache powder, then a nap and then a walk in the fresh air. And I always forget what a lovely city this is to just wander around in down in the old parts. All those red tile roofs and cobblestone streets."

"It does seem hard to imagine on some days that there is a horrible war going on in parts of the world while walking around Lisbon."

Philby sat down in a comfortable leather chair and lighted a cigarette. "Anything new?"

"As a matter of fact, I met earlier today with the OSS Chief here in Lisbon, a relatively young man named Charles Worthington. He informed me that General Donovan, accompanied by one of his aides, Duncan Lee, is arriving in Lisbon tomorrow. Staying here just one or two days and then flying on – making some sort of swing through the Med area of operations."

Philby raised an eyebrow, but didn't say anything.

"Yes, Charles and I had the same thought. Quite a coincidence isn't it that the directors of the Abwehr and the OSS both just happen to arrive in Lisbon on practically the same day!"

"Indeed it is," replied Philby as he stubbed out his cigarette.

"Don't suppose there's anything you want to tell me as to why you're really in Lisbon, is there?"

A fleeting panic crossed his face until he realized that Nigel was referring to "something" related to Canaris and Donovan, not his earlier secret meeting with his NKVD handler. "I've told you all I know. Dusko is supposedly here to tell Canaris that the answer is no. If there's something more devious going on, no one trusted me to know about it."

Nigel finally simply shrugged his shoulders much as he had with Charles and repeated practically the same mantra. "I guess if there's something we need to know, someone will eventually tell us what it is. By the way, would you like to meet General Donovan? Charles told me that his Ambassador is likely to host a dinner or something for Donovan and to keep my evening social calendar free for the next two days. I suspect that I could get you included on any such guest list if you're interested."

"No thanks. I spend enough time around overbearing Yanks up in London." He switched to his best American accent. "You've met one and you've met them all!" In fact, he would have loved to have been at a dinner with General Donovan to pick up any indications of what he was really doing in Lisbon, or just general tidbits of gossip, but he figured he needed to keep his nights as free as possible to make any further meetings if necessary with Maria. He was growing ever more skeptical of the story of the Director of the OSS "just happening" to pass though Portugal while Canaris was there as well. He felt a genuine migraine headache coming on.

## Chapter 7

Admiral Canaris used the first day in Lisbon mostly to recover from the long plane journey. The next night Colonel Karsthoff hosted a dinner at his residence in his honor, which included everyone from his Abstelle with the rank of major and above. Even with that limitation there were some thirty guests. Colonel Ewald Gehlen pleaded not feeling well and remained up in his bedroom, and for some reason Karsthoff's secretary, Elizabeth, was also absent without any explanation being offered. The table was set with the best plates available and the room lighted only by candles all along the long wooden table, giving a definite Valkyrian atmosphere to the evening. German waiters in white gloves served delicious food and drink for several hours. Canaris cynically thought to himself that he was glad his men in Lisbon weren't suffering from food rationing and shortages of most everything except potatoes, as were their colleagues back in Berlin or on the Russian Front. He now understood why he never received requests for transfers from anyone assigned to Lisbon.

Elizabeth was in fact off fetching Mr. Da Silva from his home to come to a discreet meeting at von Karsthoff's residence that evening. The banker thought it a bit odd that Karsthoff had insisted at their last meeting that he come to his home in this manner, rather than Da Silva simply driving himself as he normally would do. Upon arrival at the house, she drove around and parked at the back of the house and led Da Silva up a back staircase to an upstairs study. Colonel Gehlen was waiting there for him. Elizabeth made the necessary introductions and then went and waited in Karsthoff's bedroom – a room she was quite familiar with from previous visits.

"Unfortunately, Admiral Canaris is tied up at the moment with a formal dinner downstairs. He asked that you and I go ahead and start discussing details of the upcoming operation which will involve your bank. He should be able to join us before you leave and confirm all the steps that we have agreed upon in the meantime."

"Very well. I apologize in advance for my limited German, but it is rare that I actually speak it here in Portugal."

"Nonsense. You speak beautiful German," replied Gehlen. "I understand that your mother was from the Hamburg area."

"A suburb of Hamburg, Klein Flottbeck." He then briefly repeated his family's history in case Karsthoff had not already provided it to the Colonel.

Bankers and professional soldiers generally get along very well because they both like getting directly to the business at hand. "Mr. Da Silva, by mid-November we would like to begin the first of perhaps two or three large shipments of gold and diamonds via Portugal to Brazil. By late November, we will arrange for men and their families to start arriving in Portugal, with the idea of them also sailing to Brazil. The final number remains undetermined, but will probably be at least two hundred in number. They will be documented as citizens of Switzerland or perhaps a few other countries. There will be no citizens of Germany making the journey.

"I understand." Da Silva proceeded to explain, as he already had to Karsthoff, how the shipment of "goods" and people would work, with there being no records of either existing after the trips. "I have a good relationship with the owner of a company that fishes for cod, then dries them and ships much of the catch to Brazil. Many Portuguese have moved to Brazil over the decades, and many still like the traditional foods from the Continent. There will be certain 'fees' to be paid to the owner of the company and to each ship captain that sails for Brazil. At most, each ship will be able to accommodate about thirty passengers, so this will take a number of sailings over a number of weeks, perhaps even a couple of months, depending on how many people and when certain ships will be sailing. Depending on whether your 'passengers' will be arriving in Portugal all at once or not, it might also mean having to quietly house our guests somewhere for many weeks, before it is their turn to sail for Brazil."

Colonel Gehlen decided he would save Da Silva the awkwardness of mentioning his own fee and brought it up himself. "We understand that you are assisting out of a sense of patriotism to the homeland of your mother, but Admiral Canaris has instructed me that you are to be well compensated for your service just as the others involved in this transportation operation will be."

"Thank you. That is very generous of the Admiral."

"We will leave to you to explain to the various ship captains that just as we are generous to those that assist us, we would be equally passionate in dealing with anyone who betrays us."

"I can't imagine that will become an issue, but I shall pass along your 'comments' to those playing key roles in our operation." Da Silva thought that that had been the most tactfully phrased threat he'd ever heard.

"Now as for the 'fees,' I don't believe that up to this point that you and Colonel Karsthoff have discussed this in precise numbers."

"No, we haven't, but this is simply because I've been waiting for an indication that this operation was indeed going forward and also quite frankly, I will need to talk to several other people to determine what their costs will be. I can then give you or Colonel Karsthoff a precise cost per person and as for the gold and diamonds, probably as a percentage of the value of goods being discreetly shipped."

"That will be quite acceptable." Gehlen then poured each of them a cognac and conversation turned to what life was like in the Sao Paulo region of Brazil, while they waited for the arrival of Canaris. Gehlen had already explained that on such an important matter, the Admiral himself would want to meet Da Silva personally before formally launching the operation.

Some fifteen minutes later, Admiral Canaris entered the room. "My apologies, Mr. Da Silva, but I had some duties to perform downstairs. You understand."

"No problem at all. Colonel Gehlen and I used the time productively to work out I believe to everyone's satisfaction most of the details of this operation and to get personally acquainted."

Gehlen nodded discreetly to the Admiral that all seemed in order.

"I'm sure that you have, but perhaps you can now just give me a summary of the major points of our agreement."

Da Silva took a seat. "With pleasure." He then ran over the plans in great detail for the Admiral, appreciating that the ultimate "yes" depended on Canaris and Canaris alone.

Gehlen did intercede towards the finish to explain that the precise final cost of "fees" would not be available until Da Silva had had a chance to speak with certain individuals whose cooperation would be needed.

"Naturally," replied Canaris. "Well, I think we're all in agreement for the present. Mr. Da Silva will start making his plans on this end and come up with a precise budget, while we start making plans for the transportation of goods and people to Portugal by late November."

Ewald poured glasses of cognac for all three and they stood for a toast. "To our mutual success and happiness," stated Admiral Canaris. The first domino had been pushed over.

General Donovan and his personal aide, Duncan Lee, arrived at the American Embassy the following afternoon. His first stop was in the Ambassador's office, as a matter of courtesy, then he came down to the OSS section. Charles was still contemplating the amazing coincidence of Donovan and Canaris both being in Lisbon at the same time, and at a time when the head of German Military Intelligence was seeking a separate peace with England and America. But if Donovan had come for a discreet, secret meeting with the Germans, by coming to the Embassy, Donovan was letting half of Lisbon know that he was in town. Charles toyed with the idea that Donovan was trying to outwit any observers – that by being so open about his visit, he would make people think he wasn't in town for any clandestine purpose, but then he would sneak away to meet Canaris. The more Charles thought about that reverse logic methodology, the dumber it sounded. He finally concluded that he was wasting his time, given that in just 15-20 minutes Donovan would be in his office and if something very secretive was afoot, the head of OSS would shortly be seeking his assistance.

General Donovan came to the OSS offices and first went around and shook hands with all his people and inspected the office space the Embassy had provided them. Finally, he was settled into a comfortable leather chair in Charles' private office.

"How are you Charles?"

"Just fine, Sir. Did you have a good flight?"

"I always hate flying over an ocean. Would make for a very long swim if the plane goes down! Before I forget it, I saw Vincent recently. I bumped into him at some boring cocktail party there in Washington just a few days before I started this trip for President Roosevelt. At the time, I didn't think I would be stopping here, so no particular message from him. We were originally planning on flying directly to Gibraltar, but the British are doing something hush-hush out of there in the next few days and didn't want to potentially draw German attention to the island by me making a visit, so you got me!"

It certainly sounded to Charles that it was indeed pure serendipity that Donovan had arrived in Lisbon at this time, but he thought he'd just blatantly ask. "Ah, so that's the explanation. Quite frankly, when I learned that Admiral Canaris is in Lisbon and then heard you were about to suddenly arrive as well, I put two and two together and got five. I thought perhaps you were having some super secret meeting with the German."

It was always possible that General Donovan wasn't going to reveal to a mere Charles Worthington of Lisbon Station, but if he was about to have a clandestine meeting with Canaris, he was certainly a great actor. He looked as surprised as anybody that Canaris was in town.

"First I've heard of such a visit. Do we know why he's here?"

"As a matter of fact we do, courtesy of the British, who briefed me a couple of days ago. He's come down here supposedly to personally meet and debrief two of their sources, a Yugoslav codenamed TRICYCLE who normally resides in England and OSTRO, who resides here in Portugal. And just to make life interesting, the Yugoslav is actually a double agent for the British and the second fellow is a complete con artist, but whom the Abwehr thinks is wonderful with all sorts of subagents within England and even America!"

"Ha! And Admiral Canaris thinks these are two of his best sources. No wonder they're losing the war. Still, a little odd that the head of the service comes all this way, and perhaps even at personal risk of being kidnapped or assassinated by the British, just to meet with two agents. What do you think might be going on?"

Charles couldn't resist smiling. "Well, Nigel, the MI6 rep, and I contemplated that perhaps you'd come to town to hold a secret meeting with Canaris."

"I wish that were true. But honestly, we were diverted to here at the last minute quite literally because the British didn't want us coming to Gibraltar right now. Don't take it personally, but Lisbon wasn't even going to be a stop on this trip when it was first planned."

"I take your word for it, but I fear Nigel is going to be a bit disappointed. He had this all worked out in his mind, and it even explained for him why Kim Philby of his Headquarters had really come down to Lisbon and not just for the TRICYCLE-Canaris meeting."

Donovan grunted. "That annoying prat is in town? I've met him twice at functions in London and once in Washington. He's the most anti-American Brit I've ever met. He can't go two minutes without making one of his oh-so-witty remarks poking fun at America. London sent him down to Lisbon just to be present for an agent meeting with Canaris?"

"Does sort of make you wonder just what's so important that's to be discussed at that TRICYCLE-Canaris meeting?" replied Charles.

"Maybe Canaris is going to defect while in Portugal? I'm only half joking. We've had a number of incidences during the fighting in Italy of German officers, up to the rank of Lt. Colonel, just showing up unexpectedly at some frontline guard post with a cart-full of personal possessions and wanting to surrender. One even brought his Italian mistress with him, instead of his wife!"

"You know, Sir, half of Lisbon knows that you're in Portugal and the Ambassador is hosting a dinner for you tonight, which will guarantee that the other half learns of your visit. I wonder if Berlin and Hitler will have the same suspicions about you and Canaris both being in Lisbon at the same time as I had?"

"You do have a devious mind, don't you! I'd always heard that about you Harvard men."

Charles smiled at the poke of fun from a Columbia Law School graduate. "I was just thinking, if you were to include some remark at the dinner tonight about how it's reaching the point of the war where a lot of people will soon have to be deciding where their futures lay. I could make sure that a couple of prominent locals who we suspect are informants for the Germans are on the guest list, so that your comments get to the German Embassy."

"So those words get back to the Gestapo in Berlin and they start worrying about what Admiral Canaris was really doing in Lisbon…

hmm, that's an interesting angle. Let me think about that a bit, but go ahead and get the informants added to the guest list for tonight."

"Just one more item, while we're alone. Have you made any progress in figuring out how the Italians learned about our operation into the Japanese Embassy?"

"Not really. I brought over from New York two totally trustworthy men, who had worked with me on that mole situation for Vincent Astor. They're completely unknown in the Embassy and I've had them out doing discreet background checks on Embassy personnel. The only faint possibility so far is Solborg, because of some Italian ancestry and his being upset at being fired by you, but he shouldn't have even known about that operation. I'll keep working at it."

"I know this is a tough assignment, suspecting all your colleagues. Hopefully, it will turn out to be something totally bizarre to explain how the Italians learned of the Japanese operation that has nothing to do with any of our people, but we need to track this down if we can. Well, I should continue on my rounds around the building."

Donovan rose and headed for the office door, but then stopped and returned to the coincidence of Canaris and he being in town at the same time. "You know, I hope the FBI doesn't hear about Canaris being here in Lisbon, that paranoid moron Hoover might decide I'm working for the Nazis instead of thinking the Admiral might be working for us!" They both smiled broadly.

While Charles was attending the Ambassador's dinner for General Donovan that evening, Dusko Popov was standing in front of a small tobacconist shop, smoking a cigarette and waiting for Elizabeth to come by and pick him up.

Once in the vehicle, he leaned over and gave her a kiss on the cheek. "Good evening beautiful lady." He did that because he liked kissing beautiful women, but also because he'd seen that the owner of the shop had been watching him out his window for several minutes, probably wondering why he hadn't moved on after purchasing the package of cigarettes. This way, the Portuguese man could jump to whatever conclusion he was so inclined – probably that one or the other of them was married and not to each other. It was indeed a secret rendezvous, just not the kind the tobacconist suspected. It was thinking about such little things that had helped allow Popov to have successfully played his dangerous game of double agent for several years.

"And how is my good friend Ludovico?" he inquired of his lovely chauffeur.

"He's been behind closed doors practically since our special guest arrived. When I saw him at lunch, he seemed to be in a terrible mood."

"Any idea why?" Popov was always looking for any signs that the Germans might have tumbled onto his being a double agent. He stared intently at her face for any signs of a non-spoken answer, even if she gave him one verbally.

She paused a few seconds before answering. "I have the impression that some of the news that the Admiral brought with him about how the war is going is very bad." Having heard her answer, he then understood her hesitation in answering. Good loyal Germans were never to speak in defeatist terms, which she just had. She had probably been worried whether Popov would report her to Ludovico, or even worse, the Gestapo man at the Embassy.

As if he could read her mind, he responded, "Don't worry, I won't report your 'defeatist' talk to anyone." He gave her a reassuring smile and reached over and patted her arm. "If the director of the Abwehr can speak of such things, surely you and I are allowed to do so in private as well. Was there anything in particular that they discussed?"

"Mostly about how badly things are going on the Russian Front and that we've lost Italy as well, and…" She paused. "And that it is now just a question of when, not if, Germany loses the war."

"Have you and Ludovico made any plans for what you might do, if the war does…end badly?"

"Not really. Of course, he has a wife and children back in Bavaria that he has to think about, so I'm not sure just where I would fit in to any post-war plans, win or lose."

They were almost to Karsthoff's home, so he brought the conversation to a close by simply saying, "Let's speak of this again, when you and I have more time."

Karsthoff himself greeted Popov and Elizabeth at the front door. He indicated for her to go to the living room and wait while he escorted Popov directly to the upstairs study where Canaris was waiting.

Once he entered the room, the Admiral rose and came to greet the Yugoslav. "Good evening Dusko. Very good to see you again."

"It's very good to see you again so soon, as well," replied Popov.

Karsthoff poured drinks for all three gentlemen as they settled into comfortable chairs grouped near the large fireplace. He then pulled out a small notebook, in case Popov had anything that needed to be recalled in detail.

After several minutes of small talk about whether anything new was playing at the West End theaters in London and the weather back in England, Canaris turned to business. "So, what information do you have that necessitated so soon a return to Lisbon?"

"It's about Allied plans for creating many new bases in England, starting in January, for the anticipated arrival of tens of thousands of American troops. They are to be part of the First United States Army Group, which is to eventually comprise some 800,000 men. This FUSAG is who will eventually lead the cross-channel invasion of France." He handed over to Karsthoff a sheet of paper upon which he had written the names of English towns and villages where these bases will be built. "Most of them appear to be to the southeast of London, out around Dover, Canterbury and Ramsgate. At this stage, the British Army is simply going out and doing surveys and making plans for all the wood, cement and steel that will be needed to build the thousands of barracks, dining halls, etc. that will house these hundreds of thousands of men."

Canaris looked at the names on the sheet. He recognized a few of them. "Well, we've all known that eventually the Allies would launch such an invasion, which is why we have been constructing 'Fortress Europe' along the beaches of France, Belgium and Holland to defend against such an invasion. I don't suppose you obtained any information to indicate where the invasion will fall in Europe?"

"Unfortunately, to date, none of my subsources have learned anything of substance. Naturally, there are rumors that the invasion will be anywhere from Norway down to the beaches of Estoril just five miles from here!" All three men laughed.

"The Portuguese would be very upset to have their summer bathing upset by an invasion next summer!" responded Canaris.

"I was able to learn this: there is to be a top level summit before the end of the year involving Churchill, Roosevelt and Stalin to agree upon a date and the location of this invasion. Naturally, I have offered all my subagents a substantial bonus for any details on such a summit."

Popov's intelligence was very intriguing and confirmed everything that the Germans already suspected, but underneath the smoke, he really had no details on the actual fire. Still, Canaris and Karsthoff were pleased that Popov was diligently working on the problem and had shown the initiative to bring them what he thought was important information. He said he wanted to be able to pass along his impressions, not just the names of towns as he could have done via shortwave radio.

After some 45 minutes of discussion, the Admiral suggested that they take a little break and stretch their legs. "Come Dusko, let's take a little stroll out in the gardens. It's a beautiful night." Karsthoff had not made colonel by not understanding when he was not wanted. He remained in the study making notes on some of the points that he would want to include in the reporting cable to Berlin first thing in the morning.

Once they were alone in the garden, Canaris got right to the point. "Did you meet with Menzies while you were in London?"

Always looking for an opportunity to make himself look good, Popov started by saying, "This was not easy to arrange, even through my good contacts in the British Army, but I was finally able to call in a favor of a good friend. He thinks I just wanted to ask Menzies for his assistance in getting an import license to bring certain products in from Portugal to England. And once I met with Menzies, I explained that you had sought my assistance through a relative of mine in Belgrade. I explained that you have been good friends with him for many years and through him, you knew that I occasionally traveled between London and Lisbon."

"Yes, yes, excellent work." Canaris was getting impatient. "And what was Menzies' answer to my proposal?"

"I'm sorry to report that the British government completely rejected your proposal. When I met again with Menzies two days later, he said that he had spoken with Mister Churchill and his response was simply that Allied policy is for unconditional surrender. He would welcome the removal of Hitler from office, but that alone was no basis for negotiations with you or anyone else as the new leader of Germany. Apparently, Churchill did not even bother contacting the Americans about your proposal."

The two men walked along in silence for almost a full minute. Finally, Popov felt that he needed to say something to get the conversation going again. "I'm sorry that I have not brought you a better answer."

"It's not your fault. You have done well and I thank you for your effort. All I ask of you now is that you completely forget that we ever had these conversations. As you can imagine, it would not be in the best interest of either of us for these details to reach certain other organizations of the Reich." Canaris took an envelope out of his pocket and passed it to Popov, without saying anything.

"I understand perfectly."

"Let's return to the study and continue our conversation about the information that you have brought from London."

Canaris walked on ahead of Popov along the gravel path, who noticed the now stooped shoulders of the Admiral and a slightly slower gait. Even though he had said nothing, clearly he had taken the answer from London badly. If the war was going as poorly as Elizabeth had told him earlier, it may well have been that Canaris had seen his offer to Menzies as the last hope of Germany avoiding total destruction. He almost felt sorry for the man. He stopped and took a quick glance in the envelope. As he suspected from the feel, it contained money – a thousand English pounds. At least the Admiral paid well for efforts on his behalf and presumably for Popov's continued silence.

Later in the evening after Popov had left, Gehlen joined Canaris and Karsthoff in the study. Canaris did not share even with these most trusted colleagues the true details of Popov's mission to London, nor of the negative response he'd received from Menzies about the idea of a separate and negotiated peace between a Hitlerless Germany and England. He did confide in them his profound pessimism for the future of the war and the horrific conditions that would befall Germany as the Russian Army marched across his beloved homeland. He couldn't understand why Churchill and Roosevelt did not appreciate the dangers that would come with a Soviet Union that occupied at least half, if not more, of the European continent. If they had been concerned about a Hitler that wanted to control all of Europe, why couldn't they understand the threat from a man and an ideology that wanted to control the world? He feared that their blind desire for revenge against Germany was ruining their calculations for the future.

"Gentlemen, it is clearly time to move forward and with some haste on Operation Grandfather. We seem to have found the proper banker in Mr. Da Silva. Hopefully he will be back in touch soon with you, Ludovico, on the fine logistical details and on the final price for the movement of our 'goods' and of our people to Brazil. Once Ewald and I are back in Berlin, we will push forward on the preparation of false documentation for our junior officers who will be the first to go, and for their families. We still need to work out how we can get a number of these officers the correct assignments that will allow for their travel to Portugal. I have a few ideas on how these officers and their families can disappear without immediately raising alarm with the Gestapo, but this clearly needs further attention. It will make it easier if we begin the movement of people out of Germany as the holidays approach in November and some of the absences can be explained by people off on Christmas leave. I'm also thinking that we might have to resort to there being a horrific bus crash or perhaps a building fire in which afterwards, specific bodies could not be identified."

Ewald spoke up, "Wilhelm, I've been giving this some thought as well and have started putting together a prioritized list of people who are to be moved to Brazil. In some cases, it's a question not just of merit, but the geographical realities of where some officers are assigned or their families are living. There are some very deserving cases, but for whom it would simply be impossible to arrange for their transfer back to Berlin in order for them to begin the clandestine journey to Portugal. I suggest that we also have a secondary list, in case we are very lucky and can continue in a few months the extraction of even more people, without the Gestapo becoming aware of our activities. Obviously, the Gestapo and the SD people would find our plan quite traitorous and when it is eventually discovered, as surely it will be, we must be prepared for the consequences."

"To the extent possible, those consequences will fall mostly on me, but both of you should depart early once in the process."

Both of the others started to speak in protest, but Canaris raised his hand. "This is not a question that is open for discussion." A very tired and depressed-looking Canaris rose from his chair. "Good night gentlemen. I'll see you for breakfast in the morning."

The following night, Canaris went ahead and held his meeting with agent OSTRO, the Czech businessman, who ran a number of very good subagents within England and even several in the United States. Even though he'd concluded the night before that the war was hopeless, his sense of duty required that he at least continue to try the best job that he could for his country. And in any case, for appearances sake with the Gestapo men watching most of his moves, he had to make the meeting which was one of the justifications for the trip. He did let a small smile come to his lips at his own cleverness. He had the British thinking he'd only come to Lisbon over his offer of a negotiated surrender and his own government thinking he was there just meeting Abwehr agents, while he was truly in Portugal to make arrangements for the clandestine movement of many of his trusted junior officers to a new life in Brazil. "Ah, what a tangled web we weave," he heard himself mumbling. As for the idea of doing away with Hitler, what was now the point? If the British were still going to insist on unconditional surrender and not be willing to protect them from a Russian invasion, how could he convince fellow German officers to take such a risk, if they gained nothing? No, the German nation and its folk were going down a dark path to destruction and there were no alternatives.

Paul Fidrmuc was brought into the same upstairs study where the meeting had been held previously with Popov. It might have seemed strange to some to bring such important agents to the home of the Abwehr Chief of Lisbon, but it really was the perfect place to meet. It was located in an isolated area, with high walls and a number of guards. There were several roads that led quickly up to the front gate, so that you could easily smuggle in someone in a fast moving car, as they had done with both of these men. Plus, there was the psychological aspect. Neither the Portuguese Service, the PDVE, nor the British would ever think that the Germans would actually use Karsthoff's home for such a purpose.

Canaris turned on his charm as he entered the room. "Paul, so good at last to get to meet you in person." He extended his hand.

"It is an honor to meet you, Admiral."

They took their seats and began a wide-ranging discussion about conditions in England. Canaris always liked to hear about how the average citizen was faring in the enemy countries, for he knew it was a good indicator of how hard the soldiers of those countries would fight.

Paul seemed to start a number of his answers with the phrase, "Well, as I've recently learned in a secret writing report from my man in London, or Portsmouth…" He clearly liked to emphasize how well sourced his information was that he passed to the Abwehr.

"And what are you hearing about preparations for new bases to house American troops that would come at some point to England, in order to be part of an invasion force?"

"Mostly just rumors so far. Everyone is of course expecting such a build-up prior to any invasion attempt, which I'm sure will be repulsed, but there will be an invasion in the coming year." Fidrmuc was always politically correct in his comments. Hitler was busy building the coastal defenses for 'Fortress Europe' and had said in many speeches how Germany would repulse any such invasion attempt.

Canaris continued to press. "Any word yet as to where in England these new bases will be built?"

"No, because no decision has yet been reached on where the invasion will take place. The Pas de Calais area of France is, of course, the natural choice, being the shortest distance across the Channel, but that then makes it the obvious choice and where Germany would have the most troops ready to resist the invasion."

Canaris began to notice that while Paul spoke a lot, he never actually provided a firm answer to any question. He was full of speculation and rambling possibilities, but very few hard facts. Canaris began to think that he now knew how the ancient Greeks must have felt when they went to consult the Oracle at Delphi and went away, after paying in gold, with vague answers that could be interpreted in one of many ways.

Towards the end of the conversation, he did lean forward and reveal one nugget. "I received word just a few days ago that within the next few months, there will be a high-level summit of Churchill, Stalin and Roosevelt, if his health will permit the travel. It is at that meeting that they will decide on a date and place for the cross-channel invasion."

"And where will this summit take place?" asked Canaris.

"That's still being negotiated. Stalin does not wish to travel far from his country. Churchill thinks this is because he's perpetually worried about being overthrown and doesn't want to be away for more than a few days."

"Well, thank you very much for coming by. It has been very informative. I want to personally convey to you on behalf of the Fuhrer our gratitude for your excellent work on behalf of the Reich."

Not to be outdone, Fidrmuc replied, "It is an honor for me to serve such a great cause."

Karsthoff escorted his star agent back out to the car and he was driven quickly away to be discreetly dropped off back in the city. Canaris remained by himself in the study thinking. He knew that the evaluations of OSTRO's reporting had continually been very good, but he certainly didn't impress the Admiral in person. Listening to him reminded Canaris of some of the briefings he had attended by Hitler's scientific advisors who were supposedly developing incredible weapons that were going to totally reverse the situation on the Eastern Front, in Italy and take England completely out of the war with self-guided flying bombs. Like OSTRO's answers, those briefings were full of vague generalities and even beautiful models, but what Canaris never saw were actual weapons being produced. Not that it really mattered much anymore, but he wondered just how many subagents that clever Czech actually had in England?

## Chapter 8

Two days after his first secret meeting, a car driven by a local once again picked up Kim Philby and brought him to the special NKVD apartment building in one of the working class neighborhoods of Lisbon. Maria was waiting for him as before, though he noticed that she seemed to have taken some effort about her appearance for this meeting. She had at least carefully combed her hair and had put on a little bit of lipstick.

He waited until she had closed and locked the door before speaking. "How are you Maria?"

"I am well, comrade. I take that you have more news to me?"

"Yes, I do. I have the results of the meeting between Admiral Canaris and the British double agent, Popov. And also a related matter, but let me first tell you about the meeting with Popov." Philby proceeded to relate to Maria the same information that Popov had given to him and Nigel the day before, about his meeting with Karsthoff and Canaris while meeting together. More importantly, about the private conversation with just the Admiral, while the two walked in the garden. Maria once again took some notes, but listened in silence to Philby's report. It had become obvious to her during their first meeting, that Philby did not appreciate being interrupted.

"Popov did not seem have had much to say about reaction from Canaris to rejection from Menzies about surrender proposal. There nothing more?"

"According to Popov, Canaris said nothing after hearing of the rejection, other than to thank Popov for his efforts." Philby shrugged his shoulders to indicate that there was nothing more.

"And what this second item you have to report me?"

"I learned that the Director of the American spy organization, the OSS, arrived unexpectedly in Lisbon a few days ago. The local OSS Chief, Charles Worthington, told my colleague, Nigel, that General Donovan was just passing through on his way to North Africa and that he had no real purpose in stopping in Lisbon, other than the logistical necessity of needing a refueling stop. I, however, am skeptical of this. I find it an amazing coincidence that Admiral Canaris and General Donovan arrived at the same time in Lisbon. I emphasize to you, my surprise that the British Government so quickly turned down the offer by Canaris for negotiations and also the lack of an emotional reaction from Canaris that the British response was a negative one. Perhaps he reacted so calmly, because he had already also reached out to the Americans and had gotten a more positive response. Perhaps that explains why Donovan really came to Portugal?"

When Maria heard the name of Charles Worthington, she had to catch herself from responding. She was quite taken by surprise to learn of his presence in Lisbon and was immediately elated. She also needed to suppress a small grin over the 'brilliant analyses' by the pompous Philby, as to the real purpose of Donovan stopping in Lisbon. She already knew the real story, and it was in fact a simple logistical necessity, not some secret mission to meet with Admiral Canaris. However, she could not share with the Brit that she knew the real reason, for it would have revealed to him that the NKVD had a source within the OSS and very close to General Donovan. The fact was, less than twenty-four hours earlier, Duncan Lee, personal aide to Donovan, had been sitting in the very chair where Philby now sat. Along with many other important details about the work by the OSS he'd passed along, he had assured her that the stop in Lisbon was because the British at the last moment had told them it would be unwise to make a refueling stop at Gibraltar. So much for Philby's insights.

She simply responded to Philby that his theory of a secret Donovan-Canaris meeting was quite interesting and that she would immediately report it on to Moscow. "Anything else you learn on this subject, without endangering you, will be appreciated in future."

As opposed to their first meeting, she had no interest in prolonging this one and didn't care if he was feeling lonely or not. As soon as he had finished his oral report to her, she ushered him out the door. She could only explain staying in Lisbon for a few more days and needed to move quickly in order to discretely contact Charles, if that was even possible. She hadn't really thought of him for many months, but the mere mention of his name had immediately brought back to her all of her fond memories of him in New York. She admitted to herself how much she had missed him. She made certain that there was nothing left in the apartment and departed. Besides her radio operator who had traveled with her from Spain, she also had the name of a low-level support asset in Lisbon, a Communist sympathizer, in case she needed assistance while in Portugal. She'd actually met with him once before on a previous brief mission to Lisbon and had found him a very pleasant, old man. He reminded her a bit of her own grandfather. She was certain that she could obtain his assistance in finding a home address for Charles, without having to give the old man much of an explanation.

Just a few hours later, she was enjoying a glass of wine with this local contact, using Spanish to communicate with him. He was a retired plumber, who now worked a few afternoons a week in a tobacco shop owned by his son-in-law. His hair was mostly grey, but there was still a twinkle in his eyes, surrounded by seventy years of facial wrinkles. He was still waiting for a socialist revolution to come to his native Portugal. Occasionally assisting the NKVD made him feel as if he were still part of the good fight. Portuguese and Spanish were close enough that they could make themselves understood reasonably well one to the other. He also knew her as Maria and was pleased to see her again. After the pleasantries, she got down to the "work-related" matter that had brought her to their meeting.

"I need to discreetly acquire home address of someone from American Embassy, a Charles Worthington. Do you know anyone who might be able to get that information?"

"I have a cousin. I think his wife has a brother who works as a mechanic for the Americans. He might be able to come up with the address. How quickly do you need this?"

His answer had not surprised her. Most every Spaniard or Portuguese with whom she'd dealt with to date had a cousin who knew a man who knew a man… "I'm afraid that I need the address as soon as possible. I'm on a timetable and am willing to pay well for this information."

Antonio finished his glass and stood. "In that case, let me be on my way to my cousin. I'll meet you back here at 9:00 p.m. tonight."

Maria remained at the small table, sipping her wine. She contemplated whether she was insane for seeking out Charles. If the NKVD learned of this, they would not understand at all and she would no doubt be shot immediately as a traitor – America being an ally or not. She concluded fairly quickly that yes, it was worth the risk. Since the death of her husband and then saying goodbye to Charles in New York, there had been a hole in her soul. She knew lots of people talked about and even joked about the "Russian soul," but there was something to it and hers was now incomplete. She didn't know what would happen even if she could arrange to see him in the next day or two, but she knew that she needed to try, regardless of the outcome.

Gray-haired Antonio showed up promptly at 9:00 p.m. as promised and simply passed her a slip of paper and wished her well. He offered no explanation as to exactly how he had acquired the address of the American diplomat. She found a taxi and had the driver take her to an address a few numbers off from the one in which she was interested. She then she walked away and stopped near the corner at the end of the block. She stepped into a doorway and lighted a cigarette. She waited. Charles being the head OSS man in Lisbon, there were a number of organizations who might regularly watch his apartment. She was curious to see if anybody was loitering up or down the street, on foot or in a car. There were a few obvious residents of the street coming and going, but nothing that looked like surveillance. It was nearly 10 p.m. and few people on the street. There could always be an observation post in an apartment window on the street across from his building, but she would just have to take that chance. She walked slowly down the cobblestone sidewalk on the side of the street opposite his building. If there was an O.P., she'd be out of sight until the last moment, when she would cut quickly across the street to the door of his building. She'd put a scarf over her head to at least partially disguise her appearance. She couldn't know from the outside which one was his, number 4. Sometimes, you just have to march forward and hope for the best. In this case, that he was home and that he was alone. It had been some twenty months since she'd said goodbye to him in Manhattan – a lifetime ago. He could be married now or at least have a girlfriend, or he could have friends in the apartment that night for drinks. She just didn't care. Having gotten this close, she was going to knock on his door and take her chances.

She did actually stand silently outside his door for about thirty seconds, to see if she heard voices from inside. All was silent, so she knocked and waited. Suddenly the door opened and there he was, just as she remembered him.

"Hello. Would you like go dancing at Roseland?" she asked very softly. She hoped that he too remembered that very special evening.

He instinctively muttered almost in shock, "Olga." Then for several long moments, he simply stood there in silence. Finally, a big smile came to his face and he pulled the door completely open. "I love what you've done with your hair. Please, come in."

As soon as the door was closed, she fell into his arms and they hugged and kissed like two young people who hadn't seen each other in a very long time, which in fact, they had not. He finally stepped back a little from her. "My God, is it really you! There hasn't been a day since you left New York that I haven't thought about you."

She knew that had to be a lie, but she liked hearing it anyway. "So, you don't have wife or two or three Portuguese girlfriends?" she teased him.

"Girlfriends, yes. You're lucky you didn't show up earlier. One of them just left about an hour ago." He laughed and she laughed. It was as if they had never been apart. They were right back to kidding each other as if it had only been a day or two since last they'd been together.

He led her over to a small sofa. It was a hideous brown color, but comfortable. "I have so many questions for you I don't know where to begin. How long will you be here in Lisbon? Or do you live here?"

"I only be here couple more days, then must return Spain, which where I normally live and work. God, my English so terrible become!"

"No, you're doing just fine." He kept tightly holding her hands and staring into her eyes. "This is so wonderful," he kept repeating. "Are you still a journalist? You don't look like a journalist and what's with this black hair. Where are your beautiful red tresses?"

"I supposed be Bulgarian refugee and now simple poor peasant girl. I hear you big OSS spy – this truthful?"

Charles thought to himself that her English certainly hadn't improved since last he'd talked with her, but he didn't care in the least. "Bulgarian? Can you actually speak Bulgarian?"

"No, but nobody in Spain speak Bulgarian, so no problem." She smiled. She'd tried to clean herself up as best she could that afternoon, but there was only so much she could do. "I know. I terrible look, but there war on you know." She tried to laugh.

"You look beautiful as always to me. And yes, I'm big OSS spy now. How about you, you still working for the NKVD?"

"Yes, I still little spy and I very hungry. No chance eat since breakfast. You rich American capitalist have food?"

"Yes, of course. Let's go into the kitchen and we'll find something for you to eat." From hugging her, he'd felt that she'd lost many pounds since New York. "How long have you been in Spain?"

"Almost year. I some Spanish knew in past and now speak pretty good, but now never no English speak, as you tell." She almost blushed in embarrassment over her poor English.

Over the next hour, the two caught up on what both had been doing for the past twenty months. She had been in Portugal initially and from there she had sent the postcard to Charles, and then she had been briefly in Yugoslavia. Because she did already know some Spanish, the NKVD had finally sent her to Spain.

Charles explained to her how the mole hunt in New York City had ended, but tragically just a little late to do any good about preventing the Japanese attack on Pearl Harbor. "Then I joined the Army and was immediately picked up by General Donovan for the OSS, took some training in Canada and then England and have been here for close to a year."

"And you will stay safe here till end of war?"

"It's beginning to look that way; although, there seems to be less and less to do here. Initially, there were concerns that Germany might just invade and seize Portugal, but that risk has certainly passed. German armies seem to be retreating from everywhere. So what brings you to Portugal? You said you've been here several times."

She loved Charles, but duty was duty and she could not bring herself to reveal to him how she had just met with NKVD penetrations of the British and American intelligence services. She finally settled on the short answer of, "Work. I come here for work."

He had gotten to know her well enough back in New York to know that there was no point in pressing her for more details. He presumed that the NKVD had a few agents within the Portuguese Government, or maybe even at the large German Embassy. They drank a bottle of wine and there had been the emotional and draining effect of seeing each other after so many months. Before long, she was snuggled up against his chest and they spoke less and less. Finally, they were both asleep. It was the first time in a long time that she felt truly safe and she was able to truly let herself go into a deep sleep. Back in New York neither of them would have said they were in love. They both needed each other at the time because of their own personal tragedies, and they both really enjoyed each other's company, but it wasn't necessarily love. Now, both of them realized that things had changed. The poets say that war changes people and their feelings. The two hadn't been together in actual fighting for the last twenty months, but the pressures of war did make people understand better what was truly important in life. They hadn't realized it until just a few hours earlier, but they needed each other now and had fallen in love. What they could do about it, given their professions – that was a whole different question and one that could wait till morning.

The morning sun woke Olga first. She slipped out from under his arm and headed into the kitchen. She found the coffee tin, opened it and deeply inhaled the smell. It had been many months since she had smelled and tasted real coffee. Most of the time she had been living with a farmer and his family up in the hills of Spain, without such luxuries as real coffee. She started brewing a pot of coffee and exploring his cupboards to see what she could fix him for breakfast.

A few minutes later, Charles staggered into the small kitchen, still half asleep. "For a minute, when I first woke up and you weren't there, I thought it had all been a dream, but you really are here." He went over and wrapped his arms around her and kissed her. "I'm glad it wasn't just a dream."

"Me too. And your kitchen just like in Manhattan; you have almost nothing to eat here. How you expect defeat Nazi spies without food!" They both laughed.

They enjoyed the coffee and some bread and jam he had, then they took turns using the tiny bathroom and shower.

She came out of the bathroom with just a towel wrapped around her. "How come you have such small apartment? Aren't you big shot OSS Chief?"

"Secretly, I am big shot, but on the Embassy list I'm a lowly Third Secretary and the State Department Administrative Officer said this is all I merited as a bachelor."

She shook her head and with mock seriousness said, "After revolution, I have him shot."

"Small shower, but let me show you what a big bed it has," he responded with a lecherous grin and led her back into the bedroom. She no longer needed her towel. They made love and then went back to sleep till almost noon. He finally got out of bed and went into the living room to his phone and called his office.

When his secretary answered, he simply told her he was occupied with something and wouldn't be in to the Embassy until the end of the day. Being a spy did at times have its advantages -- one of them being to just disappear for almost an entire day and colleagues assumed you were out engaging in espionage and combating the Nazi menace. It also helped that Mary Beth was an experienced secretary, who could handle most anything that came up whether Charles was in the office or not.

"Let's go somewhere outside the city for lunch. I know a little family-run place out at Sintra, which has wonderful food." They both also had the same professional thought – that out in the countryside, they were unlikely to run into anyone who would recognize either of them and wonder who the other person was. Being intelligence officers for different countries did complicate their lives!

In the latter half of their lunch, Charles did bring up a work-related question. "Don't suppose you know anything about the Italian Embassy here in Lisbon?"

"Not much, I remember it small, compared to hundreds of Germans at their Embassy. Why you interested in Italians? Hasn't Mussolini surrendered?"

"I don't know quite where it stands; the Government in Rome may have surrendered, but the Fascists have set up another capital in northern Italy, so I'm not sure if even the Italians know what's going on. As for why I care about the Italian Embassy in Lisbon…" Charles hesitated before asking, "We still our own private intelligence service?"

She remembered their "agreement" back in New York for working together on the one special project without informing the NKVD of what she was doing. She smiled. "Yes, we still our own special service."

"Well, without boring you with details, it looks as though there might be a mole in my Embassy and maybe even within the OSS office itself, passing information to the Italians. I'm to investigate this danger."

"You have so many moles in your government! You always looking for a mole." She was referring to his hunt in late 1941, back in New York, for an American intelligence officer who was working for the Japanese. That was when their paths first crossed, initially only socially, but then they cooperated professionally, in an informal arrangement.

It was his turn to smile. "It does seem that way doesn't it? Anyway, I'm quietly investigating all of my own people here and of course, there is a CI investigation going on back in Washington DC."

That got Olga worried. She didn't want the OSS to find her Soviet mole while looking for an Italian one. She decided that it would be advantageous if she could help Charles find the leak to the Italians and bring the OSS mole search quickly to an end. "There anything I can do help in your search?"

"If you could somehow find out who in the Italian Embassy is with their Intelligence Service, I might be able to conduct the search from the other end, instead of just investigating Americans."

"I have no office where I can search records like New York for you, but I know few people around Lisbon. I ask here and there."

"Thank you. On a different topic, I've been thinking more about why Canaris was here in Portugal. I just can't buy the idea that the head of the entire Abwehr comes to Lisbon just to have a chat with a few of their agents. There must be more, but I can't think of what that would be at this stage of the war. A year or two back, maybe he'd be here preparing for a German invasion of Spain and Portugal, but now?"

"Hmmm. I can't think any reason either." She'd slipped her foot out of her shoe and had extended it up to Charles' calf and was running it up and down his leg. "Maybe, we have better ideas if back in your bed," she added with a completely straight face.

Charles looked over at their waitress and raised his hand. "Check please!"

Once they were back in the bed at Charles' apartment and had finished making love, she was laying with her head upon his chest, his arm wrapped around her. She felt so safe in that position.

He'd been postponing an important conversation with her because he was afraid of what her answer would be, but the time had come.

"I lost you once when you left Manhattan and don't want that to happen again. How do we arrange for us to always be together?"

"I do not know," she softly replied. She'd also been thinking about their problem. "I must return Spain in next day or so. I have duties."

"Have you ever thought about retiring from your duties? Just stay here with me. Become Mrs. Worthington. Be a mother to little Worthingtons?"

She smiled. She did like that idea, but knew that life wasn't that simple. "I have important work just as you have your work. I cannot just retire. Plus, I think General Donovan not like you not married to Soviet spy."

Fortunately, Charles had listened to her English many times back in Manhattan and did actually understand her strangely worded sentence. Russians seemed to always put double negatives in sentences. "Yes, that might be a small challenge, but I'm sure we could find some solution around that issue. Plus, this war will be over in a year, two at the most and then I'll be leaving the OSS and returning to Wall Street. I can be married to anyone I want. Mr. Astor could care less."

"Maybe." She lay there in silence for almost a minute. "I try explain to you something. I must believe in something. That something me since little girl been 'scientific socialism.' Maybe right, maybe wrong, but Olga must believe in something, like my mother believed in Russian Orthodox Church and one grandmother believed in… well, she believed too. I cannot go just live, make money, and make children, no matter how much I love you. I not explain good, but you understand?"

"Sort of. But can't you believe in something and love me at the same time?"

"Maybe. Better maybe after war. Now, must deal with Hitler."

"You do have a point about dealing with Hitler and the evil of his regime. I don't know how much you've heard, but General Donovan was telling me about the stories that we're starting to get about death camps. Jews weren't being treated well before the war, but it looks like the Nazis have started killing them by the thousands every week in these special camps. They're gassing them to death. How can you kill that many of your own people?"

Olga thought to herself how naïve Charles and most Americans were. She too had heard stories, but they weren't about Germans. They were from the 1930s when Stalin had shipped hundreds of thousands of Russians out to camps in Siberia and most of them died. What she had never understood was how so many other Russians could have carried out these commands. Stalin didn't load all those people on train cars by himself and didn't build those camps. Thousands of others did that to fellow Russians. All those people sent to camps couldn't have been capitalist or Nazi spies. And now Hitler and many Germans were killing other Germans because they were Jews. She started to cry. She couldn't remember the last time she'd cried.

Charles saw the tears. "I'm sorry. I shouldn't have gone into such details."

"One of my grandmothers was Jewish," she whispered. Other than that night at his place when she'd gotten word about her husband's death, he'd never seen her cry. She'd always been so tough. It was as though nothing could shock her. He pulled her closer and held her. "God, what a shitty world we live in," he thought to himself, or maybe he'd actually said it out loud. He couldn't be sure.

They both finally fell back asleep. Once they'd woken, he wasn't sure if he should inquire about her Jewish grandmother or if she considered herself Jewish. He decided that just dropping the subject might be best. He didn't want her to start crying again.

## Chapter 9

Olga had left Charles' apartment about 6:00 p.m. She'd explained that she had to go meet with her radioman and see if any further instructions for her had arrived from Moscow via coded shortwave radio messages. Charles spent the time alone thinking. First, about what might Canaris have really been doing in Lisbon? There had to be more than TRICYCLE knew or that ULTRA intercepts by the British had revealed. Second, what had brought Olga to Lisbon? She hadn't offered a word about why she was in Portugal. He was thrilled that she'd come, had learned of his presence and had sought him out, but he couldn't help be curious as to what mission for the NKVD had brought her to Lisbon in the first place. He concluded, mostly from her having served before in America, that she was an "American specialist" or at least an "English-speaking specialist." A smile came to his face, maybe General Donovan was secretly a Communist mole working for "Uncle Joe" Stalin and that was why he'd stopped in Portugal. His smile vanished when he thought of an alternative reason -- that maybe she'd been told back in Spain that he was in Lisbon and she'd been instructed to come to town to target him? He quickly dismissed that idea on the grounds that no one could be that good an actor. He preferred the thought that she'd come to town to handle her secret penetration of the OSS, one William Donovan, over the idea that she was targeting him! He started fixing himself a little food, as he wasn't sure when Olga would be back. As he stirred some "English-style bean soup" from a can on the small stove, he thought of Kim Philby. He makes an unneeded and somewhat unexpected trip to Lisbon and suddenly Olga arrives as well. Suddenly, there was a knock on the door and he heard Olga's voice and all such crazy thoughts about moles in the OSS or MI6 vanished from his head.

He opened the door and there she was with several sacks in her arms. "I saw that you had no real food in your kitchen, so I brought things make you real dinner. You know, you either need learn cook or find wife."

"You know, in the last few days, I've been thinking that myself. I might put an advertisement in the local newspaper – wife wanted, must be able to cook well."

Olga picked up a wooden rolling pin from the kitchen counter and waved it at Charles. "Be very hard get married if you dead!" They both laughed. "I cook you tasty Russian dinner."

Charles opened a bottle of wine and they drank and laughed while she cooked. He found himself again picturing life with Olga in it, seven days a week for the next 40-50 years. When she announced that the food was almost ready, Charles set the table and even lighted two candles to create a romantic mood. He thought the smell was wonderful, but waited till she brought the large ceramic bowl full of the food to the table.

"What a wonderful smell. What is it?"

"This called beef stroganoff. Old famous dish of the czars." She placed it on the table and then returned with a smaller bowl full of large flat pasta noodles. She dished out the noodles and then the meat sauce with onions and mushrooms on top of them. "Now you have enough strength to properly fight Nazis!"

They raised their wine glasses in a toast. Neither of them had anything clever to say as a toast, so Charles finally simply suggested, "To us, for many years to come."

"To us," she replied.

Charles took his first bite of the stroganoff. "Hmmm, this tastes even better than it smells. It's wonderful." They chatted some about how and from whom she'd learned to cook, and then about what were new shows back in New York City.

Charles finally decided that they were both so relaxed and slightly drunk from the wine that he'd inquire a little about her Jewish grandmother. "Have you always known about your Jewish grandmother or is this something you've only found out about in the last few years?"

"Just a few years ago. I had aunt tell me just shortly before she died. Neither of my parents had ever said anything before their deaths. As you may know, being Jewish in Russia or now in Soviet Union isn't really good thing. If someone has Jewish ancestry, but not Jew now, they usually don't talk about their history. I never really knew much about Jews, but have had plenty time in Spain between tasks and have been reading some about them. Very interesting history."

"Indeed they have, going back to Biblical times. Can't say I know much about the Jews in recent centuries, other than there has been a group of them in last decade or so who have wanted to create a Jewish homeland back in the Middle East around Jerusalem."

"You know any Jews?"

"I knew some back in Chicago while growing up. Never really thought of them as being Jewish or not. In most parts of America, nobody cares or even asks what religion you are. If you're an American, you're an American. As long as you believe in the basic political ideas of the United States and you're a patriotic American, that's about all anybody cares about. Doesn't matter what country your ancestors came from or what religion you are."

"But don't you lose your heritage that way – is that correct word, heritage?"

"Yes, heritage, but you also give up old hatreds and prejudices. If you came from Serbia, you don't have to automatically hate a Croat, or a Pole hate a Russian. Seems like that's half the problems of Europe. When you get to America, you're supposed to sort of forget about such things. You're an American first and maybe one day in March you're Irish for St. Patrick's Day, but you don't have to hate Englishmen the rest of the year."

"I have to think about this. I don't want forget I Russian."

Charles sensed the conversation was getting way too serious. He commented to her that "I don't think of you as Russian or Jewish. I think of you as Olga and your personality, your behavior, your sense of humor – that's what makes you Olga, not where on the planet you were born."

She reached over and grasped his hand. "Ya lublyu tebya," she said softly and stared into his eyes. Charles didn't have to know Russian to understand the most common three-word phrase in the world said by a woman to a man.

"I have special dessert for you."

"What's that?"

"Me!" She stood, gave him her most seductive smile and led him off to the bedroom. As the two naked bodies started to get passionate and vocal in his small bed, he bizarrely caught himself thinking what any listener of any possible hidden microphones in his apartment must be thinking at that moment – probably what a lucky fellow Charles was!

In the morning, over coffee, she announced to Charles that she was leaving for Spain that afternoon. "I am needed back in Barcelona in few days."

He realized that she must have known that as of yesterday afternoon when she'd met with her radioman, but had kept it to herself till the morning. "I shall miss you every hour you're away. Any idea of when you might be able to come back to Lisbon?"

"Maybe two, three weeks I again have work here. No way to inform you. I just show up your door some night. You better be alone!" She gave him one of her great smiles.

"I be alone." He noticed that he was beginning to speak English like Olga, leaving out various parts of grammar. His Harvard professors would be appalled.

She dawdled as long as she could, but the time finally came when she had to depart. They didn't even speak by the door. They just held each other tightly for several minutes and then she was gone. After closing the door, Charles again found himself thinking, "God, this war sucks!"

Charles showed up at the Embassy just before lunchtime. Nobody even commented on how little they'd seen of him for a few days. Such was the nature of clandestine work – people came and went at odd times and disappearing for several days was not all that unusual. And no one was going to question the chief on where he'd been. The head code clerk did come see him, once he'd heard Charles was around. He carried a sealed envelope with him. He tapped on Charles' door, but then just entered without waiting for any reply.

"I have a special 'Eyes Only' message for you. Arrived this morning."

"Anything interesting?" Charles and he made no pretense that the head code clerk didn't read everything that arrived, regardless of to whom it was addressed and with how many super secret classifications it had. You can't decode a message without reading it!

"Yes, interesting, but not clear just what you can do about it."

Charles took the envelope, unsealed it and read it immediately. He was not allowed to keep such messages down in his office safe. They could only be kept up in the code room itself.

"Hmm," was his response. "OK, thanks."

The code clerk left. Charles put his feet up on his desk, interlocked his fingers across his stomach and closed his eyes. His traditional position for thinking. The message reported that there had been an intercept from the Italian Embassy in Lisbon back to Italy, which simply reported that OSS Chief Donovan had made a secret two-day visit to Lisbon, which included a dinner hosted by the American Ambassador. No further details available.

Charles had hoped when he started reading the intercept that there would be some detail as to the source of the information. "According to secret agent X," or "according to a friend at the PVDE" would have been helpful, but there was not a word about the source of the report. Either it was perfectly understood who was the one and only source of intelligence in Lisbon, or the Italians sent that information via diplomatic courier, but how that could happen these days, given the war conditions in Italy, was a mystery. There were literally dozens of Americans at the Embassy who knew of General Donovan's visit and no doubt a number of local employees overheard who was there. The intercept showed that whoever the "leak" was, he was still in touch with the Italians, but it didn't help at all as to who that might be. Charles decided that perhaps it was time for another lunch with the Lisbon Chief of the PVDE and a reminder that given the current direction of the war, perhaps it was time for "neutrals" to start making friends among the Allies. He reached over to his phone.

"Captain Lourenco, Charles Worthington here. How are you?"

"Ah, my good friend Charles. Have you called to let me know that the war is over?"

Charles could visualize the Captain sitting at his desk with a large grin on his face. "No, I think it will be a few more months yet and then I'll be gone, so I figured I'd better invite you to lunch now. How's your schedule this week?"

"Could we make it dinner one evening? I'm actually rather busy during the daytime this week; crime is running rampant in my beautiful city and I must work hard during the day to arrest criminals."

"Certainly, how about Wednesday night at the Hotel Atlantico? But just out of curiosity, don't criminals work at night in Lisbon as well as daytime?"

"Never! This is a Mediterranean country. Evenings, even among the criminal class, are reserved for dining, relaxing and romance. Would 8:00 p.m. be a good time for you on Wednesday?"

"That will be fine. Till Wednesday."

Charles then headed out to meet up with Salvatore and Lou, to see if they might have made a miraculous discovery as to the identity of the mole. He'd had them continue to rotate their evening surveillance on various "possibles" out of the Embassy, including Solborg.

Both men seemed to have adjusted just fine to life in Portugal. Charles hadn't seen either man in his typical pin-striped suit for several weeks. With their Italian-complexions, attired now in local clothing, they could pass for a Portuguese – until they opened their mouths and spoke Italian, which was actually Brooklyn-Italian, not native Sicilian. They were already seated at a small coffee shop with a nice view of the beach around Cascais when Charles arrived.

"Hard to believe der's a war on, ain't it?" opined Salvatore. "Just look at dat beautiful beach!"

"Indeed it is." He wasn't sure if Sally was referring to the beach itself or some of the late-afternoon female sunbathers, but both were beautiful. "Hard to imagine thousands of men storming a beach like that and dying, as they did over around Italy."

Both Sally and Lou stared down in to their coffees. "Youse sure know how to ruin a nice mental image of a beach, Mr. Charles," commented Lou.

"Sorry about that fellows. I guess sometimes I start feeling a little guilty about spending the war here in comfortable Lisbon while other guys are doing real fighting."

"Yeah, well, maybes we's three could go out some night and beat up some of these Nazis that are all over the place. There's hundreds of 'em all around this city. Bet that would make you feel better!"

"There are a bunch of Germans around, that's for sure. I'm told there are supposedly over 400 Germans assigned at their Embassy here. God knows what all of them do!"

"So they's wouldn't miss one or two some night," added Sally with a broad grin.

"Probably not, but I have more important work for you. We just got news that whoever is the mole has again just sent information to the Italians here in Lisbon. This time about General Donovan's recent visit. We have to find who or what is this leak."

They both shook their heads, somewhat in embarrassment at not having discovered anything useful to date. "We's been watching dem guys on dat list youse gave us, but we's ain't seen nothing yet. There's a whole lot of drinking and screwing, but nothing that looks like spying."

"I understand. I guess, we just have to be patient. I'm having dinner Wednesday night with Captain Lourenco, head of the secret police here in Lisbon. Maybe I can find a way to convince him to provide a little information about the Italians here in town. Then we could possibly go at this from the other end – watch whoever at the Italian Embassy is involved with intelligence work and see if that leads to seeing any contacts with American Embassy personnel."

They both nodded in agreement that that sounded like a good idea. "At least we'd have somebody different to follows around!"

Charles finished his coffee and left the boys to watch, the ocean.

Two nights later, Charles arrived promptly at 8:00 p.m. at the dining room of the Atlantico and found Antonio waiting for him. One nice thing about meeting fellow intelligence officers, everyone was punctual. As they walked towards each other, Charles thought he detected a slight limp in his dinner guest. He was hesitant to ask, in case he just somehow hadn't noticed it before, but Charles was usually quite observant about people.

"Good evening, Charles. You Americans are always so punctual, as are the Germans, but as for the English, well, I shall say no more."

Charles extended his hand to shake Captain Lourenco's hand. It always struck Charles what a very firm grip he had. He suspected that you didn't want the fortyish year old secret police chief to personally interrogate you.

Once seated, they chatted some about Antonio's brief summer vacation, out to the countryside with his wife and two children. It was the first time he'd mentioned any details about his family. Then they discussed the latest war news as was available over the BBC, most of which was pretty bleak for the Germans.

By the time they were finishing their main courses Charles decided he'd adequately set the scene enough to launch into the purpose of the dinner. He'd also concluded that Antonio was not a person with whom being subtle served any purpose.

"Antonio, this war isn't going to end in the next few months, but it is becoming ever clearer as to which side is going to win. You're a very practical man; isn't it about time you start guaranteeing your future and friendship with that winning side?"

"Portugal is neutral. There will be no winning or losing side for me."

"Let's not be naïve. Salazar is already showing signs of 'favoring' England with some of his recent remarks about traditional Portuguese-English ties. He knows from where trade and aid will come in the years ahead and naturally, he will want to show that all the important positions in his government are held by people who 'always' were friends with England and America. Just something for you to think about, if by chance you've been thinking about someday being the Chief of PVDE, not just the head of the Lisbon office."

"Ah, the future is always tricky. But I suppose being the national chief would be a nice position to hold one day. And just how would a simple man like myself ensure that he was considered a 'friend' of America? Naturally, you're not suggesting that I betray my loyalty to my own government or leader, are you? And surely you're not talking about money, for then I would have to arrest you for attempting to bribe a government official." He smiled. Charles smiled.

"Oh, nothing like that even crossed my mind. I was simply thinking that there might be occasions when Portuguese and American interests coincided and two friends discussing their work might logically share views on certain topics."

Antonio dismissed with a quick wave of his hand a waiter who'd arrived at their table to inquire about dessert orders. "Naturally. And what might be an example of a topic of mutual interest?"

"Well, I suppose one example might be the Italian Embassy, such as, who are the intelligence officers there and how active have your people found them to be here in Portugal?"

Charles could almost see relief on Antonio's face, that if that was all the "assistance" it took to be considered a "friend" of America, this wouldn't be too difficult on his conscience. "Well, there are only three intelligence officers in that Embassy, plus a code clerk or two. I could have my driver drop off an envelope tomorrow at your Embassy with their dossiers, but I don't think you need to be worried about the Italian threat to America. Assistant Air Attache Luigi Biachi is the only one who seems to even go through the motions of doing his job. He's out and about a bit, getting to know people like a good intelligence officer should."

"That will be great. It's just always good to know who's who in town. And with the chaos in the government back in Italy, you never know who might come knocking on the front door of my Embassy one afternoon. Would be good to be prepared in advance on knowing who to invite in for champagne and who to just offer a cold beer out on the front steps."

Antonio laughed. He thought that an excellent analogy. Not every "walk-in" volunteer was equal. Some might have valuable intelligence; others would be worth a half hour of conversation and only a small donation to their future meal fund. Then they'd be shown the door and given a wish to have a nice life. Charles was right about what would be happening as it became clearer who would win the war. A lot of people would start taking or trading sides. Yes, he thought to himself, Charles was right. It was good to be at the front of that coming wave. Some, of course, would hold to their ideological beliefs or their sense of duty right to the end, but he suspected that even among the Germans, a few might start looking for life rafts in the not too distant future.

They wrapped up their dinner and strolled slowly out of the dining room and across the lobby of the hotel. Informants for the Germans, the English, the Americans and his own PVDE discreetly made mental notes of the two being together that night. By noon the following day, there would be a report on Colonel Karsthoff's desk about the dinner between Captain Lourenco and the American OSS Chief Worthington. Lourenco had counted on that when he'd agreed to meeting Charles in such a well-known place. He figured that Karsthoff would offer him a far better vintage of wine and a more exquisite meal the next time he went to his home for lunch, as a result of his having had dinner with the American that night. It was always good for the foreign security services working in his country to wonder a little for whose side he might be working – the truth was that Lourenco was working for Lourenco.

# Chapter 10

# Berlin

Since his return from Portugal, Admiral Canaris had noticed much more obvious surveillance on him whenever he was away from his office or home. Apparently, the Gestapo had decided that it was best that Canaris clearly be aware that he was being closely watched – perhaps they considered that a preventative measure. He actually considered the blatant coverage a good sign that they probably weren't aware of him being up to anything traitorous in particular; otherwise, it would have been very discreet surveillance on him in hopes of actually catching him at something.

He and Ewald were taking a post-lunch stroll out in the gardens of the Abwehr grounds, not that there was much left of the gardens. Between a few unfortunate bomb hits and the need for manpower doing other things, not much was still growing in the garden by mid-September. Still, it was better that the Allies were destroying roses and not the building with his office in it – at least not yet.

"Ewald, is it just my imagination or are the bombing raids getting heavier every week?"

"I can check the statistics, but I think you're correct. The production of bombers in America must be tremendous. It doesn't seem to matter how many of their planes we shoot down, they put more and more in the air. At the same time, the loss of our fighter planes is reducing ever more what we can do about their attacks. We're losing control of the skies even above our own cities, never mind above the battlefields."

"Have you spoken with Wolfgang in recent days? How is he coming on creating false documentation for the chosen officers?"

"Technically, they are genuine documents; it's simply that they have false names on them. And yes, things are going slowly, but well. He says he will have the needed 200 'packages' ready by mid-November. He can only generate a few a day, so that anybody who might be watching him or tracking the work of his administrative officer will notice anything unusual."

"Good, good. I try to have no particular contact with him, as I don't want to draw any attention on him. And how is your review process going in selecting those that will be sent to Brazil?"

"I have some one hundred officers selected so far. Part of the question is merit and part is the practical question of who can be posted in late-November in the right places, so that they and their families can 'disappear' and travel to Lisbon and then catch the ships for Rio de Janeiro. A few officers have already come complaining to me as to why they've been given shit jobs around Berlin, when they want to be off fighting and earning promotions and medals."

Canaris laughed. "Ha, winning medals. Ah, Ewald, were we that stupid as well when we were their ages?"

"You must have been. You wound up an admiral while I am but a lowly colonel!" They both smiled.

"Well, just keep making the correct assignments, but don't say anything yet to any of them about their exfiltration until the very last moment. We can't afford gossip by any of them reaching the wrong ears. When they're informed, I think we'll make it an order to them, as if I'm sending them off on a secret mission. They can thank me once they're in Brazil."

"Actually, it's arranging for travel of the families of the married men, or even the serious girlfriends of some of the single men."

The Admiral lighted a cigarette to help him concentrate. "Hmm, what if instead of trying to hide their travel, we actually publicized it – the fact they'll be traveling, but not the truth about the destination. As we approach the holiday season, let's hold a raffle among the officers of the Abwehr in the Berlin area of operations, with ten lucky winners and their families receiving a week's leave and transportation down to Bavaria. You personally do up the orders for the "winners" with no more than ten to a batch, so hopefully none of the Gestapo informants around here will notice that it's a hundred or more, not just ten officers getting on buses at various locations. They take different routes out of Berlin, so if any lowly corporal at a road block stops and checks a truck, he's told that these are simply the lucky winners of the Christmas vacation drawing."

Ewald was smiling broadly. "Now I see why you wound up the admiral and me a mere colonel! That's brilliant and we can then even have the German Army pay for the travel of our people."

"I do rather like the idea, even if it was my own. We'll start advertising the contest at the start of November. This might even help provide an avenue for the movement of the gold."

Ewald left the room and Canaris returned to thoughts about how Germany could rid itself of Hitler, even if the Allies said they weren't interested. Not having a promise from England of certain terms for a negotiated surrender would make it a harder sell to fellow officers, but still not impossible to convince some that the situation had to be better without Hitler in the picture.

Two days later, Ewald returned for another stroll of the garden with his boss. "How quickly do you think our people will be able to leave Portugal for Brazil? I'm trying to calculate how many days we have before offices back here in Berlin start to wonder where the hell their officers who went off on this brief vacation trip to Bavaria are?"

Canaris looked pensive. "Good point. I'm not sure what the answer to your question is, but I think it means that we'll definitely have to fly people from Bavaria to Portugal. There simply wouldn't be time to travel by bus all the way to Lisbon, never mind the issue of crossing several international borders."

"That would be better. Any chance of making arrangements with the Luftwaffe for five or six transport planes?"

"That should be possible. It isn't like we have any spare troops sitting around Berlin waiting to be flown somewhere to fight. But, it might be better if you were to make the request, rather than me. Asking for planes for vacationers seems rather trivial for the Chief of the Abwehr."

"Good point."

"I did just think of who at the Luftwaffe Transportation Office you should approach. That would be Major Otto Schmidt, and be sure to take at least six bottles of good French cognac with you. Otto is an alcoholic, though he tries to hide it, and I understand that it is getting harder and harder to get such bottles out of France now. He'd probably appreciate a token gesture, in advance, of your appreciation for his assistance."

"Maybe I should make it a full case of twelve bottles?" suggested Ewald.

"No, that would be too much. He might start wondering why these flights are so important. And let's tell the Luftwaffe that our people will only be staying three days in Bavaria, which should mean that the planes will simply stay at the airfield there, instead of flying elsewhere and returning when needed. Tell whomever you deal with that the Abwehr will be happy to cover the expenses of their crew members to vacation with us – that should guarantee their acceptance of our proposal," Canaris added with a smile. He understood well how bureaucrats of any military service thought. "That way, when you suddenly tell the air crews at the airfield in Bavaria that they are part of a secret Abwehr mission and they are flying on to Portugal, hopefully their Headquarters back here in Berlin won't wonder for at least three days what has happened to their planes."

"And if the crews insist on checking with their Headquarters before flying on to Lisbon?"

"Tie them up and put them on the planes. We should have enough men in the selected group who can pilot a plane if necessary, so we can go on even without their cooperation. Once you land in Portugal, keep the air crews locked up until you are ready to sail, then release them at the last moment, but don't let them hear about ships or Brazil."

"True, we don't want to provide any clues to the Gestapo as to where our officers and families have gone."

"No, we don't. Besides, do you know what the survival rate is down to now for a Luftwaffe pilot? We also don't want any of them asking at the last moment to go with you to Brazil!"

Ewald laughed. "It's going to be a very interesting day for you back here in Berlin when those pilots fly their planes back to Germany and tell their superiors what has happened!" commented Ewald.

"I suppose, but I shall be shocked when I learn that you have kidnapped my officers and shanghaied Luftwaffe crews, and I shall immediately order your arrest! I fear, you're never going to make general, after this blight on your record." They both laughed.

"No matter. I have no family left alive in Germany and I will be physically gone, but will the Gestapo and the SD believe your story that I did all this without your knowledge?"

"Of course not, but they will have a dilemma. No one at the Gestapo or the Army General Staff will want any publicity about this. To the extent possible, it will be covered up and if possible, no one will want to tell Hitler. Even if it made me look bad, it would make the others look even worse, because they didn't detect this was going to happen."

"So, it will be a stalemate."

"Exactly, but they will be watching me very closely after this." He gave a small grin and added, "Lucky for me, I am totally loyal to the Reich and the Fuhrer and there will be nothing for them to discover."

"Naturally!"

"By the way, what story are you giving the officers that you are interviewing as candidates for this extraordinary journey?"

"I have said nothing about the nature of the trip or its destination in the first round of interviews – only that they are being considered for a very sensitive, secret mission for the Abwehr. Along with other background questions, I inquire about their family situation and relatives and if being gone for several months would be a real hardship? Anyone who has told me that he has a father or mother or someone who needs him here on a weekly basis is rejected. It's a bit unfair, but if someone can't be missed for a few weeks, they probably wouldn't want to disappear forever."

"Very true. I do not envy you your job of selecting the men to make this journey."

"It's a golden opportunity, but a curse in some ways at the same time."

"OK, I think that's all for now. Keep me apprised of the request to the Luftwaffe for planes. I'll weigh in if I have to do so, but I'm hoping you can arrange this yourself, particularly with the assistance of the thirsty Major Schmidt."

# Chapter 11

# Lisbon

Mary Beth brought in to Charles a folder full of operational expense claims from a number of his officers. This was one of the most boring aspects of being the Chief of Lisbon Station. This was certainly not the glamorous and exciting lifestyle that the general public held of someone being a spy!

She returned a minute later with a cup of coffee for him. "You look rather tired today," he commented to his wonderfully efficient secretary. "Were you out partying again last night?" he teased the 43 year-old, rather plain-looking, single woman. Actually, there were rumors that she had had a short and very unpleasant marriage back in her early twenties, but she never made any reference to such an event and always introduced herself as "Miss Short."

She gave a facial expression as if a young girl who'd just got caught with her hand in the cookie jar. "No. I think I'm coming down with a cold and didn't sleep well last night."

Charles regretted having made his funny remark. It had either struck a nerve because she wasn't out having "late nights" or she had been out on a date and didn't want people in the Embassy to know about it. He hoped it was the latter. She was a charming woman, even if not the most attractive, but he couldn't remember an occasion in the last year or more when he'd heard that she'd been out on an actual date. He quickly turned the conversation to the financial reports. "I presume you've already looked these over as usual?"

"I have."

"Anything obviously bogus, other than some of mine?" He looked up and was glad to see that she was smiling again.

"Well, Gary continues to hold a number of his developmental meetings in the exotic dance clubs of the city, but since you've approved those before, I presume you shall again." She said that in a tone of total disapproval of American taxpayer money be used to pay strippers! Charles had learned when it was best not to reply to some of her comments and simply kept his head down staring at the forms on his desk.

Fortunately, about halfway through that boring bureaucratic task the direct line number on his desk rang.

"Charles Worthington speaking."

Someone speaking, sort of with a bad French accent, got directly to the point of the call. "Monsieur Worthington, your laundry will be ready promptly at 5:00 p.m. for pickup."

"Fine, thank you. I'll send someone to get it." He then quickly hung up the phone, before he started laughing. Salvatore trying to speak with a French accent was truly amusing. He assumed that all the lines into the Embassy were tapped, certainly by the PVDE and possibly by the Germans as well, so he saw no reason for a caller to pretend it was anything but an operational call. As long as it was simply an open code call, as this one had been and made from a different public phone each time, what did any listener really learn. As long as the PVDE didn't know what the message meant nor who made it, what had they learned? That he was involved in espionage work? He even occasionally had one of his own officers call the number from out and about Lisbon and pass some insane comment about what time the sun would rise the following day, just to confuse the PVDE – adding trees to the CI forest. Salvatore's "code" that day simply meant he needed to meet at the prearranged spot and it was understood that it would take place one hour and fifteen minutes earlier than stated on the phone.

Charles looked at his watch and quickly finished signing all the accounting forms. If somebody was trying to cheat the government out of $10 that day, they would succeed.

"Have to go to a meeting," he shouted to Mary Beth as he blew by her on the way out.

Charles arrived at the appointed small bar promptly at 3:45. Salvatore and Lou were already seated at a corner table with a bottle of wine and three glasses. Lou was playing solitaire; his back to a small window.

"You don't have aces and eights, do you?" inquired Charles, referring to the famous "dead man's hand." Another Charles comment that went straight over the heads of his two pals. This had happened enough during the two periods of their working together that they had learned just to ignore such comments.

Once the glasses were filled with a nice Portuguese vinho verde wine, Salvatore got straight to the point for having triggered an unplanned meeting. He grinned, leaned forward and lowered his voice. Charles knew something good was coming, as he also leaned forward in a conspiratorial physical movement. "Guess who just bought a brand new car? And not some cheap Vauxhall, but a big new Packard!"

"My, my," was Charles' subtle reply. "What you think a new American car costs in Portugal, particularly in wartime, when getting one shipped over here would certainly add to the total price?"

"Gotta be at least $6,000-7,000 here in Lisbon," replied Lou who followed the price of cars in America fairly closely, be they new, used or stolen!

"How much does Jack Solborg bring in a year as an Army officer?" asked Salvatore.

"Nowhere enough to afford a $7,000 car! Has he sold the car he was driving?"

"No,' replied Sally with another big grin. "Accordings to the nosey old lady across the street from Solborg, he gave it a few days ago to a young woman named Maria, who he tells everybody dat she's his niece."

"Hah," added Lou. "I shoulds have such a female relative!"

"Well, a man could get lonely with his wife currently visiting relatives back in America and naturally he'd enjoy the comfort of a distant relative here in Portugal," stated Charles with a perfectly straight face. "But it does make me wonder from just where Solborg is coming up with such money. And I'd guess that the car isn't the only thing that he's giving Maria!"

The other men nodded.

"Although, there are rumors that there are a number of ways for a foreign diplomat to make money on the side here in Lisbon – selling diplomatic booze, making sure somebody gets an American visa, etc. So, his extra money wouldn't have to come from selling secrets, but still…

"It's a serious coincidence," observed Sally.

"Indeed it is, but of course our problem now is, how do we prove our suspicions about Solborg?"

Gene Coyle

"Don't suppose youse just let me and Lou questions him some night?"

"I think we need a little more evidence against him before we question him, in the daytime or the nighttime." Sally and Lou both expected such a response from Charles, but were still a little disappointed.

"So, what's we do now? Just two guys can't follows him round day and night for long befores he spots us."

"No, and that could take forever to catch him at something. But maybe we could lure him into action if I bait him with a little tidbit of 'hot intelligence.' Then we could really concentrate on him, or that Italian diplomat for the next couple of days."

"Sounds like a good plan, boss."

"OK, let me think about what can be a plausible bit of news that would force Solborg to go running to the Italians, if he is the leak. In the meantime, see what you can learn more about this Maria, like how long she's been seeing him."

Instead of driving straight back to the Embassy, he headed over to the beaches of Cascais. There were a number of overlook spots with benches. He picked out a deserted spot he'd have all to himself. He loosened his tie and leaned back on the beach, staring out into the ocean. There was a storm starting to roll towards the coast. It was still far out to sea and he'd learned from his previous fall in the country that it would still be an hour or more before rain started on shore. He loved watching such storms form and roll in. He wasn't sure why, but he found it very relaxing and even conducive to thinking. What tidbit of news could he let slip to Solborg that would sound important and timely, yet still believable that Charles knew it? Charles was soon dozing.

The next sensation he had was being grabbed by both arms by two locals in their early twenties, while a third one was hitting him in the stomach. Not much of his OSS self-defense training was particularly applicable since the men on his sides had him quite secured. He did manage to kick the man in front of him in the balls, which staggered him back for 10-15 seconds, but mostly seemed to make him exceptionally mad. Just as the third man was coming back at him, he heard a car sliding to a stop on the small stones of the parking area. A few seconds after that, two shots were fired in to the air. The one in front of him got in one last good punch to Charles' stomach, then they dropped him and the three youths ran off, shouting curses in Portuguese.

Charles was still laying on the ground in pain when a man and a woman came up to him. Charles saw the Lugar pistol in the man's hand and figured that was where the shots had come from.

"Are you good?" asked the man in English with a heavy German-accent.

"Not good, but I'll live." A little blood was coming out of his mouth. "Thanks for your help," he managed to gasp out.

They helped him back on to the bench. "I take it those were not your friends?" asked the German.

"No, not my friends." Charles reached inside his suit coat chest pocket, checking for his wallet. It was gone. "Damn, they got my wallet. What was the point of beating me up?"

"Sadly, the youth of this country have no manners. Should we get you help or will you be able to drive yourself back to your Embassy?"

"I should be OK in a few minutes." He suddenly looked up with a puzzled face at his rescuers, wondering how they knew he was from an embassy. "Do we know each other?"

"I don't believe we've ever met, but I saw that you have diplomatic license plates on your automobile. My secretary and I were just passing by here and had slowed down to admire the lovely view, when she observed that someone was getting beaten up rather badly. I turned in to see what was happening and if I might be of assistance."

"Well, I'm certainly glad that you did stop. Three against one wasn't very good odds." Charles tried to grin, but it hurt too much. Apparently, his stomach wasn't the only part of his body they'd been hitting.

The German held up his Lugar. "Fortunately, I had an equalizer with me. Soon as I fired two shots, they ran off. It was only afterwards that I noticed you had diplomatic plates. I'm glad to have been of service to a fellow diplomat."

Charles extended a hand. "Charles Worthington, of the American Embassy." He saw a slight reaction on the face of his benefactor.

"I am Colonel Ludovico von Karsthoff, of the German Embassy." They both smiled at the irony of a German saving an American in a neutral country. "And this is my secretary, Fraulein Elizabeth."

Charles nodded graciously in her direction. Charles instantly recognized the name as that of the head of the German Abwehr in Lisbon.

"I don't want to sound too inquisitive, but what were you doing sitting here all alone at this rather deserted spot, where you could be robbed?"

"I like coming out here. It's very peaceful and quiet. I find that I can think well, sitting here, looking out at the ocean. I especially like watching the storm clouds come towards the shore."

"Ah, well, we have that in common. We also like driving out here and looking at the ocean. With a name of Worthington, I do not think that you have any German ancestry, but we do share a common taste in views of nature."

"Apparently so," replied Charles as all three slightly laughed. "Well, this will certainly make for a great story back at my Embassy. I'd invite you both to come let me buy you a drink at a nearby bar to thank you for your assistance, but I suspect both our ambassadors might find that a bit odd, given that we're at war with one another."

Karsthoff held up his Lugar. "Perhaps you could tell your Ambassador that I forced you at gun point to buy me a drink!" He laughed, but then shrugged his shoulders. "But what could I tell my Ambassador?"

"Well, thank you again for your kind deed. Perhaps once the war is over, I will be able to buy you that drink."

He holstered his gun, clicked his heels and bowed slightly. "I shall hold you to that promise." They both shook hands and the two Germans returned to their car to depart.

Charles waited until they had driven off, just so they wouldn't see how much pain he was in as he walked to his own car. He felt stupid enough at having fallen asleep and been mugged, but to have been rescued by the Chief of the Abwehr of Portugal, of all the people in Lisbon! He definitely wouldn't be telling that story to anyone at his own Embassy; he'd never hear the end of it. He drove straight to his apartment. He took some aspirin and poured himself some very good scotch for the pain. Whether his brain was stimulated from the pain or the scotch he didn't know, but while recuperating in his most comfortable living room chair, he did finally have an idea of how to lure Solborg into action.

His clever plan had to be put on hold the following morning as he read the morning cables that had arrived overnight from Washington. According to a "sensitive source," Germany was planning on parachuting enough soldiers into Portugal so as to seize the country, in cooperation

*Nazi Gold, Portuguese Wine, and a Lovely Russian Spy*

with pro-Nazi Portuguese groups. Charles had been in the OSS long enough to have figured out that the term "sensitive source" on occasions covered everything from super-restricted Signals intercepts to some politician's mistress who'd heard it from her hairdresser. Nevertheless, Charles and the entire OSS Lisbon team were ordered to hit the streets and question every asset, semi-asset or street peddler of rumors for any information on this alleged invasion. It took three days, but Charles finally arranged an appointment with Lisbon PVDE Chief Lourenco at his office to raise this "rumor" with him.

After the opening pleasantries were complete, Charles got to the point of his visit. "Don't suppose you've heard anything about a supposed parachute invasion of Portugal by Germany, in connection with local pro-Nazi groups?"

Antonio laughed out loud, which pretty well answered Charles' question. He thought Charles was making a joke, but when he saw that Chief Worthington wasn't smiling, he formally answered the question. "No, I've heard of no such plans, and as the head of the secret police for the capital, I certainly should have. From where did you receive such information?"

"From Washington," replied Charles.

"Well, I can't speak for the German Army, but I can assure you that no pro-Nazi Portuguese groups are planning such a coup. I have assets in every such group watching them and I have assets watching the assets. All is safe." He leaned back in his comfortable leather chair, like some corporate executive who'd closed a large, profitable deal and was waiting for admiration.

"Very glad to hear that. I can now tell Washington that they can cancel the plans to move the US Third Army from Italy to Portugal, and I can get back to more important things."

"Excellent. Anything else I can do for you today?" Antonio started to lean forward to rise from his chair, not actually expecting any further "work-related" requests from Charles that day.

"I am still interested in Italian Assistant Air Attaché Biachi. Anything new about him come to your attention recently"

Captain Lourenco leaned back in his chair to his former position. "Luigi Biachi, let me think." The Portuguese official tapped his fingers together in front of his face for several moments. "No, I don't believe so. I believe he does still come into their embassy, as opposed to many

117

others, who simply stay at home waiting for word from Italy if they still have a job. And then there are a few Italian diplomats and their families who have simply quietly vanished from Lisbon in the last month or so as the Mussolini government collapsed. Personally, I think they have secretly sailed on some cargo ship for Sao Paulo, Brazil, where there is a large Italian community already and they hope to just disappear for good."

"Interesting, I wasn't aware of the Italian community in Brazil. Is it difficult to arrange for such 'discreet' passage out of Portugal?"

Antonio smiled. "Most everything can be arranged in Portugal for the right amount of money – women, drugs, exit visas, even murder. Unfortunately, wartime has strained the legal and ethical standards of many of my countrymen. Even some of my own officers have been known to take a bribe or two over the last few years."

Charles noticed the hand-embroidered motto, in Portuguese, in a lovely wooden frame on the wall behind Captain Lourenco: "Charity Begins At Home." He wondered if that was a subtle suggestion to anyone thinking of bribing anyone within the PVDE – start at the top of the bureaucratic chart, not with some lowly sergeant. "So Biachi does appear to be going to the office and working?"

"My dear Charles, what is your American expression – 'Let's lay our cards on the table.' Why are you so interested in Biachi? His country almost doesn't exist anymore. Of what threat could he be to America?"

Charles knew he should have checked directly with General Donovan before revealing anything to Lourenco, but this seemed to be a golden opportunity that shouldn't be missed. "Let's say, speaking hypothetically, that there might be a leak of information out of my Embassy winding up in the hands of the Italians. You tell me that Biachi appears to be the only active Italian intelligence officer in town. Knowing what Biachi is up to in his evenings might help me identify this leak."

"Ah, I understand now. How long has this 'hypothetical' leak been going on?"

"For at least 3-4 months that I know of, but it could well have started long before that date.

"Well, to be honest, we haven't been paying much attention to the Italian Embassy as the participation of Italy in the war, shall we call it, has dwindled in 1943. What have you been doing about this problem?"

"I've narrowed my suspicions down to a few people within my Embassy, but it's thin circumstantial evidence. I'm now considering 'baiting the trap' with a particularly tasty piece of cheese and seeing what happens over the following few days."

Lourenco nodded in agreement. "Very clever. And you'd like me to watch Biachi on those few special days and see if someone brings him some cheese?"

Charles smiled. "I can see why you're the Lisbon Chief of the PVDE!"

Antonio knew he was being flattered and he liked it. "And I suppose such coincidental coverage by my people of Biachi on these days would count on your tally sheet of who'd been a good friend of America in these dark days?"

"Absolutely."

"I would need at least a day's notice to properly prepare for the large and subtle surveillance that would be needed. It might also help if you might be able to help financially in paying the overtime salaries that such coverage would entail. Then I wouldn't have to explain to my superiors why I was spending money on such an insignificant target."

"Of course. I would be glad to assist in compensating your best surveillants for a few days and nights." Charles glanced again at the embroidery – Charity Begins At Home.

As Charles drove back to his office, he began working out in his mind the final details of just how he would place the cheese in front of his suspected rat. He already had worked out what the "cheese" would be. It was now just a question of how to float it past the nose of Solborg, without being obvious, and then wait to see what happened next.

## Chapter 12

Charles was a busy man in the coming days, making all the arrangements for testing whether Solborg was his Italian mole in the American Embassy. He met with Salvatore and Lou to bring them up date on his plan and to arrange for them to cover Solborg nonstop starting that coming Thursday evening and all through the weekend. He also had to brief his head code clerk as to what he wanted to happen that coming Thursday afternoon. Finally, he made a brief phone call to Captain Lourenco's direct line to inform him that Thursday would be a good day to start the party and to keep drinking through Sunday night – their agreed upon code phrase for the Portuguese to lay heavy, but subtle, surveillance on Italian Assistant Air Attache Biachi. Again, Charles figured it didn't matter who else might be listening in on the call. There was a multitude of things that the conversation about a "party" might mean.

At about 2:00 p.m. on Thursday, Charles asked Mary Beth to phone over to Major Solborg in the Military Attache's office and see if he had a few minutes to spare, and if so, could he come see him now. Upon hearing from Mary Beth that he could come by in about fifteen minutes, Charles phoned up to his head code clerk and advised him to bring down the "package" in twenty minutes. Charles then leaned back in his chair, closed his eyes and waited to launch his plan.

Charles' door to the outer office where Mary Beth sat was open, but Solborg still stopped and knocked on the door to wait to be invited in before entering.

"Bob, come on in. Thanks for coming over." He put down the sheet with a variety of names on it and came around to the front of his desk to shake hands with his guest. "Have a seat." The two engaged for a couple of minutes in the usual obligatory polite chit chat, even between military men, before getting down to business. Finally, Charles reached over on his desk for the sheet with names of various Portuguese military officers and handed it to Bob.

"I wanted to get your opinion on who to invite to a dinner in a couple of weeks time from the Portuguese side. Not to target them or anything in particular, but I thought it might be good to at least be on friendly terms with some of the key people in the Army. You never know what might happen one day in a dictatorship like Salazar's. I figure it would be prudent to at least have a few home phone numbers of the important players in case something weird does happen one night. You know these guys pretty well. Have I missed anybody that ought to be invited?"

Solborg started scanning down the list. "Got a pencil?"

Charles handed over a pencil from his desk. His guest added a couple of names to the list and crossed off two names as well. "These guys have been transferred down to the south and are now irrelevant. Don't know who they pissed off, but their careers are pretty much over."

Solborg was still scribbling one more name when the code clerk came in to Charles' office and handed him a sealed envelope marked EYES ONLY.

"Thanks Ted. Excuse me Bob while I take a look at this." Charles returned to his chair behind his desk and used a pearl-handled letter opener to open the sealed envelope. He also called out to Mary Beth in the outer office. "Could you bring us two cups of coffee?"

She came to the door. "Black for both of you, if I recall correctly?" Both men nodded affirmatively to her. Charles wanted to make sure that Solborg wouldn't rush off before his plan was executed.

A minute later, as she brought in the two coffees, Charles finished reading the EYES ONLY cable and looked over at Bob. "Hey, I got something else I could use your opinion on. Keep this to yourself, but apparently the Allies are considering making an offer to General Badoglio, head of the Italian Army, which includes him and other key people staying in their jobs, if they arrange a surrender of Italian forces behind the German's backs. If they do this, they're thinking about approaching at the same time some of the Italian ambassadors still outside of Italy and enlisting their support for such a surrender. The idea is to get them to contact Badoglio and say it would be a good idea. You think the Italian Ambassador here in Lisbon carries any weight back in Italy?"

Solborg didn't hesitate to even give it any consideration. "Complete waste of your time. The old hack here in Lisbon has only had the job because his wife's sister was married to somebody within Mussolini's inner circle. I don't even remember now who that was, but the Ambassador has been here for four or five years and I don't think he's ever made one trip back to Rome."

"OK, thanks. I'll pass that along to Washington about the local guy, but still, might help end the fighting on the Italian peninsula sooner, if some deal could be reached directly with the Italians."

"Indeed, it could. Years ago, I vacationed once in that central region of Italy where most of the fighting is going on now. Don't envy anybody trying to attack defensive positions in that mountain region of the country." He handed the dinner guest list back to Charles. "I've put a few more names down at the bottom for you to consider. I have to take off. I have an appointment over at the British Embassy shortly." He finished the rest of his coffee and stood to leave.

"Thanks again for your help, on both items."

"Not at all, glad to help." He almost bumped into Mary Beth as he was exiting Charles's office. She was filing some reports in a cabinet right outside the door. "Thanks for the coffee, Mary Beth," he said as he passed by her.

Charles put the special message back in the envelope and resealed it with some tape. "Mary Beth."

Her face almost immediately appeared in his doorway. "Yes?"

"Will you please run this back up to Ted. He'll know what to do with it."

"Certainly. Don't forget the Ambassador wants to see you at 3:00."

Charles was left alone in his office, thinking to himself, "The game is afoot."

Across the city, in a small, low-cost restaurant frequented by seaman, the Portuguese banker Pedro Da Silva was conversing in low tones with the captain of one of the Portuguese-flagged cargo vessels in port — one that made regular trips between Lisbon and Rio de Janeiro. It was the third such conversation he'd had with cargo ship captains in as many days, inquiring of their willingness to "discreetly" take a few passengers to Brazil and whether they might be in Lisbon in the latter part of November? Unfortunately, this captain was willing, but would be down around Cape Town in that time frame, and another could not be convinced to carry passengers, no matter what the "fee" he would be paid, but a third one was willing and was tentatively scheduled to depart in late November. Da Silva would have to continue his search for other captains. He would need at least two more ships and preferably three, depending on what the final headcount that Karsthoff would supply him no later than October 15th was. Technically, having a couple ship captains aware that something was afoot in November for smuggling people out of the country was a threat, but these captains were no great friends of the PVDE and it unlikely either of them would go running to the police to tell their story. Besides, neither man would want to risk getting a reputation as a snitch for the police – wouldn't bring them any under-the-table business in the future.

After his chat with the cargo ship captain, Da Silva headed down to the nearby fishing village of Sesimbra. A business acquaintance had recently mentioned to him that there was a small hotel down there that was about to go out of business and would probably be closing up by late October. This might be the answer to his need to find some place to house the traveling Germans until they all could board onto the different ships, which would likely be spread over a 7-10 day period. Colonel Karsthoff had also advised him that the travelers might be arriving at different times over a weeklong period. Simply having an entire hotel available a short distance out of Lisbon seemed the perfect solution to Da Silva's problem.

While he'd never personally been to this hotel before, his directions were good and he found the Hotel Pescador without trouble. It was still technically open for customers, but from the almost empty parking lot to the completely empty lobby, there was little sign of hotel guests. Granted, the peak of the summer tourist season was over, but if not for a very elderly doorman/porter who opened the front door for him and seeing a middle-aged man behind the reception desk, he'd have thought the hotel had already gone out of business. He approached the front desk.

"Good afternoon, Sir. Welcome to the Hotel Pescador. Do you have a reservation?"

Da Silva thought the question almost comic. Of the likely one hundred or so rooms in the hotel, he suspected that at least ninety, if not all of them, were available. "No I don't, but I'd like to speak with the manager about some future reservations. Is he available?"

"I am the manager, Sir, when might you need a room?"

"It would be at the beginning of November."

"Ah, that might be a problem. The hotel will likely be closed by then." He shrugged his shoulders and raised his palms in a gesture of "it was a problem beyond his control."

"Perhaps I should speak with the owner. I'm in need of a number of rooms."

"I am the owner, Sir. How many rooms do you think you would need?"

"How many rooms do you have?"

"We have 120 rooms with two beds, twenty with single beds and ten suites."

"I will want to book the entire hotel for perhaps ten days, if we can come to agreement on a reasonable price. My guests will also need three meals a day here in the hotel restaurant. Is that possible?"

Da Silva presumed that his request would bring a broad smile to the owner/manager/desk clerk's face. He was not disappointed.

"As I said, we normally would be closed by that date, but I'm sure that for such a large number of guests, we could make special arrangements. As for a price, it would take me a day or so to calculate the costs for such a large group."

Da Silva was a negotiator at heart and wanted to get as good a price as possible, so that as much profit as possible accrued to him for arranging such accommodations. He therefore needed to let the owner know that he knew in what a difficult situation was in. "My understanding is that your hotel is about to be put up for sale, not just closing for the season. Therefore, I believe you need me much more than I need you. Do keep that in mind while you are calculating the total price." Da Silva gave the man a broad smile, just to show him there was nothing personal in his driving a hard bargain.

"Absolutely, Sir. I can assure you that you would get no better deal anywhere else in the Sesimbra area. Might I inquire what is the group that will be staying with us? Perhaps we could arrange some excursions and guided tours for your guests?"

It's a group of clients with my bank, mostly from Switzerland, who are arriving for financial meetings. A few of them are bringing their families with them. I'll have the final numbers for you within a week or two. I am Mr. Da Silva, a vice-president of Banco Espirito Santo."

The owner extended his hand. "Mr. Da Silva, of course, I should have recognized you. I can assure you that your Swiss guests will be very comfortable here with us during their stay."

"I'm afraid that there won't be time for excursions. The guests will be mostly staying within the hotel and regardless of my final number of guests, I will want to book the entire hotel. You know the Swiss, they do value their privacy. And we will want to keep their presence here as confidential as possible." The banker gave a facial expression indicating that the Swiss are of course strange, but with all that money, he had to cater to their whims.

"Of course, of course. We are a family-run hotel and even the people working here who are not my relations have been with me for several years and know how to keep their mouths closed." In fact, that was very true. A number of Portuguese businessman and politicians had been known to bring their "nieces" down to the hotel for midweek visits in recent years and there had never been any rumors spread to newspapers or spouses.

Da Silva wasn't completely confident what documents the Germans would be traveling on, and since the hotel owner had been quite cooperative so far, he thought he would just take care of one more possible difficulty right then and there. "Again, on the privacy issue and the convenience of our Swiss guests, since I am renting the entire hotel for a private function, I presume that all our hundred plus guests won't have to bother with the customary procedures of checking in and registering?"

The owner was starting to smell something just a little bit illegal about this booking and felt emboldened. "I'm sure that we can work out some procedure that will make your guests feel comfortable. There are, of course, police requirements for registrations; however, for a small additional 'registration fee' for the special handling of their arrivals, I'm sure that we can find a solution." It was now the turn of the owner to anticipate a smile from Mr. Da Silva, and he got one.

"Certainly, that would be reasonable. Just calculate that in with the total cost for ten days. And don't bother phoning me at the bank. I'll be back down here in say three days and we can settle the fine details of the booking, including a small advance down payment to secure the reservation."

"Would you like to look at some of the rooms and our dining room?"

Da Silva saw no point in stretching this façade any further. "No, I'm pressed for time today and I'm sure everything will be fine for our visitors."

They shook hands once more and then he headed back to his bank in downtown Lisbon. He'd wait to advise Colonel Karsthoff until he'd finalized everything in three days time, but everything was shaping up well. He just needed to find a couple more ship captains and his end of the deal would be completed.

Salvatore and Lou were in their car, waiting for Solborg to pull out of the Embassy parking area. Just like clockwork, at five minutes after five, he pulled out onto the street and headed north; the direction of his home.

Lou was behind the wheel. "Dat guy must have been a banker in civilian life. Never seen nobody who's so punctual about quitting time!" observed Sally. They hung back as much as possible without risking losing him, but it was fairly simple. He didn't drive fast, nor did he make any sudden turns. If he was checking for surveillance enroute to a secret meeting, he was sure good and gave no telltale indication that he was doing so. Within twenty minutes, he was pulling in o the driveway of his home.

"Maybe's he's staying home, or maybe's he's gonna sneak out after dark," observed Lou. They tossed a coin to see who got to stay in the comfortable car and who had to go stand on a small street behind the house, in case he tried slipping out on foot in that direction. Salvatore won. He seemed to frequently win.

"Next time, we's using my coin," commented Lou, as he got out of the car. Salvatore waited in the car a short way up the block from the house, while Lou leaned up against various trees on the street out back while smoking almost a pack of cigarettes. They waited until the lights in the house all went out around 10:00 p.m. They hoped that might mean something would soon happen, but it didn't. The two men waited

*Nazi Gold, Portuguese Wine, and a Lovely Russian Spy*

another two hours and then decided at midnight that the target wasn't going anywhere and they went home.

They were back on duty by 7:30 a.m. the next morning and dutifully watched him drive in a perfectly direct route to the Embassy, so as to be at his desk promptly at 8:00 a.m. They waited around the Embassy until a little before 10:00 a.m. when they headed off to meet Charles at one of the five different coffee shops that they used on a rotating basis as meeting places.

Charles arrived promptly at 10:00 and came over to join his guys at a corner table. He looked expectantly at the two as he approached, hoping for a quick resolution of his test, but he could tell by their faces that they had little to report.

"Nothing boss," stated Salvatore. "Da guy drove straights home and stayed der. He turned out his lights by ten. We's waited till midnight, den we's went home. Dis morning, he drove straight to the Embassy."

Charles obviously looked disappointed. "Unfortunately, I don't have any idea how often Solborg regularly meets with the Italian, or if he even has some emergency signal to trigger an emergency meeting. Maybe his regular meeting is in the next day or two and he decided to just wait for that meeting." Charles shrugged his shoulders.

"Well, maybe tonight we'll get him," observed Salvatore. Charles left first. The other two waited five minutes before leaving, as Charles had taught them, so as not to be perfectly obvious to someone waiting outside that the three had just had a quick meeting. Charles returned to his office, in case Captain Lourenco phoned with any news from the coverage of the Italian diplomat, and the boys again took up their waiting position near the Embassy with a view of the front door and the exit from the parking area. It would be a long, slow day. Solborg never left the Embassy.

That evening was an exact duplicate of the previous day, except that Lou won the coin toss, using his coin, and he got to sit in the car that evening. Solborg drove directly home and stayed there all evening and again turned out the lights by ten o'clock and apparently went to bed. It had started to rain about 10:30 and Lou did feel a little sorry for Salvatore, standing out there getting wet. He showed up at the car at 11:30, soaking wet and said, "Fuck it, let's go home."

Charles had remained optimistic till Sunday morning, when they once again reported that Solborg had done nothing. They'd all hoped that maybe on Solborg's day off, he'd take advantage and go to a meeting with the Italian. Nothing. Salvatore observed to Charles at the Sunday morning meeting that he was beginning to doubt the guy really even had a mistress. "He nevers goes nowhere!" Charles had told them to stick it out till Sunday night then pack it up.

It was a nice Sunday. The rain clouds had passed, but Charles could generate no motivation to go anywhere or do anything. He was trying to read a book, when suddenly his apartment phone rang.

"Charles Worthington here."

"Hello Charles. It's Antonio here. I thought you might be out practicing your Portuguese with one of our country's beautiful women?"

Charles laughed. "I was out with one of them Friday night, but I need my rest on Sundays."

"Well, if you're just sitting around resting, perhaps I'll come by and you can offer me some of that good American bourbon?"

Charles immediately perked up when Antonio suggested he come by. He optimistically assumed that Lourenco's men had observed something of interest and he was coming to pass it along to Charles.

"Sure, how soon will you be here?"

"About twenty minutes, if that is convenient?"

"See you shortly." Charles got out the bottle of bourbon and placed two glasses on his dining table. He presumed that Solborg had simply waited till the wee hours of the morning to go out and that was why his guys hadn't seen him leave his house.

Charles was still contemplating just how he would confront Solborg with the incriminating evidence when there was a knock on the door.

"Antonio, good to see you. Do come in." He pointed in the direction of the table where the bourbon awaited.

"Thank you." He saw the bottle and two glasses on the table. "Ah, a man of his word."

Charles poured them both a modest amount of the golden brown liquid. He was too anxious to engage in any polite chit chat before hearing whatever news Captain Lourenco had brought, which apparently couldn't wait till Monday. "So, what news do you bring me?"

"The first couple of days and nights produced nothing of interest, but then last night our Italian bachelor had a date. My men at first thought that it was just a man being a man on a Saturday night, but fortunately, they took a photo of the woman leaving his home very early this morning. Apparently, he doesn't even offer his overnight guests breakfast before he throws them out in the morning!" Antonio laughed. "I think these stories of Italian being great lovers are overrated."

Charles was bewildered - a woman? Was Solborg using some woman as an intermediate?

Antonio pulled a photo from his vest pocket and slid it across the table to Charles. "Do you recognize this woman?"

Charles looked and almost dropped his glass. "It's my secretary, Mary Beth Short!"

Antonio made no pretense of not already knowing who it was. He presumably had a photo album of all the Americans at the Embassy. "Yes, I thought that it was her, but I'm glad to hear your confirmation. I presume this is a surprise to you that she is 'dating' Biachi?"

"I had no idea." Charles could barely speak, he was so shocked by this turn of events.

"I can see by your reaction that you're telling the truth. At first, I thought that perhaps you were using your secretary to go after the Italian attaché, but clearly that is not the case."

"No, there was no targeting of him in any manner and certainly not by using my secretary to seduce him." Charles quickly toyed with the idea that Captain Lourenco might be conducting some twisted ploy against him, but just as quickly dismissed that idea.

"May I ask what information you had floated around, that prompted her to make a visit to her lover?"

"I let Major Solborg learn about an alleged proposal, supposedly being contemplated, to the current Italian government to surrender to the Allies and join us against the German troops in Italy. This was done in my office, but Mary Beth had been right outside in my outer office and could have easily heard most of my discussion with Solborg. I also had her hand carry a fake telegram back up to the code room. She could have easily read it before returning it."

"I ask because I had considered the possibility that her having a sexual affair with the Italian was purely a coincidence, but now that I hear of the bait you had put out and how it was done, I have to believe she is likely your leak."

"I'm afraid that you're right. That's too much of a coincidence on the timing of the two events. I'm surprised she waited until Saturday to meet him."

"Who knows what the reason was for waiting till Saturday night, but the passage of such information may explain why he threw her out of his bed so early this morning. And also why he then drove to his Embassy about 9:00 a.m. this morning. He was there almost two hours."

"Yes, that would seem to clinch our suspicions about Mary Beth. She tells him about the planned Italian peace proposal and then he rushes to his Embassy to send off a message to Italy."

"What do you plan to do about her?"

"God, I don't know. I'm still in shock. I'll have to think about that today and then confront her tomorrow morning. May I keep this photo of her leaving his house early this morning?"

"Certainly. I'll keep you apprised if we observe Biachi doing anything else of a suspicious nature."

Once Lourenco had departed, Charles poured himself another large portion of the bourbon. The Captain's news had certainly been an unexpected twist and he did indeed need to think about what to do next.

## Chapter 13

Captain Lourenco had been gone from his apartment for almost two hours, yet Charles still sat at the table pondering the news Antonio had brought. He'd picked up a pencil and had been doodling on a piece of blank white paper. Some people made intricate patterns when they doodled, or even sketched people. Charles just made random scratches over the page, as he had no sketching or drawing skills. He was still trying to think of any plausible explanation for Mary Beth's actions, other than the obvious one, which was that his secretary was the source of leaks from the OSS office to the Italians. Charles had the facts and the photo, but he couldn't understand the motive. If he'd had to make up a list of possible suspects out of the OSS staff, or even the entire Embassy staff, she would have been at the bottom of that list. She was your typical Irish-American, patriotic to her core, dependable and loyal. What could the Italian have had on her to possibly blackmail her in to cooperation? He couldn't bring himself to get up and move. It was as if he felt that if he simply concentrated on the situation long enough, he would suddenly have a flash of brilliance to explain the facts as known to him and prove her innocent. No flash ever came and finally he had to get up because he really had to pee.

He dabbled about his kitchen a bit, fixing himself a little early dinner and turning his mind to the next dilemma. If she was guilty, exactly what should he do next? Thinking as a lawyer, he knew that what he had in hand would never convict her of anything in an American court of law. Even if the SIGINT guys intercepted a message out of the Italian Embassy in Lisbon back to Italy in the next few days with the dummy information Charles had let Solborg, and unintentionally Mary Beth, learn, that would still not constitute legal proof that Mary Beth passed it to the Italians. A good defense attorney would tear his circumstantial evidence to shreds, beginning with the second-hand information from the PVDE that she had spent the night with Biachi. Who were these surveillants? Why aren't they available in a Washington DC court room to be questioned by the accused's lawyer? The only hard evidence, the photo, showed Mary Beth walking along a street in Lisbon at some early morning hour. So what? Granted, it was wartime, and the OSS could certainly fire her on the spot and ship her home in disgrace, but if she was to be punished for espionage, she'd have to confess. How could he get her to do that? General Donovan would be pleased that the leak had been plugged, but he'd want his pound of flesh as well. As would Charles, if it weren't for the fact that he personally knew and liked the leaker so much. He decided not to wait until any SIGINT confirmation possibly came in. Donovan wouldn't want him to reveal to Mary Beth that intercept capability anyway, nor was there any longer any doubt in his mind that Mary Beth was guilty. Monday morning was going to be an interesting one at U.S. Embassy Lisbon.

He did phone the small pension where Salvatore and Lou were staying. They'd be going home in a few days. There was no longer a great worry about hiding their connection to himself. He simply told them to meet him at the Embassy at 7:00 a.m. the next morning. He offered no explanation as to the reason. Sleep finally came to him about 2:00 a.m.

Charles met his two friends at the front gate of the Embassy at the planned hour and escorted them to his office. He'd already brewed the coffee and had a pot sitting ready on his desk with three cups. "It looks as though we've found the leak from our OSS office."

The two looked at each other and then at Charles. "So, is it dat Solborg fellow?" asked Salvatore.

"Nope. Despite all the signs it was him, it turns out that it's almost certainly my secretary, Mary Beth Short." He explained to them what Captain Lourenco had reported to him on Sunday afternoon and how he planned on confronting her that very morning, with their assistance. The two drank their coffee and listened to what their role was to be during the interrogation of her. Then Charles arranged a number of thick files on his desk, which were to be part of his ploy.

Mary Beth arrived promptly at 8:00 a.m. as she always did, but to her surprise found the coffee already brewed and Charles at his desk.

"Goodness, you're in early. Has something important happened?" She was halfway through his office door when she noticed Salvatore and Lou seated off in a corner by the window. "Oh, I'm sorry. I didn't know you had guests." She started to retreat.

"No, please come on in, Mary Beth, and have a seat," he said in a very quiet and serious tone. He pointed at the chair in front of his desk. Salvatore went over and closed the door. He didn't introduce the two strangers to her. He offered no pleasantries, nor made any inquiry as to how her weekend had been.

"These two men have been here in Lisbon for many weeks now at my request, watching you during your evenings and weekends." He pointed at the files in front of him then slid across the desk the PVDE photo of her from Sunday morning, just outside the gate to Biachi's home. "So, exactly how long have you and Biachi been friends? Does he always throw you out of his bed so early in the morning?" He actually felt bad inside his head about saying those words with a tone that implied what a sleazy whore she must be, but he needed to immediately crush her spirit. He wanted her to think that Charles and these two men knew all.

She sat motionless and silent for close to a full ten seconds, then she broke down in to tears and repeated several times, "I'm so sorry" while bringing her hands to her face.

Charles took a handkerchief from his inner suit pocket, walked around the desk and handed it to her. "Why don't you tell me how this all started. You'll feel better." He then waited in silence. He still harbored a suspicion that the Italian had somehow been blackmailing her into cooperation.

It took a full minute for her to be able to bring her crying under control and even look up at Charles. "It was on a sunny Sunday afternoon, back in April. I'd taken some food and a blanket and had gone to one of the beaches with a book. I get tired of sitting..." She briefly hesitated. "Of being alone at my apartment." She looked over at Salvatore and Lou as a few more tears rolled down her plain face. It was bad enough having to confess her personal life to Charles, but the presence of two strangers in the room was simply mortifying.

Charles sensed that as well and waved at the two men to leave the room, hoping that would make her words flow more freely. "Go ahead. You'd gone to the beach one fine Sunday in April."

"Yes, it was a gorgeous day, yet there were very few people at the beach that day. I was laying there, reading, when a very handsome man, who looked to be in his late twenties, came up and simply asked in Portuguese what I was reading. I answered in English that I spoke only a little Portuguese and he switched to very good English and introduced himself as Luigi." She went on for many minutes about how they chatted about her book, the weather and the way he kept looking at her with his lovely hazel-colored eyes. They had chatted for almost an hour when he invited her to come up the beach to a small café for some wine and some food.

"And did he tell you that he worked at the Italian Embassy?"

"We had almost finished the wine before he passingly mentioned that he had to enjoy that Sunday because he would be very busy as usual come Monday morning and he had to go to work at the Italian Embassy. I think I laughed a little, with embarrassment, when I told him that I worked at the American Embassy and how technically we were at war. He laughed and replied that on Sundays no one was at war with anyone. We chatted another half hour or so and he never asked anything about my work or even about in what section of the Embassy I worked. We were about to go our separate ways and I suppose we'd have never seen each other again had he not shyly asked if I came to the same beach every Sunday?"

"And had he mentioned to you that he was married?"

"As a matter of fact he had told me. He'd told me how his wife was back in Italy and that he was really very lonely and that was why he had walked up to a perfect stranger, simply to have someone with whom to talk on such a lovely day. And at that moment I told him that it had been very nice to have someone to chat with and that indeed I came there most Sundays. He was like a young schoolboy, he was practically stuttering as he came around to suggesting that possibly he and I could meet and chat again the following Sunday."

"I replied that I would look forward to speaking with him again on the beach, and then we parted."

Charles was trying to keep a neutral face, but her story was sounding more and more like a bad romance novel. They'd actually talked about this sort of recruitment approach to lonely, middle-aged women back in OSS training. He felt that surely the OSS would have given some sort of defensive briefing about this sort of approach to their own female employees, but he didn't really know. It took her almost an hour more of explaining her interactions with Biachi, before she got to the evening that they were having dinner by candlelight, alone at his house and how they'd both drunk a lot of wine and then he'd kissed her and how she'd wound up in his bed. At that point, Charles wasn't sure who was more embarrassed – Mary Beth or him? Frankly, she was giving him much more detail than he really wanted to know, but figured it was better to receive too much than too little.

"When did he start asking you about your work here at the Embassy?"

"I don't know. It wasn't a specific date that sticks in my mind. Over time, our conversations naturally started to include how each other's week had gone and the people I worked with and then eventually, what my work was."

"And then he started asking you specific things?"

"Well, the first 'favor' he asked me for was simply a copy of our Embassy's phone book. He said it would make his work easier, if he knew who was in which sections. It isn't stamped classified or anything, so I gave him a copy." She was looking more and more embarrassed over how she'd started down such a ridiculous path.

"And then?"

"He told me several months back that his government was thinking of recalling him. They didn't think he was accomplishing much as the assistant air attaché here and he needed to improve his reporting and he asked me if there was any information out of the American Embassy that I could share with him. Nothing really classified, just little tidbits of gossip. So, I started telling him little things. And it just progressed. It sounds so stupid now, but I loved him and he loved me and I wanted to make sure that he stayed in Lisbon." Mary Beth started crying again.

Eventually, she got around to telling Charles that it was indeed she who had passed the information about the operation against the Japanese Embassy in Lisbon and much more recently about the visit of General Dovovan. He'd told her about the praises he was receiving from Rome and she was proud that she'd been able to make the man of her life a success. Charles had been writing down on a pad some of the details of what she'd been telling him for over two hours.

"What will you do with me now?" she finally asked.

"The first thing is that I will send off a private message directly to General Donovan about all this. I suspect that the OSS will want you sent home in just a few days and they'll decide on whether you will face formal prosecution charges for treason or just how they plan on dealing with you. Maybe you will simply be fired, but you could also be facing several years in prison. In the meantime, you will stay at your apartment. You will not come into the Embassy and I want your word that you will not phone nor try to see Biachi."

"I promise." She seemed to be over her crying phase and was regaining her composure. "I suppose this will come out in the press and there'll be quite a scandal after I arrive back in America?"

"I don't think General Donovan would have any interest in publicity, but you know Washington. There are plenty of people over at the Pentagon who don't think much of the OSS. If they get wind of this, I fear they won't pass up a chance to embarrass the organization."

She nodded in agreement. "Probably not." She then sat there in silence, staring down at the floor.

"I'll have those two men drive you home and I want you to stay there. I'd suggest that you go ahead and start packing some things to take with you. I'll arrange later for everything else to be packed up and shipped back to Washington."

"I don't suppose I should take my cat with me when I go?"

"No, I don't think that would be advisable. You know anyone here in Lisbon who would want the cat?"

"I'll give that some thought. And my car is here. How will I get it back to the apartment? It shouldn't be left out on the street in front of the Embassy."

"I'll have one of these men drive you and the other man will drive your car."

She stood up abruptly. "The clutch on that old thing is quite tricky. I'll drive it and your men can follow right behind me."

Charles hesitated until she added, "I promise I shan't make a break for the Spanish border!" She offered a little smile.

"Alright, we'll do it your way." He opened the door and spoke to Salvatore and Lou. "Please escort Miss Short out to her car. She will drive it to her apartment and you will follow her home, to make sure she arrives safely, then you'll wait outside till you hear further from me."

They nodded in agreement, while Mary Beth gathered up her purse and a few personal items from her desk. She turned to Charles just before leaving. "It's been a privilege working for you, Mr. Worthington, and I appreciate your courtesy shown to me this morning." She quickly shook his hand and the three of them left.

Salvatore waited with her by her car while Lou went several blocks away to retrieve their automobile. He felt like saying something, anything, to break the awkward silence, but having overheard bits and pieces of the conversation between her and Charles in the inner office, he knew in general what she had just confessed to in the interview. For once, Sally couldn't think of a thing to say that seemed appropriate. Lou finally pulled up behind her car. "OK, we'll just follow behind you on your way home," he said as he went to join Lou.

She nodded and smiled. She started to give her address, but then stopped. "Oh, of course, you gentlemen know well where I live. Though, as this will likely be my last chance to see the sea shore, I think I'll take the coastal rode to home."

"Dat's fine ma'am" replied Salvatore. In fact, he didn't have a clue as to where she lived. Neither Salvatore nor Lou had ever been near her apartment. The story by Charles to her that they had been surveilling her for months had simply been a bluff. They pulled out right behind her black-colored Vauxhall.

"Stay pretty close," Sally said to Lou. "It's no secret we's following her and since we's not got a clue as to where she lives, better not lose her."

"OK. Pretty hards to believe dat nice lady is a spy for the Italians," observed Lou.

"Didn't sounds to me likes she's a real spy," responded Sally. "Just anothers poor, lonely broad who got fooled by some smooth talking guy into thinking he loved her. Dem women will do anything when dey's in love."

Lou nodded in agreement. Then they drove along in silence for a while. Once they were out on the coastal road, she sped up.

"She lives clear out here?" asked Lou.

"Naw, she just told me dat since this likely her last chance to see the seashore, she was going to take the long route home."

Mary Beth accelerated even faster.

"Dat broad sure likes going fast," observed Lou.

As they came up on the next curve, her car suddenly crossed the road and drove right through a small wooden guardrail and straight off a cliff onto the beach below.

A half hour later, Charles was called and told that he had two visitors down at the front entrance. He could tell from their faces that something bad had transpired, but the three walked in silence through the hallways until they were back in his office. "So why aren't you at Mary Beth's apartment?"

As the older man, Salvatore had been chosen between the two of them to speak first. "Der's been an accident. She's dead."

"What!"

"We's were headed along the coastal road and she went straights over a cliff. We finally made our way down to the wreck and she was definitely dead."

"She lost control of the wheel?" asked Charles, but he felt that he already knew the answer.

The two looked at each other, hesitant to speak. "It didn't look dat way, boss. We's think she wents over intentionally. She didn't break or nothing. In fact, it looked likes she was speeding up as she headed for the guardrail."

"OK guys. Look, I have a number of things I have to do, beginning with calling the police, but let's regroup for dinner about 7:00 p.m. at that seafood place where we ate a couple of Sundays back."

"Sure, we'll waits for you der. I don't thinks you needs to phone the police. There were a couple of them at the top of the cliff lookings down just as we's were leaving da spot."

"Good." They left as Charles was phoning for Captain Lourenco. It would be best if the PVDE took charge of this, instead of just the local traffic police, which was probably who had stopped first at the scene. As the victim was from the American Embassy, the PVDE could claim jurisdiction. He plopped down in his chair and thought to himself, "God, how could this have gone so wrong?" Why had he agreed that she could drive herself home! He knew exactly why she'd done it. The embarrassment. She couldn't stand the thought of the embarrassment to herself once she'd gotten back to Washington and the story had gotten out. Not only to herself, but to her parents, and she had a younger brother somewhere in the U.S. Navy. He phoned up to his chief code clerk and told him to gather up everyone who was around the building, to meet in Charles' office in ten minutes. He tried phoning Captain Lourenco, but he was out, so he could only leave a message for him. He then started to write out by hand a message to go immediately back to OSS Headquarters in Washington and another one, EYES ONLY, to General Donovan. He realized that the Embassy Administrative Officer should also immediately be advised. He bizarrely thought to himself that Mary Beth would be upset that she was causing so much trouble for the office and the Embassy. As much as he loved his work, there were days when he hated his job and this was certainly one of them!

Once he had all the staff who were in the Embassy that morning gathered into his office, he broke the news to them. "I'm afraid that there's been a terrible accident today; Mary Beth's car went off the road and over a cliff out on the coastal road. She was killed instantly. I've contacted the Admin Officer, the police and sent word up to the ambassador. I've been drafting up a cable to go to Washington, but I wanted all of you to hear this from me first, before rumors get going around the building as to what has happened." He turned to Sarah, another one of the secretaries, "Sarah, if you would, I'd like you to take charge of packing up her personal things in the next day or so, and there's also the question of what to do with her cat. If anyone is interested in a cat, here is your opportunity."

"I'd be happy to take care of her things. To where will they be sent?"

"We have an address for her parents somewhere out in northern Indiana. Someone in Washington will be getting in touch via phone with them in the next day or so to find out if they really want all her clothes sent there, or perhaps just personal things, like photos, etc. Any takers on the cat?"

He looked around the room. Sarah finally spoke. "Well, Sir, the fact is that her cat is this horrible creature, as any of us who've been to her apartment knows, so it might be a little difficult finding anyone to adopt it. I'll check with a veterinarian that some of the Embassy people use. Perhaps he will know what we can do with it."

"Good idea. I'll leave that in your hands, as well as the packing of her things, soon as we know what is going to America and what might just be passed along to a charity here in Lisbon. As soon as I know anything further, about funeral services and such, I'll pass word along."

The staff started to file out. Charles called out to the head code clerk to stay behind. "I have a draft of a message to go out now in personnel channels about the accident. Go ahead and send this one and then come back in about a half hour. I'll have another message for you."

He took the handwritten message. "Right boss, I'll take care of this right away."

Charles sat back down at his desk and continued writing the second message. The first one told the truthful story of an auto accident and that would be the story spread around the American community. The public knowledge of her relationship with the Italian and passing of secrets would serve no purpose now. It would only bring more pain on her family. There was no doubt in his mind that that was part of Mary Beth's decision to kill herself by going over the cliff.

A half hour later the code clerk returned and Charles handed him the sheets for the second message. "Read this here before you go up, to be sure you can read my handwriting."

He quickly read through the draft and then softly muttered, "Jesus, Joseph and Mary." He looked up at Charles. "There's no doubt about this?"

"I'm afraid not. I just confronted her this morning with the evidence and she confessed to me all that had gone on with the Italian diplomat, but at this point I see no reason to trash her memory. In so many ways, she was such a fine woman. Let's just leave her memory for most everybody as it was. Nobody, and I mean nobody, sees this outgoing message or any response. Soon as you send it, you burn this. If this gets out, I will personally come up there and throw you out a window. We clear?"

"Absolutely."

"When does the next diplomatic pouch go out of here for Washington?"

"In two days time."

"OK. I'll have a full report about all this typed up by then and ready to go to America, as an EYES ONLY envelope for General Donovan."

"Yes, Sir." He started to leave the office, but turned around to face Charles. "I'm very sorry about her death, regardless of the circumstances. I know that you two were friends and, well…" He was at a loss for words to finish the sentence, so he just turned and left.

Charles closed his eyes and leaned back in his chair. Yes, he thought, they had been friends and that was what made the whole affair that much harder. Had the discovered traitor been relatively unknown to him or preferably, a perfect stranger, it would have still been an unpleasant situation, but for the mole to turn out to have been someone he considered a friend – that really sucked. He then started thinking about whether there was something he could have done to have prevented the whole mess. Maybe if he'd included Mary Beth in more social events outside the Embassy or been more attuned to how lonely she had been. He obviously knew she was single, but she was always so cheerful around the office, he really had had no sense of how lonely she must have felt if she'd gone down the path of falling in love with a married man from an enemy country. She was such a bright woman. How could she have fallen for the lies of Biachi? But had they been lies? Maybe he really had started out just looking for some company out on that beach, or had he targeted Mary Beth from the get go? Whichever the case, he'd still like the chance to punch Biachi in the nose. It wouldn't bring Mary Beth back, but he knew it would make him feel better.

His phone rang. "Charles Worthington here."

"Charles, it's Antonio. They told me that you'd called earlier."

"Yes, some very bad news, I'm afraid." He quickly filled him in on the confrontation with his secretary that morning, her confession and then her suicide at the wheel of her car. "The story I'm putting out, even here at the Embassy, is that this was simply a tragic automobile accident. I don't see that it serves any purpose to say anything more."

"Yes, yes, I quite agree. Spare her family embarrassment. I assume there is family back home in America?"

"Parents and a brother. We're working on notifying them now."

"If there is anything I can do to be of assistance, please only ask."

"Thanks. The traffic police are already at the scene, but I'd appreciate it if you and your people could be involved and make sure everything is done correctly. There will probably be a small service here in Lisbon in the next few days and then her body will be sent back home to America."

"Certainly, I will personally see to things. Have no worries. Anything else?"

"Well, I don't know quite what it will achieve, but could you keep your men for just a few more days on that fine gentleman we've been discussing?"

"Consider it done. By the way, your secretary was not the only single woman that this man has been dating while in Lisbon, with his wife and children back in Italy. We can speak of this the next time we meet in person."

"Thanks. Goodbye." Charles again closed his eyes. He was sad, of course, but he noticed that he'd not cried, not even once he was alone. Maybe he had simply known too much death already in his young life. His fiancée back in New York, and the Jap he'd killed out on that South Pacific island even before the war had begun. The deaths he officially heard about concerning some of the other young men who'd gone through OSS training with him and then the ones who'd parachuted into occupied France and with whom contact had been lost and they were presumed dead. He was not yet thirty years old and he'd already known enough death to last a lifetime. God, he was sick of this war.

## Chapter 14

Charles, Salvatore and Lou met for dinner that evening as planned. They drank many toasts that evening to the good memory of Mary Beth. Charles had given them all the details that had come out during her interview with him in his office that morning. No matter what foolish things she'd done, they felt that that was not the way a life should end. The latter two being good Catholics, they also knew that suicide was a mortal sin for an Irish Catholic lady, just as it was for an Italian.

"So, she really was in love with dat bum?" Salvatore had asked for the third time over the course of the evening.

"It certainly appears that way. You hear of such stories, but you never think that anybody as smart as Mary Beth could have fallen for such a con game by that bastard. And from what Captain Lourenco has told me, Biachi was playing this same game with a number of single women in town, while his wife and children were back in Italy."

"Dat bum's lucky he didn't do this to a woman connected with a Sicilian family, or he wouldn't have to worry about making any plans for the coming weekend!" Lou made a gesture with one finger slicing across his throat. Charles had never been particularly religious, but he did have a strong sense of justice. The more he drank, the more Sicilian he was coming to feel that night. Mary Beth was dead and Biachi was still walking around enjoying life – just didn't seem right, regardless of what a court of law might say.

Lou drove all three of them to Charles' home, as Charles was in no shape to drive anywhere by the end of their time at the restaurant. As the two Brooklyn boys would be leaving in a few days, once at his apartment, Charles invited them up for a farewell drink. One turned into two. Charles woke up the following morning in his own bed. Upon wandering into the living room, he found Salvatore asleep on the sofa and Lou was in the kitchen brewing coffee and trying to find anything to cook for breakfast.

"Good morning," whispered Lou, not wishing to disturb his partner still horizontal in the other room.

"Good morning." He went over and showed Lou where he could find some eggs and bread and jam.

Everyone was moving a bit slow that morning, but eventually the three were cleaned up and dressed and sitting at the table finishing the breakfast prepared by Lou. He'd also gone out and found a morning paper. Mary Beth's death had made the bottom of the front page. The article cited eyewitnesses as to how the driver had tragically lost control of the wheel on the dangerous turn and had accidently gone through the guard rail and over the cliff. Clearly Captain Lourenco had made sure that the press coverage took the correct spin on the story.

Lou refilled everyone's coffee cup and then calmly asked of Charles, "So, when does we's go kill dat SOB?"

Salvatore turned to look at Charles. "Yeah, what day we going to whack him?"

Charles gave them both a blank look.

"Dons't tell me youse don't remember! It was youse idea, rights here at dis table last night. We's was discussing how dat bum Biachi shouldn't be able to gets away with what happened. You smiled and said he wouldn't, then you took your gun off your hip and laid its rights here on dis table." Salvatore emphatically stabbed with his finger at a point on the table not twelve inches from Charles' right hand. Charles took a long sip from his cup. It was in fact coming back to him. Salvatore was absolutely right. It had in fact been his idea to kill the Italian and his two friends not only agreed with him, but had volunteered to assist in any way needed. They were going to toss coins to see who would actually get to shoot him, but Charles had insisted that as Mary Beth had been his friend and secretary, it was his right. They had yielded to him on that point of honor.

"Yes, now I'm remembering what we discussed last night."

"Youse hasn't changed your mind have youse?" inquired Salvatore.

Charles hesitated a long moment. He quickly remembered his philosophy that people didn't do or say something when drunk that they didn't really want to do and he replied out loud, "No, haven't changed my mind. It's just a matter of what day and how to do it."

His two friends smiled. "Good. The idea last night was dat we let's maybe a week go by, so he relaxes and thinks dat everything is fine – then we grabs him," stated Salvatore. Lou nodded in agreement that that had been the plan.

"Sounds about right. I'll get Lourenco to have his men keep an eye on him this week to make sure he doesn't suddenly head for the airport. I'll get the reports on where he goes and what he does. Then we can come up with a plan as to the best time and place to grab him, maybe even at his own home, if he's alone at night."

Salvatore and Lou were always amazed at how an upper class guy like Charles, who'd gone to Harvard could think so "street-wise" and plan a hit like one of the boys. They, of course, didn't know of his real background of having grown up in Chicago and having had his father accidently killed in one of the wars between Al Capone and a rival gang. Charles had indeed gone to Harvard, but that was out of the sympathy of one of Capone's lieutenants, who felt sorry for the young boy. He'd created the name of Charles Worthington and came up with the needed letters of recommendation and outstanding school record so that the young boy could go off to Harvard on a "scholarship" as an undergraduate and then law school. Not even Vincent Astor had learned that part of his past. Only his NKVD friend, Olga, had managed to learn back in Manhattan the truth of his origins and she had promised to keep that to herself.

The following morning Charles received an Immediate EYES ONLY cable from Washington telling him that General Donovan's personnel aide, Duncan Lee would be arriving in a few days to discuss the "situation" with him. The next few days were a blur for Charles. Between arrangements for a small, private funeral, packing of Mary Beth's personal possessions and shipping of them and her body back to Indiana. He'd also had a face-to-face meeting with PVDE Captain Lourenco to see how Colonel Biachi was reacting to the news. He'd actually had an "overnight" date with another woman the day of Mary Beth's death, but after the story had appeared in the newspaper, the Italian had only left his home for a couple of quick trips to his embassy.

The rest of the time, he was holed up in his home. Lourenco noted that it was as if he was afraid of a reprisal against him by the Americans. Charles did learn that after dinner each night, Biachi's cook and servant left till the following morning. Charles was still contemplating how to grab the Italian, but nothing particularly clever had yet come to his mind.

In a rather bizarre gesture, on the third morning after the newspaper article had appeared about the death, Charles received a small personal note via the Portuguese postal service from Colonel von Karsthoff. It simply said that he had heard of the accidental death of Charles' secretary and wished to offer his sympathies over her tragic death. At first Charles thought there might be some weird angle or veiled threat in the note, but finally decided that Karsthoff was "old school European" and even to an enemy, such a note of sympathy was simply considered proper etiquette. Charles had received a number of similar notes from other Allied or neutral diplomats in Lisbon. Karsthoff was the only German who wrote him and in such beautiful handwriting. It was hard to believe it was the handwriting of a colonel of the German Abwehr! But then, there were a lot of strange things going on in the war, as Charles would come to learn.

It was after dark when he arrived at his apartment that night and he was tired. He unlocked the door and started to step through the doorway. He wasn't so tired that his nostrils didn't notice the smell of cigarette smoke in the air and noticed the small glow of a burning cigarette at the far end of the living room. He instinctively rolled forward on the floor, pulling out his gun as he came up in a kneeling position, as he'd been taught at OSS school. He paused there motionless.

He heard a female Russian accent from across the room. "You don't shoot lonely Russian girls do you?" And then a light laugh, as if from a little girl. He remained on one knee.

She switched on the small light on the table next to her. "Very impressive Major Worthington. They taught you very well at OSS school!" And again the laugh.

Charles saw that it was Olga. "You know how close you just came to being shot? Why are you sitting here in the dark?" He rose to his feet and came towards her.

"I only wanted to surprise my American secret agent."

He grabbed her and hugged her tightly. "I don't need any more surprises this week. If I had shot you…" His voice trailed off.

"Ah, yes, I heard about the tragic death of your secretary. Very sad. That's part of reason I come see you."

"It didn't say anything in the newspaper about her being my secretary. How did you hear that?"

She smiled. "You think you are only secret agent who has friends in the PVDE and around Lisbon? Portuguese people love to gossip and love conspiracy theories. Secretary of OSS Chief does not have simple accident. By time story had reached Spain, your Mary Beth had not only had car accident, but had been shot several times, stabbed and poisoned by the Germans, the Japanese and a jealous wife!"

Charles smiled, for the first time in several days. She was right. For the Portuguese, nothing ever happened in a simple, straightforward manner; there was always some triple-layered conspiracy behind every action. He was also smiling because he was so thrilled at seeing Olga. He pulled her tight once again. "Oh how I've missed you," he whispered in her ear. "Ya lublu tebya."

And she responded, "And I love you." Then she pushed him back in mock outrage. "Who been teaching you how to say 'I love you' in Russian? How many Russian girlfriends you have?"

"You taught me that. You have so many American boyfriends that you forget which ones you've taught to say 'Ya lublu tebya'?" They both laughed. Charles went back and closed the front door. He was rubbing his shoulder as he returned to her. "God, I haven't done that since my training early in 1942 – that hurt!"

"Maybe you need warm shower and Russian massage to make you feel better?" She started to unbutton her blouse.

"Yes, I'm sure that would help." He started removing his own clothing as he led her into the bedroom.

Within a minute, they were both naked in the shower, kissing and letting the warm water cascade down over them. He hadn't realized how much he'd missed her until now that she was back. It appeared that she'd been eating a little better since her first visit; she was returning to her more naturally sounded shape in all the correct parts of her body. Aside from her personality and her brains and her sense of humor, he did admit to himself that he loved her sensual body – and that she knew what to do with it in pleasing a man.

After they'd made love, they both drifted off to sleep for a while. She always felt so safe with his arms wrapped around her. She was the first to awake, at first thinking she was only having a dream about being with Charles, then realizing it was genuine. She started to rise to go explore his kitchen for something to eat, but her movement awakened him and he pulled her back on top of him.

"I'm starving. Let me go find us some food in your kitchen."

He finally relented, in part because he too realized that he'd never gotten around to eating lunch that day and he could use some dinner himself. She quickly made some sandwiches and brought them back to the bed, along with a bottle of wine and two glasses.

Once their growling stomachs had been satiated, Olga finally brought up the topic of the secretary's death, trying to be as delicate as she could be. He shouldn't be sharing such classified information with an NKVD agent, but he so felt the need to be able to discuss the whole mess that had led to Mary Beth's death with someone, he told her almost everything. He skipped the detail about how the US Army was able to intercept and decode Italian communications and simply vaguely referred to learning of the leak of information to the Italians from a "sensitive source."

"I feel responsible to some degree for her death, since she decided after I had confronted her that morning to commit suicide. I'm certain that she couldn't face the humiliation to herself and to her family that she was certain would be coming."

She reached over and squeezed his hand. "Not your fault she kill herself. You only doing your duty. She was guilty of treason, no matter what the reason."

"Being a Catholic, by her beliefs she committed a mortal sin by committing suicide. I don't know what's the view of the Russian Orthodox Church, but for a practicing Catholic, that's a pretty big deal."

"I was not brought up as religious person and don't know what Russian Orthodox priests say. Most of them are hypocrites or even informants for NKVD." She then hesitated for several long seconds, as if she was deciding whether to tell him something or not. "As I told you last time, I found out that I have grandmother who was Jewish. I happened to meet some Jews in Spain and have been learning about this religion. I think it good one. I feel very peaceful when I am talking with these people."

"I didn't know there were any Jews in Spain. You never hear about any such people in Spain."

"There probably are not many. There once were many, but King Ferdinand and Queen Isabella expelled them back in 1492. But one of the families that helps hide me from Franco Regime is Jewish."

"Have you converted to Judaism or whatever the term would be to formally become a member of a synagogue?"

"No, nothing official like that, but Yuval, the wife of this family, has been teaching me much about their religion. And how all the Jews want to return to their homeland back in the Middle East, in area that now called Palestine."

Charles knew nothing of this movement and for that matter knew very little about the religion. Naturally, around New York City there were a number of Jews, but they seemed to keep pretty much to themselves in certain parts of the five boroughs, sort of like the Italians or the Chinese did. He wasn't quite sure how to respond to her news. Finally, he said, "If it makes you feel comfortable and peaceful, then I guess this is a good thing. There are so many different religions and beliefs – Christians, Muslims, Buddhists, Jews – hard to say who is "right." He was also thinking to himself about some of the rumors that were coming out of Germany about what was happening to Jews under the Nazis, but didn't figure then was a good moment to get into that topic.

"You've never told me, Charles, what religion are you, if any?"

"I guess you'd say I'm a Christian, but can't say that I've been much for going to church on a regular basis. I'd show up at Christmas time and at Easter like a lot of folks, but have just never been much into a particular church. I suppose there's a God and all that, but it's hard to believe he intercedes much in our lives anymore – given all the horrible things that go on in the world, particularly these last few years."

She silently nodded, as if in agreement with him, but he wasn't sure as to exactly what part of what he'd been saying that she was agreeing with, or just acknowledging that he'd stated something. He decided to return to the issue of Mary Beth. "I don't know what the religious position would be, but I think there is a question of 'justice' that mere men and women can decide on and I've decided that Mr. Biachi bears some of the blame for Mary Beth's death and he is going to pay."

She was slightly confused. "He is going to pay? What does that mean? What is he going to pay – money?"

He smiled. He understood how idiomatic English phrases could be confusing to foreigners. "No, it means that as a matter of fairness, of justice, he's going to suffer the same fate. He's going to die."

Now it was her turn to smile. "Ah, you speak of revenge. We Russians understand this word very well. When will this happen?"

"We're still in the planning stage, but hopefully, soon."

"Who are we?"

"You remember Salvatore and Lou from New York City?"

"Oh, yes. The two nice men who I barely ever understood what they say!"

"That's them. Sometimes, I don't even understand what they're saying! They are here in Lisbon right now, helping me on a few things. They were actually the ones who watched Mary Beth drive over the cliff. That's why we know that it was no accident. This Italian Air Force officer, Biachi, is pretty much just staying in his home. It's going to be tricky how we can get to him."

"Hmmm. From what you tell me about how much he likes women, maybe you need pretty woman on your assassination team."

"And just what would this woman do?"

"I do not know. Maybe I lure him out of home, or he open his door to let me in? You big OSS Chief. You decide."

"So, you think you can seduce a man?" He gave her a lecherous grin. "Show me how you do that. Maybe, it will give me an idea on how to get to Biachi!"

She moved her naked body closer to his. It was an hour later that they got back to a discussion of how to get at Biachi.

The following day was a Saturday, so he could sleep in, except for two reasons. Having an incredibly beautiful naked woman next to him in bed didn't make him think much about sleep. Secondly, Salvatore and Lou were coming to his apartment at 10:00 a.m. and it would probably be more proper if he and Olga had clothes on when the guys arrived. Once they were both awake, he told her of the pending arrival of the two Brooklyn boys, which made her immediately jump out of bed and run for the shower. "I look horrible. I must shower and shampoo my hair before they arrive."

"Oh, so it's OK for you to look horrible to me, but for Salvatore and Lou, you have to look nice?"

She stopped at the bathroom door, turned and stuck her tongue out at him. She gestured with her hand at her neck to the top of her head. "They only get to see this small part, so I must make sure that this part looks nice!"

By the time the two guests had arrived, she was clean, dressed and had prepared coffee for all of them.

As Charles opened the door for his two assistants, he told them, "I have a nice surprise for you." He ushered them in and said, "You remember Olga, from Manhattan, don't you?"

They were indeed surprised, but Salvatore recovered fairly quickly. "Of course. How's could we's forgets such a beautiful and charming woman." He went over and shook her hand. Lou followed.

"Gentleman, it is indeed small world! How nice see you both." She felt a little self-conscious, as she knew that she certainly didn't look as good nor was she dressed as well as when they had known her back in New York City. She stroked at her hair and laughed. "I'm afraid that I have changed since last you me saw and not for better."

"Nonsense," replied Salvatore. "A beautiful woman is always beautiful, no matter what she's wearing."

Olga genuinely blushed. Charles thought that he must remember that line! "Let's all sit down."

Olga poured the coffee and then they quickly got down to the topic of how to assassinate Mr. Biachi.

They reviewed what they knew about him and his travel patterns. Charles thought it best to hit him while enroute to somewhere from his home, rather than in the home, as they knew nothing about the interior nor what weapons he might keep at his home. They all agreed it would be beautiful symmetry if Biachi's car also went over a cliff, but that would be difficult to arrange.

Olga had remained silent though most of the discussion, but when the conversation of the known facts was winding down, and it was apparent there was as yet no concrete plan, she spoke. "Gentlemen, one fact about Biachi that you are certain is that he considers himself real woman's man – that all women adore him. Let us use that weakness."

Charles wasn't sure he liked where her suggestion was headed, since she was the only woman on their team. "And how do we do that?"

"I get him to come out of his house one night and then you three men grab him and kill him." She made it sound so simple.

"And exactly how do you get him to come out of his house?"

"You said he speak English pretty well?"

"Yes, he only spoke English with Mary Beth," replied Charles, still puzzled over her plan.

"You one minute wait here. I come back." She went into the bedroom and closed the door. The three men stayed at the table, looking at each other, but following her instructions.

About two minutes later, she opened the door and walked back into the main room, wearing a beautiful red dress, cut low and wide in the front. Her bra was gone and when she leaned over and put her hands on the table, her large, lovely breasts almost fell out of the dress. Salvatore and Lou were speechless.

"I remember that dress from New York City," blurted out Charles.

She turned towards Charles and smiled. "Yes, is one thing I have saved from those days. I brought from Spain this time to wear for you. You still like?"

"Very much," he replied, trying with little success to keep his eyes focused on her face.

"Good. Can one of you get me very expensive-looking car to use one night?"

Salvatore and Lou both nodded in the affirmative.

"OK. That car break down in front his house. I walk up in this dress and knock on his door. I say, 'Oh, dear sir, my car suddenly stop working. Could you please see what problem? I must get to dock with my luggage to catch my ship.' When he comes out, you grab him."

"He's very paranoid right now. What if he says he can't help you? That he knows nothing about cars."

"Then I ask if he have car to take me to dock. He still have to stop at my car to get my bags."

Charles was shaking his head in the negative. "I don't know. He might still just say that he can't help you and close the door."

"Ha! You really think man with such big sexual ego going to close door on me?" She then gave a big friendly smile and looked so helpless.

Salvatore and Lou immediately shook their heads in agreement – Biachi would never say "no" to her. Even Charles, as much as he hated to involve Olga in this way, had to agree that the odds were very much in her favor. "OK, let's go look at the layout in front of his house. We need to see if there's good cover somewhere, where we three can be hiding and jump him as soon as he gets to your car. We also need to confirm if there is some ship sailing at night from Lisbon in the coming days. He might just be the kind of guy who follows such activities as sailings. You need to have the name of an actual ship sailing that night to tell him."

Lou volunteered to check the newspapers for details on ships sailing in the next few nights, while Salvatore would investigate where to get the needed luxury car.

"Good. You two take care of that and Olga and I will go check out what the street looks like out in front of his house, but first I have to see Captain Lourenco and get him to pull surveillance off of Biachi. Hopefully, he can see me on Monday, that gives us Tuesday evening to go check out how the neighborhood looks around eight or nine o'clock at night and then we do it Wednesday night, if we have the right car by then."

"I can find a car by Wednesday," Sally assured the others.

"The timing should work out OK. I'll have to spend most of Tuesday with some big shot flying in that morning from America, but I can dump him on one of the other guys from the office to entertain him Wednesday night."

They had one more round of drinks to toast their plan. Salvatore and Lou figured that Charles and Olga would have no objection to them then leaving immediately, giving the young couple some privacy. Olga went into the bedroom to remove the lovely red dress. She came back wearing only a dressing gown of Charles, which she left half open for Charles' viewing pleasure.

"Hard to say in which outfit I like you better," he teased her.

She came over and sat down on his lap. "I glad you remembered my red dress."

"How could one forget the view of your lovely body in that dress?" Before they wound up back in bed, making love, Charles was curious about one thing. "By the way, anything else bring you to Lisbon this week, or was it just to console me over Mary Beth's death?"

"I have a few small tasks to do while I am here. That is how I explained to everyone in Spain why I needed to come to Lisbon."

Charles knew not to press for info on her NKVD duties, but he was still mildly suspicious that visiting him was the main reason she'd come to town. But he didn't really care what reasons had brought her. He was so glad to see her and hold her.

Neither was in the mood to cook anything that evening, so they walked to a small tavern nearby that served several kinds of soup along with the drinks. Charles loved to find little hole-in-the-wall places such as this one. Mostly because the food was good, but also because he would rarely run into any of his diplomatic colleagues in such moderately-priced establishments. There was really nothing more to discuss about the Biachi operation and he'd already expressed his joy at her being back in town in a dozen different ways, so he decided to give that theme a little break.

They were mostly enjoying watching a young couple in one corner of the restaurant, clearly flirting with one another, and in a far corner, a very elderly couple who ate almost in silence. However, every once in a while, their eyes would meet and a little smile would appear. Given their appearances, Charles guessed that they'd been married forty or even fifty years and were obviously still in love. Olga had noticed them as well. He nodded at the two couples. "Young love, old love. Will that be us fifty years from now?"

She reached over and squeezed his hand, "Maybe. I think that would be very nice, but we first have to get through this war."

"With us working together, how can the Allies possibly lose?" he teased her.

A minute later, she changed the subject and asked, "Who this big shot from Washington who coming to see you? You getting promoted? General Donovan coming to congratulate you on stopping the leak to the Italians?"

"Not quite. He's sending his assistant and I don't think it's to promote me. He's coming to hear the details of how Mary Beth wound up dead."

"But he will be gone before we kill Biachi?"

"No, he's going to go see some places down on the southern coastline of Portugal after he meets with me and then back to Lisbon for another day or two before he heads back to Washington."

"Guess, I better leave Lisbon soon. Probably not good he find Russian spy girl in your bed while he here!" She then gave him one of her classic big smiles.

"Probably not, but I'd like to keep you here as long as possible. Preferably, forever."

## Chapter 15

Charles and Captain Lourenco met for lunch on Monday at one of the most popular downtown restaurants among the Lisbon elites. Everything Lourenco did from the time he got up in the morning till he went to bed at night served a purpose, so Charles assumed that his selecting a very high profile location versus a seaside restaurant on the outskirts of the city, where they had usually eaten in the past was not a mere coincidence. Now that the war seemed to be swinging in the direction of the Allies, presumably the Lisbon Chief of the PVDE wanted important people around the city to see him lunching with an American diplomat, particularly "insiders" who knew what Charles' real job was at the Embassy. Apparently, Lourenco had decided who was going to win the war and would presumably from here on, become ever more amenable to requests from Charles for "small favors."

Charles was happy to play along with the captain's little game, as it served both their agendas. Once other important people in Lisbon saw which way the Portuguese Government wind was blowing, Charles could expect ever more Portuguese citizens to want to get on board the Allied ship before it sailed, as Lourenco was doing.

Charles loudly and warmly greeted his luncheon guest upon his arrival at the restaurant, so that all the other guests would hear and see. "Antonio, how are you?"

"Just fine, my friend, and you?"

The obligatory diplomatic pleasantries continued for another ten minutes, before Charles quietly inquired if the surveillance of Biachi had revealed anything interesting?

"No, not really. My people tell me that he is still simply staying at his house, except for perhaps one quick trip to his Embassy every other day. He's not had visitors, official or female. He is laying very low."

"OK. I didn't know if anything would turn up, but thought it was worth a try. Thank you very much for your assistance. Why don't you just wrap up the coverage tomorrow morning. Let your men get back to more useful assignments."

Antonio was a bit surprised by Charles's suggestion, but indeed, he did have other things for his surveillance teams to be doing, other than watching someone who never left home. "Very well. If anything changes with him, we can resume the coverage at a later date."

"Anything new in Portugal I might find amusing?" inquired Charles over dessert.

Antonio smiled at Charles' phrasing of his request. "Amusing, well, let me think. There is a rumor that two German diplomats have defected from the Lisbon Embassy and have fled to Brazil on a cargo ship."

"A rumor you say. Is anyone missing from the Embassy?"

"Colonel Karsthoff personally assured me that everyone is present or has recently rotated back to Berlin."

"Do you believe him?"

"A return to Berlin would explain why the apartments of two German officials are suddenly unoccupied and most of their clothing gone. However, that then leaves the question of who the two German diplomats we briefly detained boarding a freighter at the port last Wednesday were?"

"Briefly detained?" inquired Charles with a grin.

"Well, they held valid passports and they purchased exit visas right there on the spot from my deputy, so there was really no legal reason to detain them."

"You know, someday this war will end and you might have to go back to living on your actual salary!"

"That's why I'm saving my money now. Besides, is Herr Hitler really going to miss two lowly diplomats? And, the two lovely, Portuguese women they were travelling with would have found the voyage to Rio very boring without them."

"Ah, you are a true romantic." He raised his wine glass in a toast to Antonio. "To your retirement plan, my friend. May it always grow."

Antonio raised his glass. "Thank you. Do let me know if you ever need an exit visa. I give a discount to my friends."

"I'm sure Brazil is very lovely, but I don't see any situation in which I would want to travel there any time soon."

"Oh, you never know. Perhaps one day you might find a lovely young woman who you'd like to take on a slow, romantic journey to Rio de Janeiro."

Charles forced a laugh, but did wonder if perhaps the captain knew about Olga or was simply making a joke. He'd like to someday settle down back in New York with her, but then one never knew. There could be narrow-minded men in Moscow, or Washington, for that matter. It was always good to have a Plan B, and he could think of a lot worse places to live than Brazil.

That evening, Charles stopped on his way home and bought food that he and Olga could prepare at home, and thus avoid any possibility of them being seen together out on the streets of the city. He didn't want to be paranoid, but being prudent was a good step. He was already home when she arrived and was pleased to see that he'd stopped and bought ingredients for dinner. Olga had spent a good bit of the day out doing "things," but didn't offer any specifics and he didn't press.

As they were cooking dinner, he did slide into the topic of how perhaps it was time the two of them gave some thought to their post-war lives.

"You're right, of course, that first we have to finish this war with Hitler, but that day is clearly coming and I'd like to talk about the possibility of us spending the rest of our lives together, probably back in New York City."

She reached over and stroked his cheek. "You don't want to come live in Moscow with me?"

"Granted, I've never been there, but from what I've heard, I think we'd be much happier in Manhattan, particularly with all the destruction that's occurred there during the war."

"That's true. But would your government let an NKVD officer come live in America?"

"Would probably be a lot easier if you were an ex-NKVD officer!"

"You know what one big difference there is between Russians and Americans?"

"What?"

"You Americans always planning years in advance what you will do and become and where you will live. Maybe because life so much more unpredictable in Russia, but we Russians live much more day to day, or maybe month to month at the most. It not that I don't love you muchly and idea of living with you sounds wonderful, but to bother planning so far in future just seems pointless. And, I don't think America and Russia stay friends once war with Hitler is over. I would feel funny living in America. I have been brought up that I should have a purpose in life. Is just living in love enough of a purpose?"

"OK, what about Brazil as an alternative to New York? What if we just moved and lived in a nice third world country like Brazil?"

She laughed. "There you go again, planning years in future, even in different countries."

"OK, enough for now, but do think some about your future and of a future with me in it."

"OK, I dream about it when I sleep. Now, go set table."

"I can do that. Remember, I'll be busy most of tomorrow and into the early evening with my visitor from Washington."

"I remember. I be little busy tomorrow into early evening myself."

On Tuesday morning, Charles was waiting at the Pan American Clipper dock at 9:00 a.m. when the flight from New York via the Azores arrived and down the ramp came Duncan Lee, General Donovan's personal assistant. Charles waved and Lee headed towards him.

"Welcome back to Portugal. How was your flight?"

"Very smooth all the way, although I don't seem to sleep very well on airplanes. That humming of the engines seems to put a lot of people to sleep, but not me. Don't know what it is."

"No matter, you'll have a chance to catch up on your sleep today. You want to go directly to your hotel now?"

"No, let's go to the Embassy and have a chat first. The curiosity to hear all the details on this Biachi affair will keep me awake for a few hours anyway."

Lee quickly fetched his bags and cleared immigration controls with his diplomatic passport. Charles had seen Lee before, but it still surprised him each time what a small, shy-looking man he was. He seemed barely older than Charles himself, but having worked in Donovan's law firm before the war certainly hadn't hurt his career. Soon as the OSS was created, Donovan had immediately brought him in as his personal aide. That might well be a perfect position for him. Charles certainly couldn't see Duncan parachuting behind enemy lines and garroting some sentry in the dead of night.

During the ride to the Embassy, Charles asked Duncan about his past. "I've heard second-hand that you're a descendent of General Robert E. Lee. Is that true?"

Duncan laughed. "Everybody winds up asking that sooner or later. Yes, that is true. I have all sorts of famous Lees of Virginia on my ancestral tree. Although, I was actually born in China. My mother and father were missionaries out there."

"How about you, are there Worthingtons that I should remember from American history?" asked Duncan with what Charles would come to learn was Lee's dry sense of humor.

"No, I don't think so. I grew up out in Chicago, but I think the Worthingtons who moved out to Illinois in the days after the American Civil War probably did so to avoid some arrest warrant back east."

"Yes, well if you look closely at the Lee family history, we have a few who just barely avoided being hung ourselves." They both laughed.

They waited until they were behind the closed door of Charles' office before they got down to the topic of Biachi and the death of Mary Beth. Charles explained in detail how events had progressed and the fact that Mary Beth had committed suicide, not just had an accident that morning after he'd confronted her.

Duncan finished the last of his coffee and sat the mug on the corner of Charles' desk as he rose and began to pace around the office. "I completely agree that you did the right thing in just spreading the rumor that it was simply a tragic automobile accident. It would serve no real purpose to embarrass her family, nor give our enemies over at Army Intelligence any more material to attack General Donovan and the OSS as an organization than they already have. Fortunately, being overseas, you're spared watching all the backstabbing that goes on around Washington DC. If it isn't General Strong of Army Intel, it's that egotistical maniac Hoover complaining that somebody from OSS is stepping onto his turf. I swear to God, he'd prefer that some Nazi or Jap spy would escape arrest rather than have anybody other than the FBI make the arrest, so that they can hold a press conference.

"We hear bits and pieces here in Lisbon, but you're right, it's nice to be close enough to the actual war so that most everybody here at the Embassy focuses on getting the work done, and not worrying about who is going to get credit for accomplishing something."

Duncan continued to pace. "So you think that Mary Beth was the sole source of information getting out of the Station?"

"It certainly looks that way from what she confessed to me. The few things that we know from intercepts that the Italians had learned, she specifically mentioned telling Biachi about those items. I guess it's always hypothetically possible that there is another mole in Lisbon, but I doubt it."

"Good. That's certainly what General Donovan was hoping would be your answer. We're starting the planning now for a cross-Channel invasion of Occupied Europe by next summer and we need to be absolutely certain that there are no more traitors within the OSS. Given the role our organization will play in the intelligence gathering for that invasion and for the deception plans, we can't afford to take any chances if there are any doubts about anyone."

"Agreed."

"By the way, how are your relations with the British here in Lisbon? You exchange much information with them?"

"I've met their chief and a number of their officers. The chief doesn't speak a word of Portuguese, but other than that strange oddity, they seem a qualified bunch of chaps."

"Good. Do you think they're accomplishing anything worthwhile here? I mean, do you think they've made any good recruitments to report on the Germans or anywhere down in the Balkans in those puppet regimes?"

A weird sensation went up Charles' neck. He would have thought that General Donovan would have briefed Lee on the couple of very sensitive double agent cases that involved the MI6 Station in Lisbon – the ones he'd been sent over to learn about from the British themselves. But Lee sounded much more like he was fishing for sensitive information he wasn't being given back in Washington DC. Clearly, Charles thought to himself, this job was truly making him paranoid about everyone. Still, he replied to Duncan's question with a vague, "They're not much on sharing with us." General Donovan had told him to discuss the British cases with no one, and he planned to stick with those orders.

"Oh, well, was just curious." He looked at his watch. "You know I'm suddenly feeling quite sleepy. Perhaps I should go to my hotel and try to get some rest. I presume there's some dinner arranged for this evening."

"Naturally, the Ambassador never lets anyone visiting from Washington over the rank of a sergeant come to town without throwing a dinner in his honor, so he can pump you for the latest stateside gossip, if nothing else!"

"What time is that?"

"It's at 7:00. I'll swing by and pick you up about a quarter till and we can go to his Residence together."

"Excellent. I don't want to trouble you, but I presume we can find someone to run me over to the hotel."

"Absolutely, that's all arranged."

"Oh, by the way, Mary Beth's replacement should be out here in about two weeks. She was being prepared to go to London, but she's happy to come here instead, it being an emergency situation and all."

"That will be good news to everyone who has been helping out here in the front office. I'll take you out to the car and then I'll see you at 6:45 p.m."

By noon, Duncan Lee was registered at the Hotel Britannia and settled in his room. He'd told the Front Desk that he wanted no calls put through to his room until 6:30. He also hung the DO NOT DISTURB card on his door knob. He looked up and down the corridor. Seeing no one, he closed and locked his door and then headed for the back stairway of the hotel, carrying a copy of Shakespeare's *A Midsummer Night's Dream*. Once out on the street, he pulled the brim of his hat low and headed off at a moderate pace. He checked his watch. He still had an hour before he was to be at the rendezvous point, so he needn't rush. Rushing simply brought attention to oneself. It was better to just walk moderately, as if simply out for a midday stroll. He knew Lisbon reasonably well. When he'd been a student at Oxford years earlier, he and some other students had come down to Portugal on a two week summer holiday. He headed in the direction of the central bus station. He stopped at various shops along the way. By one o'clock, he was standing near the sign for buses destined for Oporto.

An attractive woman came up to him and asked, "Are you enjoying William's book?"

*Nazi Gold, Portuguese Wine, and a Lovely Russian Spy*

"Not as much as Hamlet," replied Duncan.

The two then strolled away from the bus station, chatting as if they were old friends.

"Your hair color is different, but you look remarkably like Elizabeth, my 'friend' in Washington with whom I meet regularly."

"Well, then you will feel quite comfortable in talking with me once we get to the apartment. My name is Maria."

They arrived at the safehouse about fifteen minutes later.

"How much time do you have for us to talk before you have to return to your hotel?" she asked.

"I should be back by five o'clock at the latest."

"Good, we will have plenty of time. I do have some questions that I am to ask you, but please, let us begin with anything you have for me. I believe it was you who requested this emergency meeting in Portugal."

"Yes, I did. I was sent on this trip by my boss, General Donovan, on short notice, and so it would not have been possible to meet with my regular contact in Washington on the 15th as normally would occur." Duncan had realized that he shouldn't have used Elizabeth's real name with this Maria, but it was too late to do anything about that now.

"Do you have something to give to me?"

"No, I never pass documents and I hope you were instructed that you are to write nothing down until well after I have left our meeting."

"Yes, I am aware of this rule of yours. I trust that you have nothing very complicated to tell me, so I won't forget anything before I can write it down." Maria thought to herself that this 'rule' of his might make some sense in America, where rules of evidence and law mean something and as a trained lawyer, he was concerned about there being no evidence to use against him in a charge of espionage, but this was Portugal. If the PVDE thought something was going on, they would just beat him and her until at least one confessed. But, if it made the man feel better, fine. He seemed quite a timid, little man.

"Well, what I had just learned before leaving America is that General Donovan is sending a delegation to Moscow for meetings with your service to make plans to coordinate on deception operations that will be part of the plan for the cross-Channel invasion of France next year. The NKVD should know that this is genuine, not part of any trick against Russia. However, Churchill has been sending messages to President Roosevelt proposing that the invasion come as soon as possible and include planning after the landing so that the British and American forces move east as quickly as possible. This is to keep the Soviet Army areas of occupation as far back from central Europe as possible."

"I can see how you know of things within the OSS, but how did you manage to see these messages from Churchill to Roosevelt, that presumably go directly to the White House?"

"I have several friends who work at the White House, with whom I went to school. Sometimes, they tell me things that they think I might like to know, which is how I know about these messages."

"Are they fellow travelers? And what are their names?" This was the NKVD term for people who believed in socialist ideology, but were not formally working for the NKVD or the GRU.

"I don't know if they'd officially qualify as 'fellow,' but they are certainly of a like mind on politics to myself and believe that the Soviet Union should be treated fairly as a true ally against Hitler. As for their names, I don't think they would want to have their names in some NKVD file."

"It would certainly make your report much more believable, if it included the name of who told you of such messages from Churchill."

"If your organization doesn't want to believe my information, they are free to ignore it. Do as you wish, but I will not be providing anyone's name who simply occasionally tells me interesting information in confidence."

Maria backed off. Her instructions from Moscow had warned her that he was at times a difficult source. "I still think it would make for a better report, but we are grateful for whatever you are willing to tell us to help the cause of the Soviet people and of working people everywhere."

Duncan looked very satisfied. He was quite accustomed in life to having things done the way he wanted them done. "Good. Well, I believe you said that you had a few questions for me." He placed emphasis on the word "few" and looked at his watch after his comment. Duncan figured that he knew what information was worth passing to the Soviet Government and about which he had regular access. He had made clear at several previous meetings with his handler back in America that he had no intention of going around and soliciting information from other agencies for which he had no justification. He had no intention of winding up in a federal prison for espionage. This was why he never brought documents with him, nor wanted anything written down by his usual cut out, Elizabeth Bentley, back in Washington. If the FBI suddenly burst in on a meeting with her, he could always simply claim that he was just having a sexual affair with her, if there was no physical evidence to prove otherwise.

Maria asked her questions, to which Lee claimed he had no information whatsoever. She suspected that he might have known at least a little bit of information, but he seemed to consider it a point of pride that only he knew what were valid topics upon which he should report. After five minutes of him repeatedly saying he had no information, she brought the meeting to an end.

"Very well. Thank you for your valuable information. It now best that you return to your hotel. Is there anything you wish me to relay to Elizabeth in connection with your next meeting around Washington DC?"

"No need. We arrange everything between ourselves." He regretted that he had mentioned Elizabeth's true name and worse, that this Maria had remembered it. "Thank you for your assistance. I shall leave first. Will you be returning immediately to Moscow?"

"Yes, I will. I leave tomorrow and in just a few days will be personally reporting your information to the NKVD Chairman." She didn't like this man and if he wanted to be so secretive, she could be as well. It was none of his business that she worked out of Spain and she could tell that by saying she would reporting his information directly to the NKVD chairman, that it would stroke his large ego. "Thank you and goodbye."

Lee left and Maria locked the door immediately behind him. She then took out sheets of paper and started writing down what she had learned from him. If they were going to be arrested, it would have happened by now. She didn't need some upper class American, weekend socialist telling her how to do tradecraft of espionage! She found people like Lee and Philby quite intriguing. Neither of them had probably ever even shaken hands with a real working man in his life, yet they wanted to spy for the worker's state.

After she had written out the report to be sent to Moscow that night, she left the apartment and headed off to meet her radioman to pass him the report. He would take care of encoding it and sending it. Once that duty had been performed, she headed back to Charles' apartment, to await his return and have a final run through for Wednesday night's kidnapping and murder of the Italian.

It was almost ten before Charles arrived from his dinner with his Ambassador in honor of Duncan Lee's visit to Lisbon. Salvatore and Lou had arrived an hour earlier and Salvatore had taken her out to make sure that she knew how to drive the car that he had "borrowed" that afternoon. It was a 1938 Bugatti sports car. It was silver in color and beautiful. She knew it was but a symbol of capitalist pride and wealth, but she did feel a little touch of sorrow that such a beautiful object would be going over a cliff and be destroyed in less than 24 hours. She had handled the car just fine.

Charles finally arrived and the four sat down to discuss the fine details of the operation for the following night.

"Did you get the information about what ship is sailing and when tomorrow night?" Charles inquired of Lou.

"Yeah, we's in luck. The Cristobal, a freighter, mostly carrying dried cod fish, leaves Wednesday night around 10 p.m. for Rio de Janeiro and it does carry a few passengers."

Olga repeated the facts and nodded that she had them memorized.

Lou added the address of a very fancy house on a street full of rich people just a mile or so from Biachi's house. If necessary, she could claim that she had been staying with a friend at that address and was headed for the port when her car had broken down.

"And what about the car?"

"I found dis gorgeous 1938 Bugatti. It's almost a crime to plans on destroying such a car!"

"Will it be missed soon?" asked Charles.

"Naw, I gots it outta a rich guy's garage and he's off in England till da end of da month."

Charles walked them through the plan one last time and then there was really nothing left to say. The boys went back to their little hotel and Charles and Olga got undressed and climbed into bed. They'd both had a long day and were tired. Neither was even interested in sex. She just curled up in his arms and was sound asleep in a matter of minutes.

Charles got a lucky break on Wednesday morning when Duncan Lee announced that he'd decided to head on down to the Algarve region of the country in the south that afternoon, instead of traveling on Thursday. That meant that Charles would be completely free that night for "Plan Biachi."

## Chapter 16

On Wednesday morning, Charles went to the Embassy at the usual hour and had just a few minutes more with Duncan Lee before his Washington visitor caught the train to go to the southern coast of the country. Olga vaguely alluded to conducting a little more business in the city, but said she would be back to the apartment no later than 4:00 p.m. Salvatore and Lou spent the morning exploring once more the coastal road north of the city, still searching for the perfect quiet spot at which to send Biachi over a cliff. Salvatore had carefully been wearing gloves when he "borrowed" the Bugatti and had made Olga wear them as well when she had her driving lesson Tuesday night, so there would be no link to the "team" even if the car didn't catch fire when it landed down on the shore. They always found waiting on the day of a hit to be the hardest part of the operation.

They had settled on 7:45 as a good time for Olga to approach Biachi's front door. Charles had made them change it from precisely 8:00 because of some training class he'd had where they told him never to plan events on the hour or half-hour. In this situation, it might seem odd to Biachi that a stranded motorist comes to his door precisely at the top of the hour. It would be fairly dark by that hour, and most people would be home by then and street traffic would be very light. Olga had put on her fancy red dress and had carefully prepared her hair and her makeup. She'd also placed a small derringer in a home-made holster on the inside of her upper left thigh – just in case things didn't go well at the front door. The men put several expensive suitcases, which had been bought the day before, in the Bugatti.

The three men dressed in suits, nice dark ones. Salvatore claimed that a man in a nice suit and tie always attracted less attention, even if seen hiding in bushes, than a man dressed in casual clothes. The latter might be considered a mugger or a thief, but the well-dressed man, even if hiding in the shrubbery might be taken for a drunk or at worst, a detective trying to catch a cheating husband. They followed Olga in Salvatore's car, leaving Charles' at his apartment. They didn't want a car or a license plate associated with the Embassy to be seen near the scene of the upcoming crime.

As she neared Biachi's home, she pulled over and let the men in their car pass her, so they could have a few minutes to stash their car and get in place in the bushes near the spot where she would soon stop with her "car failure." At 7:45 she pulled up to the curb at the end of the drive of Biachi's house. She killed the engine, but then started it up several times, but immediately shut it off each time – just on the odd chance that Biachi was somewhere where he could see or hear the car. She wanted it to genuinely appear as if she was having car trouble. She then exited the car and walked up the driveway towards his front door. It was only some 50 or 60 feet to the three steps that led up to a medium-sized porch. Fortunately, he had the porch light on, so it would be easy for him to see her through the security peep hole. Just before ringing the door bell, she made sure that the top front of her dress was pulled low so that her large breasts were at least half on display. No one came to the door within twenty seconds of her first ring, so she pressed the button again. She heard it ring, so she knew it was working. This time she could see that lights in the hallway beyond the front door had been turned on. A few seconds later, she could discern that an eyeball had come up to the peep hole. She gave a nice smile and said loudly in English, "Hello, I need help."

A few moments later, a handsome man in his early thirties opened the door. He appeared to be Italian and stood tall and straight. Before he could speak, she said quite rapidly to him, "Do you speak English? I'm having car trouble and desperately need help." She pointed haphazardly over her shoulder at the end of his driveway and then just smiled.

He smiled at her. "Yes, I speak English. What has happened to your car?"

"Oh, who knows with that Italian piece of crap. It spends as much time in a repair shop as it does out on the road. It just died on me and it won't start. But I'm on the way to the dock and just have to catch my ship for Brazil tonight. Do you know anything about cars?" She and Charles had spent thirty minutes carefully practicing these sentences, in which she carefully used articles of speech and tried to sound as American as she could manage.

He smiled broadly at her and didn't even try to conceal his staring at her breasts. "I'm not a mechanic, but perhaps I could be of assistance to you. Would you like to come inside and have a drink while I go out and examine that Italian piece of crap?" He gestured towards the hallway.

"Thank you for the offer of a drink, but I think I had better come out with you to the car while you check it. If you can find the problem, perhaps I'll have a quick drink afterwards. My ship doesn't sail for a couple of hours yet, but I do need to know that I will be able to get there in my car." She put on her biggest smile.

"Of course. Let me just grab a torch so that I can see better and we'll go see together what might be the problem." He returned just twenty seconds later. He had a torch in his hand, but she also noticed that there now seemed to be a slight bulge in his right-hand coat pocket. She suspected that he had added a gun to his needed tools for checking her car. A very careful man, she thought to herself. He closed the door and took her by the arm to help her down the steps. "And what is your name?'

"I'm Suzy, originally of New York City, but I have been living over in Spain for the last couple of years. Unfortunately, my husband just died a month ago and now I'm taking a trip to Brazil, to help me get over that tragedy. I was afraid to go on a ship by myself – you hear such terrible stories – but my friends who live just up the road with whom I've been staying for a few days told me that it would be just fine."

"I'm sure that you will be quite safe; although I am sad that I meet such a beautiful woman, and she is about to leave the country." He continued to hold her arm as they walked down the driveway.

"You have a bit of an accent. Are you Portuguese?" she asked.

"He laughed. No, I am Italian. The people who make those crap automobiles!" He was now close enough to see that it was a Bugatti sports car that she was driving. "Normally, that is a very fine machine, but let us have a look."

She giggled like a 16 year old girl. "Oh, I am sorry. If I'd known you were an Italian, I would have never made such a comment about Italian cars. Do forgive me." She gave his arm a squeeze.

They reached the car. He cautiously looked around the car and up and down the street. Charles was the closest, but even he was a good twenty feet away. He opened the driver's door and slid in behind the wheel. "Let me just check a few things, like whether you have gasoline." She giggled and replied, "Oh dear me, I'm going to feel like such a fool if I've run out of gasoline." He handed her the large torch. "Here, hold this and shine the light onto the dashboard for me."

"Certainly." She took the torch as directed. She heard just a little rustle of braches of a bush, which was Charles starting to head for the car. Unfortunately, so did Biachi. He was starting to turn his head in the direction of the sound, when Olga smashed the foot long torch into the side of his head. He went out like a light.

All three of her co-conspirators had now reached the car, but quickly saw there was nothing for them to do. Biachi was slumped over in the seat.

"That was quite a swing," commented Charles.

"I told you once that I used to work on tractors. Was no problem." She had lapsed back in to her Russian-accented English.

Salvatore and Lou lifted Biachi out of the car and moved him over to the passenger seat. They then tied his hands and feet, in case he started to wake up during the ride. Then Salvatore got behind the wheel. Amazingly, the car started right up. Olga, Charles and Lou went and got into Lou's car and both vehicles started slowly and quietly down the street. No reason to disturb the neighbors, or give them anything to remember to possibly tell the police in a few days, if they came around. Soon, they were headed out on the coastal road.

Having reached the chosen, deserted spot, they returned Biachi to behind the steering wheel. Salvatore told Olga and Charles to wait off to the side. "Leave's dis to da professionals."

Lou held open Biachi's mouth while Salvatore poured the brandy down his throat and splashed some on his clothes and face. They tied his hands to the steering wheel with some light silk rope. The brandy started to revive Biachi. Salvatore had brought along a piece of wood, which he used to depress the clutch and a shorter one soaked in gasoline, which he used to jam the accelerator down. Lou started the engine and put the gear stick into second.

Salvatore called over to Charles. "Youse got anything to say to dis bum before he departs?"

Charles came over to the car. Biachi was coming around, wondering at first why his head hurt so much, then why were his hands tied. He looked up into Charles' face. Lou had gone around to the back of the small car, ready to give it a push to help get it moving.

Charles looked hard for a few moments into Biachi's eyes. "Mary Beth sends her regards."

If anyone wanted to know what real fear looked like on a man's face, Biachi's was a perfect example. Charles nodded to Salvatore. The latter set on fire first the wooden stick holding the gas pedal down, then the silk rope. The fire would take care of evidence that this might have been a staged accident. A split second later, he pulled out the wooden piece holding the clutch pedal down. The Italian sports car lept forward. It had gained a speed close to 30 by the time it crashed through the guard rail and went over the cliff. Biachi was screaming like a small child who'd fallen off his bicycle.

All four of them felt like justice had been served, maybe not courtroom justice, but justice after all. "Anyone hungry besides me?" asked Olga. "I'm starving."

"I could go for some pasta," replied Salvatore. He was beginning to like Olga more and more. They headed for their car. It had started to lightly rain. Charles couldn't remember the title of the novel he'd read years before in a college literature class in which rain started to fall after a death, but which he remembered seemed quite fitting in the novel and now here in real life. Salvatore was thinking how the rain would help cover up the fact that there were no braking skid marks on the pavement, which normally there would be, if a driver had found himself hurtling towards a guard rail in front of a cliff. Olga hurried to the car; she didn't want her dress ruined. Lou liked rain. He walked slowly over to their car with his head turned up to the heavens, not thinking of anything in particular.

The death of Italian Assistant Air Force Attaché Biachi made the Lisbon newspapers two mornings later. Part of the article even addressed the fact that this was the second death of a foreign diplomat along that stretch of coastal road within as many weeks and questioned if any safety features needed to be improved on that highway.

Around mid-morning, PVDE Captain Lourenco phoned Charles. "Have you seen this morning's local newspaper?"

"Yes, I read it over breakfast. Anything in particular I should focus on in today's paper?"

"I thought you might have noticed the article on the front page about the accidental car death of Mr. Biachi."

"Oh, of course, I noticed that. I thought you might have been referring to some nugget of information more buried elsewhere in the paper."

"Quite a coincidence, isn't it? The death of your secretary, who'd been acquainted with Biachi, along that road and now he has an accident along that same stretch of highway."

"The newspaper didn't identify specifically where along the coastal road that he had his accident, so I couldn't notice whether it was a coincidence or not, but if you're telling me that it was the same part of the same road where Mary Beth died, then yes, that is a coincidence. The newspaper said that the car caught on fire after it crashed. Is that true?"

"Yes, it is. Fortunately, the impact of hitting the beach from that height probably instantly killed him, so he would not have suffered from being burned alive."

"Too bad he didn't suffer," responded Charles. "He wasn't my favorite person in Portugal, you know."

"Yes, I know. You want to hear something peculiar about this accident?"

"Certainly. What?"

"Biachi was driving a stolen car when he died."

"You mean he was a car thief as well as an Assistant Air Attache?"

"Possibly, but a woman came to the Traffic Police this morning after seeing the paper and she told them that she was supposed to meet Biachi at his home at 9:00 p.m. the night he died. But that he never answered the door, so she finally gave up and went home after about fifteen minutes. Seems odd that he would be out driving around in a stolen vehicle just an hour before he had a lovely female guest coming to his home for drinks."

"I suppose it does. Any idea of why he was out? Perhaps, he needed to procure some good wine or some food for his anticipated guest?"

"But in a stolen car?"

"You sure it wasn't his? Perhaps he'd just recently bought it or had only borrowed it?"

"Anything is possible. Well, we'll be investigating his death. You're a very clever fellow, Mr. Worthington. I just thought I'd see if you had any insights on how his death might have occurred?"

"No, not really, but then I haven't given it much thought, as I think the world is a better place without Biachi in it."

"That may be true. Well, I suppose I should get back to my duties. Perhaps, we can arrange dinner one night next week?"

"I'm sure we can find a mutually good night. Give me a call when you have a specific date in mind."

"I shall. Good-bye for now."

"Good-bye," replied Charles as he was hanging up the phone.

He then leaned back in his office chair. It didn't seem like anything to worry about. Antonio was clearly just fishing. He could suspect all he wanted, but he had no evidence to go on. Charles checked his watch. Duncan Lee should be back in town in the early afternoon from the south of the country. They'd probably have dinner together and then Lee would be leaving the following day to fly back to America. He debated whether to even tell Lee about Biachi's death, but finally decided that given Biachi's role in the recent death of Mary Beth, that Duncan would find it odd if he eventually learned of it and Charles hadn't even mentioned it that day.

Charles had invited several other Station officers to the dinner, which was to be held in the restaurant of Lee's hotel. That would keep Duncan from having any real opportunity to privately discuss Biachi's death with Charles, or any possible link to Mary Beth. As it turned out, Lee's train was late, so Charles was spared seeing him or talking to him one-on-one at all that afternoon.

At one point, over drinks before they all sat down to dinner, Charles just casually mentioned that there'd been another car accident of a diplomat out on the coastal road. He added, "It was the Italian, Biachi, so perhaps there is a God."

"Have the police investigated the accident yet?"

"I heard second-hand that they have and concluded that it was a case of drunk driving; they found a half-empty bottle of brandy in the car and the medical coroner concluded that Biachi had been drinking."

Duncan smiled slightly. "Well, I guess that pretty well closes my security investigation into the leaks that we'd been having. And, yes, I guess there is a God."

"So my mother always told me," Charles replied, then turned to talk to someone else. He wasn't certain if Lee wasn't just trying to be funny or if he suspected that Charles had had a hand in Biachi's death, but even if the latter, he gave no indication that he cared or planned on investigating anything further. That was a relief. He was glad they did it, had no doubt that Biachi deserved it and now he could consider the whole matter closed.

When he arrived back at his apartment, he found Olga already there, wearing a pair of her work-style pants and one of his flannel shirts. Even in such ill-fitting clothes, she looked beautiful and sensual. She was on the couch, drinking some coffee and thumbing through some of the old American magazines Charles had in his home. She did like looking at what women were wearing in America. They were very impractical, but they did look pretty. She remembered some of the nice clothes she had worn when she was in Manhattan. Those days with Charles, dancing with him at the Roseland Ballroom, lunch at the Harvard Club.

"How was your dinner with your visitor?"

"Nothing special. The only important news is that he doesn't seem to care about the death of Biachi. Maybe he believes it was an accident, or maybe he thinks I had something to do with it, but either way, he doesn't seem to care."

"That is good. That all behind you now." She indicated for him to come over and sit down next to her on the couch. "I have little news for you that I learn today and I share with you – just for our private intelligence service." She gave him a grin.

"OK, super agent Olga, what is your information?"

"Have you heard anything about Germans looking for cargo ships to travel under to Brazil?"

Now it was his turn to smile. She still had trouble with certain participles in English, like on, by, under and with. "Not really, other than two German diplomats recently fled from their Embassy and caught a ship with their Portuguese girlfriends to Rio de Janeiro."

"No, this not past trip, but planning for future trips and many people."

"Where did you learn this?"

"Many dock workers are socialists. They sometimes hear things and pass along. According to one man, some Portuguese banker been asking around about cargo ships who would take passengers to Brazil and he claim they all Swiss who want to travel quietly."

"That is interesting, though I'm not sure exactly what it means? Did that dock worker know the name of the Portuguese banker making these arrangements?"

"No, he not know, but I don't think any rich Swiss people travel on freighters and want to keep their travel secret."

"No, that doesn't sound very Swiss, does it? Any chance of finding out anything more?"

"Not this trip. Maybe next month when I return."

This was the first Charles had heard anything about her departing and obviously his face showed disappointment.

She leaned towards him and stroked his face. "I will be here two-three more days. No need to become sad already."

"This gets harder every time you come here. One of these visits, I'm not going to let you leave," he teased her.

She gave him that "wise mother to a naïve son" look. "That is way life is now. We both have important work to do. And mine is mostly over in Spain."

"Doing what, working so that Stalin can replace Franco as dictator? Doesn't it bother you working for a man who has killed millions of his own people – your people? If word about this has gotten as far as America, surely you must know about the camps out in Siberia and about all the people who just disappeared in the night." He regretted saying what he did as soon as he'd said it, as it probably wasn't going to help the situation, but he was tired of watching Olga devote her life to a cause run by a mass murderer.

Her nationalistic pride had been attacked and she didn't like it, even coming from a man she loved. "For man who never been in Russia, you seem to think you know very much what go on there." She got up and went to the kitchen. Running away from an argument wasn't her style. He had a gut feeling.

"You know the truth about Stalin, don't you? You know about all the people who have disappeared, even the thousands of your fellow NKVD officers who have been killed."

She stood for many seconds facing away from him. When she finally turned around to face him, he saw that she was crying.

"Yes, yes, many people have had to die for the revolution, for the cause, to build a better society. Even my husband had to die so we can build scientific socialism in Russia. He had become counter-revolutionary. I learned the truth of what happened to him after I left New York." She was practically shouting and the tears continued to roll down her cheeks. Charles remembered from Manhattan days that she had gotten word that he had died fighting the Nazis.

"You don't really believe that about your husband do you? Nor about the millions of other people who've died. If a government has to kill that many of its own citizens, then it isn't much of a government. Stalin is just a paranoid murderer." He stepped forward and took her in his arms.

She finally stopping crying enough so that she could speak again, almost in a whisper. "Yes, but if he is monster, then everything that I have believed in for almost all of my life is lie. The whole purpose of my life, since I was little girl and became a Young Pioneer, has been to build this new society for Russia, by fixing tractors and then by working for NKVD. If I believe these things are true about what happened in 1930s, then my life has no value and my soul is worthless."

Charles was a bit at a loss as to what to say to her, but drawing from his own hard experiences as a young boy in Chicago, he finally tried to console her. "All it means is that you have to find a new purpose for your life. Not everyone solves big political issues, or brings world peace. What if your real purpose in life is simply to have a good family – to love a husband and help raise good children?"

"Maybe," was her only response. She lapsed into silence, just continuing to clutch him very tightly. He was afraid to even move with her to the couch and break the spell. He'd known her long enough to sense when it was best to leave her alone with her thoughts. He lost track of how long they'd stood there – 10 or 15 minutes at least – then she pulled back from him and simply said, "Let's go to bed. Hold me all night, please."

They disrobed and crawled into bed. There was no kissing, no sex. She simply curled up into his arms and put her head on his chest. Charles fell asleep in that position and when they woke up some eight hours later, she was still in his arms. There was nothing more said in the morning about Stalin or of her needing a purpose in life. She was as happy and chipper as he'd ever seen her. She fixed them breakfast while Charles showered and shaved and dressed to go to the Embassy.

As he sat down at the table and saw the wonderful breakfast, he teased her by saying, "You know I'm getting spoiled by these daily meals by you. I might tell Liliana that she's going to have to improve her cooking when you're away, or I will start looking for a replacement for her."

Olga laughed. "How much you pay this Liliana?"

"Pay her? We just have a barter system." He grinned.

She picked up a piece of roll and threw it at him. Then she stood and came around the table and kissed him passionately. "Does she look as good in your robe as I do?"

"I never let her wear my robe."

She stuck out her tongue at him. "I am leaving now. You can have Liliana clean table."

He smacked her on the butt as she walked away from him. "Do you have plans for today?"

"Just few things I need to do, then I go see my radio man and learn if there are any new messages for me from Center – then I will have better idea of when I will return to Spain."

"OK. Just in case you have to leave tomorrow, tonight, let's go out to a nice restaurant, somewhere out along the beach and celebrate."

"What we are celebrating?"

"Well, given that there is world war going on, just the fact that we are alive and we are in love."

She gave him a wonderful smile; the kind of smile that could keep a man going for months when he wasn't able to see his girl because of a war. "Yes, those good reasons we celebrate."

She went in to the bedroom to put on clothes. Before she put on a turtleneck blue sweater, she took from her suitcase a Star of David necklace and put it around her neck. The sweater hid it from view. She stopped once more on her way out to kiss Charles goodbye. "See you tonight my love."

He liked the sound of that – "my love."

Charles arrived home at 5:00 p.m., accompanied by Salvatore. When he'd heard earlier in the afternoon that Olga might be leaving soon, he'd suggested he come by just for a quick farewell drink, before the two young lovers went off to their romantic dinner.

He unlocked his front door and shouted, "Hello! Make sure you are dressed, I have Sally with me." He noticed that there were no lights on in the apartment. Once he turned several on, he noticed the note on the table: Had to suddenly leave this afternoon, so could catch truck ride back to Spain. Be back in few weeks. Take care of my red dress while I away! Love, Olga.

He saw her red dress draped over a chair. Amazing how he could go from being so happy to being so sad in the time it took to read three sentences on a piece of paper. He felt like crying.

Salvatore could see the look on his young friend's face. "I gotta use the can. Be back in a minute." He wanted to give him some privacy.

When Salvatore returned several minutes later, Charles had recovered his composure and had gotten out a bottle of good Irish whiskey he'd been saving for a special occasion. He'd poured two glasses and had already started on his.

Sally lifted his in a toast, "To Miss Olga. May she travel safe."

They clinked classes. "Youse really in love with dis gal, ain't ye?"

"Yes, I believe I am, but we just can't catch a break. I wish this stupid war was over."

"Well, I suspects there's lots of people share dat opinion with youse. Listen, dis will all work out. I knows women and I can tell dat she's really in love with you."

"I hope you're right, because life just doesn't seem complete without her in my life." Charles picked up the bottle and poured both of them another round.

## Chapter 17

First thing the following morning, Charles phoned Captain Lourenco to make an appointment for as soon as possible. It was 9:00 a.m. when he called and learned, not much to his surprise, that the captain normally arrived about 10:30. Charles wondered if warfare over the centuries around the Mediterranean had also been conducted on such a leisurely time schedule as the PVDE Headquarters maintained. Lourenco returned his call just before 11:00.

"Charles, how are you?"

"Good Antonio, how are you?"

"Fine. I understand that you have something urgent to discuss with me."

"Something has just come to my attention and I'd like to get your opinion on it, before anything happens. When are you free for a cup of coffee today?"

"I have a lunch at 1:15, but if you'd like to meet me at the Café Antonio at 12:30, that would work for me."

"That would be fine. Tell me, do you own this café, since it is named after you?"

The captain laughed. "No, not after me. After Antonio the Sailor of the 16th century! Me, I get seasick just walking close to the ocean! I'll see you at 12:30. You know where this café is located?"

"I'll find it. I come from a long line of great navigators!"

Charles then called several of his officers in and tasked them with inquiring of any of their assets who had anything to do with shipping or the port to see if anyone had heard of this rumor of Olga's about Germans looking for passage to Brazil.

When he arrived at the Café Antonio, the namesake was already seated in a quiet back corner of the place.

After the opening banter, Charles turned to business. "I remember you telling me about those two German Embassy officials who were sailing for Brazil. Have you heard any rumors about more Germans looking to book similar passage?"

"No, I don't think so, but I can have my people make some discreet inquiries around the port. Is this story from a good source of yours?"

"Not really a source, more of just a rumor that reached me. Also, it's supposedly a Portuguese banker who's doing the arranging for these Germans."

"Ah, that makes it a different situation. That makes me wonder if someone is sending money as well as people to South America. My prime minister doesn't like when people try to smuggle money out of our poor country."

"Without paying an 'export fee' you mean, to his government?"

"Exactly!"

"Perhaps this is just a rumor, but if there is some kernel of truth to it, I thought it best that I passed this along to you as soon as possible. With the war turning against Germany, there might be more and more people trying to escape."

"Very much a possibility. And some of them might be trying to take things with them besides their clothes!" Lourenco smiled broadly. "I hear that all sorts of artwork and bank gold reserves have disappeared from the countries that the Nazis conquered. Moving to South America with wealth would be a lot more pleasant for Germans than arriving down there poor!"

"No doubt. But I'm sure that your government wouldn't allow stolen property to pass through Portugal. There's no 'license' a German could buy to export stolen goods is there?"

"None whatsoever."

"I and my government are glad to hear that."

Less than a mile away, Colonel Karsthoff, in civilian clothes, was having a coffee with Mr. Pedro Da Silva of the Espirito de Santo Bank. The banker gave Karsthoff an envelope which contained all the details of the accommodations for the "visitors" and the names of the ships and their captains who had agreed to discreetly carry passengers and cargo to Brazil towards the end of November.

"Of course, the dates of sailing can only be approximate, this far in advance, but the actual dates will likely be within a week or so of those listed here."

"Excellent work, my dear friend. I should be able to give you at least a week's advance notice as to when the travelers will arrive in Lisbon."

"That will be satisfactory."

Karsthoff slid a plump envelope across the table to the banker. "This is a down payment towards the total cost and associated fees for this travel. We will settle up at the time of the sailings."

"Very good." He then looked Karsthoff directly in the eyes. "Is there any chance you might be one of the people sailing to Brazil?"

The colonel looked quite offended. "Of course not. My duty is here in Lisbon. Why do you ask such a question?"

"No offense intended by my question. It's just that the passenger accommodations on one of the ships are much nicer than the others. If you were going, I would book you on that one."

"That's very considerate of you, but I will definitely not be going."

Upon return to the German Embassy later that day, Karsthoff wrote a letter to Ewald and then sealed it in an envelope with a wax seal, which he then put in another envelope similarly sealed. He then called in one of his junior officers who was to leave late that evening with the courier pouch for Berlin. Not only did he trust him implicitly, but he had also subtly hinted to the young officer what would happen to his wife and young child should anything happen to the letter enroute to Ewald. It was to simply go in his pocket, not in the official pouch.

Around 3:00 pm, Charles' sweet tooth was calling to him. He was also in the middle of trying to write some obligatory quarterly report, which was incredibly boring to do. His solution to both was to put down his pen, put on his jacket and announce that he was going out for a bit. He knew of a wonderful little shop down on the Avenida de Republica that made Italian gelato. At that time of the day, the shop was fairly deserted and once he had obtained his tasty treat, he made himself comfortable in a small alcove with a window view of the street. Just a few minutes after he entered, an attractive woman came in, apparently with the same gelato craving as had called to Charles. She seemed vaguely familiar, but he couldn't recall who she was, until he heard her speak. It was the woman who had been with Karsthoff that day that they had rescued him from being robbed.

Once she had her cup of the delicious Italian treat, she had headed for the same alcove. She was practically in the motion of sitting down before she noticed that someone was already tucked away at the table. Finally seeing that the table was occupied, she'd mumbled "desculpe" and had started to turn away when Charles spoke, "Fraulein Elizabeth."

She quickly looked back, somewhat startled, but then recognized the American. "Ah, Mr. Worthington, how are you?"

He smiled and pointed at his half-eaten bowl. "Much better now. I see that you also have an appreciation for gelato."

She smiled and said, "Yes, I discovered this treat when I first got to Lisbon and have become quite an addict while here. Sometimes, in the middle of the afternoon, when I need a little break from my work, I sneak off here and indulge my 'sweet tooth,' as we say in German."

Charles gestured at the other chair. "Please join me. We have the same phrase in America – sweet tooth." Charles suspected that his ambassador wouldn't quite approve of him enjoying gelato with the enemy, but since she had been responsible for his rescue from muggers that day, he figured she was a special case. He doubted that he was going to undermine the Allied war effort by sharing a table with the woman while they enjoyed their gelato!

She took a seat and stuck a spoon into her cool treat. "Have you avoided falling asleep on any more park benches?" she inquired with a smile.

He liked her sense of humor. "Yes, I learned my lesson that day when you and Colonel Kartshoff came to my rescue. Thank you once again."

"May I offer my belated condolences about your secretary. That was such tragic news. Had she been with you long?"

"Yes, she was here when I'd arrived about a year and a half ago."

"The newspaper didn't say. Was she married or have children?"

"No. She had a brother and her parents, but she'd never gotten around to a husband."

"Ah, that is too bad. It does seem rather ironic to die from a silly auto accident, in the middle of a world war." She seemed to regret having said that as soon as she'd completed the sentence. "I'm sorry for such an inappropriate comment. My Portuguese is not very good and sometimes what I say doesn't come out very good."

"No, there was nothing wrong about your comment, and as for your Portuguese…some of the things that slip out of my mouth are truly horrible. I can always tell when I've said something in Portuguese quite wrong when the person I'm talking to shows a slight smile, but they're too polite to tell me what incorrect phrase I've mistakenly used." They both laughed as she nodded in agreement to that phenomenon.

Charles had finished his lemon gelato and decided he should get back to his Embassy. He was also running out of things to say to a member of the enemy's embassy. "I trust Colonel Karsthoff is well. Do give him my regards."

She laughed. "I shall. He will find this quite amusing." She extended her hand for Charles to shake. He did so and wished her a pleasant afternoon.

By the time he'd reached the door, he'd reached a decision. This encounter was never going into any report to Washington!

The following several weeks were quite uneventful. Captain Lourenco's people had turned up no information about Germans booking secret passages to South America, other than the usual crazy rumors about how Goring, or even Hitler himself, had been seen boarding a ship at midnight disguised as an Irish priest. The war in Italy continued going well for the Allies, as they pushed ever further in to the northern part of the country. The Soviets were claiming great victories on the Eastern Front, but Charles put about as much faith in Russian news releases as he did German ones. Hearing reports about Russia, however, did make him think of how soon he might see Olga again. Her departure note had mentioned that she might be back in a few weeks. He hoped it might be sooner. He missed her terribly.

At the start of November, the weather in Lisbon had finally turned to its normal fall behavior -- cool and rainy with heavy cloud cover and strong winds.

On a Monday afternoon, three men arrived unannounced at Colonel Karsthoff's residence. They wore rather cheap-looking suits and identical grey cloth trenchcoats. Once the butler had opened the front door, they showed him their identification cards as being with the German Security Service, the SD, and demanded to immediately see Colonel Karsthoff. He escorted them to the upstairs library where Karsthoff was seated before a good flame in the fireplace.

Once the butler had opened the door, the three waited for no introductions. They simply pushed past him. One stayed by the door, with his right hand in his coat pocket, giving the appearance of a man holding a gun in it, in case anyone resisted. The other two strode over to Karsthoff, who had risen from his chair, to see what was happening and had drawn himself up quite straight in his uniform. The slightly elder visitor, a man of about 40, had a face that appeared as though he'd been in many street fights earlier in life.

"I am Oberfuhrer Otto Schmidt of the SD. I am here to replace you as the head of all intelligence operations in Portugal." He didn't bother taking out and showing his identity card.

Karsthoff remained at attention. "Upon whose orders are you replacing me?"

Schmidt didn't reply. He simply moved over closer to the warmth of the fireplace and was removing his coat.

"Upon the orders of whom are you making this claim? I have received no such notification from Abwehr Headquarters."

"Upon the orders of Brigadefuhrer Schellenberg."

"I take my orders from Admiral Canaris, head of the Abwehr, not from the SD."

"Colonel, you are now taking your orders from me." The other SD man placed his right hand in his trenchcoat pocket, which clearly held a gun.

"Shall we phone Admiral Canaris in Berlin and clear up this misunderstanding?" suggested Karsthoff.

"There is no need to phone anyone. You are to be flown tomorrow to Berlin. Once you're there, feel free to phone whomever you wish."

"Am I to understand that I am under arrest?"

"You are, I believe, being transferred to the Russian Front, but if you interfere with my activities, I am, of course, allowed to simply shoot you here and now."

At just this moment, Elizabeth came through the open door of the library, carrying a silver tray with a pot of tea. She saw at once that something serious was underway, particularly with two unknown men with their hands clutching guns in their pockets. She proceeded, without really thinking, to bring the tea pot over to the table by Colonel Karsthoff. He took the pot from the tray and poured some of it into a cup from which he'd already been drinking. He then brought it up to his lips and took a sip.

"Ouch! He shouted. "Didn't you check the temperature of the tea, you stupid cow?" He threw the cup on the floor, shattering it by her feet. "Get out of here and close the door on your way out. And inform the chef that there will be no dinner plans." Totally bewildered by his conduct, she looked at his face. She'd heard his voice of anger, but his face was fleetingly a glance of love.

"Yes, Herr Colonel. I'm terribly sorry." She then rapidly turned and headed for the door. She was afraid that the unknown man by the door might stop her, but he didn't move. She heard Karsthoff say, "Since you're taking over, I suggest you find a new secretary as well. This one has been quite hopeless."

She still didn't know exactly who the three visitors were, but she knew that she'd never see Ludovico again, at least not alive. She closed the door behind her as she'd been instructed and returned to the kitchen. She quickly grabbed her outer coat and left via the kitchen door. She started the car and drove away from the house, somewhat surprised. She interpreted his comment about informing the chef about no dinner plans, that she was to somehow inform Admiral Canaris about what had happened.

She drove directly to the German Embassy. She inquired of the German guard at the front door whether any special visitors had arrived that morning. He told her that he'd been on duty since 8:00 a.m. and that no one other than regular Embassy employees had arrived. She was relieved to hear that. She proceeded to the radio room on the top floor of the building. She was good friends with most of the code clerks who worked on that floor. The Abwehr had a small room separate from the others within the Communications Center. She tried to appear calm as she entered the Abwehr section.

"Hello, Werner. How are you today?"

Werner didn't bother to stand, but did turn her way so that he could get a good look at her body. "I'm excellent, and how are you?"

She gave him a big smile. "Much better since seeing your handsome face, Werner," she said with a blatantly flirtatious tone to it.

He knew she was about to ask him for some favor, but he didn't care, if it got him that sort of treatment from her.

"I forgot to do something yesterday for Colonel Karsthoff and must take care of it immediately. Can you manage to put a phone call through to Colonel Ewald Gehlen back at Abwehr Headquarters?" She'd walked over and was standing with her hands on the sergeants shoulders. She was giving him the most wonderful smile.

"I believe that is possible, though it might take just a few minutes."

"There's no rush. I'll wait. You don't mind if I just wait here with you?"

"No, not at all. Would you like some coffee while you wait?" He started to rise, to go over to a coffee pot in the corner of the room.

She stopped him. "I'll get us both a cup, while you place the call." She poured two cups of coffee while he worked on making the call, impressing upon every operator he had to deal with that this was a priority call for the German Ambassador!

After about five minutes, a smile came to his face. "Colonel Gehlen is coming on the line now, Fraulein Elizabeth." He handed over the phone to her.

"Oh, thank you so much. Werner, one more little favor. Your coffee is a little bitter for me. Would you run down to the cafeteria and get me some sugar, and see if they have any buttered rolls left today?" She'd already undone several buttons of her blouse and leaned forward while she made her request. With the lovely view of her half-exposed breasts in front of him, Werner would have gone out and milked a cow to get the liquid and churned it into butter for her roll.

"Yes, of course, gladly." He closed the door behind him as he left.

"Colonel Gehlen?"

"Speaking."

"This is Colonel Karsthoff's secretary calling from Lisbon."

A lovely vision flashed through Gehlen's mind. "Yes, what can I do for you?"

"I was told to inform you that Colonel Karsthoff's replacement safely arrived today and that he will be flying back to Berlin tomorrow. All is fine, but he said to tell you that with such little time before he departs, he won't be able to finish several reports to you. He has finished the arrangements, but he won't have the opportunity to write any reports."

There was a long silence, but then she heard Colonel Gehlen's voice smoothly replying, "Not to worry. There's no rush on the written reports. They're not particularly important anyway. Can you pass that along to him?"

"No, I don't think I'll have an opportunity to speak with him again before he leaves. He's quite tied up with his visitors and his replacement."

"No matter. If there are any last minute questions, are you available to clarify small points?"

"Yes, I think I should be able to do so. Probably best to reach me at my home telephone number. I'm going to take the next few days off from work."

"Very good, Fraulein Elizabeth. Thank you for your call."

The line then went dead, just as Werner returned with a mound of buttered rolls on a tray and a massive cup of sugar.

Once she'd consumed several of the rolls and let Werner enjoy the view of her breasts for several more minutes, she departed the Embassy, without even going by her office in the Abwehr section of the Embassy. She needed to go somewhere and think. She headed to the gelato store. Even though the weather didn't really make one desire a cold dessert, it would be a nice quiet place to ponder what to do next.

# Chapter 18

# Berlin

As soon as Colonel Gehlen finished the phone call with Fraulein Elizabeth, he headed to Admiral Canaris' office to apprise him of the development in Lisbon of the SD taking control. His primary secretary informed him that the Admiral was occupied with a phone call from General Jodl and could not be disturbed. He managed to mumble something to the effect that it was nothing very pressing, but he would wait a few minutes in case he was about to become free. His voice might have sounded nonchalant, but he suspected his face showed the panic that was growing within him. He sat there chain smoking cigarettes for another ten minutes and reading a newspaper. He had just stood up to leave, when she nodded that the call had ended. She buzzed the Admiral and advised that Gehlen was waiting, and then nodded for him to go in to the office.

Gehlen had no sooner opened the door than Canaris was coming out of it. "Let's walk. I need to stretch my legs."

"Certainly."

It was cold and rainy outside, barely above the freezing mark, so it would have made no sense to go outside to walk. Fortunately, the Abwehr Headquarters building had numerous long corridors, where there could be no prying ears or microphones.

"Have you come to tell me something about Lisbon?" asked the Admiral.

"Yes, I just had a phone call from Karsthoff's secretary, informing me that he has been replaced by some SD man and is to be flown to Berlin tomorrow. Perhaps our entire Plan Grandfather has been blown?"

"Well, I just got off the phone with General Jodl. He informed me that Hitler has approved that the SD now be in charge of all intelligence operations in seven different countries, so if it's any good news, the SD hasn't singled out Portugal. Perhaps, they are not aware of our 'travel' plans. Did the young lady have anything else to tell you?"

"She indicated in double talk that all our plans are arranged at their end, but if there were any further questions, she could be reached by phone at her apartment. Said she's taking the next two days off from work."

"OK, that's good, but I don't know if Karsthoff is actually being returned to us, or he's under arrest. If the latter, it won't be long before he would tell all he knows under their interrogation techniques."

"I guess we will know tomorrow when he's allegedly returning to Berlin."

"True, but in any case, I suggest that we move the departure date up to one as soon as possible – before the end of the week, if that is possible. Go immediately to our friend at the Transportation Department and see if there are planes available in the next few days?"

"I can go this very afternoon. The good news is that the gold and diamonds are all packed and ready to go."

"Where are they now?" asked Canaris.

At the supply depot near Templehof airfield. They are in crates, marked as desert boots."

Canaris laughed. You have a warped sense of humor, Ewald!"

"Well, since our great Afrika Korps is no longer in existence, I figured no one would accidently try shipping them off to Tunis!"

"From my phone conversation with Jodl, it sounds as if this takeover of our operations in different countries is just a power bid, not an action because of the SD's knowledge of our plans. But the longer we wait, the more danger of a leak. Come back and see me once you have an answer as to when the planes can be ready."

## LISBON

Despite the weather, Elizabeth did indulge in a raspberry-flavored gelato. Perhaps, it was the mental link of Charles to gelato that made her consider one option for her future. She had concluded that despite Ludovico's valiant attempt at his house earlier in the day to make the SD men think that she was a poor secretary and had no special relationship with him, she still faced real danger in the near future. If he was to be arrested upon arrival in Berlin, he would eventually talk and her days would be numbered as well. At this point, the question before her was how to provide for her own survival. The American Charles Worthington seemed her best bet. She asked the owner if she might borrow his phone and his phone book for Lisbon.

After speaking with the switchboard receptionist and then a secretary in the Political/Military Affairs section, she had Mr. Worthington on the line.

For the benefit of any PVDE listeners, she put on her sexiest voice. "Hello, Charles. This is your gelato-eating friend. I've been missing you so. Could you join me right now and we could share a bowl?"

For the first several seconds, he thought one of his colleagues was pulling a prank on him, but then it sank in that it was Fraulein Elizabeth. "Well, what a coincidence. I was just thinking about wanting a lemon gelato. I could be there in about fifteen minutes, if that would be good for you?"

"Yes, that would be fine. You know, they taste better when you're naked!" she added, and then laughed.

"See you shortly." He hoped the phone intercept man on duty that day was enjoying himself!

Charles did arrive at the café in fifteen minutes precisely and saw Elizabeth sitting in the same alcove as before, albeit with clothes on. "I'm not certain why you phoned me, but given all the people who probably listen to my phone calls, it might be best if we moved on to some other location for a chat."

"I agree. Wherever you suggest is fine with me." She had done a nice acting job on the phone, but it was clear from her face that she was afraid of something.

"My car is just around the corner. "Let's get moving in that and then we can decide upon a destination."

They had been driving for some twenty minutes when Charles decided that nobody was following them. He pulled into the roadside stop along the coastal highway; the one where she and her boss had saved him from the mugging that day. It had started to rain quite heavily just as they arrived. They weren't likely to have anyone else come pulling in to enjoy the view that day.

They had ridden in silence. He turned off the engine and turned to face her. "A pleasure to see you Elizabeth, but I presume this is not just a social call on me."

"Colonel Karstshoff has been arrested and my own life may soon be in danger. I am looking for a 'life boat,' as they say in Abwehr terminology. I would like to trade my safety with you for information that I presume your Agency would like to know."

Charles liked a person who got right to the point. "Why don't you tell me precisely what has happened and then we can go from there."

"First, you tell me if there is a way that you can give me safe haven, before I waste any time telling you things and then just have to go to the British Embassy anyway."

This was no weak and panicked little woman. She intended to drive the best bargain for herself that she could and Charles respected that, so he began treating her as any lawyer would, who was looking out first and foremost for his side. "I do have the authority to offer safe haven to some degree or another, depending on how valuable your information is to America. That might mean simply giving you some money and wishing you well, perhaps providing you an apartment in the south of Portugal for a few months, or perhaps an airplane ticket to America and a new life." He paused several seconds for effect. "So, let's hear what you came to tell me."

"Three men from the Security Service, the SD, showed up with guns in their pockets at Colonel Karsthoff's home this morning. One of them informed Ludovico that he was replacing him as the chief of all intelligence activities in Portugal and that Karsthoff will be flown tomorrow to Berlin, allegedly for onward transfer to a unit on the Russian Front."

"Do you believe that is what will happen?"

"I doubt it. Lots of people who are taken into custody by the SD simply disappear. First, they are interrogated, and then they are no doubt shot."

"But why are you in danger? You're simply his secretary, correct, doing your job as ordered?"

"Because I am aware of certain 'projects' and facts that will likely come out during his interrogation, and then I too will be on a flight to Berlin." She explained how Karsthoff had tried protecting her with the hot tea performance in front of the SD men, but doubted that sham would protect her for long.

Charles gave Karsthoff credit for at least having tried to give his secretary and mistress some distance from himself, but Elizabeth was correct, that ploy wouldn't last but a few days, depending on what Karsthoff would be giving up during interrogation – if that indeed was what was about to happen to him.

"And what are these certain projects and facts that you are aware of that put you in danger?"

She hesitated. "Mr. Worthington, that day that we shared a gelato in the shop, I felt like you are a decent man. I hope you truly are."

Charles remained silent. There was only the continued sound of the heavy rain drops pounding on the metal roof of the car.

"Does the name Dusko Popov mean anything to you?"

"No, I don't think so. Should it?" was his verbal response. His brain was racing in panic. God, what was she about to tell him about one of the supposedly best British double agents? Or, was this whole thing some elaborate test by the Abwehr to see if Popov was a double agent?

"The man is a Yugoslav, who works for the Abwehr in London, but occasionally travels to Lisbon. Ludovico is convinced that the man is really working for the British and that everything he tells us is part of a British deception campaign."

"And how long has this agent been working for you?"

"Perhaps two years, I'm not sure."

"If Karsthoff is convinced the man is a double agent, why has he continued to meet with him?"

"Because Ludovico has never told Berlin of his doubts about Popov."

Charles was becoming ever more confused and presumably his face showed it, so Elizabeth immediately continued her explanation.

"Hitler thinks Popov is wonderful. He thinks all of our agents in England are wonderful – because everything they report agrees with what the Fuhrer already believes. If you ask me, I think it's all ganz quatsch!" She searched her memory for the correct English word. "Nonsense, that's it, nonsense."

"And Ludovico has himself told you that he thinks Popov is a double agent?"

"Yes, one night when we had been drinking a lot of champagne. He'd received a telegram that day, supposedly from Hitler, congratulating him for his recent reporting from Popov, which had confirmed for Hitler that England was near collapse, etc, etc. He was being awarded the Iron Cross, second class, for his service. I was congratulating him as well, in my own special way." She smiled.

"I understand completely," replied Charles, with his own smile.

"And that's when he told me that he didn't believe a word Popov reported, but if he wanted to keep his nice position in Lisbon, he repeated the nonsense to Headquarters, which reported it on to Hitler. Everyone was happy and Ludovico avoided being sent to the Russian Front, which was what he figured would have happened if he'd said that the 'emperor has no clothes.' This way everyone gets medals and promotions and keeps that madman Hitler happy."

Charles concluded that if this story by Elizabeth was simply part of a CI test by the Germans to determine if Popov was legitimate or not, she was the greatest actress in the world! Given the reputation of the German military for centuries of being so professional and honorable, it was a little hard to believe that so many of its intelligence officers would go along with such a ploy, but then, they'd never served a Hitler before. He'd obviously have to pass this story along to the British, but for the moment, there was the question of what to do with Elizabeth.

"That is quite a story and I shall pass it along to the appropriate high authorities. Do you have any other information of that quality?"

She hesitated. "Let's speak of what you are going to do for me, before I tell you anything further."

Charles found himself thinking that he'd hate to play cards against this woman. "I don't make the final decision, but I'm prepared to recommend to Washington that you immediately be flown to America for full and complete debriefings of everything you know about Abwehr operations. I'm sure there are lots of small details to tell us, but to help me write as strong a case as possible for your flight to America, do you have any other gems like the Popov situation?"

"I don't know the specifics, but when Admiral Canaris came to Portugal some weeks back, there were very secret discussions between him, Colonel Ewald Gehlen and Ludovico. It is a plan called 'Grandfather' and involves the shipping of gold and many, many Abwehr officers to Brazil. This is to happen before the end of the year. Ludovico has been negotiating with some Portuguese banker to arrange for the sailings on various ships. This is so sensitive that it's never even mentioned in encrypted Enigma machine radio messages with Berlin."

"Is this to be an advance team of officers to Brazil to prepare for an invasion or something?" Charles again had that confused look on his face.

"Not for an invasion, but for an escape, before Germany loses the war. As Ludovico explained it to me, given the situation in Italy and on the Russian Front, Admiral Canaris is preparing a way for many of his younger officers to escape to South America to start new lives, before the Russian Army eventually rolls over Germany and kills everyone."

Charles was contemplating how he could possibly write up a telegram to Washington, without everyone back at Headquarters thinking he'd gone mad or was quite drunk!

"I know you and Ludovico are, well, quite close, but why did he discuss such a secret operation with you?'

"We've been lovers for over a year. He discussed this with me in the context of whether he and I should go on one of the ships, if there was room."

"Is Canaris himself fleeing to Brazil?"

"No, this is supposed to be for young officers, who might have a future, especially since they are going with money."

"Yes, you mentioned gold? A lot of gold?"

"He never mentioned amounts. Just that they are smuggling gold as well as people on these ships."

"And you don't know any of the specifics?"

"No, he only talked with me about this in the context of he and I possibly going as well, which he concluded was not realistic. He has a wife and children in Prussia and Ludovico could never desert them. It was left for me to think about whether I might want to go alone."

"Are there plans of this exodus in Ludovico's home or office that the new SD man is going to find in the coming days?"

"I doubt it. He recently sent a handwritten report to Berlin with details of the preparations. He had a young officer he quite trusts hand carry an envelope directly to Colonel Gehlen. As I said, there was never any mention of Plan Grandfather in encrypted radio traffic, which by the way, Ludovico didn't trust."

Charles was becoming ever more impressed with Colonel Karsthoff. He'd figured out that Popov was a double agent and suspected that their radio communications had been broken by the Allies as well!

"Of course, if they start interrogating him, I imagine he will tell them everything."

Charles had heard stories of the brutality of the Gestapo and imagined that the SD was just as ruthless. "Yes, I suspect he would."

They then just sat there in silence for several long moments. It was getting quite dark and the rain still hammered on the roof. The weather seemed quite appropriate for the topics they'd just been discussing.

"Well, we have much more to discuss, but I think it's time we took some steps right now for your safety. I presume that you're not planning on returning to your Embassy for any reason, nor possibly even to your apartment?"

"Certainly not to the Embassy. I don't know about the apartment. My clothes and things are there, but I suppose the SD men could by now be waiting for me to show up there."

"Let's do this. I'll have a couple of my friends go with you to your apartment to quickly pack up some clothes and then take you somewhere safe for tonight."

"These SD men are very ruthless and have guns."

Charles smiled. "My friends also have guns." Charles was willing to match Salvatore and Lou against any SD men! He reached over and took hold of her hands and gave them a squeeze. "Don't worry, you're safe now and I'll see if we can learn anything about what has happened to Ludovico."

Charles drove back to the edge of the city and found a small café with a phone. He was in luck and Salvatore was at his pension. He gave him brief instructions simply to come immediately with Lou to a particular restaurant at the north end of the city.

And not that it was likely a necessary reminder, but his final words were, "Be sure to bring your guns."

Salvatore smiled. He liked the sound of this upcoming car drive.

Within a half hour, the four had rendezvoused and Elizabeth had been transferred into the safe hands of Salvatore and Lou. They confirmed that they thought that there were empty rooms at their pension and would check her in there once they'd fetched some of her clothing from her apartment. Charles was glad to hear that there were rooms available there. His other option was to put her up at his place and he knew that tonight would naturally be when Olga suddenly showed up. He really didn't want to have to explain to a fiery Russian why a gorgeous German Fraulein was staying in his apartment!

While the boys set off on their mission, Charles headed back to the Embassy to start writing up several IMMEDIATE EYES ONLY messages back to Headquarters. He checked his watch. It was past 5:00 p.m., but fortunately, one of the code clerks stayed late on regular work days, to handle just such emergencies. Given the time difference back to Washington, his messages would reach there during normal office hours for action and thus he could count on having a reply and hopefully some specific instructions when tomorrow's work day arrived in Lisbon. He was still trying to think of how to phrase some of what Elizabeth had told him, so as not to sound like a total lunatic to OSS Headquarters.

## Chapter 19

On the following morning, Charles received from Headquarters agreement in principle that "the woman," as she was oddly referred to in the message, could be flown to America within a few days. This would be done in return for her cooperating fully in a debriefing on Abwehr operations in Portugal and anything else she knew of value to the Allies. He was to keep her safe and himself continue for the present with the debriefing of her, particularly on local matters. As for the story of Colonel von Karsthoff's removal, HQS said it would have a further response in a few days. As for the alleged plan to smuggle Germans and gold to Brazil, there was no comment at all from Headquarters. Charles guessed that that meant that different offices were still arguing over the information and they couldn't agree on what to say and therefore, Headquarters simply said nothing.

He received in a separate EYES ONLY message instructions to immediately go over and discuss with the British MI6 Commander in Lisbon the information about how Karsthoff believed agent TRICYCLE was a double agent. Washington advised that the OSS Office in London would approach MI6 HQS in a day or two, but as a matter of courtesy, would wait so that the MI6 office in Lisbon would have an opportunity to itself advise London of these developments. The telegram noted that regardless of what Karsthoff might believe of the validity of the case, if Karsthoff had been relieved of duty over suspicions of disloyalty, German authorities in Berlin might conclude that Karsthoff had tipped the British off about Popov's role as a German spy. In other words, they might jump to the correct conclusion about Popov being under the control of the British, but for the wrong reasons.

Charles called the British Embassy, only to discover that Nigel Pendergast was out of the city until the following morning and his secretary claimed not to know his schedule once he returned – best to call back tomorrow and speak directly with him. She couldn't make an appointment for him. That made Charles suspect she really didn't know when he was returning, but he would indeed try phoning again tomorrow.

He then called to Captain Lourenco, hoping for a better response. The captain was free for lunch that very day at 1:00 p.m. As Charles was going to be asking for a favor, several in fact, he figured the least he could do was buy Lourenco a very nice lunch. As he would be free until lunchtime, he then left the Embassy and headed via a rambling route, so he could check for surveillance, to the pension where Elizabeth was being hidden. He presumed that by that morning the Germans had noticed that she hadn't shown up for work at the Embassy or Karsthoff's home and the newly arrived SD men would start some level of search for her. Once they checked her apartment and noticed a lot of her clothes and suitcases gone, they'd correctly conclude that she'd fled somewhere. Depending on just why her boss had been relieved of his position, her disappearance presumably wouldn't help his cause. Charles made a mental note to have his officer who handled a couple of assets at the airport check to see if Karsthoff was indeed put on a plane for Berlin that day.

He found Salvatore sitting in the small café right next door to the pension.

"Lou just took some coffee and rolls up to da lady in her room and will stays with her tills we's switch at lunchtime."

"Any sign of nosey people coming around last night or this morning?"

"No, alls been quiet and no new guests at the pension."

"Good. Keep your eyes open. The Germans will have figured out by now that she's gone missing and will be searching for her. I'm going up now to talk some more with her." He was several steps away from the table when his companion called to him.

"Oh, knocks three times, den two times, so Lou knows you ain't no German, and shoots you through da door," said Salvatore with a grin.

"Thanks for telling me that!"

After the proper sequence of knocks and calling his name through the door, Lou admitted Charles into the small room. Elizabeth was enjoying her coffee at a small circular table in one corner. Her suitcases were stacked in another. She'd not made any attempt at unpacking much of her stuff, as she'd not known if she'd be staying here a few days, or moving on immediately.

"Did you sleep well? How are you feeling today?"

She rose to greet Charles. "I slept very well, thank you. Your two friends have been very helpful and very comforting, knowing one of them was always on duty in the hallway all night."

Lou grinned from over by the door. "I'm going downstairs for some more coffee."

"Yes, you're pretty safe with Sally and Lou."

After Lou had left the room, she asked, "Are they New York gangsters? They look and talk just like gangsters from all those American movies."

The impact of Hollywood on the world always amazed Charles. "Gangsters? Heavens no, they were both kindergarten teachers before the war."

She sensed that Charles was teasing her, but decided not to challenge him on his claim. "So, have you received any word from Washington about what to do with me?"

"Yes, Headquarters has agreed that you will be flown to America in a few days for detailed debriefings."

"And will I then be allowed to stay in America, after the interrogation?" she asked rather anxiously.

"That wasn't precisely addressed, but I can't imagine they would go to all the trouble to fly you back to Portugal afterwards." He offered a reassuring smile. "It's probably more a question of precisely what to do with you after the questioning sessions. They won't want to lock you up as a POW, but on the other hand, they won't want an Abwehr person just wandering around wherever you want in America."

"Understandable. I am quite a dangerous threat all by myself." It was her turn to grin.

Charles joined her at the small table. "Let's talk some more about this Plan Grandfather that is about to happen. Tell me again what your understanding of the purpose of this operation is?"

"Ludovico had discussed it with me in terms of me going to Brazil on one of the ships, since he didn't see how he and I could go together. Admiral Canaris believes we will lose the war and that when the Russian Army comes across Germany they will rape all the women and slaughter the men, because they are uncultured barbarians. He wishes to give as many younger officers and their families the chance for a new life. The only way to do that is to escape now, to Brazil."

Charles suspected that many a Russian thought the Germans were "uncultured barbarians" as well, given what SS troops had done when they had rolled into wide stretches of the Soviet Union in the first year of the war. But straightening out that ethical and intellectual debate over who was more barbarian was not his task.

"And where is this gold that is to be shipped with them coming from?"

She shrugged her shoulders, indicating no precise knowledge. "I presume that it's gold that was taken from various banks of conquered countries, or from 'Untermensch', like gypsies and Jews."

And just when Charles was almost starting to like her, he realized she really was part of the Aryan race with that opinion that she and other "real" Germans were superior to lesser groups. It wasn't just a few thousand top Nazi Party officials who had that attitude; it went right down to the blond, blue-eyed secretaries of the "master race." The American saying was that "politics made strange bedfellows." Wartime necessities made even stranger ones. Giving this woman sanctuary in America would obtain for the Allies very important intelligence, but it didn't make him feel good in having to deal with her. He planned on taking a long, hot shower once he got home later that day.

"And how are all these German Abwehr officers going to arrive in Portugal, so as to catch passage for Brazil?"

"I have no idea. I don't know how many and I don't know precisely when. I don't know whether the officers are traveling with their families or everyone is traveling separately."

"Families? That's the first time that you've mentioned families."

"Of course they are bringing their wives and children, those that have them. What sort of German officer would run away to South America and leave his family behind in a defeated Germany!" Her opinion of Charles as being a fairly bright man was beginning to slip.

Charles asked the same questions from various angles over and over, but always with the same results. A witness being asked over and over by a detective who suddenly remembers some key clue apparently only happened in the movies. Elizabeth was a reasonably bright person and had told him everything she knew. There weren't going to be any last moment recollections. What she'd told him was indeed important, but actually finding all these German Abwehr officers with wives and children and gold was going to be his task. A task for a good policeman. Charles thought of Captain Lourenco and looked at his watch. It was about time for him to being heading to his luncheon appointment with Antonio. He'd risen to his current position by being politically astute, but he'd started out life as an everyday policeman and apparently had been a very good one. Finding people and hidden gold sounded like a perfect challenge for an old-fashioned police detective.

"Thank you for your patience with all my questions. I have to go now to another meeting, but will be back this evening to check in on you. I'm also trying to confirm whether Colonel Karsthoff flew out of Lisbon today, as the SD man said would happen."

"Thank you, Charles. That would be very nice of you if could confirm what has happened with Ludovico."

Charles arrived at the restaurant precisely at 1:00 p.m. Captain Lourenco was already seated and had started on a very good bottle of Portuguese white wine.

Once seated, he looked at the label on the bottle and saw that it was from a very exclusive and expensive estate. "Are you celebrating something in particular?"

"Is your presence not enough of a reason to celebrate?" responded Antonio with a smile. He poured Charles a glass of the wine and raised his in a toast. "To your continued good health."

"And to yours, and to all our colleagues in the intelligence business!"

Lourenco gave Charles an odd look. "Somewhat of a peculiar toast?"

"Well, I was just thinking of Colonel Karsthoff. I'm not sure his sudden replacement and departure for Germany bodes well for his continued good health."

The captain smiled. "Ah, I see word has spread very quickly." Antonio looked at his watch. "Actually, I don't think his plane is leaving for another hour or so, but your knowledge of all that has happened at the German Embassy probably tells me that my service can quit looking for his secretary. The German Ambassador phoned this morning asking for our assistance in finding the lovely Fraulein Elizabeth. He feared she might have been kidnapped or some harm had come to her. I presume she is safe?"

"Yes, I believe she's quite safe – wherever she might be."

"That's good. I believe the German Ambassador was simply concerned with her safety. Not that he was asking me to return her to her embassy or anything like that."

"Good. I doubt she'll be in Portugal much longer, so she will be of no concern to their ambassador, or to you. I am curious what you make of Karsthoff's sudden removal? Have you met his replacement?"

"I suspect you probably know more than I do. All I know is that some fellow named Schmidt has an appointment with me tomorrow, to introduce himself as Colonel Karsthoff's replacement."

"I do believe that is the name that I heard is the replacement."

"Have you heard anything else that might be of interest to a lowly Portuguese official like myself?"

"As a matter of fact, there is one thing. A young lady very recently told me that a large group of German officers, some even with families, will be arriving in Portugal before the end of the year. A Portuguese banker has supposedly made arrangements with various cargo ship captains to provide discreet passage for all these Germans to Brazil. And secondly, that they will also be smuggling stolen gold with them to Brazil, which they will use to start new lives for themselves in Brazil."

"My, that is quite a story. Did Elizabeth, I mean, this anonymous woman, happen to say who is arranging all this back in Germany?"

"She said it's Admiral Canaris himself, as he has concluded that Germany will lose the war."

"My, you are full of interesting news today. And is there a name to go with this alleged Portuguese banker who is making all these sailing arrangements?"

"Not a clue, but I figured that is where you might be of some value. Have you heard of such rumors, or have any insights as to which bankers might have such connections with ship captains?"

"Hmmm, I can think of five or six off the top of my head who might have such connections, but I will have to make some discreet inquiries. I presume that you'd not like for word of such an investigation to get back to the German Embassy?"

"I think it would be best if no one around Lisbon knew of our hearing of such a plan. According to my source, this plan has been held very tightly. It's never even been discussed in Abwehr cable traffic with Berlin."

"But with the disappearance of Karsthoff's secretary, won't Canaris and whoever else is involved with this plan, presume that it has been reported to you or the British?"

"According to my source, she did not officially know of the plan. Her good friend had simply discussed it with her one night in the context of whether she might like to sail for Brazil as well. And in any case, as long as there is no public news of her, nor anything so crude as her walking out to a plane in plain view at the Lisbon airport, Canaris might conclude that she is hiding with some farmer down in the Algarve."

"What a lucky farmer!" Antonio replied with a lecherous smile. Well, let me discreetly talk with a few good friends around the city and see if anything turns up."

"By the way, speaking of Karsthoff: is his departure from Lisbon being done voluntarily? I know he's my enemy, but I have a distant impression that he is a decent man. I hate to think of him being dragged off unwillingly to Berlin for 'unpleasant' questioning."

"From my dealings with him, I do believe he is a decent man, an old-world European gentleman, as I believe you Americans like to call such people. I have my deputy and a number of my men standing by at the airport. My deputy, who Ludovico knows, will personally stamp his exit visa. If there is any indication that the colonel is being forced onto a plane, my deputy has been authorized to forcibly detain Colonel Karsthoff on suspicion of currency violations – and he will be held at the airport until I arrive to sort out the situation. If he misses his plane today to Germany, well, he misses his plane." Antonio shrugged his shoulders. "The law is the law, even for someone with a diplomatic passport."

Charles smiled slightly. "I'm glad to see that you enforce Portuguese law, even for diplomats."

"All this talk of smuggling people and gold has made me very hungry. Let's order. The head waiter told me that the swordfish is excellent today."

"Yes, let's order. I know you can't do your best work, if you are hungry!"

Two days later, Charles finally got in to see Nigel at the British Embassy, who offered no explanation as to where he'd been for the last several days. He might have been off on a secret mission, or he might have just taken a few days off to hike in the woods. Charles had concluded that the British intelligence people quite enjoyed promoting an air of mystery about all of their movements, even if they had simply been at home, puttering in their backyard garden.

Charles brought him up to date on the sudden removal of Colonel Karsthoff, the defection of Fraulein Elizabeth and her story of how a "large group" of Abwehr officers, with families, would soon be passing through Portugal on to new lives in Brazil, funded by stolen Nazi gold. He saved the best for last.

"Elizabeth claims that Karsthoff has believed for some time that TRICYCLE is a controlled double agent, being used by you British to send false information to Germany." That did take the perpetual look of superiority off his face.

"We've seen nothing in ULTRA intercepts to indicate any suspicions about his status and loyalty to Germany. How has Karsthoff reported these suspicions to Berlin?"

"She claims that Ludovico never reported his suspicions – as that wouldn't have been career enhancing, given that Hitler loves this agent, and his handling of TRICYCLE has helped keep him Portugal, instead of being transferred to the Russian Front."

"Any chance the woman is just making this all up? To make herself sound more attractive and valuable to the OSS?"

"I suppose it's possible. She is very bright, but my gut feeling is that she's telling the truth about what Karsthoff had privately told her. The danger now, depends on just why he was pulled from here as the Abwehr chief? If he's in real trouble and is about to be interrogated by the SD or the Gestapo, he may well reveal his doubts about TRICYCLE. Or, if the SD suspects him of treason, for whatever reason, they'd fear that he's told you Brits or us about TRICYCLE, and the others being run by the Abwehr. And thus the same damage; the Germans will stop believing anything that TRICYCLE reports."

"Hmmm, that would be most unfortunate, as this agent is to be one of the key players in the deception plan to deceive the Germans about the location and timing of the D-Day invasion across the channel." A very unpleasant look had come to Nigel's face, caused no doubt by this sudden thought of complications that could arise from Karsthoff's removal, but also the unpleasant prospect of having to report all of this to London.

*Nazi Gold, Portuguese Wine, and a Lovely Russian Spy*

"I was told that in another day or so, Chief OSS London will be going over to discuss all of this with Menzies, so you'd best get a report in to your Headquarters pretty quickly."

"Right. Wish you'd given me a little more warning, old boy," said Nigel as he rubbed his left ear.

"I've been trying for three days to see you, but kept being told by your secretary that you were incommunicado."

"Oh, yes, right." He seemed lost in thought for several moments. "Is the girl still here? Might I have a little chat with her?"

Charles looked at his watch. "I'm afraid you just missed her. One of our planes landed here last night, which included several female passengers. While the ladies were enroute back to the airport this morning, we did a switch of Fraulein Elizabeth for one of them, who's also an attractive blonde. She'll lay low for a few days, then catch another flight out. Hopefully, none of the usual informants at the airport will have noticed the swap and our 'guest' should now be safely on her way to the Azores and then on to Washington for further debriefings."

"Very clever. Have the Germans been looking for her here in Lisbon?"

"The German Ambassador did phone the PVDE the first morning she went missing, but simply claimed that they thought she might have been kidnapped by local criminals or had an auto accident somewhere. He wasn't making a demand for her return or anything."

"And what is Washington thinking of her story about dozens of Germans being on their way to Brazil with stolen gold because Canaris thinks Germany is going to lose the war?"

"I haven't had much of a reaction. OSS Headquarters has informed me that ULTRA intercepts have confirmed Karsthoff's replacement by an SD man named Schmidt, and of the planned return of the former to Germany. They also reported that they've rechecked all the back intercepts for several months and there's been absolutely nothing about travel of a group of Germans to Portugal and onward. That didn't surprise me, as Elizabeth told me that this was being kept very tightly controlled and messages about it were being hand carried, not sent in regular radio traffic. I've put out some feelers around the port for any such rumors, but so far nothing. Would appreciate anything MI6 might be able to learn locally."

"Yes, of course. We'll make some discreet inquiries."

"Well, I'll leave you to write something up about implications for TRICYCLE and get that off to London."

"Yes, I'll do that, but the more I've been thinking about this, the more suspicious I'm becoming of this woman's claim. The idea that a senior German Abwehr officer would suspect someone is a double agent, but not report it to his Headquarters. It just seems a bit fanciful," he concluded as he again rubbed his ear.

Charles made his farewell and headed back to his own Embassy. He thought while riding in the car that naturally, Nigel didn't want to believe that one of his star agents had been tumbled by Karsthoff and whether he'd officially reported those suspicions are not, he surely would have been downplaying TRICYCLE's reporting all these months. And there was now the danger of what might happen with Karsthoff's removal, his forced flight back to Berlin and possible interrogation.

When Charles got back to his office, there was another EYES ONLY message awaiting him:

1. Be advised that a search in southern Germany for a missing flight from Lisbon to Berlin had ceased after three days. Explanation for the end of the search was because of press of other issues, combined with fact that flight had presumably gone down in heavily wooded areas and slight chance that anyone who might have survived the crash landing would still be alive three days later.
2. Most of the intercepted radio signals about this event were in normal, emergency channels (not encrypted), so we had initially attached little importance to the event. We finally made possible connection between this crash and the flight of Colonel Kartsthoff from Lisbon once we had an ULTRA intercept from Berlin to Lisbon, informing them of the crash.
3. One of the radio signals intercept personnel in Italy who had initially heard the transmissions about the crash "thinks", repeat "thinks", he'd heard mention that there had been a disturbance on the flight just before the plane signaled an emergency and went down. This was followed by another operator telling the first one to shut up and to make no further reference to a "disturbance."
4. Please confirm that this flight was the one that you believe Colonel Karsthoff was supposed to be on from Lisbon, and also,

if you pick up any information locally, confirming his death in this plane crash.

Charles read through the message several times. He was glad that Elizabeth had already departed Lisbon and it would not be his task to inform her of Ludovico's death. He also debated if this crash had truly occurred and Karsthoff was really dead? He concluded that no doubt the Germans could have put out fake radio messages about search and rescue efforts, but to what end and for whose benefit? To make the Allies think Kartshoff had died, or to fool the Abwehr? And then there was the tantalizing tidbit about a "disturbance" on the flight just before it went down. He didn't speak German, nor know what the use of that word might imply in aviation circles. He had a mental image of Karsthoff deciding that he didn't care to face interrogation in Berlin and deciding to take whatever secrets he had to a grave in the mountains of Bavaria, and thus he had somehow caused the "disturbance" on board leading to the crash.

Presuming he really was dead, the plane crash did insure that plans for a large exodus of Germans through Portugal for Brazil stayed secret. He thought, however, that the sudden removal of Karsthoff might prompt Admiral Canaris and whoever else was involved in Plan Grandfather to move up their departure, before anything else happened. OSS Lisbon simply didn't have the coverage of the port that was likely to turn up this sort of intelligence in advance of a sailing of Germans. They might hear rumors in the weeks after, but not before a ship or several ships departed for Brazil. And he doubted if MI6 had any better coverage of the docks than the OSS did. No, Captain Lourenco was going to have to come through for him on this one, and he was certainly more likely to determine what Portuguese banker might be involved. Charles would have to do what he hated most – wait and be patient!

# Chapter 20

# Berlin

Admiral Canaris and Colonel Gehlen went to lunch at a small, modest restaurant – not one that the Gestapo would automatically have covered in advance with informants or microphones. With the onset of bad weather, walks in the "garden" seemed absurd and they could only stroll together up and down the corridors of the Abwehr Headquarters building so often without drawing obvious suspicion that they were hiding something. Simply deciding on short notice to go out to lunch seemed the solution. Canaris spotted what he thought was surveillance by the Gestapo as they rode to the restaurant and a lone diner in a cheap leather coat came in for lunch shortly after they did. Fortunately, he was seated at a table on the opposite side of the room. There was no way he could overhear what the two men were saying. Canaris was glad to see that wearing an admiral's uniform still merited some respect in a Berlin restaurant. He and Gehlen were given an excellent table off by itself, with a nice view of the entire restaurant. Both men smiled and laughed over their lunch. The surveillant would report later that it appeared as if the two men were indeed just enjoying a nice lunch out of the building – on a day when the low cloud cover was giving a respite from heavy daytime bombing raids.

"So, can we have the needed planes for this coming Saturday?"

"Yes, all is set on that point. It's good we're leaving soon; I've given over the last bottles of French brandy I could find anywhere in Berlin to that drunken fool!"

"And our people are ready?"

"As ready as we can be, with a few last moment adjustments. Lt. Breithaupt is unfortunately in the hospital with an appendicitis, so he is off the list and another man's wife is within days or even hours of having a baby, so he has agreed that they should not travel as well. There are 61 officers going, with a total number of travelers of 109, counting all the wives and children. It should be 110, but we have the peculiar situation of one man who does not want to take his wife with him!"

Canaris laughed out loud. The Gestapo man presumed that Colonel Gehlen had just told him a very funny joke. "And what has he told this poor woman as to where he is going this weekend?"

"Apparently, he simply told her he was going off on a secret mission for several weeks to the Russian Front. She told him to stay as long as he wished and she hoped he died there. A few minutes later, he spotted her going through her clothes closet looking for a nice black dress, suitable for a funeral."

"Yes, perhaps it's best if he travels alone to Brazil!"

"I know you wanted an opportunity, if possible, to say goodbye to your men and I think I have found a solution."

"If it can be done without jeopardizing the mission, I would like to say a few words to them."

"Fortunately, Admiral Donitz is having a large birthday party this Saturday night, to which you have accepted an invitation. I think it will be possible to sneak you out of there for at least an hour, so you can come to the departure point and then return without the Gestapo even realizing you are not at the party."

"That would be good. And the crates of 'desert boots'? You have trusted men taking care of their shipment?

Gehlen smiled. "All is set"

Canaris raised his wine glass for a toast. "To you good health, my old friend. Be careful in that strong Brazilian sunshine in the first few weeks!"

Towards the end of the meal, Canaris noticed that the poor Gestapo surveillant alone at a table had ordered nothing but soup for his lunch. He called over their waiter. "Do you have any of that marvelous apfel strudel today?"

"Yes, Herr Admiral. It's getting harder and harder to find all the needed ingredients, but today you are in luck." As soon as he said that, a panicked look came to his face. He hoped he'd not sounded critical of the Reich. The newspapers and the radio were constantly telling the public that there were no shortages.

Canaris gave him a reassuring smile and patted him on the arm. "Don't worry. My cook at home makes such comments all the time."

"A piece for each of you?' asked the waiter, much relieved. "And some coffee?"

"A small piece for each of us, and do you see the man eating soup all by himself over there?" Canaris nodded discretely in the direction of the Gestapo man.

"Yes."

"Take him a very large piece and some coffee and simply tell him it's from a German citizen, grateful for his patriotic service."

"Ah, is he your driver or your body guard?"

Canaris smiled. "Something like that."

A few minutes later the waiter brought the strudel to Canaris and Gehlen and then took the third piece over to the lone man. He looked very confused and looked over at the Admiral. Canaris picked up a piece of the dessert on his fork and tipped it towards the Gestapo man, with a smile. After a moment's hesitation, he smiled back and cut into his large piece of dessert.

"Why are you being nice to that thug?" asked Ewald.

"No doubt many Gestapo men are, but that one just looks like some poor bastard doing what he's told to do and they didn't even send him out with enough money to buy a decent lunch while supposedly watching us. Besides, having your surveillance team like you might come in handy someday."

Ewald didn't really agree, but didn't think it worth arguing over.

"Is there any need to try to contact Fraulein Sahrbach in Lisbon, regarding the arrangements for the travel, or is everything all set?" asked Canaris.

"We know all of the plans that Karsthoff had arranged. We simply needed to tell the banker of the change of dates, but I decided to just send the man an innocuous-sounding telegram from one of our cover companies, rather than risk phoning her to notify that man."

"Yes, you're probably right. The death of Ludovico is certainly a tragic event. I still can't make up my mind if this was truly an accident, or if perhaps he did something to intentionally crash the plane? Of course, that crash story could all just be a blind by the SD or the Gestapo, so they can interrogate Karsthoff at their leisure. No plane wreckage has yet to be found."

"I doubt if we'll know for certain before I leave this Saturday, but it's prudent that we've moved up the departure date, regardless of what's the true story with the plane."

When the bill came, Ewald reached over and took it, over Canaris' objection. "What am I to do with all these Reich marks that I have in my possession after this Saturday? I may as well spend them now, and I will be especially generous in my tip to our waiter!"

"Good, I may want to come back here again. The chef must know his way around the black market if he could come up with the ingredients to make such a wonderful strudel. He may be an important man to know in the future!" They both laughed as they rose from the table. The Gestapo man silently mouthed "thank you" as the Admiral passed his table.

## LISBON

Charles arranged to have lunch with Salvatore and Lou that same day as Canaris and Gehlen were lunching in Berlin. Salvatore had managed to find a small restaurant actually run by a real Italian and his wife, and who with advance notice that you were coming, would prepare a few genuine Italian dishes. While they were eating the delicious food, Charles raised a question to his two colleagues.

"I would guess that you've both smuggled an item or two in and out of the ports of the New York area?"

They both smiled. Salvatore responded for them both, "And maybe even through Boston."

"Good. While I'm waiting to hear back from Captain Lourenco with any information he might be able to find about this alleged smuggling plan of people and gold out of Lisbon, let's approach this from a different perspective. If you were in charge of this Plan Grandfather, what would be steps that you'd take to make all the necessary arrangements? Who all would you need to bribe to make this happen?"

"Well, first is da ship captain. Nobody or nothing comes on board a ship without da captain's approval," observed Lou.

"And then there's da Customs official for the port, or whatevers dey calls such a person here in Portugal. He'd have to be taken care of so ders no surprise inspection of youse cargo, or of who mights be in some passenger cabin," added Salvatore.

"Would it be the same person who approached the captains who makes a deal with the Customs official?"

The two "experts" looked at each other. "Hmmm, it woulds be more natural if each captain made his own arrangements with Customs and den da captain would feel more certain that the fix is in, rather than dependings on some third person to makes da deal. But we's don't knows how many ships are needed, do's we? If dat number was going to be above 3 or 4, then maybe it would be easier if one man made the arrangements for all da ships with da Customs man."

Charles nodded in agreement with all the two had told him so far, which was interesting, but didn't yet point the way for their own investigation around the Lisbon docks – a place notoriously closed-mouthed to outsiders. "Anybody else come to mind?"

"Well, der's always a money guy involved with sailings and shipping. Some guys got to put up da insurance for the cargo and for da ship itself. Dat kinda banker guy would have all the right connections with dem people we discussed who'd need to be bribed."

"Excellent, so presumably there are certain bankers who specialize in dealing with ship captains and everyone involved in making a sailing happen – getting the cargo arranged and securing whatever exit permits are needed?"

"Correct. Find dems guys and you'd have yourself a short list of suspects for arranging these sailings dat interest you. And one mores thing. Dependings on the number of peoples going, maybes they can't all gets here from Germany at once, so you'd needs some place for dem to lay low until their particular ship was ready to set sail for Brazil. If it was me, I'd trys to find a small hotel out of town, to stash my people in tills the night of da sailing. Youse don't want to draw attention to a bunch of Germans wandering around Lisbon!"

"That's great guys. You've given me several good ideas of where to look for signs of some discreet sailings for Brazil being prepared. I'll be back in touch soon."

Charles had forgotten to bring back to the Embassy that morning several books that he'd borrowed from a colleague, so he swung by his apartment after the lunch. As he walked up to his apartment door, he noticed a small card pinned to it, saying: "your cleaning lady is working inside." As Charles had no cleaning lady, he didn't quite know what to make of the note, so he opened the door as quietly and slowly as he could. He saw Olga asleep over on his sofa, under a blanket. He came closer and just stood there in silence for a bit, admiring her beautiful face. The floor creaked as he started to step away and she slowly opened her eyes. She saw who it was and she smiled, followed by a big yawn.

"Hello there, sleepyhead."

"Hello."

"So, you're my cleaning lady now?" He sat down next to her.

"Well, last time I arrived unexpected, you almost shot me, so I thought it best to warn you I'm in here." They both grinned.

He reached over and stroked her face with the back of his right hand. "How can you get more beautiful every time I see you?"

"You just say such things because you want sex with me."

"Yes, but that doesn't mean it isn't true." He leaned over and kissed her. A minute later, he picked her up and carried her into the bedroom.

It was hard to say which of them was more in the mood for sex than the other? Besides the emotional bond between and appreciation for the other's sense of humor and intellect, they both had a serious physical attraction for the other.

Afterwards, as they were laying snuggled up to each other, Charles noticed that she was wearing a Star of David pendant around her neck. He'd seen a few such pendants on people he knew were Jewish earlier in his life, so he was fairly certain that's what it was. He pointed at it. "I see that you're getting more into your Jewish heritage and faith."

She'd not known quite how to bring up her new found religious belief, so she was glad that he'd noticed her Star of David, and that he understood what it meant. "Yes, I've been receiving instruction from family I'm staying with in Spain. I don't understand everything yet, but I feel more comfortable, is best word I know in English or Russian, to describe how I feel after I've prayed."

"Then this is a good thing," replied Charles.

"I've been hearing rumors of terrible things happening to Jews in Germany. You think such stories true?"

"I've heard similar rumors about camps where all the Jews are being sent. Sadly, I suspect that to a large extent they are true."

"According to this family, Jews suffer everywhere and only solution is for all Jews to go back our traditional homeland, in area of Middle East that British call Palestine. There are Jewish groups who had been fighting British before war with Hitler started, and once it over, they will go back to fighting English to make this happen."

"I know nothing about such Jewish-English fighting, nor of who owns what lands. Haven't Arabs always lived in that area as well?"

"Only after they stole from Israelites land that God told Jews was their land."

Charles sensed this was not a discussion he really wanted to get into, particularly since he knew so little of the facts of the history of that area. He decided to bring the conversation back to more local issues. "Let me bring you up to date about this alleged plan to smuggle a bunch of German Abwehr officers and gold to Brazil."

This did grab her attention. "Yes, tell me what is happening. Is there such plan?"

"The former Abwehr chief here in Lisbon, Colonel Karsthoff was suddenly recalled to Berlin, but his plane went down and he was killed, or so we think. His secretary, and mistress, Elizabeth, came running to me for help because she was afraid that the SD might haul her back to Germany as well. She is now in America being debriefed, but she gave us more details about this plan. She didn't know the specifics, but I believe her story."

"And what you doing to find details?"

"I went to the chief of the Portuguese PVDE for Lisbon. He is trying to find out which specific ship captains might have been approached to help smuggle these Germans to Brazil."

"When this to happen?"

"She thought before the end of the year, but my gut feeling is that with the mysterious sudden recall of Karsthoff, that Admiral Canaris might move up the timetable for departure, before details get to the Gestapo and SD."

"Why Canaris sending these soldiers to Brazil?"

"According to Elizabeth, he thinks Germany will lose the war and he wants to send these young officers, and their families, to where they will be safe before the Red Army arrives and slaughters all these people."

"I hope so. Hopefully, they kill all Nazis."

"Well, regardless of what happens when the Russian Army gets onto German territory, for the moment, my problem is to stop this plan and to stop the smuggling of this gold to South America."

"How much gold?"

*Nazi Gold, Portuguese Wine, and a Lovely Russian Spy*

"I don't know. Elizabeth didn't know. I presume Canaris would send all he can, particularly since I don't completely believe this humanitarian story of him simply wanting to give his young officers a new life. What if that is simply a cover story most of them have been told, but it's really a plot to continue on the Nazi movement in South America?"

She nodded in agreement. "That sounds more like what the head of Abwehr would be planning, rather than crazy idea of starting new lives in Brazil."

"I mentioned the idea of us starting a new life in Brazil after the war – am I crazy?" He gave her a big smile.

"You didn't mention us having lots of gold with us!" She managed to keep a straight face for several seconds, before breaking out in laughter.

"You know, for being a good Marxist, you're pretty mercenary. You wanted to meet me in New York City because I worked for Mr. Astor, richest man in America, and now you want to know if gold comes with the invitation to move to Brazil!"

The phone rang, bringing to an end their joking about gold. Charles got up to go answer the phone in the living room. Olga lay back in the bed and stared at the ceiling and whispered the word, "gold."

Charles returned in a couple of minutes. "I have to go back to the Embassy. Will you just be staying here the rest of the afternoon?"

"No, I really should go do a few things myself."

"You have any idea of how long you will be here this time?"

"Maybe week or so. Is that problem for you? Maybe you have other girl booked here later in week?"

He threw a pillow at her. "I'll be home about 7:00 – have my dinner ready!"

Once Olga showered and dressed, she surveyed the kitchen and determined, as she suspected, that there was not much of anything in there that could be turned into a home-cooked dinner. She would have to do a little shopping that day as well as spying. Most of the agents with whom she met that day were local Communists who were providing the NKVD information that could be used one day to overthrow the Salazar regime. She had to admit to herself, that little that she did in Portugal had anything to do with fighting the Nazis. While meeting with one man who worked for a shipping company, she did venture onto the topic of any rumors of things being smuggled to Brazil by anybody. The man agreed that it wouldn't be terribly hard, for the right price, to smuggle people, gold or elephants onto a cargo ship headed for Brazil. And that at the other end, Brazilian officials were even more corrupt than their Portuguese counterparts, so there'd be no problem at the other end of the voyage either. Unfortunately, the man knew of no specific facts or rumors about anything being smuggled at that very moment. He had seen Pedro Da Silva, a banking official of the Espirito Santo Bank making a number of visits in recent days to various ships, but that wasn't all that unusual, as his bank was involved with the financing of many cargos headed to South America.

Charles paid a call on Captain Lourenco at PVDE Headquarters to see what information he might have obtained about gold or Germans headed for Brazil.

"Charles, how are you my friend?" asked Antonio, as he came around from his large desk to greet the American.

"I'm fine, thank you, and yourself?"

"Still poor and humble, but healthy at least," he replied with a smile.

Charles doubted the first two claims. "Well, I'm glad that you're at least healthy."

"Sit down my friend. Shall I send for some coffee?"

"Thank you, but not today. I'm rather pressed for time today and unfortunately, need to get directly to business and then depart. Have you come up with anything related to the possibility of gold and Germans being smuggled through Portugal on the way to Brazil?"

"Nothing concrete, as you'd like to hear from me. However, a friend, shall we say, at Espirito Santo Bank tells me that one of their senior officials, Vice-President Pedro Da Silva, has been quite friendly with several of the Germans from the Embassy this past year. Apparently, his mother was German. And in the last month or so, he has been having a number of appointments with cargo ship captains. He had also made some internal bank inquiries about some hotel in the Lisbon area that was on the verge of bankruptcy, but which now has managed to again start making its monthly payments."

Charles looked quite excited at the last bit of news.

"Unfortunately, there is no information about which hotel that is, nor of which ships he has visited."

"Still, this man Da Silva sounds like a good person to focus some attention on in the coming days. For my part, all I have for you is a theory. It seems to me that if Admiral Canaris really did have such a plan in the works and then all of a sudden, his man in Lisbon, Karsthoff, is replaced and then Karsthoff's secretary disappears – if it were me, I'd move my plans up to as soon as possible, before any details of the planned movement of people and gold leaked out."

"I agree with your logic, but if that's the case, then we probably don't have a lot of time to carefully and discreetly investigate Plan Grandfather. While we're being clever, we might read in the Rio Times how a hundred Germans just landed."

"True, but what's the alternative?"

"Well, I could have a friendly chat with Mr. Da Silva, on behalf of Prime Minister Salazar, and appeal to his patriotic feelings."

"I don't have any feel for the man. You think that might work?"

Lourenco smiled. "It's amazing how patriotic some citizens become while chatting with me in the basement of our building."

"Ah, that sort of 'patriotism'!"

"No, no. I think, Charles, that you've never been involved in questioning people. Physical pain isn't what makes people talk. It's the psychological fear of what physical pain might be coming to them. The fear is in the anticipation. It's almost like how the anticipation of being in the arms of a beautiful woman is more pleasurable than actually being with her. There are all sorts of rumors around Lisbon about what goes on in the basement of the PVDE building. Perhaps Da Silva has heard such rumors? If I merely invite him to join me for a cup of coffee tomorrow morning, he might volunteer certain information that he thinks that I should know, particularly if he is assured that there will be no repercussions for him personally. And, I will have a surveillance team on him before I make the phone call inviting him here – just in case he decides to do something foolish after receiving my invitation."

"It certainly sounds like it would be worth a try. And if he's not personally involved, perhaps he would at least have some ideas on who else you might invite over for a cup of coffee."

"Exactly. I know you're busy, so let's leave it at that for now and I will phone your office tomorrow if Da Silva tells me anything interesting."

Charles had barely returned to his office when he received a phone call from Captain Lourenco. "Charles, I tried making an appointment with that gentleman we were discussing, but I was told he's out of town till late Sunday night."

"Do you believe that story, and if he's out of town, could that be an indicator that he's involved in what we discussed?"

"His secretary told me this and generally, secretaries really know what their bosses are doing. He has gone out to a small village in central Portugal; it's his elderly father's birthday. And if that's truly where he's gone, I doubt he'll be doing anything more than eating birthday cake. It's a very small village, with barely a telephone in the village. However, I will send a couple of men out there tomorrow to at least confirm his car is there."

"Well, I guess all we can do then is wait until Monday. Perhaps, this is a sign that nothing is happening this weekend, or he'd want to be in the city?"

"Perhaps. He has an appointment to come see me for coffee Monday afternoon."

"OK. I'll pursue a few minor leads from my end and talk with you on Monday."

Charles hated to just sit around idly and not be pursuing some avenue, but he was at a loss at to what else to do for the moment.

## Chapter 21

When Charles arrived at his apartment that evening and opened the door, he was greeted with a wonderful smell emanating from his kitchen. He shouted out, "Not only does my cleaning lady clean, but she can cook! I should marry this woman."

Olga appeared in the doorway of the kitchen, with one towel around her body and a smaller one around her hair. "You're home early. I'm still at work making me beautiful. Go out and buy us bottle of good champagne!"

"Are we celebrating something?"

She let the towel drop from around her body, displaying her spectacular body. "You don't think having this for dessert with your dinner merits champagne?"

"I'll go get two bottles!" He headed out the door while she headed for the bedroom to put on her makeup and her special red dress. The lamb stew continued to slowly boil in the kitchen.

When Charles returned, she was fully dressed and indeed looked beautiful. He missed her red hair, but otherwise, she fulfilled all his dreams. He put the two bottles of pre-war French champagne in his small refrigerator and then came over to her and wrapped his arms around her. After a long, deep kiss, he told her," I love you so much. I'm only happy when you're here with me."

"I loved you. I love you. I will always love." She then laughed.

Charles didn't understand why she thought that was so funny. She tried explaining that it was a play on an old Communist Party slogan about how "Lenin lived. Lenin lives. Lenin will live." Charles still didn't get it.

"That smells wonderful. What is it?"

"Lamb stew, Olga style," she replied while laying her head against his shoulder. They were a perfect fit for each other, with Charles just a little taller than she was.

"And just what does 'Olga style' mean?"

"It mean I put in whatever I could find in your kitchen!" You have worst prepared kitchen in all Portugal or Spain!" She pointed over to the table. "I prepared you list of things you should buy for this kitchen – basic foods, spices and even certain tools of kitchen. How you ever find good wife if you not have well-prepared kitchen?"

"Does that mean you'll marry me if I have a well-stocked kitchen?"

She gave him a very serious face. "Would definitely help your cause – make up for your poor sexual talent!" He smacked her on her perfectly round, firm butt.

"Go set table. I give you sex test later," she said to him in a very low, sultry voice.

While eating, she told him what she'd learned from a man who worked at the port. "He told me that this one particular banker has in recent weeks been a number of times to visit several ship captains. His name Pedro Da Silva." She looked very proud of herself. Charles didn't have the heart to tell her that he'd learned of the lead to Da Silva earlier that day himself from Captain Lourenco.

"Very good. I'll check on him tomorrow."

"We still make our own very good spy agency, yes?"

"Yes, we do. We're better than Nick and Nora Charles!"

At first she had a blank stare, but then she remembered. "Ah, yes, you told me of these movies back in New York City. Tell me, what we going to do when we find these Germans and their gold?"

"Well, as for the gold, that's easy. It will be turned over to an Allied Commission on stolen property that was created recently, which hopefully will be able to determine from whom it was stolen and at war's end, return it to them. As for the people, God only knows! The military officers should wind up in a POW camp somewhere, but technically, they will be in a neutral country, so it will depend on what the Portuguese Government says should happen to them. The Portuguese could send them back to Germany, which of course would mean a death sentence. And nobody will have a clue as to what to do with their wives and children. I hope they never get here. It's going to be a mess of giant proportions if we actually catch them."

"You think gold will ever get back to the people it was stolen from?"

"Maybe for a few national banks, if they can prove that the German Army stole gold from their vaults, but unless it has stamped on each gold bar, 'property of Holland or France' or something definitive like that, how do you decide who a gold bar belongs to? And for individuals, it will be even more unlikely that a person will ever get back a few gold coins that were stolen and melted down."

"I've heard stories of Nazis pulling out gold teeth of Jews after they've been murdered in those camps. How do you give back two teeth worth of gold to the relative of a dead Jew?"

"As I said, it will be a mess."

"I think Allies should give all gold Nazis have to Jews who manage to survive."

"A very kind sentiment, but who represents 'the Jews'? And what about gypsies or ordinary Frenchmen who have been murdered by the Gestapo while fighting for the Underground? And what of the tens of thousands of Russian civilians who've died? Do they all deserve a payment from a pile of German gold?"

She made a grim face. "Yes, I see what you mean – very complicated on how to be fair."

"That's one of the real problems of war; there isn't much that's 'fair' or just. But I do have one thought about the gold. If it gets into the hands of Salazar, it isn't ever going to go to anybody but him and his political regime. If we can ever find the gold, we need to have some way of seizing it for the Allies and immediately take it out of the country, before the Portuguese government has a chance to lay their hands on it."

"Maybe you and me should just take it all and move to Brazil? That would solve whole problem of who gets what percentage. Gold just disappears. We disappear and then rich Mr. and Mrs. Smith show up in Brazil." She poured them both more champagne.

"What about all those suffering Jews and Russians and gypsies we were just discussing?"

She grinned. "I was just testing you. You too honest to steal all gold. You sure you really capitalist?"

"Just on my mother's side." He leaned over and gave her a long kiss. "When am I getting this dessert you mentioned earlier this evening?"

When they awoke in the morning, with headaches from too much champagne, she turned to Charles and said, "I have solution."

"A solution to what?"

"You have men in your office with guns. I have friends in town with guns. We don't need PVDE police to seize the gold. We can do it. If we can learn where it is."

"You make it sound so easy. And what do we do with all the Abwehr officers and their families?"

"Very simple. Let them go on to Brazil. But their gold stays here and is turned over to Allies. Or maybe, I even give them one or two bars of gold so they get to Brazil and not starve in first week."

"You're getting very generous in your old age, with gold that isn't yours!"

"You one who said what mess it will be on what do with German officers and their families. Just let them sail off to Brazil. Auf Wiedersehen!"

His initial reaction of questioning her sanity was fading. He could never get official permission from OSS Headquarters for such a solution, but if the German group somehow just "slipped" through Charles' fingers, well… Who's going to miss 50 or even 100 Germans? And maybe even one or two bars of gold, as Olga suggested? "You know, you might just have a solution to one problem."

## BERLIN
### Saturday

The large German trucks with canvas tops started picking up Abwehr officers, family members and their suitcases from their homes around five o'clock. Colonel Gehlen had observed that there were usually gaps in the Allied bombing runs at that time of the day, with the Americans finishing their daytime bombing around 4:00, but the British not starting their "nighttime" bombing until 9:00 or later. He'd also noted that Saturdays were the lightest days of all. Apparently, the American GIs liked to have Saturdays off. Gehlen had personally drawn up the routes the trucks were to use for the pickups and then their travel to the airbase. The seven different trucks then drove directly into a large hanger, where the people were sat at tables and were given food. It would be many hours before there would be another opportunity to eat. Their suitcases were taken directly to the planes and loaded, along with seven crates, marked desert boots. A couple of the officers observing this wondered why on earth would they need desert boots and also that the crates seemed to be awfully heavy, the way the workers were straining to move them. The selected officers had never precisely been told to where they and their families were headed on this "secret mission" – only that they would be gone for several months, but that their families would be much safer than if they remained behind in Germany. Speculation among the men had ranged from some place in Africa or South America, or even China. Colonel Gehlen had promised them that Admiral Canaris would address them that night at the airport before their departure. He hoped that would indeed happen.

At 8:00 p.m. sharp, Admiral Canaris' vehicle arrived at the home of Admiral Donitz for the latter's birthday party. He had a beautiful mansion, which had been in the family for many generations, just outside of the city, which made it seem less likely to be bombed. They did avoid any outside lighting and kept all the curtains carefully drawn, so as not to appear a potential secondary target to any enemy bomber that might have gotten lost enroute to his assigned target. These safety precautions would also make it easier for Canaris to slip away from the house in a small truck, without attracting any attention from Gestapo guards around the grounds of the mansion.

When Canaris was dropped at the main door on the ground floor, he left his coat at the check room, but then rather than immediately going up the grand staircase, he headed for a bathroom down a side corridor. Waiting there was one of his men, who gave him an enlisted man's winter coat and hat, and an empty wooden crate that had held potatoes. The officer escorted "Sgt Canaris" towards a side door and into the back of a small supply truck. The truck drove slowly out of the compound and headed for the airport, where the special flight was waiting.

The truck arrived with 30 minutes to spare before the flights were to depart. Colonel Gehlen greeted the Admiral as he climbed out of the back of the truck.

"Congratulations, Colonel on a brilliant plan. If only we could do this well on the battlefield, we'd be winning this war." They both laughed.

They walked over to the officers and families who had gathered up in a semi-circle on the cold, concrete floor of the hanger. Canaris had still been thinking during the ride in the truck on exactly what to say to these young men, all of whom he knew by first name. His men admired and respected him, but he had never been known as a particularly warm and open individual, and he saw no reason to suddenly pretend that he was such a person now. He walked with purposeful strides to the center of the half-circle and began immediately to speak.

"Good evening, gentlemen and ladies. You are about to start on an arduous and dangerous mission, but I promise you that within a week or two you will have started a whole new stage of your careers and your lives." Timed perfectly, there were some distant explosions of bombs hitting German soil. "Lives which will be free of fear from bombings. Colonel Gehlen will brief you in detail in just a few days as to where you're headed and your specific mission, but let me say to you now, I shall be proud of you and Germany will be proud of you in the months ahead. The war is not going well here in Europe. It's time to prepare for alternatives and your futures. Good luck." A few men noticed that he'd said "Germany," not the "Reich." He then passed along the front of the crowd and shook hands with each of his officers. It was understood without saying that they would never see him again after that night.

As all of the other passengers started loading into the planes, Ewald and Wilhelm drew off to one side. "Ewald, you have a difficult mission ahead of you, but I have complete confidence that you will make this happen, for the good of our men and their families."

"I shall succeed. We've been friends for more than 20 years. It's hard to say farewell, especially since I know that this coming week will be quite unpleasant for you."

Canaris smiled. "Me -- wait till you read someday the nasty things I'm going to say about you at your courts martial next week!"

Gehlen stood erect and saluted his commander and his friend for the last time. Canaris returned the salute, then turned and headed back to his potato truck, while Gehlen headed for the plane. He was the last man to board.

By the time the planes were all airborne and well to the south of Berlin, Admiral Canaris was safely back mingling with all the other guests at the mansion and was there in plenty of time to sing Happy Birthday to the guest of honor. During the ensuing investigation of what happened that Saturday night, Canaris' Gestapo watchers would testify that he'd been at the Donitz mansion the entire evening.

## Chapter 22

The German planes landed at a small, Portuguese Army airfield near Lisbon just before the sun was setting on Sunday evening. It had been a long and arduous flight and everyone was glad to be on the ground. It was essential that they had arrived while it was still daylight, as there were no lights or even barrels of oil to light to accommodate nighttime landings at this secondary field. They'd been lucky so far on this bizarre odyssey. When they had landed in the early hours of Sunday morning back in Bavaria, all the pilots of the planes were quite young, relatively new to the Luftwaffe and readily accepted orders from a superior officer without much question. So, when Colonel Gehlen had told them that there had been a last minute change of plans and they were flying on to Portugal as part of a secret mission, none of the crews raised any objections. They thought it strange, but then, that was what the Abwehr did. They didn't understand why a bunch of women and children were along on a secret mission, but the German military trained its personnel to follow orders, not ask questions.

Colonel Karsthoff had made all the necessary arrangements many weeks earlier with an elderly Portuguese Army captain who was in charge of the airfield on weekends. It had been necessary for Gehlen to phone early that week and double talk the new instructions to the Portuguese banker Pedro Da Silva. Eventually, he understood that he was to contact this captain and let him know that the arrival date had been moved forward and to make the necessary changes at the hotel. As they came in for the landing, Gehlen was pleased to see that they did seem to be expected. There were several buses and two trucks standing by to haul the passengers and the crates of "desert boots" from the field as darkness fell. The first step of Plan Grandfather had gone smoothly. The pilots were instructed to spend the night in their planes, refuel the next morning and then depart for Bavaria, maintaining radio silence during the return flight until just before landing in Germany. As for any questions when they got back in Germany, the pilots were to simply say they had been acting under the orders of Colonel Gehlen and refer all questions to Abwehr Headquarters. As all the "missing" officers had been given leave until the following Saturday, there hopefully wouldn't be any great concern about their whereabouts for six more days. All of Gehlen's group was scheduled to depart on different ships over the next several days, with the last to depart that upcoming Friday. With just a little luck, everyone and their "special" cargo would be well out to sea before the alarm went up back in Berlin.

All of the German officers were in civilian clothes, but only idiots would not have recognized the men of the arriving group as some sort of military personnel from their physical shapes and bearing, though the presence of women and children confused the few Portuguese ground personnel who were on duty that evening. Colonel Gehlen gave the Portuguese Army captain a large envelope of British pound notes, just before the buses departed, to "help" him and the airfield crew forget about any planes having arrived there that Sunday evening. The buses bounced along the rough Portuguese roads for several hours, but finally reached their prearranged hotel around 10:00 p.m. Gehlen had one young officer with him who spoke Portuguese and he was brought forward to deal with the hotel owner and the few staff members present. He explained to the owner how they were all Swiss bankers and tourists, and after checking the large envelope full of British pound sterling notes, he pretended to believe the story. By midnight, everyone had had a light dinner of cold cuts and bread and had managed to settle into their assigned rooms. Gehlen made a mental note to himself to congratulate this Portuguese banker when finally they met on his efficiency. So far, everything was going according to plan. Three of the single officers were given handguns and told to guard till morning the truck sitting behind the main hotel building that was carrying the crates.

By that same Sunday evening, Charles and Olga had completed their independent preparations for action, IF they ever somehow got word of a group of Germans traveling with an undetermined amount of gold. On Friday, Charles, in consultation with Salvatore and Lou, had come to the conclusion that Olga's idea for how to handle this very odd situation was indeed the correct one. Charles had standing by ten of his younger officers, who had all been issued with rifles in addition to their usual handguns, to be part of the "raiding party." Olga had reported that she had about the same number of locals with guns and two trucks standing by to assist in the "rescue" of the gold from the German travelers. Charles had also checked with the Army Air Corps representative at the American Embassy about planes and learned that on almost every day of the week, there were two or three cargo planes on the ground in Lisbon that could handle carrying several large crates out of the country. Having a day or so advance notice would be useful, but he could arrange for cargo transportation on short notice if necessary.

Charles and Olga had also reached the conclusion that the Germans, if it really was a group of young officers traveling with wives and children, would simply be allowed "to escape" during the raid to seize the gold. Salvatore and Lou were to play an important role in that part of the plan, so that no others of the OSS officers besides Charles would have to be direct participants in their crazy plan. A plan which might get Charles dismissed from the OSS and possibly even prosecuted if Washington didn't believe the story that all the Germans, and their personal luggage, had all "escaped." Charles was sort of hoping that his Headquarters would focus on the successful seizure of the gold and not dwell on the fleeing Germans.

He and Olga had even agreed that, depending on the amount of gold seized, a small amount might even be left with the German travellers, so that they could at least complete their plans to reach Brazil. After advice from Salvatore and Lou on how smuggling was normally done, they'd concluded that the secret travel on cargo ships would only have been partially paid up front and that the Germans would need some money to pay certain bribes to be allowed to board the ships and sail for Brazil. This all presumed that Fraulein Sahrbach's story was actually true and there really were dozens of Germans with wives and children sneaking through Portugal on their way to new lives in Brazil with boxes of gold! As Charles fell asleep that Sunday night with Olga snuggled up to him, he was strongly hoping that Captain Lourenco would be able to force some interesting answers out of banker Da Silva that coming Monday afternoon.

Pedro Da Silva stayed Sunday night at his father's house in the countryside, instead of returning to Lisbon that night, but left very early on Monday morning. Enroute to the city, he stopped at the "closed" hotel in Sesimbra to see if the Germans had arrived. After a brief conversation at Reception, he was taken to the room of Colonel Gehlen.

When the door opened, he introduced himself in German. "Good morning. I am Mr. Da Silva, an acquaintance of Colonel Karstoff. Welcome to Portugal!"

"I am Colonel Gehlen. The leader of our group. I understand that you are responsible for all of these arrangements?"

"Yes, I have arranged for the hotel and for your onward journey to Brazil."

"I must compliment you, on how well everything has gone so far. Please come in and let's chat about the next steps."

"I must say that your sudden change of dates has not made my life easy, especially in terms of arranging with enough ship captains to handle all of you, but all has ended well. However, with a couple of the captains, they are now demanding more money."

"And why does departing sooner cost more money?"

The banker smiled. Obviously, the good Colonel had never dealt much in arranging illegal affairs. "It's not that the true cost is higher; it's just that the captains sense that with your need to suddenly depart sooner, there is some reason for this and that they can squeeze a few more pounds out of you. They do rather have you over a barrel, as the English say."

Gehlen nodded his understanding. In a world where everything is done for money, naturally, the players want to maximize their profits. "And just how much more will departing as soon as possible cost me?"

"I have managed to keep it down to only twenty percent more, by implying that there might be further such passenger business for them, if this first time goes well."

"Very well, that is acceptable, but with one change of plan. I want to put my people on the ships by Tuesday night, regardless of when they are actually sailing. It's hard to say what sort of reaction there will be out of Berlin once the pilots who brought us here are questioned. There might be pressure on the Portuguese Government to find their 'missing' citizens. It would probably be best if none of us were still on dry land after Tuesday."

"To be honest, you might be more secure here at this hotel until a ship is actually ready to sail, but if your desire is to load everyone by tomorrow night…" Da Silva shrugged his shoulders, as if to say, "Well, it's your money, so we'll do whatever you prefer."

They continued discussing the fine details of how the buses would take everyone and the cargo to the different ships around midnight, hopefully on Tuesday night. That would mean leaving the hotel no later than 11:00 p.m. Gehlen's ship and the special crates would actually sail on the morning tide Wednesday. Two more ships on Thursday and the fourth and final ship on Friday.

"It won't be very pleasant for your men, wives and children who are not sailing for a day or two, but they must be kept out of sight below decks, until the ships are well out to sea on their departure day."

"Understood. I will explain this to my people today. We shall be prepared to depart by 11:00 p.m. tomorrow night."

"Very well. I will go directly from here to the port to negotiate this last change to the plan. Approximately half of the fees have already been paid. The rest of what is owed will be paid upon arrival at the ships on Tuesday night."

"Fine. Will I see you tomorrow night?"

"No, there will be nothing more for me to do after today. I will leave with you now the figures of how much more needs to paid, but you and your people on the different ships will pay that directly to the ship captains."

"Do I owe you anything more?"

"No, Colonel Karsthoff was most generous in his payments to me already and it's an honor in any case, to serve the Fatherland."

"You have been most helpful. But I must admit, that this additional 20 percent will just about clean us out as far as cash goes, until we reach Brazil."

"Understood. By the way, have you heard from Colonel Karsthoff since his return home?"

"No, have you?" he answered correctly, but quite deceivingly, as he knew that Karsthoff had died in a plane crash.

"Actually, there are a few rumors going around Lisbon that he was killed in a plane crash on his way home, and that his personal secretary has disappeared from Lisbon as well."

"I regret to inform you that in fact there was a tragic accident on his way home and indeed his plane did crash in southern Germany. As far as Fraulein Sahrbach, she is simply back home on vacation. Fortunately, she and Colonel Karsthoff were on separate flights." Gehlen saw no reason to tell Da Silva that she had in fact vanished about the same day that her boss had been informed of his recall and nobody knew where she had gone.

"Well, that is tragic news about the Colonel, but I'm relieved to hear that his charming secretary is safe and well."

Gehlen and Da Silva stood, shook hands, and then the banker was on his way. Da Silva proceeded directly to the port to get agreement from the captains that their "passengers" could board Tuesday night, regardless of when the ship was actually sailing. The captain of the ship that wasn't sailing until Friday particularly didn't like the idea, but for yet another small added fee, he finally agreed. Knowing how cash strapped the Germans were, Da Silva simply paid that amount out of his own fee already paid him. He truly was a German patriot.

Mr. Da Silva arrived at his bank around noon, at which time, his secretary informed him that he had an appointment at 4:00 p.m. with Captain Lourenco of the PVDE. That made him nervous, but the message was that Lourenco simply needed some assistance with a minor banking question – shouldn't take much of his time at all.

When Da Silva arrived at PVDE Headquarters later that afternoon, a young Lieutenant greeted him at the main entrance and announced that he was to escort the banker to his meeting with Captain Lourenco. Da Silva was a bit mystified when they started going down the stairway instead of up. He presumed that the Captain for the Lisbon region of the PVDE would have a nice office on an upper floor. Instead, he soon found himself in a sub-basement and sitting on a hard wooden chair behind a very small desk in a windowless room. This was clearly an interrogation cell, and Da Silva didn't like the signs of where this alleged "assistance with a minor banking question" was headed. One heard such horrible rumors of what went on in the basement of the PVDE Building!

Captain Lourenco left Da Silva sitting alone in the interrogation room with only one light bulb in it, for about twenty minutes before entering the room. He wanted to give time to the banker for his mind to be contemplating the worst possible fate that was awaiting him that

Monday afternoon. Successful interrogation was all about psychology, not the physical treatment of a suspect. Shortly before Lourenco entered Da Silva's room, he had one of his young officers scream loud and long from a room down the hallway. His colleagues had to suppress their inclination to laugh. This went on for several minutes. Lourenco knew that Da Silva had a number of well-connected political friends, so he'd have to treat him much more politely than some typical street criminal.

Da Silva almost leaped from his chair when the heavy metal door of his room opened and in came Captain Lourenco.

"Good afternoon Mr. Da Silva. I am Captain Antonio Lourenco. So good of you to stop by to offer your assistance with one of my inquiries."

Da Silva managed to regain a little of his composure. "Of course, Captain. Our bank is always happy to cooperate with the PVDE in its important work for our country." He managed a small smile.

"Actually, I've just very recently had a breakthrough in this investigation and I believe that I have a pretty good understanding of what was being planned, but you might be able to clear up just a few minor details."

"What can I do for you?"

I understand that you were acquainted with Colonel Karsthoff of the German Embassy, until his recent recall to Berlin?"

"Yes, I was. He was a most charming host at some dinners I attended at his lovely home, and as I presume you know, my mother was German."

"Oh, really. I wasn't aware of that familial connection to Germany." There proceeded several minutes of conversation about his mother and how she had grown up in Brazil. Lourenco pretended this was news to him and Da Silva pretended that he believed Lourenco's claim of not knowing of his mother's background.

Captain Lourenco finally got to the point of his request that Da Silva drop by that day. "Mr. Da Silva, are you aware of a group of Germans who are planning to visit Portugal in the near future? Germans who are planning to move to Brazil?" Lourenco stared hard into the eyes of the banker, as his face took on a stern look. It gave a message of, "you don't want to lie to me."

Da Silva knitted his brow as if deeply thinking about the question. "No, I don't recall hearing of any Germans passing through our country."

"Or possibly you've heard about any plans of smuggling Nazi gold through Portugal on its way to Brazil?"

"No, definitely, nothing about gold. There would be a number of forms that would have to be submitted to the government in connection with any such transfer of gold, and I've heard nothing about any such forms being prepared."

"No, I didn't think that you would have, or as a patriotic citizen you would have reported any such rumors to the government – actually, to me."

This roundabout conversation continued for another half hour.

"Captain, I'm beginning to think that you suspect I have something to do with this smuggling scheme that you keep referring to in your questions. If that is the case, I would like to have my lawyer come be present at this meeting. Given my position, I demand proper treatment before this questioning will proceed."

Lourenco sat in silence.

Da Silva sat in silence.

Lourenco was coming around to the conclusion that Da Silva's interrogation would take much longer then he'd initially hoped it would -- before the man told him anything of consequence -- though his gut feelings of being a policeman for twenty years told him that Da Silva was up to his freshly starched collar tab in this whole business. So much for subtle intimidation, he thought to himself.

"Your lawyer? Ah well, those screams you heard when you first arrived – that was your lawyer. I don't think he'll be available to give you any advice for some time. I'm going to go take a piss. Why don't you search your memory to see if you can't remember making visits recently to chat with certain ship captains and what the subject of those conversations was? I'll be back in a while." He stubbed out the cigarette he'd been smoking while staring directly into Da Silva's eyes, then walked out of the room without saying anything further.

He did in fact stop at the lavatory on the way back up to his office. He then immediately phoned Charles at his office.

"I've been having a relatively friendly chat with that fellow for the past half hour, without much progress. He denies knowing anything, but the longer we chat, my instincts tell me he knows a great deal."

"So what do we do now?" asked Charles.

"Are you free to come over to my office to have a chat? Perhaps there is something that you can do to assist me."

"Certainly. I can be there within about thirty minutes."

"Excellent. I was about to send out for some dinner. Would you like something as well? We could be here awhile this evening."

"Fine, I'll have whatever you're having. See you soon."

When Charles arrived a half hour later, Captain Lourenco had just started on his dinner at his desk.

"Come in Charles. Your timing is perfect. Our food has just arrived. I trust you like our chicken piri-piri?"

"I do, very much. An excellent choice. So, has our friend come around yet?"

"Nothing since I spoke with you on the phone. I've just left him down in one of the interrogation cells to think about his situation."

Antonio proceeded to tell Charles how the earlier questioning had gone, while they ate their dinner, washed down with a nice local white wine. He then reached the moment of making a suggestion for Charles' assistance.

"Part of the problem here is that I think he's very afraid of me and what might happen to him, should he admit to whatever his role has been in this smuggling plan. I am the traditional 'bad cop.' I think you should play the 'good cop.' I think that if he sees that you are part of this inquiry, he would be much more inclined to take your word as an American diplomat, that no harm will come to him personally – if he tells us the truth about what has been arranged for Germans to transit to Brazil."

Charles was certainly familiar with the good cop—bad cop gambit. "I'm happy to play a role, but exactly what 'good' things can I offer him?"

"Sometimes the PVDE's reputation helps us in our questioning, but in this case, I think he believes that he is going to wind up dead, or at least in prison for many years, if he confesses to any involvement in this smuggling plan. Perhaps, if he has the word that the Allies, and you personally, are guaranteeing his safety and there will be no repercussions… he might be inclined to tell us what he knows." Antonio nodded his head and shrugged his shoulders. "Worth a try?"

"Yes, certainly worth a try. Shall we go down now and chat with him?"

Antonio checked his watch. "Let's leave him alone for a few more hours to think about his situation, before his American white knight arrives to save him."

"Whatever you think is best. That will give me time to finish my delicious dinner!" They both laughed and returned to their food.

Around ten o'clock, Lourenco nodded and indicated it was time. They'd gone over what Charles should say to Da Silva while alone with him. Antonio said, "It's well after dark and it's been quiet down in the basement for some time. Rumor has it that rats come around to some of the cells in the evening hours. That should make a nice impression on our friend." Charles thought to himself that he'd certainly never like to be arrested by Captain Lourenco!

When they reached the room, Lourenco entered first. He found a much more subdued person than when he'd left several hours earlier. "Mr. Da Silva, I've brought you a guest." Charles entered and nodded to the banker.

"I am Charles Worthington, of the American Embassy." He walked over to the small table where Da Silva was sitting, and extended his hand. Lourenco left the room and closed the door behind him.

The banker stood and extended his own hand. "Pedro Da Silva, Vice-President of the Espirito Santo Bank." He looked positively relieved to see anyone besides Lourenco, and especially an official from another country. "I'm glad you're here Mr. Worthington. I fear there has been a terrible misunderstanding with the PVDE about my participation in some smuggling plan."

Charles sat down at the table. "Mr. Da Silva, please don't insult my intelligence. Fraulein Elizabeth Sahrbach has told me everything about the plan that Colonel Karsthoff arranged for a number of German officers and their families to travel to Brazil – and oh, yes, about the gold that was to go with them. She also told me about your meetings with Colonel Karsthoff and your role in making certain arrangements. About all I don't know is precisely when this move takes place."

Da Silva's smile and renewed self-confidence immediately vanished. He made one last effort at bravado. "I want to see my lawyer, immediately!"

"I just saw your lawyer in a room down the hallway." Charles produced a grimace on his face. "I really don't believe he's going to be of much assistance to you. Captain Lourenco seems quite skeptical that he doesn't know much about this smuggling plan, and by the way, he doesn't believe your denials either."

The two men then sat there in silence for a good full minute, simply staring at each other.

"Mr. Da Silva, I can help you, with your very 'difficult' situation."

A faint glimmer of hope showed on the banker's face. "Do please continue."

"I'm guessing that you're afraid of what will happen to you, if you confess to participation in this smuggling scheme, or perhaps what will happen to you, even if you continue to deny any knowledge of the plan. And you might well be correct. However, I can guarantee you, on behalf of the Allied Supreme Council and the American Embassy here in Lisbon, that once you've confessed and cooperated, you will not be physically harmed, nor will any legal charges even be brought against you. Does that interest you?"

"Yes, yes it would. May I have that guarantee in writing?"

Charles smiled benignly, as occasionally Olga did to him when he said something rather naïve. "If you don't trust my word, do you really think a piece of paper with a few signatures on it is really going to carry any weight?"

Da Silva sat in silence for 10-15 seconds. "No, I suppose it wouldn't. But I have your personal word on these guarantees?"

"Indeed you do. Now, are you ready to tell us what you know about this plan by Colonel Karsthoff?"

Another bit of silence, while the banker contemplated any other remaining options. "Yes, I'm ready to tell you all I know."

He then proceeded to recount in great detail his previous meetings with Colonel Karsthoff about this plan and then of the meeting one night with Admiral Canaris himself to confirm the arrangements. Charles didn't bother writing down any details given by Da Silva, as he presumed, quite rightly, that the room had to be wired with microphones.

"The final count I was given for the number of German travelers was 109, which included the wives and children. I think it was 60 some officers. There were also to be five crates, which Colonel Karsthoff implied would contain some gold and other valuables, such as paintings. These would go on the ships with the passengers. There were to be no public records of passengers or their cargo. The passengers would be spread out over five different Portuguese cargo ships, which would sail on different days over about a week's period of time."

Charles found his own pulse quickening as he thought to himself, "My god, this is true!"

"Did Karsthoff or Canaris explain to you what the purpose of sending these families and the valuables to Brazil was?"

"I know this will sound crazy, but they both claimed that this was to give these young officers and their families a new start on life. They know that Germany is going to lose the war and the situation in Germany will be very bad once the Red Army troops started arriving across Germany. Canaris believed he owed them a new chance in life."

Charles was still skeptical of such an altruistic reason for the travel of the group. "Were Canaris or Karsthoff making the trip to Brazil?"

"No, neither of them. Colonel Karsthoff explained to me that he still had family back in Germany and could not desert them. I asked him a couple of times, as it was rather clear to me that the Colonel and his secretary, Fraulein Sahrbach, had a, shall we say, 'special' relationship and I thought they might go off together to Brazil. I think there might have been some discussion of her going alone to Brazil, but nothing was ever decided before Karsthoff was recalled to Germany. A Colonel Ewald Gehlen is apparently the senior official among the travelers."

Charles was still astounded. If this was the true story, it was the most altruistic one he'd ever heard and certainly not the actions of a man who was the head of the intelligence apparatus of his despicable enemy, Nazi Germany.

"And now for the most important question, Mr. Da Silva. When will they be arriving in Portugal?"

He hesitated slightly. "They're already here and will be loading onto their ships tomorrow night around midnight."

Now it was Charles' turn to look in shock. "Where are they now?"

"Mr. Worthington, I think the rest of this conversation could be conducted much better at my bank first thing in the morning. It isn't that I don't trust you, but all I have is your word that I will be leaving here unharmed tonight and we've never met until this day."

"This is not a negotiation. You will tell me all you know now."

"Ah, but I think it is a negotiation and I will feel much more comfortable entering into an agreement with you while sitting in the office of the president of my bank, whose cousin is a general of the Portuguese Army. Once I tell you the final details of this German plan, what further need do you or Captain Lourenco have of me? Rest assured that with the information in hand tomorrow morning, you will have plenty of time to take whatever actions you might be planning."

They went back and forth over this point for several minutes, but it was clear that Da Silva saw this as a non-negotiable point.

"Very well. You will spend this night in the comfort of your own bed, but just to make sure that nothing happens to you between now and, say, 9:00 a.m. tomorrow morning at your bank, when we'll continue this conversation, several of Captain Lourenco's officers will escort you home. They will also stay just outside your bedroom door during the night and the phone will be removed from your room."

Da Silva looked appalled. "Who has a phone in his bedroom? That's what servants are for at my home. I will need to make one call when I get home. That will be to the president of my bank to inform him that he will need to come in early tomorrow to meet me there at 9:00 – normally, he never arrives before 10:00."

Charles stood and went to the metal door. He rapped on it several times, just to maintain the pretense that their entire conversation had not been listened to by Captain Lourenco. Captain Lourenco entered, with two of his men.

"Mr. Da Silva will go home and after making one call to his bank president, he will remain there under guard, until he is driven to his bank at 9:00 a.m. to finish his conversation with me. At that time, he will tell me of the current location of the Germans and the details of their travel plans for tomorrow night."

Lourenco and Da Silva both nodded in acknowledgement that that was the agreed upon plan.

"Oh, just one more thing. I suggest, Captain, that a number of your men keep the port under close watch tonight – just in case Mr. Da Silva has mixed up in his mind the date that the Germans are sailing."

"An excellent idea. Mr. DaSilva, these men will escort you to one of our cars to take you home."

After Da Silva's departure, the two returned to Lourenco's more comfortable office on the top floor.

"Do you believe what he told you?" inquired Lourenco.

"Yes, I do. I think he's too afraid of you to try lying in his current situation. The real question for us, is when do we want to seize the Germans and their possessions?"

"Good question. If we wait till they reach the harbor, there will be all sorts of commotion and no way to keep this whole mess a secret, which I believe the Portuguese Government would prefer, and perhaps yours as well. If we try to seize them at whatever location they are presently residing, they could have weapons and it could turn ugly. With many women and children present, I'd certainly like to avoid a massive gun fight. So, I think intercepting them along the road when they are in vehicles and not suspecting anything might be the best approach."

"I agree with your logic. If Da Silva's information will allow us to figure out what their route Tuesday night will be, then yes, that might well be the best approach. I have about twenty men standing by to be part of this seizure, so if the PVDE being involved at all in the raid is going to create diplomatic problems for your government with Berlin, it may be that your people will not be needed to participate at all."

Charles had been debating how best to bring up this point with Antonio, but saw an opportunity and took it. He wasn't sure how he would respond.

"Well, the political fallout of this is an issue. If this becomes public, which it most likely will if the PVDE seizes and puts in jail a hundred German citizens, the German Ambassador will be in Prime Minister's Salazar's office within a matter of hours. Germany may be losing the war, but it hasn't lost yet and thus relations with Germany are a consideration. And you and I both know what will happen with these people if they are turned over to the German government! Just what would you do with these people and the valuables?"

"Everything and everybody would be turned over to the Allied Command. It would be up to SHAEF in London to formally decide, but I could certainly arrange for the people and whatever they've brought with them to be on planes to England by early Wednesday morning. The Abwehr officers would be put in POW camps, but some sort of humane resolution would be found for the wives and children. And in this way, you could deny everything. To all questions from the German Embassy, if there are any, you just say 'what Germans?' Da Silva and any others who were part of this plan certainly won't be saying anything publicly."

"Your last point is a good one. Da Silva certainly won't be opening his mouth in public; he'll just be happy he isn't in my basement." They both laughed.

"I agree with you about what will happen to these German travelers if they are sent back to Germany. They would be treated as deserters and shot. Much better for them if they simply wind up in a nice, safe POW camp in England."

"Do you think your 20 men can handle the nighttime capture?"

"We need to hear what Da Silva tells us in the morning. Hopefully, there will be an obvious point along the road from the spot where the Germans are now located to the port, where an ambush could logically be done. However, it might not be a bad idea if you and another twenty of your men just 'happened' to be doing a nighttime training exercise fairly nearby and could rush in, in case things did turn ugly."

Antonio smiled. "My men love nighttime training!"

"Alright. I think that's all we can do for tonight. I will wait for you outside the main building of the Espirito Santo Bank at 8:45 tomorrow morning."

"Agreed."

They had discussed everything that needed discussing, and Charles wanted to get home to Olga. She might need to go out yet that night and let her people know to be ready for Tuesday night. And on top of that, he knew he only had a few more days before she thought she would be leaving to go back to Spain. He hated to miss out on any hours to be with her, and it would certainly be crazy in the day or two after Tuesday night's planned raid.

## Chapter 23

Charles found Olga sound asleep on his living room couch when he finally arrived home that Monday night. He'd stopped at a small bar and used the telephone to place a call to Salvatore to let him know the poker game was on for Tuesday night and that he and Lou should plan on coming by his apartment around 10:30 a.m. the next morning. Charles figured they'd be plenty of time in the morning to let his people know about Tuesday night – no need to alert anyone now.

He stood over her and watched her sleeping for several minutes. He loved looking at her beautiful face. He then sat down next to her and stroked her hair. She started to wake up.

"Some spy you are! Letting someone come in and sit down next to you before you even woke up."

She let out a big yawn and stretched. Then she pulled his head down to hers for a long kiss. "I knew it was you all time. You sound like American when you walk. Why you come home so late?"

"I've been busy finding out where the German soldiers and their gold will be tomorrow night!"

"How did you do that?"

"I'll go over all the details in a minute, but first a question. Our raid will be happening tomorrow night around 9:00 or 10:00 p.m. Do you need to go out now and let anybody know, so your people will be ready tomorrow night?"

She looked at the clock on the end table and then thought for a minute. "No, would be better tomorrow morning. My people already know they are to be ready on any night this week."

He proceeded to tell her about his 'good cop, bad cop' session with the Portuguese banker Da Silva and of the agreement to get the fine details from him at 9:00 a.m. tomorrow morning at his bank. "Most importantly, I convinced Captain Lourenco to let me and my men seize the people and whatever valuable cargo they will have with them. He saw the logic in my plan of getting the Germans and whatever they are smuggling out of Portugal and up to England the very next morning – before this even has a chance of becoming public knowledge around Lisbon. This will save the Salazar government from any pressure by the German Embassy."

"And you told him nothing about me and my friends helping?"

"No, I simply referred to doing the raid with my people."

"Good. You gave him no hint of letting the Germans 'escape' tomorrow night?"

"No, I didn't, but after listening to Da Silva, I'm even more convinced that letting them go on to Brazil is the best idea. It certainly sounds as if this really is a humanitarian gesture by Canaris to these junior officers and the families to leave the war and simply start over in Brazil."

"Did DaSilva have any idea of how much gold the Germans have brought with them?"

"Not really, but if this is to be the money for a hundred plus people to start new lives in Brazil, it must be more than just a few thousand dollars."

"And you still plan to give them some of the gold they smuggle?"

"They will certainly need some, so as to pay the ship captains and a few dollars to get started once they arrive in Rio de Janeiro."

She nodded in agreement with his plan.

"I wasn't sure when you would be returning, so I didn't cook any dinner, but I did bake you some cookies, like they have in New York City."

She retrieved a plate with the sugar cookies from the kitchen. Charles had horrible expectations, but they were actually pretty tasty. "Say, you might make a good wife after all!"

She went over to his record player and put on one of her favorite tunes from her days in Manhattan, an old romantic melody from the 1920s called "Always" by Irving Berlin. She only knew a couple of lines of the song: "I'll be loving you, always; With a love that's true, always."

She cuddled up with him on the couch and hummed along with the rest of the song. When it finished, she looked up into his eyes and said to him, "And I always will, regardless of what happens to us in this horrible war." Tears came from her eyes. Neither of them spoke. Charles pulled her tightly to him, and there they remained till well past midnight. Charles couldn't think of a better way to fall asleep than to have her in his arms, that night and hopefully, for the rest of their lives.

Olga prepared him some eggs and coffee in the morning before he headed off to meet Lourenco. She would wait at the apartment until he returned by midmorning, along with Salvatore and Lou, so as to make their final plans for that night.

Charles found Captain Lourenco sitting in the backseat of his official vehicle in front of the Espirito Santo Bank at 8:45 a.m. Da Silva arrived in the car with two of Lourenco's officers just a few minutes later and the three walked into the bank together.

They went directly to the office of the president of the bank, only to learn from his secretary that he had called about ten minutes earlier to advise that he would not actually arrive till about 9:30. Da Silva shrugged his shoulders and said, "Let's just go to my office and talk." He seemed to feel more confident simply by the fact he was in his building, not the basement of the PVDE. He turned back to the secretary, "Please ask Mr. Marchand to come directly to my office when he arrives. He knows what this is about." The trio then headed to Da Silva's office. He ordered his secretary to bring in coffee for the three of them.

"Gentlemen, please have a seat." He took his place behind his large ornate desk. He was definitely feeling in a better mood than the day before, feeling much more secure in his office that bespoke authority and influence. "What a beautiful fall day we are having today."

Charles decided to cut this direction of the meeting immediately, before Da Silva forgot what he had agreed the previous evening to provide that morning.

"Mr. Da Silva I did not come here this morning to discuss the weather, to apply for a loan or to sell you tickets to the policemen's charity ball next month. Captain Lourenco might have time to sit around chatting with you and drinking coffee. I do not. I have to make arrangements to capture a bunch of Nazi soldiers that you have illegally helped smuggle into Portugal, along with gold that was no doubt stolen somewhere in Europe. Never mind what the PVDE may or may not do to you now, when this war ends, I will have you arrested and extradited as a war criminal who worked with the Nazis, if you don't immediately start giving me the information we agreed upon yesterday." This time it was Lourenco who was thinking that he wouldn't want to have Charles interrogating him.

The smile and look of self-confidence had vanished from Da Silva's face. "Mr. Worthington, we are all still in agreement. I was merely making some small talk until the coffee arrived, but if you wish to proceed directly to the business before us, let us begin."

Charles leaned back in his chair. "Very well, let's begin."

"The group arrived Sunday night and were taken by several buses directly from the small, Portuguese military airfield just outside of Lisbon to a tourist inn in Sesimbra, the Alhambra. The entire inn is reserved for the group. The owner and staff were told they are Swiss banking officials, here on a holiday with their wives and children." He leaned forward and wrote down on a full sheet of paper the names of the five ships and their captains, with whom arrangements had been made for their transportation to Brazil. He wrote next to each ship name the date it would sail from Lisbon. "They will all board their respective ships tonight around midnight, even though only one of them sails early Wednesday morning with the tide. The rest will stay hidden on the other ships until their sailing dates."

Charles accepted the sheet of paper from Da Silva and handed it to Lourenco, who responded, "Yes, I am acquainted with these ships and most of their captains. What time will the Germans depart the inn for the port?"

"It is planned for 10:00 p.m., but with so many people and women and children, it's hard to predict if they will depart promptly at 10:00 or not. I will not be there." He shrugged his shoulders, as if to say, "It isn't my problem."

"What route will they take?" asked Charles.

Another shrug. "I have not discussed this with any of the drivers, but I would think that the only logical choice would be to take the Sesimbra Main Highway, until the edge of Lisbon, then turn off onto the Harbor Road. There are some other small country lanes, but this would be the logical route for large buses and a truck with several crates."

Charles looked over at Antonio, who nodded in agreement with Da Silva about the options for the travel of buses and a truck.

"Anything else you think it would be useful for me to know?" asked Charles.

"Only that this Colonel Gehlen seems like a most determined man. I don't think he will easily surrender."

Charles stood. "Thank you for your cooperation. You will now tell your secretary that you're not feeling well and are going home. You will stay at home with Captain Lourenco's men until tonight's operation has ended. Once again, there will be no phone calls or communication with anyone. If all goes well tonight, today will be the last you see of either of us in regard to this matter, nor will your name be mentioned in any reports about the seizure of the Germans or their cargo. Are we in agreement?" Charles looked to Lourenco and then to Da Silva.

"We are," replied Captain Lourenco.

"Agreed," replied Da Silva. He then extended his hand to shake Mr. Worthington's. By 9:20, all of them had left the building and gone their separate ways. Bank President Marchand had still not arrived.

Charles picked up Salvatore and Lou and the three were back at his apartment by 10:00. Olga had gone out briefly to make one phone call, but had returned and had a big pot of coffee prepared by the time the three of them arrived. She had hid from Charles the night before some of her home-baked cookies, so she still had a few to offer to Sally and Lou. They shared Charles' opinion that they were delicious. "When we alls go back to New York City, why don'ts youse comes in to business with us Olga? Sally and me will finance youse to opens a cookie shop in Brooklyn," suggested Lou.

"An excellent suggestion," added Charles. "I bet Mr. Astor would even invest a few dollars, once he tasted one of these."

Olga was actually blushing. She'd been in gunfights and had killed men, but compliments over her cookies made her blush. She retreated to the kitchen to compose herself.

The three men sat around the table and looked at a finely detailed map of the Lisbon area that Salvatore had acquired somewhere. As soon as she heard them discussing "business", she returned and joined them.

"I've been out that way a couple of times over the past year. This is a fairly steep part of the road and the buses and the truck will be moving quite slowly up that grade. This would be a good place to jump the group. It's heavy woods all along the roads out there." He pointed with a pencil at the stretch of road he had in mind.

Not knowing the area at all, the other three nodded in mild agreement. "Can we swings out by dis road early afternoon and checks it out?" asked Salvatore.

"Sounds like a good idea. You'll be far enough away from the inn where the Germans are staying, it shouldn't raise any alarm."

Olga joined the conversation. "A lone woman walking near inn shouldn't raise suspicion. I'll leave car several miles back and come over this hill. I think we should know for ourselves number of buses and trucks – not depend only on word of this Da Silva."

The three men looked round the table at each other and nodded in agreement. It was a good idea. If any Germans even saw her, they'd be much less suspicious of a peasant woman nearby than if they saw Charles or any other unknown man, especially in a suit.

"OK, you do a reconnaissance on the inn, while we three check out the ambush point near the top of this hill. Also, are we all agreed that we're simply going to let the Germans 'escape,' and they can proceed on with their plan to catch their boat rides to Brazil?"

The other three nodded silently in agreement. "And that we'll even give them a little bit of the gold, so as they can pay the ship captains the final payment for passage when they go on board?"

Again, silent nods, but then Salvatore did ask, "Did Da Silva tell youse how much more dies Germans owe? Maybe we oughts to check first to see hows much they got on 'em before handing over any gold."

"A fair point. Apparently a Colonel Gehlen is the head man. Let's figure out quickly which one he is and after explaining that we're letting them go on to the port and their ships for Brazil, simply ask him if he has enough in cash to pay the extra 20 percent the chip captains are now demanding."

"Der's just no honesty among dies smugglers. Youse don't go jacking up an agreed upon price. It just ain't kosher."

"Honest or not, that's the deal they're offering and if the Germans don't pay, they don't get on board the ships. And one last thing, if we can, I want my men doing something other than guarding the German prisoners. When I report up the chain of command how they escaped into the night and we didn't know where they were headed, that's going to be a pretty thin story to sell and I'd just as soon if possible that none of my men had to be directly involved in such an absurd fantasy."

Olga chimed in, "Once we see that these Germans aren't going to put up a major gunfight, perhaps your men could be sent back to the Alhambra Inn to supposedly check to make sure there no Germans still there?"

"That might work OK, but I wouldn't send them away until I'm about to tell the Germans they can drive away, as there would only be me, Salvatore and Lou to control a hundred Germans." He turned to Olga, "Perhaps one or two of your men could give a hand to control the buses?"

"Maybe, though these men probably not too happy to be seen by you American spies." She grinned. "But also, if you decide Germans will need little bit of gold, you could send Lou back to wherever freight truck has stopped to retrieve a sack or two to bring back to you for Germans."

"So, my men will be up front and stop the buses and your men will close in from the rear and secure the cargo truck?" asked Charles.

"Well, your men young and trained. My men mostly old and no training. Probably better, your men secure the people, while my 'retirees' secure truck, which can't shoot back." They all smiled.

There was then a brief discussion over how the truck with the gold would be taken to the American military portion of the Lisbon airport for immediate loading onto an American military plane to be flown to London.

"It will be quite dark out on that rural road. Will be difficult to stay together, but we try and if get separated we will go to main entrance of airport and simply wait there for you. In fact, neither me or any my men will want enter airport. One of you should meet truck there and drive it on airport."

Charles agreed. "OK, I think we've done all the planning we can do before we actually see that road. Olga, I know you have to go off and make some arrangements, but let's plan on all of us meeting here again at 7:00 p.m." He checked his watch. "I need to swing by the Embassy now and let my people know what's happening tonight and work out with them where they'll rendezvous and who will drive out to Sesimba." He turned to Sally and Lou, "Will you two wait here till I return?"

They both nodded in agreement.

Olga stood to leave first. "I go by self now. Must stop first and talk to my 'old men' before going out there to walk near inn. I be back here before 7:00."

Olga and Charles headed off on their missions, while Salvatore and Lou took out a deck of cards to amuse themselves till Charles returned from the Embassy.

Once at the Embassy, Charles gathered together in their conference room the eight colleagues who would be with him that night. In addition to the hand gun and a rifle they'd already been issued, Thompson machine guns were given to two men. "Hopefully, nobody will have to fire a shot tonight. I suspect that as the Germans will be there with their wives and children, once we stop their buses and make the situation clear to them, they will quickly surrender." Charles looked around to see if anybody had a question and indeed several hands were in the air.

"But if they do start shooting, are we to shoot back at buses full of women and children?"

Charles had already given that tough question a lot of thought the day before. "Yes, we will. The Germans brought the women and children with them, not us. If they set such low value on the safety of their families, then so be it. We'll try not to hit the women and children, but we will shoot back if they resist capture and open fire on us. I realize that may make some of you uncomfortable morally and if that is a big deal for any man, come to me right after we break up here and tell me so and I will find a substitute for you. But if you come tonight, you don't get to change your mind in the middle of a fire fight, when other men's lives might be affected by your ethical qualms. Understood?"

Seven men nodded in agreement. The eighth, Jack, a slightly older man with two kids of his own stood up. "Sorry, Charles, but I didn't sign up to kill women and children. I think there must be another way of doing this." He left the room.

Charles then spread the map out on the table, so that all could gather around and get oriented on where the seizure would occur that night, where they should park once they arrived in the area and finally, who would ride with whom.

"One more thing, I have two other men who will be working with us tonight. Their names are Salvatore and Lou and they will drive the two cars that will actually cut off the lead bus tonight. They'll block this narrow road and be situated so that their headlights shine down the road, which hopefully will give us enough light to see what the hell we're doing out there in the dark of night. We'll also have with us three of those big emergency battery lights that are normally up in Communications. Soon as the buses are stopped, line up one of those on each bus doorway."

"And just exactly what are we to do or say once we have them stopped?" asked Gary.

"Actually, Gary, you're going to be up near the first bus and seeing as how you have the best German among us, you'll be the one to shout out to them that they are under the arrest of the U.S. Army, that they're surrounded, and to put down any weapons they have. Tell them how they and their families won't be hurt if they cooperate. The usual stuff. Then I want you to call for a Colonel Ewald Gehlen to identify himself and come forward for a conversation with me. He's the head man of them. If I can speak quickly with him and get his cooperation, everything should go pretty smoothly."

"Did I hear you mention earlier that there will be a truck with them and some crates?" asked Gary.

"Yes, hopefully, at the back of the parade, after the buses, there will be a flatbed cargo truck with some crates. Those will be seized by the Portuguese PVDE guys, who will drive it to the Lisbon airport. There will be an Army Air Corps plane standing by to fly whatever is in the crates to London. There will be other planes standing by to take our German guests to England as well."

"What time are we going to depart the Embassy to head out to Sesimbra tonight?"

"Allegedly, they will be leaving this inn around 10:30 or 11:00, but I want to be in place by 10:00, just in case they get anxious and depart a little early. They're supposed to arrive at the port around midnight. Get yourself a little nap this afternoon if you can, get some dinner before we rendezvous and dress warmly in dark clothing. It will get chilly out there tonight. And one more thing, keep your ears open tonight for further instructions from me. This works really easy in theory, but once the show gets underway, who knows what the hell may happen and we may have to improvise on the fly. Just be listening for my lovely voice tonight!"

*Nazi Gold, Portuguese Wine, and a Lovely Russian Spy*

They all laughed. It was well-known around the office that Charles was absolutely tone deaf and couldn't sing on tune if his life depended on it. The group broke up and headed off to get ready.

Charles grabbed a few sandwiches out of the Embassy cafeteria and then drove back to his apartment in one of the Embassy's big Packard's, leaving his car at the Embassy to be picked up later. He was ready to chat with Sally and Lou, about their specific roles for that night.

He found the two of them still playing cards, where he'd left them hours earlier. "Anybody hungry? I brought some sandwiches."

"Thanks, but we went out a bit ago and found some food. So, what's da plan for tonight?"

He repeated for them what had gone on with his OSS folks earlier and how he'd "volunteered" them to drive the two cars that would block the road that night. "That's why I brought a big Packard back with me. Your car is pretty solid as well. Between the two of them, that should solidly block that narrow country road, but also, they both have big headlights and we're going to need as much light as possible on those buses so we can see what the hell we're doing and more importantly, what anybody in the buses might try doing."

"No problem, Charlie. We's gots some experience in hijacking trucks. This should be about da same thing." They both smiled at Charles.

"OK. First, I'll have my little conversation with this Colonel Gehlen, at which hopefully he'll agree to peacefully give up his cargo of gold in return for us letting them go on to the port and get on their ships. I'll also find out from him if he's got enough dough to pay the ship captains their bribes, or if we gotta give him a little of the gold. If so, Salvatore, I'll send you back to tell Olga at the cargo truck how much I need. Lou, I want you to get in the first bus and keep your gun on the bus driver, and the rest of them, to make sure they just drive directly to the port."

"I can do that."

"But before any of the buses drive off, I will tell my men to hustle back down the road to check to make sure that there aren't any more Germans still back at the inn. That way, when I report tomorrow to Washington that the Germans 'escaped,' none of my guys have to be part of my lie."

"Understood, boss. Anything else need doing?"

"No, I think we're pretty well set. We'll rendezvous with my guys out at the road just before 10:00 p.m. I guess we're ready to take a run out there now and look over this road situation. Only one other thing guys. When we rendezvous back here later with Olga, once we've finished discussing the plans for tonight, how about you two going out shopping or something, so I can have a little time alone with her?"

Salvatore and Lou grinned like proud uncles and nodded in agreement. The three then headed for the car and the drive out to Sesimbra.

## Chapter 24

When Charles, Salvatore and Lou returned to the apartment just before 5:00 p.m., they found Olga already there, relaxing on the couch and reading one of Charles' American magazines.

Charles went straight to her and gave her a kiss on the top of her head. "Did you have a successful day?"

"Yes, I had pleasant stroll in woods. I saw large truck with two big crates on back, which said on outside they were packed with desert boots. There were two young men guarding them. I don't think they full of boots!" They all smiled.

"No, probably not full of boots," replied Charles. "You see anything else of importance?"

"They have three big buses, like tourist buses, but I saw nobody who looked like Germans, other than the two guarding the truck."

Charles spread out the map once again on the table and brought everyone up to date on the planning of what his men would do that night and how Salvatore and Lou would initiate the seizure by pulling out and blocking the lead bus, headlights pointed down the road. Charles give Olga the fourth battery-powered light from the Embassy. "This may come in handy for your people to use with the cargo truck."

She took the light. "Very clever. I have six men coming tonight. We wait further down the hill and when we see Salvatore and Lou act, we act. We make sure truck not back up and also cover rear end of third bus. Make sure your men not confuse my farmers for Germans and shoot them."

"And don't lets them shoot no Italian-Americans either!" added Lou.

## Gene Coyle

Charles smiled. "I promise, we only shoot Germans, and hopefully, we won't even have to shoot any of them. Once I've had a quick chat with this Colonel Gehlen and found out if we need any of the gold from the truck, I will send Salvatore down to you Olga to tell you how much, if any, is needed. That's when I'll tell my men to head down the road to the inn. I'll tell them that Gehlen indicated that there were more Germans back at the inn and they should go there to make a quick search, then return. Once they're gone, we'll let the buses head for the port with Sally in the first truck and Lou in the second – just to make sure nobody tries anything clever. I'll drive the Embassy Packard to the port to retrieve the boys, then we'll head to meet you and the truck just outside the main gate of the airport. We can come back the next day to retrieve the other car."

The other three nodded in agreement. "OK, we'll leave from here about 9:00 p.m."

Salvatore spoke up. "Me and Lou got a few shopping needs. We's gonna go out now and return just befores nine." He tried not to grin and almost succeeded.

"Yeah, we's got errands," added Lou. They grabbed their hats and were quickly out the door.

Olga gave Charles a knowing smile. "I think you three make conspiracy during trip to Sesimbra, just so you can get little Russian peasant girl all alone."

He came over and wrapped his arms around her. "Yes, I did. What do you think of my clever plan?"

"I like very much. Otherwise, I have to find excuse to send them on errand."

After a long kiss while standing in place, they moved off to his bedroom. Neither of them wanted to say it out loud, but they were both considering that one never knew for sure what would happen that night. Desperate, fleeing men with gold and guns, suddenly surrounded by other men with guns made for a combustible atmosphere. They made love with great passion, then snuggled together. He couldn't help but think of the great line from the movie *Casablanca* when Bergman told Bogart: *Kiss me. Kiss me as if it were the last time.* He knew practically every line from that movie. The Embassy only owned about a dozen movies and they'd shown and reshown *Casablanca* about once a month for the past year and a half. Every time they showed it as the free Friday night feature at the Embassy, he swore he wouldn't go again, but there was something hypnotic about it, and practically every month there he'd be eating popcorn in the last row till Rick Blaine and Captain Renault walked across that wet airport tarmac.

Olga stirred and turned so she could face Charles. "You do know that I love you very much, more than my own life – whatever happens, I will always love you."

"Ditto." He could tell by her puzzled expression that she didn't know what that meant. "It means, exactly the same for me."

"Ah, very good." She let out the deepest, most contented sigh he'd ever heard as she buried her head back into his chest. About ten minutes later, he stole a glance over to the bedside table clock. "I hate to say this, but we better get up and get dressed. "We wouldn't want to embarrass 'Uncle Salvatore' and 'Uncle Lou' by them returning and finding us naked in bed! They'd be so shocked, they wouldn't be able to shoot straight tonight."

"You are silliest man in Portugal." She gave him a big grin and then pulled back the cover to reveal her spectacular naked body. "And probably only man in all of Europe who would tell a girl with this body to put clothes on!" Knowing there was no line he could say to top her comment, he remained silent and just stared at her lovely body. She shrugged her shoulders. "OK, I get on and put clothes up." She still had that problem with English language prepositions of on, up, down, off.

By the time Sally and Lou did arrive, after standing outside the apartment door for several minutes, talking loudly, before knocking, the couple in love were dressed and seated in a respectable manner in the living room.

Olga made some bread and butter for her and Charles, and strong, black coffee for everybody. Salvatore and Lou had eaten while wandering around the neighborhood. They'd pretty well beaten the planning to death, so for the last hour before departing for Sesimbra, they all took turns telling stories of embarrassing moments as children. They were all relaxed and in a good mood when it was finally time to leave. The only contradictory event to the happy childhood stories was when they all checked their guns to make sure they were fully loaded. Olga still had that big monster .45 she'd had in New York City several years earlier.

By ten o'clock everyone was set. Salvatore and Lou were in the two cars near the top of the hill, just slightly off the road. Charles and his men were positioned just slightly down the hill, ready to surround the buses. Olga and her Communist farmers were hidden in the bushes, still further down the road. It was a clear and cold night. Everyone could see their own breaths, or look up and see the stars. It was 10:40 when they heard the sound of large engines laboring under the strain of moving buses packed with people up the incline. Their headlights cast ghostly shadows among the trees lining the narrow road. Charles thought to himself that probably only Salvatore and Lou were relaxed. For the rest of them, this was their first roadside heist. After all the planning and waiting, the time was almost there. Charles noticed that despite the cold, his palms were sweating and his heart rate had gone up.

Suddenly the headlights of the lead bus came into view, and then the two cars were out in the road, blocking the path, and Gary was shouting in his excellent German for all of them to put down their weapons and remain in their seats. They were under arrest of the United States Army. Amazingly and thankfully, that is exactly what happened. The Americans could hear some orders being shouted in the first bus and then several revolvers were being dropped out of the windows and the bus door opened. Out came an older man, clearly an officer used to being in command. He shouted in English, "I am Colonel Gehlen. Who is in charge here?"

The battery-powered lights had come on outside all of the buses and the truck, which was some 50 yards behind the third bus. Guns were being dropped out of the windows of the other vehicles. "Nothing like well-trained German soldiers," Charles bizarrely found himself thinking. Their commander had told them to surrender and give up their weapons, and that's what they did.

Charles walked slowly into the light. The headlights from Lou's car cast a long shadow of his body down the road. "I am Major Worthington, American Army," he announced when he was within about fifteen feet of the German. As he walked even closer, the German saluted and repeated, in a normal tone of voice, "Colonel Ewald Gehlen of the German Army."

Charles stopped a few feet away from the German and returned his salute. Charles lowered his voice so that neither the people on the bus, or his own men, still off in the shadows of the trees, could clearly hear him.

"Colonel, I am aware of the purpose of your journey with these people to a new life in Brazil, and I have no intention of stopping you from getting to your ships."

A look of relief came across the Colonel's face.

"However, I'm also aware that you have with you a quantity of gold. Gold that was probably stolen from other countries or even individuals – that gold I intend to seize and it will be held by the Supreme Allied Command until the end of the war, when hopefully, it can be determined to whom it really belongs. But back to your sailings to Brazil, I suspect that you need to make some sort of final payment tonight to the ship captains for this journey?"

"Yes, I'm afraid that the good captains sensed blood when we suddenly moved up our departure date and have demanded an additional 20 percent payment."

"Very well, if you can show me how much money you actually have with you and can convince me that you need a reasonable and small amount of the gold to make that final payment, I will allow you to remove that amount from the crates back on the truck."

The Colonel smiled. "Ah, I see that you have done your homework about the crates. Well, Major, as you are being so gracious about allowing us to still leave the country, let me honestly tell you, that I have already removed from one of the crates the gold needed to make the additional payments. I give you my word as an officer and a gentleman of the German Army that it is only the amount I need for the payments, but I will be happy to show you the bag on my bus here, so you can see the amount that I have taken."

Charles noted that Colonel Gehlen referred to the "German Army," not the Reich. "Colonel, your word is good enough for me. I will tell you that you are being allowed to continue your journey because frankly, it would be a nightmare to determine what to do with all of you if we took you under control. If turned over to the Portuguese, the German Embassy would press for your return to Germany, where no doubt, all of you would be shot for desertion. If we fly you to England, your soldiers will go to POW camps, but God knows what we would fairly do with your wives and children. Are yours with you?"

"My wife was killed in an American bombing raid earlier this year. Both our sons have died on the Russian Front. There is no new life awaiting me in Brazil. Admiral Canaris ordered me to go so that there would be someone in charge that he trusted to get these younger officers and families to Brazil and to dispense the gold and diamonds to them once we are there."

"I am very sorry about your wife and sons. Just for my own curiosity, what exactly was the Admiral's plan with this journey?"

"Very simply, Admiral Canaris knows the war is lost and when the Red Army comes rolling into Germay, there will be horrible consequences. He wished to save as many of his young officers as he could from that fate."

"A noble gesture on his part. Colonel, if you will excuse me for a moment, I must give a few orders so that your buses can get on their way. How many men do you have with the truck?"

"There are only two men with the truck."

"I will arrange for them to transfer to the back bus. Excuse me. Please wait here for me."

Charles walked back to where Gary waited. "Gary, the Colonel tells me that there are still a number of Germans back at the inn. I want you to take our men and go there now, to deal with them. Just fade back into the trees until you're down the hill a bit, and then return to the road once you're past the last bus. I will get on the first bus, until you return. Lou will get on the second bus and Salvatore on the third. Go now."

Gary didn't think this was a really good idea, but Charles was the boss, so he moved off and signaled quietly to the others for them to follow him. Charles waved for Salvatore to move his car out of the way, so that the buses could get by once Lou eventually moved his as well, and then for Salvatore to come to Charles.

When Salvatore arrived to him, he told him, "You're not needed to go back to the truck to retrieve anything, so just run down there and tell Olga that we will all be moving in just a few more minutes and for her to put the Germans with the truck on the third bus. You then get on the second bus. Lou will follow us to the port, and then give us a ride to the airport to meet up with Olga."

"You got it boss."

Charles walked back to Colonel Gehlen. "Colonel, I will be joining you on your bus and another of my men on the second bus. Please go and give instructions to the drivers and your men on the second and third bus that they are to simply follow your bus to the port and continue on as planned."

The Colonel saluted once more. Thank you Major Worthington, for your kindness. I'm afraid there isn't much left of that in this war."

He turned and started for the second bus.

"Oh, Colonel, one last question – approximately how much gold is there back there?"

"Between the gold and the industrial diamonds, we estimated it at around five million of your American dollars." Colonel Gehlen then proceeded on his way.

Charles was glad that it was dark, so that the German couldn't see the expression on his face. He actually muttered out loud, "That was going to be a mighty nice retirement plan for those young officers and their families!"

Once he saw that Salvatore was back to the second bus and the Colonel was back to his, he waved to Lou to move his car out of the way, and the caravan was off into the night. Lou would follow behind the third bus. Charles thought silently to himself, "Nobody at Headquarters is going to care what the hell happened to a hundred Germans once I report that I've retrieved five million bucks!"

It took close to an hour before they had reached the port and started dropping off the passengers at the different ships. Being well-organized Germans, they had loaded the buses according to who was going to which ship. Colonel Gehlen got off at each one and went to the cabin of the captain to make the final payment, then returned to the bus. He had divided up what bit of money he had left to the leader for each ship, explaining that there would now be no further payout once they reached Brazil as originally planned, and wished them luck. At the last stop, which would be his ship, he gave all the rest of the money he had in his possession to his second-in-command and explained that he would not be making the journey. As he would no longer be needed to oversee the distribution of wealth once in Brazil, he considered his mission over. He had gotten them on the ships.

He then came back to Charles. "Major Worthington, I surrender myself to you."

Charles was surprised. "You're not going to Brazil?"

"I hate warm climates. Besides, what the hell would I do in Brazil, except grow old and fat? I'd just as soon sit in a British POW camp." Both men laughed at that comment. "Besides, Major, I suspect you may have some explaining to do about how all those Germans escaped from you. This way, you can at least show how you captured one dangerous Abwehr colonel!"

Charles instructed the three Portuguese bus drivers to return the buses to wherever they came from and to forget they'd ever driven a bus that night. He gave each of them a wad of Portuguese escudos, which brought smiles to their faces, and he watched as each bus drove away. Charles, Salvatore and Colonel Gehlen then joined Lou in his car for the drive to the airport.

They arrived at the front gate of the Lisbon airport at about 1:00 a.m. Charles expected that Olga would already be there and waiting. He hoped there had not been any difficulty in seizing the cargo truck. Then he started wondering if perhaps the truck had broken down enroute to the airport. At 1:30, he ordered Lou to head back out the Sesimbra road, hoping to see a cargo truck broken down somewhere on the side and Olga frantically waving for assistance. Alas, they drove all the way to the inn and there was no sign of the truck or the crates of "desert boots." He wondered if perhaps the men Olga had lined up to assist her had betrayed her, but slowly it started to dawn on him that he was the one who had been betrayed – by Olga. He was sure that the NKVD would be very happy and surely Olga would get a promotion, when she turned in five million dollars' worth of gold and diamonds!

He finally told Lou to head to the Embassy. The truck was obviously long gone off into the night. He might as well get started at writing up his report of the evening's events, and probably ought to just go ahead and write out his resignation as well. Reporting how he'd lost the gold and the Germans was not going to make anybody happy back at OSS Headquarters in Washington. Capturing one German Abwehr colonel wasn't going to sound like much of an achievement. Salvatore and Lou came into the Embassy, for the first time since their arrival in Lisbon, to keep an eye on Colonel Gehlen.

Charles wrote his report out by hand. His handwriting was quite legible and the communications guys could read it as well as a typewritten report. He explained how the Lisbon Station had gotten onto the lead about Germans and gold passing through Portugal on their way to Brazil from Elizabeth Sahrbach and PVDE Captain Lourenco. That part was easy. Then came the awkward paragraphs about the involvement of Olga, a Spanish-based NKVD officer. He tried to briefly explain her cooperation with him in New York City, before the war, and thus his acceptance of her offer to provide a few "reliable farmers" to help in capturing the Germans and their stolen

*Nazi Gold, Portuguese Wine, and a Lovely Russian Spy*

gold, so as not to have to involve the local police. He was quite vague about just how he'd gotten back in touch with her in Portugal or when. Finally, he briefly explained how the Germans had overpowered himself and Salvatore and all had escaped, except for Colonel Gehlen.

The concluding paragraph was the hardest. His speculation on what had happened after the Sesimbra raid and possible explanations for Olga's failure to show up at the airport with the gold, per the original plan. His final sentences read: "While it is possible that the local Portuguese Communists turned against her and stole the valuables on the truck, I think it most likely that the gold and industrial diamonds are now in the hands of the NKVD and will be turned over to the Soviet Government. It has been only about a dozen hours since the raid, but I have received no word from Olga and must presume she has fled with the gold. Suggest that Headquarters send a senior officer to oversee further investigation of this situation."

As for the final sentence, Charles figured he'd best make the suggestion himself, rather than waiting for the anticipated telegram from Washington in which Headquarters would tell him that was what they were going to do anyway. He looked at his watch; it was almost 8:00 a.m. His colleagues would be arriving shortly and he could pass along his handwritten message for transmission, and turn Gehlen over to someone to take out to the airport to put him on a plane for London – for interrogation and imprisonment. Charles had forgotten that there were three planes waiting at the airport to fly all his Germans to London that morning. He'd leave to Gary inform the Army Air Corps about the "small change" from approximately 120 passengers to there being just one! He suddenly felt quite exhausted and realized he had been up all night.

He stopped to briefly say farewell to Colonel Gehlen. "Colonel, you will be taken shortly to the airport to fly to England, where you will be questioned and eventually placed in a POW camp; although, given the circumstances of your capture, they may keep you segregated from your fellow prisoners. I've just sent off a telegram saying how your men overpowered me and Salvatore and that we were only able to capture you."

"Doesn't speak too highly of me does it, that everyone but me could escape." He smiled. "Don't worry. I intend to only give my name and rank as required by the Geneva Convention. How the Allies sort out last night's adventure is not my responsibility. I suppose your superiors will be a little upset about the missing crates of gold and diamonds as well?"

"I suppose they will."

Gehlen smiled again. "Perhaps I might mention that I never actually saw any gold or diamonds, so I really couldn't say how much, if anything at all had actually been in those crates. Your people never actually looked in the crates did they?"

"No, we didn't."

"Well, there you are. You only have some second-hand rumor from a Portuguese banker. For all you know, those crates might have been full of desert boots."

They shook hands. "Good luck after the war young man."

"And to you Colonel."

Once Charles got home, he disconnected the phone and crawled into his bed. He was sound asleep within two minutes. As he started to slowly wake some four hours later, he instinctively reached across the bed for Olga. Then he awoke, to the horrible realization that not only was she gone, but she had played him for a fool and betrayed him. He rolled over on his other side and tried to go back to sleep, but it was pointless. He was still tired from lack of sleep, but his brain was wide awake. He finally gave up and got up around 1:00. He took a long, hot shower, which helped some, then a little food. At 1:30, he plugged the phone back into the jack and phoned his office and spoke to his secretary.

"Captain Lourenco has desperately been trying to reach you, and Gary would certainly like to talk to you as well. Those two fellows you left here this morning, Salvatore and Lou, turned over Colonel Gehlen to Gary when he arrived, but as for anything else, they just keep saying to talk to you. Gary's about ready to have them locked up. You better get down here as quick as you can."

"Did Gary get Gehlen out to the airport for the flight to London?"

"Yes, he made the phone call you instructed him to make in your note that you left and we got word about an hour ago that the plane had taken off for England. That's about all the news I have for you. There's been no response back yet from Washington. It's still too early there for anybody important to be at work yet."

"OK, I'll phone Captain Lourenco right now and may stop off to see him on my way in, so it might be an hour or it might be two hours yet before I arrive. Tell Gary to treat Salvatore and Lou nicely; they work for us."

"OK, I'll tell him. Good to hear from you. A few people were starting to wonder if you'd disappeared along with the gold!"

Charles laughed. "Ha, I may eventually wish I had. See you soon."

Next, he phoned Lourenco on his direct line.

"Antonio, did you get a good night's sleep?"

"Yes, I had an excellent late dinner, then went to bed without a care in the world? How was your night? Peaceful and calm?" he asked sarcastically.

"No, it was a terrible night and morning. I've just been getting a little sleep here at the apartment. How about I come by your office in about 20 minutes and I'll bring you up to date on events?"

"That would be excellent. I'll be waiting."

When Charles did arrive in the Captain's office, he had a carafe of hot coffee and a bottle of wine standing ready on his desk. "Which would you prefer?"

"I'd like to get drunk, but I better drink the coffee. To jump to the conclusion, about anything that could go wrong, went wrong. If you have any openings for privates in the PVDE, by this time next week, I may be looking for a job." He poured his own cup of coffee, sat down and began to tell Antonio how the events of the previous night unfolded.

Fifteen minutes later, he came to the conclusion. "My one prisoner is on his way to London, all the other hundred or so Germans have escaped, five million dollars in gold and industrial diamonds are gone and I've been betrayed by a woman who I thought loved me. I've suggested that someone come from Headquarters to carry on the investigation and I presume that by this time next week, I will have been fired, if not put in prison."

"I think we should open the wine, my friend. My last night was definitely better than your last night! So, you've told your Headquarters that the Germans 'escaped' and you have no idea where they are?"

"Correct. Just letting them go ahead and leave for Brazil, without the gold, seemed the most humane thing to do with them, and it still does. Now, you can presumably send your men down to the port and gather up the officers and their wives and children, but then they become your problem and your government's problem of what to do with them. Do you really want that?"

Lourenco smiled. "Not really. In fact, one ship has already sailed this morning. The others will be leaving within the next few days. My men are watching the ships where you dropped your 'friends' off last night, but I think that is all we're going to do. I hope they enjoy Brazil. Now, the gold is another matter."

"No shit! No one in Washington is going to forgive me for losing five million dollars."

"Nor is anyone in Lisbon going to like it either. If even a portion of that gold winds up in the hands of the local Communists, you and I both will be looking for new jobs by next week."

They both just sat there in silence, staring at one another and drinking wine for several minutes. Finally, Captain Lourenco spoke, "OK, when asked, I will officially tell whomever that we have no idea of what happened to the Germans. I will have the entire PVDE out looking for the truck full of gold as soon as I throw you out of here, but I'm sure it's long since been transferred from the original truck and could be hidden anywhere in Portugal by now."

"Well, I better head back to my Embassy and see if there is a reply from Washington." Antonio was so depressed, he didn't even stand up when Charles left. This wasn't going to do anything good for his career. He picked up the phone to put out the alert for a truck with a beautiful woman and two crates of gold and diamonds. That ought to at least motivate his men to really go out and look for such a truck!

## Chapter 25

When Charles returned to his office, everyone wanted to hear what had happened the night before. How did the Germans escape? What had happened to the two crates? Charles demurred on all questions. He told his secretary to pass out to all staff members a copy of his telegram to Washington. After that, he went in to his office and closed the door. He found Salvatore and Lou sheltering in there, so as to avoid more questioning from the other OSS officers.

"Thank God youse back – that Gary was abouts to put us in a cell."

"Sorry about that, but I think that I now have that straightened out with Gary." He then gave them a quick rundown on his conversation with PVDE Captain Lourenco.

"Sure be's great if he could find that truck," was all that Salvatore could think to say. Neither man wanted to say anything about Olga.

"Have you two gotten any sleep yet?"

"We napped a little here in youse office."

"Why don't you two go back to your place and get some sleep. I'll give you a call later this evening, after I've heard back from Washington."

As the two were leaving his office, the commo tech was bringing in the response from Washington. Charles gave him an inquiring look.

"Well, I hope you weren't planning on getting promoted this year!"

Charles managed a bit of a smile as he took the paper copy of the telegram into his hand, then spun around in his swivel chair so he could put his feet up on his desk and started reading.

A few minutes later, his secretary brought in an unsolicited cup of coffee, black, just as Charles liked it. "Figured you could use a cup of coffee. I saw the telegram before he brought it in to you and I have Gary waiting outside, for whenever you're ready for him."

Charles gave her a smile. "Might as well send him in now."

Gary entered slowly. "You know why I asked for you to come here?"

"Yes, sir. Just about everybody in the office has read it. I think Headquarters is greatly overreacting, but…"

Charles rose from his desk. "Well, you've, temporarily at least, been placed in charge, so you might as well take your proper seat. I presume you'll make the arrangements for General Donovan's arrival tomorrow evening. Lucky for us he was already in London. This way, he can make decisions right on the spot. It won't be some middleman making reports back to Washington and then us having to wait days to hear from Donovan. He can be judge, jury and hangman right here on the spot."

Gary was glad to see that Charles was keeping some sense of humor about all this.

"I saw in the telegram that I'm to consider myself under house arrest. Will you be sending someone home with me?"

"Hell no. Listen, I've seen that dump you live in. If you were a crook, you'd have been stealing money all along and living much better. Just give me a call if you're going to make a run for the Spanish border. Otherwise, I'll call you if we get any news on anything that might interest you."

"OK, I'll generally be at home, if you need to ask me about anything. May I have permission to go home now?"

"Certainly, Major Worthington. And keep those two goofball Italian mobsters out of here. For two guys who were there all night with you, they couldn't remember 'nuthing.' Complete waste of time questioning them."

Charles smiled slightly. "Yes, well, with their backgrounds in Brooklyn, you aren't exactly the first person to have ever questioned them." Charles started to leave, then stopped and turned back to Gary. "Remember, you and the others were all down at the inn on my orders when the Germans escaped. You had no role in the guarding of them, nor for responsibility over the truck."

Gary nodded in agreement and Charles left. Gary continued sitting there, wondering to himself, "What on earth was on his mind last night?"

When Charles got to his apartment, he allowed himself a couple seconds of excited anticipation that when the door swung open, there would be Olga sitting inside on his couch, reading a magazine. The door swung open, but the room was still and empty, like his broken heart. He took out from a kitchen cupboard his best bottle of Scottish single-malt whisky, put a lot of ice in a very tall glass, grabbed a can of peanuts and headed to the living room sofa. He opened the bottle and threw the cap off in a far corner of the room. He knew alcohol wasn't the answer to life's problems, but there were individual days when it was the best answer available.

He wasn't sure just when he'd passed out and then slept, but it was almost daylight now. His neck hurt like hell. He'd slept most of the night in an awkward, semi-upright position. There was a light tapping on his door. Charles looked at his watch and couldn't imagine who the hell would be visiting him at this early hour. He stood and started for the door, then thought about getting his gun out just in case it was somebody unpleasant, but his head hurt and frankly, given his mess, somebody shooting him might just be the best thing anyone could do for him.

He pulled open the door, as he said, "Good morning."

Charles found a young teenage peasant boy standing there, wrapped up in several scarves, a thin sweater and a partially torn coat. Not exactly one of the upper-class citizens of Portugal. "Yes, young man, what do you want?"

"Senhor Worthington?"

"Sim, Eu estou Worthington."

"Por favor," the very uncomfortable-looking youngster replied and took an envelope from one of his pockets. Soon as Charles took the missive, the boy ran down the hallway and down the stairs quick as a rabbit.

Charles knew instantly from the handwriting that it was from Olga. He locked the door and returned to the sofa. He stared at it for several long moments before carefully opening it. He unfolded the small single sheet of paper.

> My dearest Charles,
>
> I know that you are deeply disappointed in me. You feel that I have betrayed you, which is worse than even having stolen the gold from you and your government. As you have seen, I have been getting more and more

into my Jewish roots and it is for the Jewish people I have stolen those crates. They are going to need much help after this war, in particular, we need a homeland. This gold will help greatly build a Jewish homeland, which God gave us thousands of years ago. Probably some of this gold has been stolen from Jews by the Nazis anyway, and so it is being returned at least to its rightful people. As for the gold from the banks, well, we need it more than some bank. I don't know what will happen to me in the rest of this war or after, as I try to get this gold to the right people to build Israel, but do believe that I will always love you more than even myself. Going away from you now and forever is the hardest thing that I've ever had to do, but it is something I needed to do for my God and my people.

I'll be loving you, always,

Your Olga

    Charles just sat there in silence, motionless, except for the tears rolling down his eyes. Strangely, what was flashing through his mind were good times with Olga back in Manhattan before the war – dinner at the Rainbow Room, dancing at Roseland. Not that he hadn't felt lousy fifteen minutes ago, but now, not only having lost his job and future, he knew he'd never again see the love of his life. He really did now wish that someone would come through the door and just shoot him.

    Around 9:00 a.m., there was another knock on the door, accompanied by the easily recognizable voice of Salvatore. Charles opened the door and there were Sally and Lou, in their finest pinstripe suits, with little flowers in their buttonholes, smiling as if they'd just won a trifecta at Aqueduct Raceway.

    "Come in gentlemen. Aren't you two looking resplendent today!"

    "Well, we figured, if they's gonna shoot us, we should at least goes out in style! Youse had breakfast yet?"

    "No, just a little coffee."

"Good. Didn't youse tell us once that der's some hotel here in town that makes a real breakfast, likes with eggs and ham and stuff we'd actually recognize as breakfast food."

"Indeed I did. The Britannia Hotel serves an excellent breakfast. Are you proposing that we go and indulge ourselves there for breakfast? Sounds like a great idea to me. Give me ten minutes to get properly attired."

He debated how to explain the letter to them and then decided it would just be best to let them read it, despite its personal nature. He picked up from the coffee table the letter from Olga and handed it to Salvatore. "A young peasant boy brought this to my door early this morning. It's from Olga and pretty well explains what happened that night. Read it while I'm changing."

By the time they'd finished reading it, both of the Brooklyn tough guys were also crying. Neither man looked at the other, as mobsters weren't supposed to cry. Fortunately, Charles reappeared from the bedroom and inquired, "Are we ready to go?"

"Yeah, let's go," they both replied.

All three of them noticed as they climbed into Charles' car that there seemed to be surveillance at both ends of his street, both Portuguese-looking gentlemen reading newspapers and smoking cigarettes. "Looks like I've suddenly become quite popular," noted Charles. As they drove into the center of the city on their way to the hotel and breakfast, two cars followed them, neither car making much of an effort to even pretend that they weren't following Charles. Once they'd parked, Charles walked over to one of the cars that had pulled up nearby and said to the driver in Portuguese, "We're going in here for breakfast. Be about an hour."

The driver smiled and saluted.

He rejoined Salvatore and Lou. "Those PVDE guys are always so polite. I'd guess that Captain Lourenco is simply going through the motions with surveillance on me, just so he can say to anybody who inquires what he had the PVDE doing about all this, he can say he placed me under surveillance."

"Nice joint," observed Lou as they were shown to a nice table with a white linen table cloth, off by a window. Charles ordered the "Breakfast American" for all three of them.

They were starting on their coffee when Salvatore decided he should say something about Olga's letter to Charles. "I know she stole from youse boss, but dat's the classiest 'Dear John' letter I've ever read."

"Yeah, I means, she did steal it for her church, right?" added Lou.

"Thanks guys. At least now we know what happened that night. Whether General Donovan, even being a good Irish Catholic boy, will accept what happened and forgive me, remains to be seen."

"Any ways of tracking her down boss?" asked Lou. "That kinds of doll would be worth some effort to find and marry."

"I agree with you on it being worthwhile, but if Olga wants to disappear, I suspect she does it very well. Maybe after the war, something might be done, but for now…"

"It's sure been an interesting time here's in Portugal. We're glad youse brought us."

"You've both been a big help to me and your country. Maybe I can get you both medals, or at least arrange for all three of us to serve time in the same prison."

They were starting to laugh at his bad joke when he noticed Captain Lourenco approaching. "The police are headed this way guys. Why don't you take your coffee cups over to a table at that far window and enjoy a view of the city for a few minutes."

"Sure boss."

They got up and walked away, just as Lourenco arrived at the table.

"I didn't mean to break up your breakfast, Charles. May I?" He pointed at a chair.

"Certainly. My friends had almost finished anyway. They'd never had breakfast here before and I told them that they really should enjoy it before they returned to America."

"They and you leaving soon for America?"

"General Donovan arrives tonight and I've already 'temporarily' been relieved of my position, so I suspect that yes, I will be leaving in just a few days for home. It's mostly just a question of where my new home will be." Charles smiled.

"Oh, surely they wouldn't put you in prison over a meager five million dollars!" His turn to smile.

"Any news about the missing truck?"

"Oh, we found the truck and the two crates without too much difficulty. The thieves even kindly left the key in the ignition for us.

Unfortunately, the crates were empty and not a clue as to where their contents were taken, or how."

"I presume the obvious surveillance on me is to show your boss or the American Embassy that you are right on top of this?"

"Of course, and by the way, my surveillants outside told me how courteous you were to let them know that they'd have at least an hour to go get some coffee or food for themselves while you were in the hotel."

"Well, I knew your budget wouldn't allow for them to come in here and eat while watching me, so I figured it was the least I could do."

"Any expectation of what General Donovan will do with you?" inquired Antonio with a sympathetic tone.

"For this kind of a major cock up, somebody's head will have to roll. That will be mine. It's really just a question of whether I will be recalled and discharged from the Army, or if he'll need to show to the usual critics of the OSS how tough he is and have me put in prison."

"That's a tough country you have -- putting people in prison for incompetence. Fortunately, we've never had any such silly concept here in Portugal; otherwise the jails would be overflowing with government officials!"

The both laughed. "By the way, I spoke with Colonel Gehlen, the head German of the group, just before we sent him off to a plane for England. He was quite appreciative for me letting his men go on to Brazil. He told me that during his upcoming interrogation, he planned to say that he'd never actually seen any gold or industrial diamonds go into those crates, so he had no idea of what would be the value of their contents – if there was even anything."

"Very kind of the colonel. I'll have a chat with Mr. Da Silva, to make sure his 'story' is consistent, in case anyone ever speaks to him again about this matter. In fact, I'm sure he never saw the inside of those crates. His statement was in fact based just on second-hand hearsay."

"Well, if no one can testify how much gold got away and no one catches it while being smuggled across the Spanish border, I may just wind up being embarrassed, but not court-martialed." Charles lowered his voice. "And have all the German tourists left town yet?"

"There is one ship left to sail tomorrow at dawn. After that, unless the American government wants to stop and search every ship nearing the coast of Brazil, I don't think anyone is ever going to know what became of those Germans. Maybe there never were any to begin with?" He shrugged his shoulders.

"Maybe not," replied Charles with a smile. "Well, I doubt we'll see each other again after this morning, so let me say what a pleasure it's been working with such a professional officer. I consider you a friend."

"A mutual opinion, my friend. If you receive a cake at whatever American prison you wind up in, be sure to check inside for a saw before you bite into it!" Antonio rose, shook hands with Charles and wished him, "Boa viagem!"

Salvatore and Lou returned to the table. "Any good news, boss?" asked Lou.

"Lourenco told me that they found the truck and the empty crates, but no clues as to where the contents went from that spot. The last 'tourists' will sail tomorrow morning, so the people will be gone, the gold is gone and Colonel Gehlen plans on saying that he personally never actually saw any gold in those crates. He only knew what Admiral Canaris had told him. So, perhaps it was all a scam for Canaris himself to steal the gold?"

"So, we's may not be going to prison after all," observed Salvatore. "It's all second-hand rumor and insufficient circumstantial evidence." Charles was impressed at Salvatore's knowledge of criminal law. He wondered why he'd wasted three years at law school, when one could learn so much simply by being arrested a few times.

"Once I speak tonight with General Donovan, I'll have a better idea about our futures, but I'd say that you two could safely head on over to the PanAm Clipper office and get yourselves two tickets for America as soon as possible. Tell them to bill my office at the American Embassy."

"What's youse gonna do today?

"I think I'm going to head back home and start going through my stuff at the apartment. Get myself organized, in case, I too will be out of here in just a few more days."

"Just as well," commented Lou. This war will be over by next summer anyways. Youse might as well go on home and start working again for Mr. Astor. Me and Salvatore needs to get back to ours professions as well."

"Well, technically, you two are still in the Army, but I'll speak with General Donovan tonight about that as well. Probably we'll see each other again here in Lisbon before we all depart, but if not, once we're all back in the Big Apple, dinner at the Stork Club, on me!"

The three went their separate way. Charles waved at his surveillance team as he was leaving the hotel, and mouthed the words, "To home." The driver smiled and nodded.

Charles did get started on cleaning up his place. Even if he somehow miraculously didn't get sent home, the place could use a good straightening up. Gary phoned him around 6:00 p.m. and told him that Donovan's plane was on schedule and Charles should plan on being at the Embassy at 8:00 for a meeting with him. As Charles was starting to put some things in suitcases, he realized that he didn't have a single photograph of Olga – perhaps it was just as well. He could probably forget her faster if he had no photos of her about his home, wherever that may be in the coming months.

Charles was waiting in his office by 7:45, taking a guest chair in the room, since technically, it was no longer "his" office. General Donovan, his aide, Duncan Lee, and Gary arrived about ten minutes later. Charles thought to himself, without saying anything, that the General had aged in just the four months or so since last he'd seen him. Running the OSS in wartime couldn't be good for one's health.

"Charles, how are you? Before I forget, Vincent sends his regards. We crossed paths in London just yesterday at a reception."

"Thank you, General. How's he doing?"

"He looked good – certainly better than you or me!"

"Sorry everything got so screwed up on this latest operation."

"Gary and Duncan, why don't you give me and Charles a few minutes to chat privately."

They nodded and left the room without saying a word.

"I talked with Colonel Gehlen early this morning and Gary has given me his account of that night. He's also been in touch with this Portuguese police captain to get his version. Bottom line is that you are the most incompetent officer in the entire U.S. Army, or there never were any Germans nor gold and Gehlen was only in Portugal to do his early Christmas shopping. You seem to have a lot of friends who really like you and I doubt I will ever know the truth of what happened. I'm not sure I even want to know. I presume that the mystery woman and her Partisans who were there that night is the same Russian gal who had assisted you in New York?"

"Yes, Sir, it was, but as I'm sure you've heard, she has vanished into the night with whatever may or may not have been in those crates."

"You have any plans or arrangements to see her again?"

"No, I'm afraid she has vanished into the wind and no doubt has her own duties till this war ends."

"Well, I won't drag this out. Given the contradictory and second-hand stories of what happened that night out in the woods of Sesimbra, you are not going to be court-martialed. However, apparently, there are stories already spreading around Washington about some major cock-up by the OSS in Portugal. I suspect we have the good Mr. Solborg to thank for informing Army Intelligence back in Washington so quickly. In any case, somebody's head has to roll for how those crates disappeared, whether there was gold, desert boots or tin whistles in them – and that will be yours. Fortunately, not many know about the role of the Russian NKVD gal in this mess, or we'd both be fired."

"That's perfectly understandable."

Donovan was glad to see that Charles didn't want to protest or argue the issue. "Duncan Lee will stay here for the time being as acting-chief, until I can get someone of the proper rank transferred out here. You're to pack up and come back to Washington within the next week or so. You will be honorably discharged as soon as the new year begins. Don't ask me to explain to you why, but my aide tells me that you're financially better off if I fire you in January instead of December." They both managed a small laugh.

"I appreciate your consideration, Sir. Oh, and could your aide see to it that my two personal assistants, Salvatore and Lou, are immediately discharged as well? They've been quite valuable here in Lisbon, but I'm not sure that they're really cut out for Army life back in the States."

"Consider it done. Charles, you've done some very fine work here in Portugal. I hate to lose a good man like you, but at least now, you can get on with your life back in America. Any ideas on just what you might do as a civilian?"

"I suppose I'll have a chat with Mr. Astor when I return, but there's nothing on my immediate horizon."

Donovan looked at his watch. "Well, I have to get over to the Ambassador's residence for dinner. Again, thank you for your work here and good luck to you in your next career."

They both stood, shook hands and then Donovan was gone. Charles looked around his "former" office. He still had a few personal items in drawers, but he'd deal with that tomorrow. He was mentally drained and frankly, he just wanted to get back to his apartment and go to bed. As he left the Embassy, he noticed he no longer had his PVDE surveillance team on him. Word had obviously spread quickly in Lisbon that Charles was now officially a "nobody" and no longer a suspect in having played a role in stealing gold.

He crawled into bed and slept soundly. At least now, he knew his fate and there was no more anxiety of what might be coming. He would miss not being a part of the U.S. Army when victory did come.

# Chapter 26

Charles was still sound asleep the following morning when he thought he heard knocking on his door. His bedside clock told him it was only 6:00 a.m. and it was still quite dark outside. He decided he'd been dreaming, but then he heard it again. He dragged himself out of bed to go see who was there. It must be something important, as no one else would have the nerve to come visiting at such an early hour. His first guess was Salvatore or Gary, or maybe the young peasant boy with another message. He was wrong on all guesses.

He cracked the door as wide as the safety chain would allow, he saw the clothing of a typical Portuguese merchant seaman with his seaman's bag over one shoulder, except hidden under the hat was the face of a beautiful woman – the face of Olga to be precise. Charles was in such shock he just stood there for several seconds before unlatching the chain and opening the door wide to let her enter.

"I wasn't expecting to see you this morning, or ever, given your note."

"I'm glad to hear you received my note. Were you impressed with my English? I worked very hard on writing it." She'd taken off the hat and the seaman's coat and was just standing there, looking a little bedraggled and tired. He suspected that she'd been sleeping in barns again since she'd vanished that night of hijacking the truck.

He smiled. "Yes, I noticed that your grammar was excellent!" They then stood there, silently staring at each other. "Shall I make us some coffee?" he inquired, just to break the silence.

"Let me do it. You make horrible coffee," she replied with a smile.

She started for the kitchen, but then turned back and literally threw herself into his arms. "I couldn't go away. When I wrote that note, I intended to never see you again, figuring that you could never forgive me, but yesterday when it was time to get in the truck to be smuggled across the Spanish border, I just couldn't go."

"I've missed you so much" was all he got out of his mouth before their lips met in a long, deep kiss. Several minutes later, she finally got to the kitchen to make the coffee.

"Did Germans get away on their ships? And what did Washington say about theft of all that gold?"

"Yes, the last ship with Germans on board should be leaving port just about now. All got away, except for Colonel Gehlen, who decided that as there would be no gold nor diamonds to oversee the distribution of, he had no desire to go to Brazil. He was sent up to London and will eventually be in a POW camp in England. As for me, I've been replaced, ordered home and come January will be honorably discharged from the Army."

"Oh Charles, I'm so sorry."

"Well, life goes on. So, was there really millions of gold and diamonds in those crates? I'd hate for all this to have happened and there really were only desert boots in there!"

She smiled. "No, no boots. There really was lots of gold. Someday, new homeland for Jews will be very grateful – probably should name street after you in honor of your assistance."

Charles smiled. The idea of a street in the capital of this Jewish homeland named "Worthington" didn't sound quite right. "And where is all this treasure now?"

I left it with my Jewish host, who came over from Spain to retrieve it, and me. I know I can trust him to see that it reaches right people when this war is over and fight against British to create our homeland in Palestine begins."

"But you decided not to go with the gold and diamonds and to help build your new country? What happened to your new Jewish faith?"

"I am still good Jewish girl, but I think giving my homeland five million dollars is enough of a contribution. I could not also give up man I love. I could not go away and never see you again. They get the money and I get you – if you still want me?"

The biggest smile she'd ever seen on Charles' face appeared. "Well, let's try being together for say, fifty years, then I'll decide whether to make it permanent. Of course, we may both starve. If the rumors spread far and wide about me having something to do with stealing five million dollars, it might be hard to find a civilian job."

Now it was her turn to offer a wide smile. She led Charles over to her seaman's bag, still on the floor in the living room. She opened it so he could look inside. There amongst her clothes were three gold bars. "I don't think we starve for several years."

"So, we really are thieves?"

"I decided that new Jewish homeland owed us something for all effort we went through to get them other four million and nine hundred thousand dollars!"

"Quit talking and kiss me."

As they sat talking on the couch, Charles brought up the awkward "minor detail" of how exactly they would stay together, with him being sent back to America and she was still working for the NKVD.

"Going to be a bit awkward bringing you on the Pan Am Clipper in a few days. I'm not exactly sure how to get you back to America? And how would you explain that to Moscow?"

"I'm resigning. Well, not exactly resigning. I had idea on way here early this morning. You good friends, seems me, with this Portuguese PVDE captain, yes?"

"Up until now, I'd say we were. Why?"

"Think he could give newspapers story of how PVDE shot and killed female Russian spy, who tried to illegally cross Portuguese border?"

A smile came to his face. "Ah, I see what you have in mind. Olga is dead. And I take to America, poor little Bulgarian girl?"

"Something like that. But that not solve problem of you being fired. You will miss being OSS spy, yes?"

"Well, it would have been nice to still be around when Germany eventually surrenders, but not much I can do about that now." He shrugged his shoulders. "General Donovan told me last night that someone had to be thrown to the wolves for this mess, and that someone is to be me. He even brought my temporary replacement with him from London, Duncan Lee. I'm to be gone in just a few days. I thought I might get a ride on Donovan's plane back to Washington when he leaves

Portugal tomorrow, but I guess he didn't really want to be seen arriving in America with me!"

"So, Duncan Lee is your replacement?"

Charles saw a strange look come over her face. "Yes, he's General Donovan's personal aide, but he'll fill in here as the chief for a few weeks till they can find a proper replacement."

"Darling, you made big sacrifice for me and Israel. I didn't exactly ask you if you would, but you made it in any case. Perhaps there is something I can do to make you big hero and General Donovan will ask you to stay in OSS and even give you promotion!"

"Darling, I love you madly, but I think the lack of sleep or food has affected your brain!"

She gave him a wonderful smile. "You think you could get us private meeting today with General Donovan – without Duncan Lee in room?"

# Epilogue

Duncan Lee continued on as General Donovan's personal aide until the end of the war, but for reasons never publicly explained, as of early January 1944 his duties shifted more to scheduling and travel tasks for Donovan and he had little direct involvement with actual OSS operations. The courier for the NKVD in the Washington DC area, Elizabeth Bentley, when she approached the FBI in 1945 seeking a deal, named Duncan Lee as one of the moles in the United States Government with whom she'd met to receive information. Lee never passed documents; he only orally passed along information he wished to convey to Moscow, so she had no evidence of his spying. He was clearly identified in the VENONA intercepts of Soviet Intelligence messages, but the government was unwilling to use that evidence in open court for Lee nor for many others. He was publicly accused in the late 1940s, but never convicted nor even indicted, and went on to a very successful career in private law practice until his death in 1988 in Canada.

Kim Philby was finally discovered by MI6 as a mole and fired in the 1950s, but was never prosecuted and went on to work as a journalist. He managed to slip away in Turkey when about to be confronted and questioned by an old MI6 friend in January 1963 and was smuggled into the Soviet Union. He died in Moscow, in 1988.

GARBO and TRICYCLE both survived the war and many years later, their double agent efforts were publicly acknowledged by the British Government.

Both Graham Greene and Ian Fleming went on to successful careers as writers after the war.

The Soviet Union's NKVD in December 1943 posthumously awarded Olga Moussinova the Order of Lenin, Second Class, for having given her life while on a mission abroad to Spain. Her body was never recovered. The Portuguese PVDE had reported in November in the press that a Soviet female agent known as Marie had been shot while trying to illegally cross from Spain into Portugal and had been buried in an unmarked grave.